PRAISE FOR JEANET
NOVELS OF IRELA

"Jeanette Baker spins an eloquent and intricate story that combines the lives of two extraordinary women. *Nell* is yet another shining example of Ms. Baker's exceptional gift for storytelling."

—*Romantic Times*

"Ms. Baker has put together a breathtaking novel that has the reader eagerly turning the pages. All the classic themes, including an innovative time travel twist, combine for an explosive read. . . . Ms. Baker waited for the right moment to pack on the sensuality. And it was certainly worth the wait."

—*The Literary Times*

"*Nell* is rich in the Irish history of a couple of time periods, and Ms. Baker's prose draws her readers right in. Blend this with not one but two love stories, and readers will cherish this creative masterpiece that spans two decades and the past."

—*Rendezvous*

"*Nell* has to be one of the best books I have ever read. The characters are so enchanting and unforgettable. I picked up this book at the library and finished it that same night. I was unable to sleep until I finished it because it was so good."

—A reader from Connecticut

"*Nell* is an incredibly wonderful book . . . a perfect mix of romance, history, and contemporary and historical fiction. The story and characters stayed with me long after I'd finished reading."

—A reader from Colorado

IRISH LADY

"It grips the reader from the first page to the last. . . . A wonderful mix of past and present comparing the griefs and tragedies of ancient Ireland with the heartbreak and passion of present-day Ireland, and an exploration of divided loyalties and discovered destinies."

—Diana Gabaldon, author of the Outlander series

"A delicious yet poignant read. . . . Truly one of the best and most touching books I have read—a true love story complete with a host of emotions."

—Amy Wilson, *The Literary Times*

"The pride of the Irish and their struggle for freedom from the British is brought to life with outstanding skill. Add two amazing heroines, one in the present, the other in the past, but each with a love that outlives time, and the reader is ensured of hours of joy."

—Rendezvous

"Inspired writing! Splendid! 4½ BELLS!"

—Bell, Book, and Candle

CATRIONA

"Jeanette Baker is rapidly proving herself one of the shining talents of the paranormal genre. *Catriona* is an outstanding blend of past and present that makes for inspiring and irresistible reading!"

—Jill Smith, *Romantic Times*

"Readers of all genres will cherish this prize. . . . *Catriona* . . . comes alive with the paranormal, burning sensuality, and a notable plot of outstanding quality that will have readers eagerly awaiting Ms. Baker's next book."

—*Rendezvous*

"Jeanette Baker has joined the ranks of such award-winning authors as Kristin Hannah, Christina Skye, and Barbara Erskine, who have all striven to create unique stories that blend the reality of history and time so that love will triumph. Baker's *Catriona* and *Legacy* are classics."

—Jody Allen, CompuServe Romance Reviews

"A great read!"

—Waldenbooks *Romantic Interludes*

"An absolutely stunning and unique mixing of several genres (supernatural, historical, and contemporary romances) into a great novel that will delight fans from all three. . . . One of the top novels of the year."

—America Online on the Shelves

Books by Jeanette Baker

Legacy
Catriona
Irish Lady
Nell
Irish Fire

Published by POCKET BOOKS

Colleen

Colleen—Very good.

M.D—really enjoyed it!

JEANETTE BAKER

IRISH FIRE

POCKET STAR BOOKS

New York   London   Toronto   Sydney   Singapore

This book is a work of fiction. Names, characters, places and incidents are products of the author's imagination or are used fictitiously. Any resemblance to actual events or locales or persons, living or dead, is entirely coincidental.

An *Original* Publication of POCKET BOOKS

A Pocket Star Book published by
POCKET BOOKS, a division of Simon & Schuster Inc.
1230 Avenue of the Americas, New York, NY 10020

Copyright © 2000 by Jeanette Baker

ISBN: 0-671-03407-3

First Pocket Books printing August 2000

10 9 8 7 6 5 4 3 2 1

POCKET STAR BOOKS and colophon are registered trademarks of Simon & Schuster Inc.

Cover art by Peter Fiore

Printed in the U.S.A.

This book is dedicated to Gilles Stewart, a kindred spirit, who shares my empathy for oppressed populations and whose thoughtful questions and quick understanding encouraged me to clarify, rethink, and appreciate the Celtic birthright we share.

It is with great appreciation that I thank:

My sister, Vicki, who lost her thoroughbred, The Corrigator, last year, and who guided me through the most elemental aspects of care for the breed.

Pat Perry and Jean Stewart for their encouragement, their careful attention to detail, and their enthusiasm for each new venture I undertake.

Peter and Anne Martin of Glebe House in Kilcullen, Ireland, for their wonderful hospitality, their huge sitting room fire—a must for a southern Californian visiting Ireland in November—their delicious breakfasts, and their unflagging persistence in setting up appointments for me to complete my research for this book.

Ian Lewis of the Turf Club for spending an afternoon answering my questions about horse racing in Ireland and for arming me with more brochures, books, and information than I could possibly need.

Edwina Farrell, M.R.C.V.S., Member of the Royal College of Veterinary Service at the Troytown Clinic, who gave me a personal tour of the clinic, answered all my questions about RLN disease, and allowed me to view an actual equine surgical procedure in progress.

Helen Boyce and Eileen Kavanagh of the Irish National Stud who kindly brought me up to speed on breeding practices at the stud farm. Leona Harmon, who walked me around the impressive facility and, while discussing procedures, calmed my nerves when a stallion, bearing no similarities at all to the mild-mannered geldings and mares of my experience, "escaped" from his stall and thundered past us.

Nancy Williams of "Tea & Sympathy" who regularly buys and handsells more of my books for her store than anyone in the world.

And last but not least, Loretta Barrett, my literary agent, and Kate Collins, my editor, for offering encouragement and supporting my desire to branch out into contemporary fiction.

IRISH FIRE

1

Brigid Keneally picked up a teaspoon and frowned at her reflection in the polished silver. The face that looked back at her was old. Somehow, while she was busy minding the pub and the store and raising the girls, the years had crept up on her, carving deep crevices that crisscrossed her skin like lines on a road map. She didn't feel old, not a day older than forty, but the gleaming sterling of her place setting told her differently, as did the ache in her bones from living in a house that was too big, too old, and too in need of repair to ever be truly warm.

Still holding the spoon, she stared at the flowing script of the letter in her lap. Where were her reading glasses when she needed them? She ran the fingers of one hand over the stationery and wished that her eyes were better, that Caitlin wasn't four thousand miles on the other side of the Atlantic, and that her grandchildren, the sweet rosy-cheeked, dark-eyed pair of them, would somehow, miraculously, come running into the store, throw themselves into her arms, and beg for sweets.

She sighed. Why not just wish that she was young again and that all the years she had spent wishing were hers to live over, only this time with the hindsight to do it right. Brigid looked at the clock. It was past time to open the pub. There would be men wanting their spirits even at this absurd hour of the morning. Her mouth twisted humorlessly. Pity the woman who tried to part an Irishman from his drink.

Her regulars would just have to wait a bit. A letter from Caitlin was rare enough that she wanted a moment to sit and think, to go over the pain of it again in her mind, to wonder where she'd gone wrong with her youngest, least predictable daughter.

Visions of her late husband intruded upon her thoughts. Resolutely, she pushed them away, back into the think-about-it-later file in her mind. Caitlin's letter was enough of a damper. No need to bring up Sean Keneally, yet another one of her failures.

One would think that when a daughter was grown and married, with children of her own, that the worry would stop and the sick, tight feeling a mother felt when something wasn't quite right would never plague her again. But it didn't work that way. The feeling was always there, sometimes deeply hidden, but ready to flare up again when the provocation arose. Oftentimes, Brigid reflected, adult children's troubles were worse than anything. After a child was grown, a mother had no control. Difficulties couldn't be solved by the promise of sweets or a warm cuddle in an ample lap.

Brigid concentrated until the vein in her right temple throbbed. What was it about Caitlin that bothered her so, outside of her ill-fated marriage? Not that a bad marriage wasn't enough to gather the storm clouds over a house. But

Caitlin wouldn't be defeated by something so easily remedied, not the Caitlin Keneally her mother remembered.

Fourteen years in America had changed her, something more than Sam Claiborne with his smooth tongue and polished manners, his blueblood family and their Kentucky money had done. Brigid felt it as surely as she felt the rain slanting down on Kilcullen Town, drowning the otherwise pretty village in a drab shroud of gray wetness. If only she could put her finger on the real hurt. Why wouldn't the obstinate child confide in her?

Those who recalled Caitlin in her youth frequently reminded Brigid that her youngest daughter was born difficult. A changeling, the superstitious whispered, a black-haired, dark-eyed, reed-slim throwaway from the travelers' caravan that had camped for a single night down by the river and disappeared in the morning.

Others, with their feet on the ground and their requisite share of common sense, recognized the child for what they thought she was, the spitting image of her recently departed father.

Poor Brigid, the town folk had commiserated, shaking their heads after one of Caitlin's more mischievous escapades. How unfortunate that the child born to her six months after Sean Keneally's untimely death, should be the one most like him. If they had known the truth, Brigid would have been drawn and quartered, her head a pike decoration on the ancient fortress walls of Donore Castle. Perhaps not now, but not so very long ago when Rome had its fist tightly clenched around the heart of Ireland.

Everyone knew that Sean, may he rest in peace, was a wastrel—a charming wastrel with a twinkle in his eye, a way with words, and a smile for the ladies. Not that Brigid ever complained, mind you. She had more than enough to be grateful for with five saintly daughters made in the image of herself, lovely blue-eyed, golden daughters who behaved beautifully and predictably from the moment the midwife placed them in Brigid's waiting arms, daughters who obeyed their masters at school, minded their mother at the store, kept their eyes lowered during mass and said "thank you" and "if you please," without any reminders.

Caitlin, on the other hand, was never still, never compliant and, most definitely, never predictable. She simply moved on a plane that was a level apart from everyone around her. Schedules did not interest her. She was as unlikely to arrive on time for tea as she was to appear for Sunday mass, for her lessons at Saint Patrick's Academy or for taking her turn working in her mother's store when the long summer afternoons lingered into twilight. Unmoved by threats of perpetual purgatory, bribes, or pleas to her better nature, she brought shame to her family with the regularity of Saint Patrick's church bells announcing the hour on Sunday.

No one could explain it, least of all the Dominican Sisters who had the questionable duty of shaping the girls of Kilcullen Town into an ethical, albeit indistinguishable, mold. One reproachful glance from Caitlin was enough to reduce the saintly sisters to stammering apologies. Caitlin Keneally simply went her own way. With her unmanageable black curls, foreign-dark eyes and a mouth that the women who had known Sean Keneally in his youth never failed to settle on and lose track of their thoughts, much to Brigid's disapproval, Caitlin was something of an anathema to the good citizens of Kilcullen.

None of it would have mattered if she had been unattractive or aloof, mean-spirited, selfish, or foolish. If she had been any one of those things, the residents of Kilcullen Town would have clucked sympathetically and gone out of their way to be condescending. But she was not.

Brigid's late-in-life daughter blazed with a quivering inner light that made the more imaginative think of faeries and wee folk, of the legends of Emain Macha, and the stone Celtic circles that glowed with magic.

The children of Kilcullen adored her, imitated her, followed her lead, idolized her. She was curious, fearless, tenacious, and intelligent. She could climb the lichen-strangled walls of Donore Castle with the nimbleness of a gymnast, walk its twenty foot high rampart with eyes closed and arms outstretched; tell deliciously horrifying stories in the graveyard after midnight by the light of a wind-flickering candle; calculate the odds of a two-year-old colt placing in the Two Thousand Guineas Race simply by looking at him; consume a book with an inch-and-a-half spine from cover-to-cover in two hours, losing nothing of its meaning; and ace her mathematic's examinations without ever completing a single page of practice sums. Everyone who knew the girl realized before long they were in the presence of something quite out of the ordinary.

Looking back, Brigid recalled that only one thing had really mattered to Caitlin and that was thoroughbreds—the breeding, training and racing of them—which explained her immediate and intense attraction to the Claiborne heir.

From the beginning it was crystal clear to Brigid that marriage would not suit Caitlin, not marriage to Samuel Claiborne, anyway. But the child wouldn't listen. Children never did, of course. Brigid, herself, hadn't listened when wiser minds than hers had tried to warn her away from Sean Keneally. She suffered a twinge of guilt. Marriage hadn't exactly suited her either. She hoped it was nothing she'd passed down to her daughter. But then Sean was nothing like Sam Claiborne, and Caitlin had never known her father, except through the eyes of those who had.

The truth of it, Brigid admitted to herself, was that

although she loved all her daughters dearly, Caitlin was the one who brought a song to her heart and a smile to her lips, just as her father had done in his day, and the very idea of her living in a state of unhappiness was like a festering wound that refused to heal. Brigid went to sleep every night dwelling on her daughter's predicament and woke each morning without an answer. Perhaps if she hadn't allowed the girl to visit Lelia.

Caitlin had been so very young for marriage. Not that marriage and motherhood were bad things in themselves, especially for another sort of girl. But they shouldn't drain the spirit from a woman, wipe the life from her eyes or the laughter from her face, or the teasing wit from her lips. Brigid had known something wasn't right on her one and only visit to America, but Caitlin was on her guard, Sam was charm itself, and no amount of wheedling would bring the girl's troubles out in the open.

Brigid looked down at her hands. She was past seventy and her hands, more than anything else, showed it. They were thin skinned, the veins large, ropy and blue, extending high above the crepe-like flesh. They hadn't always looked this way. Once her hands had been beautiful. When had she stopped caring about them? She thought back over the decades. It was soon after Sean's death. Hands had been important to him. He noticed them immediately. Where other men saw a woman's breasts or legs or hair, he saw hands. She closed her eyes and remembered the feel of a warm mouth against her fingers, lips pressed against her palm.

She rose on weary feet and headed for the door leading to the pub. She wasn't feeling herself lately. It was time to settle what was left of her affairs and write to Caitlin. Not that a pub and convenience store could be called a true legacy. But maybe Caitlin was ready for something less magnificent than the Claiborne mansion with its fifty rooms and a stable lit by the light of crystal chandeliers.

Brigid clucked under her breath. What was the world coming to when horses were better cared for than people? Even in horse-crazy Ireland, a man knew the difference between himself and a horse. Kilcullen thoroughbreds grazed on green grass and slept in sensible wooden barns with blankets thrown over their backs, not forced-air heat in the winter and air-conditioning in the summer. There were no bronze-coated stable roofs, simulated tracks, and speakers strategically placed to recreate the noises of a roaring crowd. The most Ireland could boast were the lantern-shaped rooftops and skylights in the box stalls of the National Stud. A horse was a horse and if he was a runner, so be it. The Irish had done well enough with their thoroughbreds thanks to the old tried-and-true methods of training.

Americans. Brigid snorted deprecatingly. Not that they weren't lovely people with lovely bank accounts, but they had no concept of age or roots. The Claibornes had occupied their acreage in Kentucky for a mere hundred years, strutting their lineage and their membership in the Jockey Club as if they were descended from true aristocrats, instead of felons dumped on the shores of a British penal colony.

Here, in Kilcullen, where a century was a mere drop in the bucket, where *old* meant that misty time when the Celts carved their circular designs in the caverns of Newgrange, they would be considered newcomers.

Brigid had nothing against newcomers. Sean had been a newcomer, his home that rocky land far to the north. A land of low stone fences, soil a mixture of sand and seaweed and, in every direction as far as the eye could see, a vast ocean and endless sky. Too late she had learned that he could never be quite comfortable in the richer, greener, more prosperous land to the south, a land of horses and gentle hills and haystacks rolled into golden bales. But that was all behind her now. She brushed away the unwelcome memory, concentrating once again on the Claibornes.

Brigid had not begrudged the Claibornes their money. What sensible mother would? She wasn't one of those people who resented inherited wealth. As for those who'd done well on their own, well she was more than happy to celebrate their success and wish them well. But the Claibornes pretended they'd always been rolling in excess as if it wasn't common knowledge that, until Bull Claiborne's father made a fortune dealing illegal spirits in America's prohibition years, the Claiborne family had never done anything more than dabble in wagering at the annual Kentucky Derby.

Brigid had never cared for pretension. Caitlin's mother-in-law, Lucy Claiborne, was so full of it that if one took a pin to her well-endowed backside, she would most likely sit several inches lower in her chair. Of course, what could one expect from people who served their ham slathered in maple syrup and ate grits dredged in bacon-cream sauce? It made Brigid's stomach heave just to think of it.

"Brigid Keneally," a loud voice called from below her window. "It's past nine. Are ye openin' the doors today or takin' a holiday?"

Brigid groaned. It was Seamus McMahon and his voice was already slurred with the drink. Unless she called someone to take him home, his wife would see nothing of the paycheck he'd already liberally dipped into.

She threw open the window and leaned out. "I won't be unlatchin' the door for another hour or so, Seamus."

The man rubbed his stubbled cheeks, stepped back into the street to look at her, and summoned a smile. "I could help myself to a wee pint or two before you come down, Brigid, love."

Brigid lowered her voice. "I'm no fool, Shay. Go home before I call our Mary."

Muttering expletives under his breath, most of which referred to the devil having his way with heartless women, Seamus stumbled down the street in the direction from which he had come.

Brigid sighed with relief. Perhaps she *would* write to Caitlin, even take a holiday. Better yet, she would call her and tell her she could no longer manage everything on her own. If Caitlin needed an excuse to come home, Brigid would give it to her.

2

❧❧❧

Lexington County, Kentucky

Caitlin Claiborne lay on her back and stared at the ceiling, willing herself to breathe naturally. Beside her, Sam snored the deep, inebriated groans of a man who had managed to barely find his bed before passing out in a drink-induced haze. Light from the stables streamed through the French doors, intensifying the sheen on the plush carpets, the gleaming cherrywood furniture and the Georgia O'Keefe originals covering the papered walls.

Sam thrashed recklessly, throwing his arm in an arc that barely missed her shoulder. Caitlin's body tensed and she waited for his breathing to normalize. Minutes passed. Finally, without regaining consciousness, he settled back into his pillow.

Caitlin inched away from him until she lay, rigid and awake, on the edge of the mattress. Hell, she decided, was sharing a bed with a man she couldn't bear touching. Not that he wanted to touch her either.

The bed had been made to order. Sam had specifically requested a king-size four poster. Caitlin hadn't objected. No bed could be too big if she had to share it with Sam Claiborne. Now, at least, she could move far enough away so that it felt as if she were sleeping alone.

If they had a home of their own, this charade wouldn't be happening. She would have her own room and Sam could come and go as he pleased. But Lucy Claiborne wouldn't hear of anyone moving. Claiborne House was Sam's home, his legacy. If privacy was so important to Caitlin, Lucy would be the one to leave. After all, how much space did a poor widow lady need?

Caitlin brushed the uncharitable thought aside. For a mother-in-law, Lucy wasn't bad. She worried about Sam, about the children, about Caitlin, and about the undeniable frost between her son and daughter-in-law with a diligence that rivaled the persistent trickle of spring sap down the trunk of a Virginia pine. It wasn't Lucy's fault that Sam Claiborne's nickname was "hound dog" in every bar between Lexington and Louisville, or that he couldn't keep his trousers zipped long enough to stop the rumors from flying.

A mosquito hummed above her head. Ignoring the reflex to swat, Caitlin blew it away. The air was stifling. Despite the Claiborne millions, Lucy didn't believe in air-conditioning. As long as she was alive, Claibornes would swelter in the heat of a stifling summer just as they had every summer for a hundred years.

In many ways Lucy reminded Caitlin of her mother. Both women were united in the belief that self-denial bred character, that without the first the second was an impossible feat. Brigid was more perceptive, of course. She was Irish. No Irish woman ever born would have missed what Lucy Claiborne had missed for three of the last five years. From clear across the Atlantic, Brigid understood that something was dreadfully wrong with her daughter's marriage.

Caitlin closed her eyes. Ireland. Beneath her eyelids, the rich compelling green of her homeland materialized and with it the image of brown turf stacked and drying beneath a milky sun, rolled bales of hay, gold against green, wooly long-haired sheep, a hint of chimney smoke, gray disappearing into a grayer sky, the first mouth-watering bite of a potato boxy, gray stone walls brilliant with fall-colored lichen, the smell of peat and oatcakes, loose tea with milk, friendly reserved smiles, and at the end of it all, her mother's eyes, always blue, always clear, always unalterably, painfully honest. If only she'd appreciated what she had.

Perhaps it wasn't unusual for a young girl to want something different. Growing up in Kilcullen she'd paid no attention to the windswept beauty of the Curragh, to the timeless sense of space and history, the friendly smiles, the weathered faces, the camaraderie, the unconditional, wondrous feeling that she belonged, would always belong simply because she was herself.

An ache built up in her chest. She breathed deeply, forcing back the tears that always came when she thought of Ireland. God, how she wanted to go home. What she wouldn't give for one clean breath of air scented with bog and woodsmoke, to wake up to rain on the wind, boiling clouds, steaming tea, her mother's soda bread spread out on snowy linen on the table in the huge immaculate kitchen where she'd shared countless meals. She missed the cornerstones of her youth with a craving beyond anything she'd felt before.

And behind it all, hovering above anything external, was a desperate yearning for her mother. It was a relief to finally admit it. If only she could go back in time, to be young again, to a place where all hurt and disappointment were brushed away by Brigid's cool hands on her hot forehead. Caitlin's relationship with her mother had been strained at times but she'd never doubted the strength of Brigid's love. No matter what she did, or how far she strayed, her mother's love was forever.

There had been a time when America called out to Caitlin, when the tiny town and the people she'd known forever wove a suffocating net around her. She had been the only one left at home. Kitty and Mary had married Australians and gone to live on a sheep station in the outback. Deirdre, up to her ears in children, lived in the north in County Tyrone, Lelia was settled in Boston with a husband and soon a new baby, while Anne, the oldest, Caitlin's surrogate mother, worked for a London newspaper.

Caitlin had dreamed of America. When it called out to her, she answered. Brigid was heartbroken. She'd wanted a university education for her youngest, cleverest daughter. Caitlin's O levels had been the highest in her class. She could still hear her mother's voice. "An education is the only democracy, Caitlin. An education levels out the haves and have nots."

But at seventeen, Caitlin didn't want college. The confinement of four more years of classroom walls and required reading wasn't for her. She barely managed to attend secondary school long enough to earn her Leaving Certificate. America and horses were in her blood.

Her naivete had cost her years of humiliation. Her cheeks still burned when she recalled the snide comments and rolled eyes of her husband's friends when she first attempted to venture into their conversations. Caitlin had her share of pride. Never in her life had she experienced the kind of condescension and outright rudeness at which Sam's social circle excelled. Looking back, with the clarity hindsight so often brings, her reaction to their cruelty had been a positive one. If they had been more accepting, if she had been less sensitive, if Sam had tried to protect her, she might never have attended college and earned a degree at all. For that, she could be grateful.

Perhaps it was time to end this bitter period of her life. Her mother's last letter hinted at poor health. Perhaps it was time to go home for awhile. The complications were enormous. There were Annie and Ben to consider. The children were settled in school and despite Sam's lack of interest in her, he loved his children and they loved him. Caitlin had no desire to see her children grow up without their father. Lucy would be devastated. Annie and Ben were her only grandchildren and she adored them.

Depression closed in on her again. She fought it off. Maybe, if everyone was reasonable, if Sam didn't lose his temper, something could be worked out. Her heart fluttered with renewed hope. An idea began to form in her mind. For the first time in months, Caitlin settled into a restorative sleep with a smile on her lips.

The Kentucky Derby held at Churchill Downs on the last Saturday in May was a Claiborne family tradition. Not only did Claiborne colts participate but the entire family, the trainer, the servants, the groomers, the exercisers, everyone who had anything to do with Claiborne horses, attended the race that began the count down to the Triple Crown. The series of three annual events beginning with the Derby and ending with the Belmont, determined which thoroughbred, if any, would go down in American racing history as the winner of the most prestigious purse in the thoroughbred world. This year the Claiborne colt, *Night Journey*, was slated to win.

Caitlin, slim and elegant in a linen wrap skirt that fell to her ankles, a white sleeveless blouse and a wide-brimmed straw hat, sat in the Claiborne owner's box sipping iced tea. Six-year-old Ben sat beside her scanning the crowd.

She glanced down and saw the worried frown on his small freckled face. Sliding her free arm around her son's shoulders, she pulled him close for an extended hug and breathed deeply. The all-consuming love that motherhood evoked never failed to astonish her. Caitlin hadn't been prepared for that kind of emotion. Sometimes it choked her and she couldn't manage the words. "Don't worry, love," she said carefully, keeping her voice light. "They'll be here in time. Has Daddy ever missed a Derby?"

"No." Ben looked up, saw the smile on his mother's face, and relaxed against her.

Across the sea of people spread throughout the stands, Caitlin's eyes found Lucy Claiborne's and connected. The older woman smiled bracingly and Caitlin lifted her glass in a salute. Lately, her mother-in-law had been unusually approachable, almost as if she approved of her.

Lucy had intervened after Sam flatly refused to allow her to take the children to Ireland. "Caitlin has a right to be with her mother," she reminded her son with a hint of steel in her voice. "And Brigid should see her grandchildren."

In the end, Sam had capitulated. No one argued with Lucy. She simply announced her position and refused to deviate from it until everyone came around to her way of thinking. It was a trait that annoyed Caitlin immensely when she'd first come to Claiborne Farms. Now, she was grateful for it.

Caitlin knew she was a far cry from the naive young girl who'd married Sam Claiborne fourteen years before. It was much more than an expensive haircut, the labels on her designer clothing, or the diamond on her finger, large but not quite large enough to stretch the boundaries of tastefulness. Caitlin radiated an aura of polished sophistication that was typically southern and purely Claiborne. A cross between wholesome and elegant, with striking cheekbones, a brilliant smile and the contrast of creamy skin against night-dark hair and eyes, Caitlin Claiborne was accustomed to her share of admiring glances.

Sometimes Caitlin wondered if her mother-in-law could read her mind. Would Lucy accept the inevitability of her son's failed marriage, wish Caitlin well and tell her to take good care of Annie and Ben? Or would she be vindictive and controlling like Sam?

Caitlin bit her lip. Her answers would come soon enough, as soon as she had the nerve to hand Sam the divorce papers she carried in her purse. Lucy couldn't possibly know of her plans. No one knew, not even Brigid, not yet.

It was nearly five o'clock in the afternoon. Churchill Downs had opened at eight that morning to a crowd of thousands flowing steadily in from Fourth Street. Across the brick-lined walkways, through the tulip and marigold beds and past the clubhouse, a sea of tanned legs and shining hair, of pink pantsuits, cut-off shorts, straw hats, lycra skirts, t-shirts, and bared backs moved to the sound of rock music, cheers, and hawkers. Inside expensive box seats, men in white suits and bucks lounged beside ladies in tasteful linen, strappy sandals, and wide-brimmed hats.

Caitlin tapped her foot impatiently. If Sam didn't arrive soon with Annie, she would be too late to speak with the jockey.

Beside her, Ben spotted his father and leaped from his seat. "There they are," he shouted, waving his arms. "Daddy, Annie."

Sam Claiborne grinned, shaded his eyes, and waved back to his son. Holding Annie's hand, he picked his way through the crowd, entered the box and sat down. "Where's Mother?" he asked.

Caitlin stood. "She's in the Sommer's box," she answered briefly. "I'll be back in a minute."

"The horse'll win with or without you, Caitlin," Sam drawled running a hand through his gilt-colored hair. "I doubt if Carlson's waiting on pins and needles for you to cheer him on."

Caitlin felt the blood rise in her cheeks.

Ben spoke up. "Can I come with you, Mama?"

Caitlin held out her hand but Sam spoke first. "Stay here with me, son. Mama'll be right back. This is something she likes to do alone."

Without a word to her husband, Caitlin kissed her children and left the box, dismissing Sam's rudeness from her mind. Horses were already coming through the tunnel one at a time. Television cameras focused on the tanbark ring. Owners and trainers converged on the paddock, locating their colors, calling out names, shaking hands. Crowds of onlookers lined the fence. Jockeys in colorful silks moved down the stairs.

Caitlin caught up with Tom Carlson when he was nearly in the mounting circle. Her eyes warmed and she held out her hand. "You know the horse, Tom, and you're the best jockey in this race. Ride it as it comes and don't worry."

Carlson, his eyes level with Caitlin's, grinned. "This one's ours, Caitie. Don't you worry."

She smiled. "Good luck."

"Mount up," an official called out. Tom mounted. Strains of "My Old Kentucky Home" from the brass band lifted the crowd to its feet. The riders led their mounts around the clubhouse making their way back down the long stretch to the starting gate. Caitlin watched as Carlson let the horse out in a slow gallop to warm him up before returning to the green and white starting gate. The jockey pulled plastic goggles over his eyes. *Night Journey* stepped into the gate and the doors slammed shut behind him. Carlson reached down, grabbed a handful of the colt's mane, and bent forward.

Caitlin held her breath. This moment, before the break, was always the worst. Then it happened. The horses surged forward. Seven tons of hard-breathing animals shot toward the straight and the first turn. Caitlin inhaled, waiting.

Carlson allowed *Night Journey* his space while maneuvering for a stronger position. *Silver Flag*, from the Burlington Stables, ran head-to-head with *Baby Rose*, a California horse, who had been in the lead. *Royal Flush*, another Burlington colt, went from fourth to fifth around the bend.

The line was thinning now with Carlson biding his time. Caitlin clenched her fists. If he didn't make his move soon, it would be too late. Then she saw it. *Night Journey* took the bit in his mouth and leaned forward. She sighed in relief as the horse moved ahead, passing *Seventh Cavalry* and *Royal Flush*, leaving the two horses in the dust.

Slowly, with the precision of an artist, Carlson urged *Night Journey* to pick up speed, to accelerate around the bend, moving faster and faster. The horse never missed a beat. Swinging out he switched leads, left to right, as if he were flying through the air. Propelling with his forelegs, he ate up the ground. The race was half over. Only two horses were ahead of him and the time was forty-nine and one-fifth seconds, a record, so far.

Effortlessly, Carlson advanced his horse, swallowing up the lengths that separated him from *Baby Rose*. Caitlin removed her sunglasses, narrowed her eyes and watched. Behind her the crowd roared. *Night Journey* was in third position and there was one quarter of the race still to go.

He sailed past *Baby Rose* while her jockey looked helplessly on. The five-sixteenths pole loomed ahead. Carlson rode in a whirl of motion, instincts alert, every movement practiced and sound. Flashing his stick beside *Night Journey*'s eye spurred the horse to a final flash of speed. Moving to the right and forward he was neck-and-neck with *Silver Flag*. The crowd screamed and rose in the stands as the two horses raced through the top of the straight. Slowly, relentlessly, *Night Journey* pulled ahead. Behind him *Silver Flag*'s jockey rode furiously, chirping, pumping, going for the whip.

Caitlin's breathing altered. "Go with him, Tom," she whispered. "It's nearly over."

And it was. *Night Journey* opened one length and then two as the horses drove toward the wire. In the lead now by a full two and a half lengths, he raced through the wire. The board flashed one minute, fifty eight seconds, a Kentucky Derby record.

In the stands and on the blankets the sea of spectators roared their approval. Carlson slowed *Night Journey* to a trot, circled the track another time, pulled the horse to a stop and lifted his helmet in salute. Reporters, photographers, and television people surged toward the winner's circle.

Sam and Lucy were already there with the children when Caitlin arrived. Lucy threw her braceleted arm around Caitlin's shoulders and hugged her tightly. A photographer snapped their picture. Everything looked as it should have, a united family jubilant with excitement.

Later, after *Night Journey* was led away for the routine urine and saliva tests, after the television crews and reporters disappeared into their favorite sports' bars, after the groomers and the pony boys had brushed, watered, and fed the horses, and sunburned tourists had retreated to their fast food restaurants and budget motels, the aristocracy of the thoroughbred community gathered together in the muted light of an antebellum plantation house. The parties would continue for at least a week.

Ice clinked against fine crystal, and ladies showing cleavage and tanned bare backs flirted outrageously with unavailable men in white jackets, their foreheads slick with perspiration, their voices whiskey-slurred, their words lazy and long on vowels, their intentions clumsy, obvious.

Caitlin stopped in for only a moment to speak to Sam. She'd planned to tell him earlier, before the drink had jellied his brain. But, as usual, she was Sam Claiborne's last priority. He had bypassed his allowed legal limit for alcohol consumption six hours earlier. A man with less tolerance would have passed out long before.

"I'm leaving, Sam," Caitlin said calmly when he'd followed her out onto the lawn. "My lawyer will contact you to settle the details. There isn't anything you can do to stop me. I want nothing from you except what's rightfully mine."

Reeking of bourbon, his voice thick, his face swollen with alcohol, he sneered at the document she'd thrust into his hand. "What's this?"

"A petition for divorce."

"Like hell it is." He downed his drink, threw the glass into the nearby hedges, and methodically tore the papers into shreds. Then he grabbed her arm, pulled her toward him, and before she had time to react, deliberately stuffed them down her blouse.

Caitlin's hands clenched. She willed herself to stand still. She would not lose her temper, no matter how he baited her. There was nothing Sam liked better than to see her explode. "There are other copies, Sam," she said reasonably.

"They'll go the way these did."

Her control broke. With shaking hands she pulled the scraps of paper from inside her blouse and dropped them on the grass. "Why are you pretending it even matters? You can't possibly want to continue this charade of a marriage any more than I do."

"I don't give a coon dog's dick about you, Caitie," he croaked drunkenly, "but I'll be damned if I allow you to take my kids away from me."

"I'm not taking them away from you. You can see them whenever you want."

"I want to see them all the time."

She laughed bitterly. "You mean between drunken binges and screwing half the county?"

"You got that right."

Caitlin sighed, threw up her hands, and began walking toward her car. "I'm not going to argue with you, Sam," she said over her shoulder. "I thought I'd tell you in person. I owe you that much. But you can't stop me."

"My lawyer will shred your appeal over his morning coffee," he shouted after her retreating figure. "Annie and Ben'll be home before the Derby dust settles."

Caitlin slipped into Annie's room and pushed the door shut behind her. The welcoming glow of the night light softened the corners of the dresser, the edges of the toy chest, and brought life to the carved features of the glassy-eyed dolls staring down at her. They reminded her of the stories she'd read as a child about the gentle guardians with eyes of obsidian who watched over the pharoah's tombs of ancient Egypt. The memory gave her courage. Carefully she walked over to the bed and sat down beside her daughter. Annie stirred, her eyelashes fluttered and separated. Caitlin waited. Annie always woke this way. A minute passed, then another. The child's eyes opened and she smiled.

"Mama," she said sleepily, "did you come to kiss me goodnight?"

Caitlin nodded and smoothed her daughter's dark hair. "I came to tell you something, too, Annie. I need to tell you before you hear it from—" she hesitated, "from someone else."

Annie waited.

She was always like this—patient, thoughtful, well adjusted. Caitlin's heart thumped. What if she didn't want to come? How could she live without Annie?

"I've decided to go to Ireland for awhile, Annie, to visit Gran. I'd like you and Ben to come with me."

Annie smiled. "I'll come. I love visiting Gran. Ben does, too."

"It will be a long visit."

"Will I miss school?"

Caitlin nodded. "A few weeks, I think. There are two schools in Kilcullen where Gran lives. We can see which one you would like best."

Annie sat up. "But it's almost summer. Why do I have to go to school in Ireland?"

"I'm not sure that we'll come back here to live, Annie. You'll have to go to school."

Annie's mouth puckered as if she'd eaten something sour. "We aren't moving, are we, Mama?"

The truth was always a mouthful, no matter how short the word. "Yes."

"Why? Daddy and Grandma won't want to move. They've lived here forever."

Caitlin's eyes filled. She took her daughter's hands in her own. Lowering her head, she kissed each knuckle. When she lifted her head, the tears were gone. "Daddy and I won't be living together anymore."

"You're getting a divorce?" There was no mistaking the horror in Annie's voice.

"Yes."

"Why?"

"We aren't happy together."

"I'm happy. Ben's happy. Does he know?"

Caitlin shook her head. "Not yet. He's only six years old.

I won't use the word *divorce* with him. He wouldn't understand."

Annie's lip trembled. "Will I see Daddy again?"

Caitlin gathered her daughter into her arms. "Of course you will. And when you do see him, he'll spend more time with you than he does now."

"What if he doesn't? Can I come back?"

Caitlin's heart broke. "If you really want to, love. I can't imagine living without you. But if you really want to, I'll manage. All I ask is that you give it a chance."

"Why do we have to go away?" Annie mumbled into her mother's shoulder. "Can't you be divorced here?"

Caitlin breathed in the scent of Annie's freshly shampooed hair. "It's complicated but I'll try to explain. I want to breed and train thoroughbreds for racing. It's all I've ever done and all I know how to do. But it takes an enormous amount of money to do that here in Kentucky or anywhere in the United States. In Ireland land and fees are much less. The chances of beginning something there are much greater than here." She kissed Annie's cheek. "Do you understand, love?"

"Yes." Annie's arms slid around her mother's neck. "Will you sleep here with me, Mama?"

Caitlin stretched out on the twin bed beside her daughter. Annie's slight form molded itself against her. Minutes later she heard the child's deep, even breathing. Pressing her lips against the soft nape of her neck, Caitlin closed her burning eyes and slept.

Three weeks later, without the anesthetizing affect of a pint of bourbon straight up, Sam Claiborne had good reason for his anger. His lawyer had called with the news that custody battles took time. Meanwhile, Caitlin's final riposte was clear, purposeful, and astonishingly well executed. Not only

had she sold exactly one half of the mutual funds she'd
invested and withdrawn half of their joint savings account,
but *Kentucky Gold*, the mare he had given his wife for a wedding gift, the dam of three Triple Crown champions recently
covered by the champion, *Narraganset*, was on her way to
Ireland.

3

❧❧❧

Caitlin woke to a loud banging on the door. Groggily she opened her eyes and focused on the glowing hands of her alarm clock. Dawn was still three hours away. The mare must be in foal. Adrenalin surged through her and she was instantly completely awake. Throwing aside the duvet, she reached for the jeans and sweatshirt she had left hanging over the back of a chair, walked to the long window and threw open the sash. An icy blast of wind cut her face like a knife. She shouted out the window. "I'm coming, Davy." The knocking subsided.

Within minutes she was ready, her mass of curls twisted and controlled in a claw clip, her jacket zipped, a denim tote bag slung over her shoulder. She paused long enough to walk down the long hall to peek into her mother's room.

Brigid was awake. "I'm off," Caitlin whispered. "*Kentucky Gold* is foaling."

Brigid sniffed and sat up. "Why are you botherin' t' tell me? With himself poundin' and shoutin', the entire town must know. Go along now. I'll see t' the children if you're not back by breakfast."

Caitlin nodded, ran down the stairs, out of the house, and into the waiting truck. Without a word she opened the door and climbed in. The man at the wheel was visibly nervous.

"I thought we'd have another week at least," he said, "but she's breathin' hard and waxin'."

Caitlin shrugged and stared out the window, her mind on what was most likely happening inside the stable. "What did the vet say?"

Davy Flynn didn't answer immediately. She knew it was her accent that he couldn't get past. Except for a certain husky timbre, Caitlin sounded nothing like herself. Fourteen years in America had nearly erased all the Irish from her voice. Her accent wasn't the only change. It was something much more subtle than that. She recognized it even if Davy didn't. She wasn't the same Caitlin Keneally who'd left Ireland fourteen years before. Education, sophistication, and more money than the blue-collar inhabitants of Kilcullen would see in a lifetime had left their mark.

"He's at the Grange," Davy said at last. "Mrs. Clarke had an emergency. There was no one else."

Caitlin turned. "Are you saying that he doesn't even know *Kentucky Gold* is foaling?"

"Not yet," replied Davy grimly.

"I thought a resident veterinarian was one of the benefits of keeping a mare at the stud farm?"

"For Christ's sake, Caitie, what was the man to do? There was no one else to go."

She stared straight ahead silently acknowledging the reasonableness of his argument. "I'm sorry, Davy," she said at last. "I'm just nervous. What about Brian Hennessey? Does he know?"

"Brian's still not back from the auction," Davy said stoically, refusing to criticize his superior.

Caitlin let out a long breath. "Well then, I suppose it's up to us."

Davy's eyes left the road to stare incredulously at the woman across the bench seat from him.

Caitlin knew him well enough to read the thoughts running through his mind. Davy Flynn, a groom at the Curragh Stud Farm, had known her since she was born. He was wondering when that wild streak he remembered from her youth, the one that she'd tempered slightly after marriage and motherhood, would resurrect itself. What Davy Flynn didn't realize was that Caitie Keneally was gone forever. She was Caitlin Claiborne now, and impulsive decisions were an indulgence she could no longer afford.

Out of the corner of her eye she saw him swallow. Flying a premium broodmare across the Atlantic when she was due to foal was a disaster waiting to happen. If anything happened to the mare or her foal, they could all be in a very bad way.

She turned back to the road. She'd played the odds. But it was her turn to win. Just this once, to make up for the mistakes she'd made, she needed a win.

The neonatal unit and foaling barn were at the end of the farm along the Tully Walk. Past the wrought iron gates with their enormous gold letters. Past the tree-lined drive and rail fences. Past the training school, the dormitory, and the kitchen. Past the stallion boxes, the museum and the Black Abbey. Away from engine noises and crowds. Near the side of the paddock where the mares chewed on lush grass, rich in lime, blue at the root—grass that bred horses unlike any other in the world. Davy drove up to the white-washed

building with its lantern-shaped roof broken by a series of
skylights, and killed the engine.

Caitlin grabbed her bag, ran across the packed dirt, and
disappeared into the black shadow thrown by the barn door.
Kentucky Gold was pacing back and forth inside her stall.
"Easy, love," she crooned, rubbing her hand against the
mare's swollen belly. Milk had congealed around her nipples
like melted candle wax. Her nostrils were flared and she was
warm to the touch.

"It won't be long," Caitlin said, when she heard Davy's
footsteps at the door. She reached for her bag, her fingers
closing reassuringly around the iodine and the enema. "Fill a
bowl with water and bring me some gloves," she ordered.

Davy watched the horse begin to circle. Then he disappeared through the door to find a bowl, returning quickly.

Caitlin glanced at him. "Don't be nervous, Davy," Her
husky voice was filled with amusement. "Have I ever let you
down?"

He sat on a low stool and watched the mare pace. "No,
lass, but we've never had so much at stake."

She nodded. At fourteen years old, *Kentucky Gold* was
already a legend, the dam of more winning bloodstock than
any mare in the history of American thoroughbred racing.
The foal she carried was a *Narraganset* foal, the Claiborne
Triple Crown winner whose syndicated shares sold for one
million dollars each. This was the mare's sixth labor. It was
imperative that nothing go wrong.

Less than an hour later, she stopped pacing and col-
lapsed in the straw on her left side. Caitlin slipped on rubber
gloves and knelt beside her, waiting. Amniotic fluid, warm
and foul smelling, gushed from the animal's vaginal opening. The foal would soon follow. A minute passed and then
another. The tip of a foot appeared. Caitlin bit her lip.
Where was the other one? Normally, the two came out

together. A full three minutes passed. "Call the vet, Davy," she said tersely. "Tell him we need him now."

Davy ran for the phone beside the tack room. Caitlin waited no longer. Gently she inserted her gloved hand into the vagina. The mare's contraction peaked and her tight muscles clamped down mercilessly, crushing Caitlin's hand. Tears rolled down her cheeks. Gritting her teeth, she waited it out. Finally, after what seemed like an eternity, she was able to feel for the foal's foot and gently untwist it.

Kentucky Gold breathed heavily, blowing through her flared nostrils. Caitlin waited for the foal's legs and then the head to appear. If all went well the shoulder would be next, followed by the neck. Both slipped out of the opening with perfect precision.

A cold draft pierced her fleece-lined sweatshirt. Someone had entered the barn. The mare panted and strained. Caitlin took hold of both legs and pulled hard.

"Easy now," said a voice as rough as tires on wet gravel, a voice that definitely did not belong to the stud farm's vet. "Don't rush her. You're doing fine."

Caitlin kept her eyes on the horse. This must be the elusive Brian Hennessey, the man in whom John O'Shea had enough confidence to turn over the reins of one of the most prestigious thoroughbred stud farms in all of Europe. The man touted as having an uncanny instinct for knowing what an individual horse needed to make him a winner. A man who had the reputation of a magician, who turned horseflesh into gold. "You took your time coming back," she said.

Brian Hennessey knelt in the straw beside her, slipped on a pair of rubber gloves and took hold of the colt's left leg. "I didn't realize I had a Claiborne thoroughbred waitin' to deliver in my stall. You neglected to mention your mare was in foal when we talked on the phone."

"She's mine," said Caitlin automatically, hearing only the first half of his sentence.

Without answering, he slipped a practiced hand inside the mare. "The shoulders are large," he said, withdrawing his hand. "He might have difficulty clearing the opening. Wait for the ribs to come and I'll guide the hips."

They pulled together for several minutes. When the ribs came through, Brian positioned his hands and eased out the rest of the body. It was a male, large of bone and shoulder, perfectly proportioned.

"Oh," Caitlin breathed, "he's beautiful. Look at him. He's perfect."

Brian Hennessey sat back on his heels and expertly sized up the foal's long straight legs, the dished-in Arabian face—a recessive trait from the *Godolphin Arabian,* father of all thoroughbreds—the blaze of white down his forehead, and the strong musculature that bespoke good racing blood. "Aye, that he is," he said at last, "a fine colt, generations of speed bred into him. If he has the rest of what it takes, he'll be a runner."

"You mean if he has heart?"

"I mean nothin' of the sort," retorted Brian. "*Heart* is an old wives' tale. If the horse can breathe enough to run, he's got a fightin' chance." Gently, he pulled the foal around to the mare's head, breaking the umbilical cord in exactly the right place. Tentatively, and then with growing confidence, *Kentucky Gold* began to lick her newborn while Brian wiped her wound with iodine.

Caitlin rubbed the foal down with a towel to dry him off and jumpstart his circulation. "The mare needs penicillin."

Brian nodded. "We'll give her a combination of penicillin and streptomycin just to be sure." He looked at Caitlin's smeared sweatshirt and cheeks. "Where in bloody hell is our vet?"

"With Mrs. Clarke, at the Grange," Caitlin replied. "There was an emergency."

Davy spoke up from behind them. "He's on his way."

Forty-five minutes later the Curragh Stud's veterinarian walked through the door in time to see the foal gain his legs and begin to suckle.

"I'm sorry, Brian," he apologized. "Clarke's mare was in trouble and I thought we had another week here."

"No harm done. Mrs. Claiborne managed on her own. You can check the pair of them out and let us know of any developments. We'll be in the kitchen."

Caitlin waited until they were out of hearing range to voice her objection. "I have to go. My children are home asleep."

"Your mother raised six children. I don't imagine another two would phase her."

"My mother is past seventy."

"Come, Mrs. Claiborne," Brian said reasonably. "This won't take long and I'll drive you back when we're finished."

She relented. "Ten minutes. That's all I can spare."

Together they walked down the long, tree-lined lane to the farmhouse kitchen. Brian slowed his pace to match hers. He wasn't particularly tall for an Irishman but the top of her head barely reached his shoulder.

He opened the door. A single light over the stove lit the kitchen. He would have flipped the main switch but Caitlin stopped him. "Leave it," she said. "I'm exhausted and the light won't help."

"Tea?" He picked up the kettle.

She rubbed her eyes. "You wouldn't happen to have any decaffeinated coffee, would you?"

He grinned and for the briefest instant her heart fluttered. Then he spoke and his words made her angry all over again.

"Wake up, lass, this is Ireland."

"Believe me, Mr. Hennessey, I'm aware of that. What did you want to talk about?"

"I heard about your divorce. I'm sorry."

"Thank you," she said wearily. "However, with the exception of two children, divorce will be the only good thing to come out of my marriage." Her eyes challenged him. "Is there anything else?"

He reached into his back pocket and handed her a piece of paper. "This."

She read it twice, quickly, then handed it back to him. "It isn't true."

"Which part isn't true, Mrs. Claiborne?"

"Caitlin," she said, quietly. "Please, call me Caitlin." She was so tired it was an effort to speak. From behind her haze, she watched him hang his jacket on the back of a chair, roll up his sleeves, and spoon tea leaves into the pot. She wondered if he'd always been like this, practical, objective, every action measured.

No one would ever call him handsome, not in the fleshy, muscular, ruddy-skinned way of Irish men. Brian Hennessey was lean, so lean that the housewives of Kilcullen Town most likely clucked sympathetically while leaving puddings and stews on his doorstep. He had thin, finely hewn features, soaring black eyebrows, and heavy-lidded eyes the clear, blue-green color typical of the Aran Islands where the Anglo-Norman influence hadn't infiltrated the general population. Under the spare flesh, his bones were narrow, capable, of the chiseled quality found in men who ate only when their stomachs reminded them it was time for a meal. The very look of him bespoke calm, reason, and competence, the kind of man whose level blue gaze and steely conviction a woman could count on when she needed it.

It suddenly occurred to her that she wanted him on her side. "*Kentucky Gold* is mine," she explained. "My husband gave her to me as a wedding gift."

He looked skeptical.

"It's true," she insisted. "I've put years of labor into Claiborne Farms. *Kentucky Gold* is all I asked for."

He leaned back against the counter and folded his arms across his chest. "I imagine Sam Claiborne thought your marriage would last."

"Well, it didn't."

"Why not?"

She stared at him. No Irishman would ask such a question. "It's none of your concern," she stammered.

Brian continued to look at her. His unblinking stare grated on her nerves.

"Did you hear me?" she asked at last.

His voice turned low and husky and his answer was the last one either of them expected. It seemed to come from somewhere deep inside of him. "I can't remember when I've seen eyes so dark against skin so fair. Martin never told me you were pretty enough to stop traffic." Then he smiled and somehow, without quite knowing why, the standard by which she had previously determined the measure of a man had been irrevocably altered.

She felt the heat clear up to her hairline. Before she could formulate a sensible reply, he was all business again.

"It's very much my concern if I'm harborin' a stolen horse in my stables," he said deliberately. "The entire reputation of the farm is at stake."

"I told you the mare is mine."

"What about the foal?"

Caitlin bit her lip. "I'm not sure yet."

"When will you know?"

Nervously, she fidgeted with her hair clip. Handfuls of

black curls fell around her face. "Sam has other foals. I only want this one."

"But is he rightfully yours?"

"I don't know," she confessed. "My lawyer is filing a petition for a court date. A judge will decide."

The sharp whistle of the kettle interrupted them. Brian poured water into the teapot. "There has been a new development, Caitlin. Your husband confirmed that his prize stallion, *Narraganset*, died yesterday from a blood clot on the brain."

She couldn't have heard him correctly. Not *Narraganset*, the greatest stallion in the history of American turf, a stallion whose breeding services were reserved ahead of time for a million dollars a covering.

"Caitlin." Brian's voice came to her as if from a great distance. Her thoughts were coming too quickly, flip-flopping inside her head. Hard fingers dug into her shoulders, and eyes, impossibly blue, peered down at her. "Listen to me, Caitlin. *Kentucky Gold* has just given birth to *Narraganset's* last foal. Samuel Claiborne may care nothin' for horses but he's no fool. He'll never give this one up."

It wasn't until later, until after he'd driven her home and left her at the door, after she'd scrubbed away all traces of the foaling barn and curled up beneath the warm duvet, until she'd gone over every word of their conversation and relived every nuance of his expression, that it came to her. How could Brian Hennessey know that a man in charge of a multi-million dollar thoroughbred farm cared nothing for horses?

Caitlin punched her pillow and flipped over on her back. It was late and the subtle changes in her appearance, obviously invisible in the soft light of Brian's kitchen, would be glaringly evident in full sunlight. Twenty-one-year-old women could manage a few sleepless nights and still appear radiant the next day. Ten years later they could not.

Her appearance had never concerned her before, at least it hadn't until Samuel Claiborne made it blindingly clear that she lacked the necessary qualities to keep him faithful or even tactfully discreet. Not that her husband meant anything to her. He hadn't in a long time. But Caitlin had never been short on pride and Sam's behavior was humiliating.

Now, in retrospect, with wisdom earned through fourteen years of experience, much of it painful, she could look back to that first year in America and see exactly why she had succumbed to his brand of southern charm, synthetic and maple-syrupy though it was.

Her two week visit to Lelia, the older sister who lived in Boston, had stretched to three months. Lelia had given her an ultimatum. Find work and a place of her own or go back to Ireland. Caitlin knew she had outlasted her welcome. Three people in a one bath, studio apartment was unbearably crowded. It was time to move out on her own.

Caitlin had helped out in her mother's pub often enough to know something about waitressing but her heart wasn't in south Boston. She yearned for country roads, fog hanging like gray lace over low stone walls, white plank fences, and gleaming horses grazing in lush grass. It wasn't long before she'd earned enough to set out for the bluegrass horsebreeding country south of Louisville, home of the aristocracy of the equine world.

Unlike Ireland, where women had yet to assume a place in male-dominated occupations, thoroughbred farms in the United States were hiring women throughout the industry. Caitlin was amazed and gratified to see women grooms, trainers, exercisers, and jockeys.

Charlie Barton, groom for the Claiborne Farms, took a careful measuring look at Caitlin's petite, high-waisted frame, her dramatic dark eyes and ivory skin, and another at the compact muscles in legs that appeared too long for her body and hired her on the spot.

"You haven't seen me ride," Caitlin had protested.

Charlie spat out the end of his cigar, pulled a piece of tobacco from his tongue, and grinned, white teeth splitting his black face in two. "Missy, ya got the body of a jockey. I'll teach ya whatever ya need to know."

As it turned out, John O'Shea, manager of the Curragh Stud, had already taught her more than anyone had expected. By the time Caitlin cashed her first paycheck, Charlie trusted her enough to allow her to begin training *Mollie's Joy*, a yearling colt sired by *Citation*, a Triple Crown winner.

So strong were the images of those early days in Kentucky that Caitlin had only to close her eyes and it would come back to her in graphic detail: the white plank fences, rolling hills, antique shops at every crossroad, the mare's frosty breath on the morning air. The light panting and thudding hooves of thoroughbreds out for their morning exercise. The brilliant orange of a southern sunrise. The Kentucky river rolling past white-pillared eighteenth century homes set back on canopied, tree-lined drives. The brilliant purple, red, gold, and green of country fruit stands, and stone walls that reminded her of her father's home in the west of Ireland.

Woven throughout it all, was an awareness of money— the decadent, surreal, eye-crossing pace at which it flowed in ways that it never could in that green country across the Atlantic where she was born.

In Kentucky, yearlings sold for more than ten million dollars, horses dined in stables lit by crystal chandeliers, and it was not unheard of for waitresses to receive thousand dollar tips from well-fed foreign buyers.

Caitlin couldn't be blamed for falling under Samuel Claiborne's spell. Sam was a gentleman, soothing, complimentary, protective. **His** oozing, relaxed confidence, his appreciative glances and his casual disregard for money were as different from a blunt, principled Irishman as Lucy Claiborne, elegant matriarch of Claiborne Farms, was different from blunt-speaking Brigid Keneally, local publican.

Lucy had disapproved of her from the beginning. Now, when she reflected back, Caitlin could see her point. Sam was a catch—intelligent, educated, and rich. His mother had wanted the very best for her only son and Caitlin Keneally, Irish immigrant with only a high school education, did not measure up.

But for once in his life, Sam had proven unusually difficult. He was set on Caitlin and none of the debutantes his mother paraded before him swayed his thinking. They met on a crisp fall morning, shortly after her nineteenth birthday. He'd recently returned from six months in Europe, a gift from his parents upon his graduation from Duke University. Sam wasn't particularly interested in horses but he was interested in business, and Claiborne Enterprises was enough of a business to warrant his full-time interest.

Because Sam was a dutiful son and because he was intelligent enough to know what was coming to him, he did not protest when his father roused him before dawn to see the latest batch of Claiborne yearlings.

Caitlin, dressed in black jodhpurs and a red sweater, dark curls twisted untidily away from her face, was exercising *Mollie's Joy*. Sam Claiborne, caught by the brilliant red and black against the colt's dark coat and the breathtaking beauty of Kentucky's fall foliage, stopped to take a second look and forgot to breathe.

Already, *Mollie's Joy* showed the promise of great speed, and when the two of them—horse and girl, perfectly formed, effortlessly aligned—thundered around the track, Sam, a connoisseur of beauty, was smitten as he had never been in his life.

Caitlin flushed becomingly when Bull introduced them. Looking back she wondered if what had happened that morning would have blown over if she had been a bit further removed from Ireland or if Sam had been less romantically inclined, or if Lucy's protests hadn't been so uncharacteristically strident, or if Bull Claiborne hadn't praised her so effusively, as effusively as any father proud of a daughter's accomplishment.

As it turned out, Lucy's protests went unheeded. When Bull Claiborne pronounced Caitlin the best little bruising rider he'd seen this side of the Mason-Dixon, his wife threw up her hands and, with the beautiful manners instilled in southern women from birth, gave up graciously and began planning the wedding of the decade.

Caitlin was a reasonable person. Although she could never really like Lucy Claiborne, over the years fairness forced her to admit that the woman was a wonderful grandmother. She'd often taken Sam to task for his philandering and assured Caitlin that no matter what happened to the marriage, her grandchildren would never want for anything.

Unfortunately for Caitlin, Lucy was no longer a major shareholder of Claiborne Enterprises. Since Bull's death, his son ran the company, with the exception of a few duties his father had stipulated Caitlin take care of. Those duties had escalated, earning her a reputation in Kentucky's thoroughbred community. They also brought Claiborne Farms a healthy profit. Sam made it quite clear that if Caitlin chose to humiliate him with a divorce, he would see her reduced to nothing.

His threat was meaningless, of course. American courts were reasonably fair to women who'd given birth to a wealthy man's children. And Sam Claiborne's idea of *nothing* in no way resembled Caitlin's definition of the term. She would have laughed in his face if it hadn't been for paragraph three in the proposed settlement, a paragraph far more chilling and cruel than his taunt to leave her penniless. He wanted custody of the children.

Sam had underestimated her. Caitlin would die before giving up her children. *Kentucky Gold*'s foal meant far more than a winning purse. It meant stud and breeding fees, foals, syndicated shares—everything she needed to break free of the Claiborne yoke and keep her children. The money would keep them until the foal reached racing age. After that Caitlin was on her own.

She had every hope of success. She was Irish, and Ireland was the place for a trainer to establish a reputatution. Fees were low, yards were inexpensive, and the Irish Curragh was the only stud in the world where horses were trained on the same track where they raced. The spindly, chestnut colt she'd pulled feet first into the world was her single hope for the future.

4

Brian Hennessey had never really loved a woman. He knew that now, at least not the way a man does when he thinks in terms of children and a forever kind of permanence, the kind found in marriage vows, insurance policies, and adjoining cemetery plots. Women and their preoccupation with order and appearance were fine in small doses, to attend the cinema or to share a meal with and, if they were willing, occasionally a bed, but that was the extent of it.

For some inexplicable reason, Caitlin Claiborne, reeking of horse blood and amniotic fluid, her arms halfway up the insides of a laboring broodmare had come closer than anyone to revealing the folly of his assumptions. Caitlin was the kind of woman who turned a man's insides to mush, the kind he could count on to keep going when everything around her fell apart and there wasn't much hope of coming about.

It wasn't just that she was willing to dirty her hands with hard work. Brian didn't know of an Irish woman who hadn't defined the phrase with a whole new dimension. Nor was it the way her eyes and mouth had gone soft when the colt finally made his appearance. Brian had known a number of women, and men as well, whose insides turned to jelly at the sight of a newborn colt. There was something incredibly unassuming about her, as if she didn't know she had the kind of beauty that scared a man witless, as if she didn't care what he thought of her.

He liked the way she persevered during her mare's delivery, working hard enough for the arteries to pop up on the sides of her neck. Women didn't normally allow a man to see that, as if strain somehow demeaned them or made them less feminine. And for a single brief instant after the colt was delivered, she'd included him in her happiness. Something told him it would be no small thing to be a part of Caitlin Claiborne's joy.

He couldn't afford to fall in love with her. It hit him that moment in the kitchen when they'd stared at one another, the absolute polarity of who they were. She was Mrs. Samuel Claiborne, with fourteen years in America behind her and the resources to stable ten mares at the Curragh Stud Farm. He was a salaried employee living in rented quarters with a savings account that next to Sam Claiborne's millions would look like pocket change.

Brian absently caressed the shapely head of his six-year-old collie, Neeve, and watched the blinking light on his fax machine spit out yet another sheet of paper into the overflowing tray. It was almost dawn. He'd been awake for nearly twenty-four hours and still sleep eluded him. He knew the reason for his insomnia. He wasn't a complicated enough person to have hidden, unprobeable depths. Only once had he misread himself.

That mistake had sent him in the wrong direction for a number of years. It was his friend, Father Martin O'Shea, who'd shown him the error in his thinking. He couldn't completely regret those years. Without them he might have followed his father to the fishing boats, a fate similar to a prison sentence in Brian's mind. Instead he'd acquired an education few fisherman's sons from the Aran Islands could claim.

The fact of the matter was that Caitlin had surprised him. There was nothing left of the girl Martin O'Shea told him about, nothing except a mass of flyaway black curls and eyes as large and dark as Raphael's Madonna, the one that had so intrigued him in the antechamber of the Jesuit rectory in Dublin. Only now those eyes didn't sparkle with mischief. They were angry and concealing and filled with an unmistakable wariness. Intuition told him the anger he saw was really something else, something he couldn't imagine associating with the Caitlin Keneally he'd heard so much about.

Neeve slipped out from under his hand, walked to the fireplace where the turf still glowed a dull red, turned around several times, and settled into a comfortable sleeping position. Brian gulped down the last of his now tepid tea, rose, and headed for the single bedroom at the back of the cottage he called home. If he was lucky he could manage at least three hours of undisturbed rest before anyone called him.

Thirty minutes later, in that twilight stage between waking and sleeping, when the edges of a solution are not yet clearly defined but the problem doesn't appear quite so difficult as it seems in the merciless, unrelieved light of day, it came to him just as it always did when the night was long and his mind was particularly receptive to association. Martin O'Shea had grown up with Caitlin. He would know her as well as anyone. The priest had a way of putting a healing finger on the heart of a matter.

After all it was Martin who'd shown Brian that a calling to holy orders was absolute, with no room for halfway measures, doubts, or portions held back in reserve. Four years in the Jesuit College with Martin had clarified the shallowness of his own religious commitment. With a sense of relief and more than a little gratitude, he had shaken his friend's hand and promised to keep in touch.

Later, when Brian needed work, it was Martin who'd convinced John O'Shea to recommend him as a thoroughbred trainer, and it was Martin who smoothed his path with the local residents who welcomed strangers, but only those who stayed from February through June, the racing season, and then went home again.

Brian's reputation had been further cemented by the training of three consecutive winners of England's Grand National, the most prestigious steeple chase in the world. The race that catapulted his face onto the front pages of *Irish Field* and the *Racing Gazette*. The race that made his name a household word in equine circles, and for the first time in his life, earned him enough of a bank balance to merit a savings account, an investment portfolio, and a platinum credit card.

When John O'Shea retired as manager of the Curragh Stud, he recommended that Brian take his place, a move that established the younger man's standing in the tightly knit community of Kilcullen Town.

Over a pint or two at Keneally's pub, Martin had shared many of his childhood escapades. He'd mentioned Caitlin often but Brian knew enough to disregard most of what he said. Memory played tricks on a man, and events seen with the eyes of youth changed enormously with age. No one person could have the qualities Martin attributed to the Caitlin Keneally of his youth.

Tomorrow Brian would call on Martin at the rectory, bring him a bottle of Irish whiskey, and ask the questions that needed answering. Maybe then he could sleep peacefully. Whatever the reason, Caitlin Claiborne, with her dark eyes and her pouting, bruised-lipped mouth, disturbed him in ways he hadn't been disturbed in a very long time.

Martin O'Shea, junior rector of Saint Patrick's Church in Kilcullen Town, answered the door dressed in faded denims and a cableknit sweater. "Father Duran won't return until tomorrow, and Mrs. Kelly has an emergency in Kinsale," he said, explaining away his housekeeper's absence. "Shall we make the most of it?"

Brian grinned and lifted the bottle of whiskey out of its paper bag. "My sentiments exactly, Father O'Shea."

"What brings you here in the middle of the week?" Martin asked when they were settled on chairs in the sitting room with two glasses half full of amber liquid and the bottle between them.

"Caitlin Claiborne."

"Ah." Martin smiled and returned his friend's gaze steadily. "It didn't take you two long to meet."

"Her mare foaled this mornin' in my stable. She was there." Brian's knuckles were white around his glass. "Sweet bleedin' Jesus, Martin. She would have delivered the colt herself if I hadn't come in."

Martin laughed. "That sounds like Caitlin, always one to throw her heart over."

"Just how well do you know her?"

"There was a time when I knew her better than anyone alive," the priest said slowly. "Caitlin and I were born on the same day."

Brian's eyebrow lifted. "You never mentioned that."

Martin looked surprised. "Surely I must have. My mother was her godmother. We grew up together. Perhaps you forgot."

Brian doubted it but he let it stand. "Tell me about her."

Martin leaned back in his chair, a fond smile on his lips. "There was never a time when I didn't know Caitlin Keneally.

Like it or not, everyone who lived here knew each other. It was the kind of town where the local publican ran the convenience store and the post office as well, where off-season a stranger could no more find a friendly pint on Sunday or after ten in the evening, than he could find a ride out of town."

"It hasn't changed much," Brian murmured.

Martin swallowed the rest of his drink and pushed the glass aside. "Is something bothering you, Brian?"

"Just a bit of curiosity. If you don't want to satisfy it, never mind."

Martin shook his head. "I'm sure Caitlin wouldn't mind. Everything I have to tell you is complimentary."

"Go on then."

"Caitie was Brigid's last daughter, the youngest of six and by far the cleverest. She was brilliant and spirited and completely without fear. I was no match for her. I can still feel the switch against my legs for the scrapes she led us into." He closed his eyes remembering. "Her disapproval was the worst. I'd look at her and her face would be closed against me in that way she had of removing herself, and I'd want to fling myself into the Liffy. But she never stayed angry for long. Caitlin never held grudges. She shouted at you and sulked for a while and then it was over."

"Just how brilliant was she?"

Martin leaned forward. "Christ, Brian. She'd read more Irish history and literature than the whole Dominican order. Her O level results are still a record for the entire county."

Brian frowned. "But you said she had difficulty in school."

Martin nodded. "The Dominicans were the teaching order assigned to Saint Patrick's Academy. They weren't cruel or particularly unkind, no more than any of the orders instructing children in the Irish Republic's parochial schools. The most anyone could say about them was they took their duties seriously and that discipline was carried out regularly and indiscriminately. But their lessons were uninspired, mostly rote memorization and rules of grammar. And they were teaching Caitlin Keneally."

"Still," Brian broke in, "they were educators. Why didn't they appreciate her mind?"

"Ego probably. Caitlin skipped school more than she attended."

Brian laughed. "What did her mother say?"

Martin shrugged. "The poor woman was besieged with the responsibilities of a pub, a convenience store, a post office, and six children. When she learned that Caitlin wasn't falling behind in academics, she left it alone." He thought for a minute. "I recall that everyone did a great deal of leaving Caitlin alone. The end result was that nothing changed. She was Brigid's last child and she managed her mother with very little effort. Even with her poor attendance habits, she was the most gifted student in her class and, I think, completely without remorse. The situation was similar to one of those underground volcanoes with pressure building, waiting for a fissure in the surface, to spill out scalding everything and everyone in its path."

Brian frowned and turned his empty glass around on the table.

"You're very serious for a man who's downed two glasses of Ireland's finest," Martin remarked.

Brian's smile flickered briefly. He didn't want to appear too interested and yet he couldn't help himself. "Why do you think she left Ireland?"

Martin shrugged. "I can't say for sure. We didn't keep in touch. She was crazy for horses. In Ireland women weren't accepted into the yards the way they are today."

It was a logical explanation, one that Brian had figured out himself. Pushing back his chair, he stood. "I've used up enough of your time. Thanks for the company."

"Have you had enough?"

"For today. My thanks, Martin. I'll see you at Mass on Sunday."

Brian was deep in thought and arrived at the gates of the Stud sooner than he expected. Everything Martin told him made sense. Caitlin was intelligent and she obviously knew a great deal about horses, but there was something missing, something about the woman herself that didn't add up. Perhaps he'd read too much into a first meeting. It had been late and she was exhausted.

There was no doubt in Brian's mind that he was overly preoccupied with her, more so than he could ever remember being about a woman. That in itself wasn't unusual. She was Caitlin Claiborne come back to Kilcullen with her million-dollar broodmare, her messy divorce, and a custody battle over a *Narraganset*-sired colt that was sure to bring Irish thoroughbred racing and the Curragh Stud some very unpleasant publicity.

There was more to it, of course. Brian was honest enough to admit that Caitlin had the power to disturb any man's hard-won peace of mind without her horse, her angry husband, or her legal suit. She was different from the girl Martin told him about—sharper, almost bitter, with a tension in her expression that he was sure hadn't been there before. But there had been a moment, a few seconds after the foal was born, when he'd seen her eyes go soft and bright, her voice tremble with wonder, and his heart twisted inside his chest.

The truth was that Caitlin was the kind of woman who could tie him up in knots with nothing more than a single glance. If he didn't pull himself together, he would have his own demons to conquer.

5

Brigid sprinkled a pinch of salt over the steaming oats, ladled healthy portions into two bowls and set them on the table.

She watched ten-year-old Annie Claiborne frown, pick up her spoon and stare at the unappetizing mass. Annie wasn't accustomed to oats but the child had to eat something. Yesterday she'd left untouched the bacon and eggs Brigid served for breakfast. Most likely Lucy Claiborne would have understood immediately. But this was Ireland and Annie's Grandma Lucy was thousands of miles away.

"May I have some milk, please?" the child asked politely.

Ben, four years younger, wasn't nearly as inhibited. "I don't like oats, Gran," he said clearly. "I want pancakes with syrup."

"You'll like these," said Brigid cheerfully, setting a pitcher of milk on the table. "I've no time for pancakes this mornin'. Your mum's been out all night. I think we should let her sleep."

"What will we do while Mama sleeps?" asked Annie.

Brigid looked surprised. "Why, you'll come t' the store with me, lass. It's old enough you are to be givin' me a hand."

"I can give a hand too," Ben piped up. "I'm old enough."

Brigid laughed. "So you are. The wood needs stackin'." She brushed the top of Annie's head with her hand, and for an instant her breath caught. The dark flyaway curls settling like a cloud around her granddaughter's face were very like Caitlin's at the same age. Brigid willed her hands to stop trembling. Black hair could be explained, but those eyes? Sean's eyes had been the sea-warmed blue of the Aran islanders, a color so distinctive that few could mistake his heritage.

Thank God no one in Kilcullen who remembered Sean Keneally had anything beyond a basic grasp of genetics, except for Father Duran, and there was nothing to fear from that corner. "Eat up now," she said crisply, "there are glasses t' be wiped and the floor t' be swept."

Annie forced the unwelcome food past her lips and fought back tears. Brigid bit her lip. Annie didn't want to wipe glasses or sweep floors any more than Caitlin had. She was crazy for horses, another trait she shared with her mother. But this time Brigid knew it wasn't horses the child needed. She wanted to go home to her own room, to her friends, and her father. Estelle, the Claiborne's cook, would have made French toast with syrup and bacon, Kentucky bacon—the thin crispy kind that curled at the edges, not the thick rubbery, undercooked slab that passed for bacon in Ireland.

Brigid glanced over at Ben and the knot around her heart eased a bit. Praise be for little boys. Ben was shoveling in oats as if it was his favorite meal.

Annie was through with pretending. She left the spoon

stuck in a mound of congealed mush. "I'm finished, Gran," she said softly.

"I'll have yours," Ben announced, licking his spoon and reaching across the table for his sister's portion.

Brigid stared down at the barely touched lump of gray in her granddaughter's bowl. Would nothing she did ever please the child? Even her buttery scones were pushed away after no more than a bite. Caitlin believed the children would acclimate. Brigid wasn't so sure. Dragging two children halfway around the world, away from everything familiar, without so much as a bit of explanation was foolish, if not disastrous. But then Caitlin had always been one to take risks.

This time, Brigid reflected, her daughter might have bitten off more than she could chew. In her own way, Annie Claiborne was as stubborn as Caitlin had been, perhaps even more so because it was plain to see that Annie had been indulged from the moment she was born. Not that Brigid wouldn't have liked to indulge her own children, but there were too many of them. There was always an endless round of work to be done, and Caitlin was such a prickly little independent thing. When she was no more than an infant, Brigid recalled finding Caitlin uncovered, her blankets kicked aside, her arms spread out in flight position even in sleep.

It was all her late husband's fault, of course, the lack of time and the unending round of work that never ceased. His death could have been prevented if he hadn't been so fond of the drink. Not that Sean was good for much more than a bit of laughter and a warm body to share the *craic* with. Still, he helped out in the pub on occasion and cooked for the girls, all the while weaving his stories of light-touched Connemara and the queer folk of the Gaeltacht until the wee ones trembled with delight, their dreams filled with visions of Emain Macha, Queen Maeve, King Conor, silkies, mermaids, druids of the summerlands, and Celtic warriors of the Red Branch.

If only Sean hadn't drunk himself into a near-amnesiac condition, he wouldn't have fallen into a trench and hit his head against the scaffolding of the old schoolhouse. Neither, would he have toppled head first into a gutter and drowned in six inches of rainwater. He died young, poor man. Brigid surreptitiously crossed herself and then remembered that her grandchildren weren't Catholic, a serious breach she would discuss with Caitlin as soon as her daughter had a minute to spare.

Calling up the discipline that was never far from her consciousness, she pushed away her thoughts and concentrated on her charges. "Pick up the dishes and put them in the sink, Annie. Your mother will wash them later. Hurry up." She shooed Ben and Annie through the door and down the small flight of stairs that was once a rectory drawing room and now served as the pub's main floor.

Brigid had tidied up the night before. Everything was in its place, unopened bottles on the polished oak shelves, breakage set out on the bar, wine glasses hanging from the rack, tumblers sitting in the residue of what was once a tub of hot soapy water, two booths to seat eight, and in the back against the wall, six small tables with two chairs, each arranged so that the girl who helped during the busy times could fetch and carry without mishap.

Hanging in every available space were pictures, pictures of thoroughbreds: thoroughbreds training, thoroughbreds racing, thoroughbreds at play, thoroughbreds in the pastures, on the track, in the stalls, yearlings, two- and three-year-old colts, veteran stallions, breeding mares. All of them done up in oil, watercolor, pastel, charcoal sketchings, photographs, silhouettes—every imaginable artistic medium known to both the accomplished and the amateur.

Because the pub had once been a residence, there were other, smaller rooms set up with tables for intimate groups. But this was where the crowd assembled, where cigarette smoke swirled like thick haze settling over the dark Mournes, and traditional Irish music brought tears to the eyes and the converted to their feet.

Brigid watched Annie's eyes shift from the uneven planking on the floor to the long polished bar and up the mirrored wall, until they settled on a large painting strategically placed high on the paneling.

"Who's that?" she asked.

Brigid rested a light hand on Annie's shoulder. "Who do you think it is?"

"She looks like me," the girl said.

Ben slipped his hand into Brigid's. "It's Mama," he said quietly. "She looks like Annie but it's Mama."

Annie stared at her grandmother incredulously.

Brigid nodded. "It's true enough. You look as if you've spied a green-eyed faerie, lass. Haven't you seen a picture of your mother before?"

"We've lots of pictures of Mama," replied Annie defensively.

"What's a green-eyed faerie?" interrupted Ben.

Brigid pulled out a chair and settled him on her lap. "Green-eyed faeries come from the western isles," she began in the rich lilting voice Sean Keneally had used when he mesmerized his daughters before the warm light of a winter turf fire. "They spend their lives searchin' for a human child they can take back with them t' the Donegal mountains. When they find one who wishes t' go, they step into his body and take it over." Brigid paused for effect just as Sean once had. "When you see a child with one green eye and the other blue or brown, you must say a blessin' quickly, because the deed is nearly done and soon there will be one more faerie on his way t' the Donegal mountains."

Ben's eyes were so wide they swallowed his dear little face.

"You're scaring him," accused Annie. "Mama doesn't like it when anyone scares Ben."

"We don't have any pictures of Mama when she was a little girl," said Ben thoughtfully, ignoring his sister's outburst.

A memory, pure and searing, rose in Brigid's mind. Reaching into her pocket for a handkerchief she blew her nose. "That's my fault, I suppose," she confessed. "By the time your mother was born, I'd forgotten all about pictures. The few that were taken are in frames back in the sittin' room."

"What about that one?" asked Annie, her eyes fixed on the oil. "Who painted it?"

Pain, not clean and sharp and breath-stealing as it once was, but recognizable in its own way, closed around Brigid's heart.

"Gran?" Annie pressed her.

"I don't remember," Brigid lied.

Annie's dark eyes widened in disbelief. Brigid sighed. The child was very like Caitlin.

"My memory isn't good anymore, love. I'm sorry."

Keeping her eyes on Brigid's face, Annie nodded.

A knock sounded on the wooden door. Brigid frowned. It was too early to open the pub. Sliding Ben from her lap, she crossed the room and turned the bolt. The door swung open and a man dressed in a Roman collar and black cassock with a thick head of snow-white hair stepped into the room.

He nodded politely and when he spoke his voice was cultured with the lovely lilt of County Kildare lifting the ends of his words. "Good morning to you all." Fixing his gaze first on the children and then on Brigid he asked gently, "Were you going to bring these children to see me, Mrs. Keneally?"

"Not today, Father," she replied.

"We're helping Gran," Ben piped up.

The priest extended his hand. "As a good lad should. I'm Father Duran. You must be Ben."

Ben took the proffered hand and shook it thoroughly. "Why are you wearing a skirt?"

"Ben!" Annie hissed.

Michael Duran laughed. "I'm a priest, lad. Don't they wear cassocks in America?"

"There aren't any priests in America," replied the boy solemnly.

Father Duran looked startled.

Brigid stepped in. "These are my grandchildren, Annie and Ben Claiborne. They're not Catholic." She squeezed Ben's shoulder reassuringly. "Children, this is Father Duran. He's the pastor at Saint Patrick's Church."

"Where is that?" asked Annie.

Father Duran turned toward her. "I'm pleased to meet you, Annie. Saint Patrick's is on the other end of High Street. Maybe your Gran can bring you to Mass this Sunday."

"She'll need to ask my mother."

"Of course," said the priest smoothly. "Invite her as well."

Annie did not look convinced. "We've never been to a church."

Father Duran sighed. "No, I suppose not. Apparently, Caitlin hasn't changed."

"She's changed," said Brigid. She had not moved from her place at the door. "Is there somethin' you particularly wanted, Father? We've a good amount of work t' finish before we open."

The priest hesitated, his glance moving from Annie's face to Ben's. "Don't let me keep you," he said before stepping out through the exit.

Closing the door firmly behind the priest, Brigid stood, hands on her hips, surveying the room. "Annie, rinse the glasses in the sink. When you're finished there's a towel in that drawer near the cash register. Wipe them dry and put them in the cupboard." She rested her hand on Ben's head. "Come with me, young man. I'll show you where t' collect the wood." She looked back over her shoulder at Annie. "If you need anythin', ask your mum. She should be awake by now. It isn't good for her t' sleep away the day."

By the mutinous set of her lips, Brigid understood that no power on earth would make Annie wake Caitlin. She hid a smile. The girl had spirit, just like her mother.

Brigid led Ben through the back door and down the dark entry to a lot in back of the pub. Fog was thick over the land, shrouding the buildings in a blanket of smoke-gray mist. With the confidence of a blood hound, Brigid walked through the wet to the pile of firewood that lay in a disorganized pile on the ground. Brigid pointed to a random stack. "A few of those will do. Pick up as many as you can carry and I'll show you where t' put them."

Ben swallowed and approached the wood as if it were alive. Tentatively, he stooped and heaved a large log into his arms. Staggering under the load, he faced his grandmother.

Brigid nodded. "It might take awhile, but you'll manage. Follow me." She led the way back through the entry into the pub and pointed to the range with its red fire and black lead dust. "Set it there."

"How many shall I bring?" asked Ben hopefully.

"Ten or twelve should do it. There's rain on the wind, but it's June after all. I can't be providin' heat for the entire village. There's turf t' add if we're short on wood. Hurry now, lad. We've dallied long enough."

Obediently, Ben ran back out the door. Brigid watched

him with a fond smile on her lips. That one was a joy. Pity she never had any sons.

Annie had finished up the glasses, found the broom, and was sweeping the floor when Brigid walked back into the main room. "I see you found everythin' all right."

The girl nodded and continued to sweep, keeping her eyes on the floor. Caitlin would have said something. Brigid held back a snort. Caitlin would never have picked up a broom in the first place.

An amused voice broke through her thoughts. "I see you have them working already."

Brigid turned toward her daughter and caught her breath. Had she changed so much or was it familiarity that had hidden what was so obvious now that she hadn't seen her daughter in years? Caitlin, with her elegant clothing, her tousled hair, her creamy skin, and those eyes, slanted and dark as a druid priestess', looked nothing like Sean Keneally. In fact, she looked like no one Brigid had ever seen before. Fourteen years in America had turned her into an aristocrat, a woman who no more belonged in a working class pub than the Queen of England. Whatever was she doing here? What had she expected of them all when she made the decision to come home?

Caitlin yawned and lifted the hair from the back of her neck. "*Kentucky Gold* foaled this morning."

Annie laughed out loud and danced around the broom. "What is it?"

"A colt," her mother answered. "Shall we think of a name?"

Annie hesitated. "Daddy likes to name our colts. Won't he be mad?"

"I don't think so," replied Caitlin evenly. "In Daddy's absence, I'm sure he would be pleased to know that you named *Kentucky Gold*'s colt, Annie."

Ben stumbled through the door, rubbing wood shavings

from the sleeves of his sweatshirt. "I've finished, Gran. When will you open the pub?"

Brigid nodded at the clock. "It won't be long now."

Ben looked at his mother. "Did you wash the dishes, Mama? We've been giving Gran a hand in the pub."

Caitlin lifted one eyebrow. "So I see. Have you had your fill or do you want to come with me and see *Kentucky Gold*'s colt?"

Ben hesitated, eyes lowered, indecently long lashes sweeping his cheeks. "Gran said she needed us to help."

Brigid's heart turned over. "You've done a fine job, lad," she assured him. "Run along now and see your mum's colt."

"You can finish up in here, Ben," his mother said. Above the children's head her eyes met Brigid's and locked. "I've still the breakfast dishes to do."

"I'll help you," said Annie.

Brigid reached for the broom. "You've both done well. Thank you."

"You're welcome," said Annie politely, slipping her hand into Caitlin's and leading her back toward the kitchen.

Ben pointed to a case behind the bar with brightly wrapped packages. "What are those?" he asked.

"Biscuits," replied his grandmother. "I believe you call them cookies in America."

"May I have one?"

Brigid laughed. "You deserve at least two. Slide the glass open and take some for yourself and your sister. She hardly tasted her breakfast."

"Annie's sad," remarked Ben wisely.

Brigid stopped sweeping. "Is she now? Why is that, Ben?"

He spoke around a mouthful of cookie, crumbs gathering at the corners of his mouth. "She misses Daddy and Grandma Lucy and her friends and her room."

"Don't you miss those things?"

Ben shook his head. "I like it here."

"More than Kentucky?"

He nodded emphatically. "Nothing's far away here and there's more to do."

Brigid straightened her shoulders. She felt lighter somehow, as if a large heavy bundle had been lifted from her shoulders.

"Perhaps, after a while, Annie will see it as you do."

Ben nodded, swallowed, and reached for another biscuit.

6

Annie picked up the bowl dripping with soapsuds, rinsed it carefully in a tub of warm water, and wiped the sides, the bottom, and the rim as methodically as if she'd helped dry dishes every day of her life.

Caitlin, warmed by a stream of milky sunlight just appearing over the roof of Feeney's hardware store and the rare camaraderie of performing a necessary chore with her daughter, was lulled into a tranquil mood. "I think I'll make some pancakes," she said, opening the cupboard above her head. "You'd like that wouldn't you, Annie? Pancakes sound better than Gran's oats, don't they?"

Annie nodded.

Caitlin began pulling sugar, flour, and baking soda from the cupboard. "Annie," she looked back over her shoulder, "check inside the refrigerator and see if there are any eggs left. We'll use butter if there's no oil."

Following her mother's instructions, Annie measured out

the ingredients while Caitlin worked quickly, sifting together the flour, baking soda, and salt. After mixing in the sugar, she formed a well and poured in the oil, egg yolks, vanilla, and a bit of cream. Humming to herself, she whipped the whites into stiff peaks and slowly added sugar. Then she mixed the dry ingredients with the wet, expertly folding in the meringue and ladling heaping spoonfuls of batter into the sizzling cast iron skillet.

Minutes later the kitchen was filled with the tantalizing smells of a Kentucky breakfast. Satisfied with her accomplishment, Caitlin nibbled at the crisp, browned edges of the pancake on her plate. Food, delicious and expertly prepared, relaxed and soothed her. She made a mental note to herself to buy maple syrup at the grocery store.

Her daughter's words shattered her calm. "Mama, why don't we go to church?"

Keeping her face expressionless, Caitlin swallowed the last mouthful of pancake, stood, and walked to the sink to slip her plate into the soapy water. She worked to keep her tone casual. "Why do you ask?"

"A priest came into the pub to see us. He knew our names."

Caitlin turned around and leaned against the sink, arms crossed against her chest. "Do you remember his name?"

Annie nodded. "Father Duran."

"What did he say?"

The girl shrugged and swallowed the rest of her pancake. "Nothing much except that he was happy to meet us. He wants you to bring us to church. I told him we didn't go."

"Oh, lord, Annie," Caitlin groaned. "What did he say to that?"

Annie, gratified by her mother's interest, continued eagerly. "He said it sounded as if you hadn't changed much and then Gran said you had."

"Dear old Mum. I always could count on her support," mumbled Caitlin under her breath.

Annie's forehead creased. "What?"

"Never mind, love. For a man who said nothing, you certainly remembered a great deal of his conversation."

"He was nice but Gran wanted him to leave."

"Did she now?"

Annie nodded. "Why don't we, Mama?"

"Why don't we what?"

"Why don't we go to church?"

Caitlin surveyed her fingernails. Three weeks of hot soapy water and no dishwasher had destroyed her manicure. Mustering her courage, she met Annie's dark eyes. "When I was a child I went to church every Sunday of my life. I longed for a day to sleep as late as I wanted and do nothing. It was different for you. If you're curious and would like to go to church, Annie, then of course you may go."

"Will you go, too?"

Caitlin gave up, anything to wipe away that anxious look from Annie's little face. "Yes, love, if it makes you happy."

Annie picked up her plate and carried it to the sink, something she'd never done in Kentucky. "I would like to try it, Mama. It will make Gran happy, too."

First church and now this. Annie's defection frightened her. "You needn't worry about Gran, Annie," Caitlin said. "She's not the type of person who can ever be really pleased about anything."

Annie's eyes widened until the ratio of brown iris and creamy skin appeared nearly the same. "Why not?"

"She doesn't think she deserves it."

"Has she done something bad?"

Already regretting her frankness, Caitlin struggled to make the truth benign enough for a ten year old to understand. "It's the way she was raised, love. She was brought up to believe certain superstitions. The fear that too much happiness can't possibly last is one of them. Do you understand?

Annie wrinkled her forehead. "I think so. Poor Gran."

Caitlin rested her hands on her daughter's shoulders. "She's not really unhappy. But she's never known any other way. It's important for you to understand that we must respect her and love her but we mustn't think we can change her. After a certain age people don't change, Annie, not unless they want to."

Annie pulled away and began to wander about the kitchen, opening drawers, fingering utensils. "Shall we tell Ben about the pancakes?"

Caitlin sighed. The subject was ended. Naivete worked every time. She'd used the same tactic herself when she was Annie's age. "I'll freeze some for him and he can have them tomorrow."

"Have what tomorrow?" Ben asked from the entrance to the pub.

His mother smiled. Ben's well-scrubbed, chubby-cheeked appeal was difficult to resist. "I made pancakes. Would you like some?"

Ben thought a minute and then shook his head and held up a small package. "Gran gave me biscuits. These are for you, Annie," he said generously.

"I'm not hungry," she said. "You can have them."

He stuffed the package in his pocket and walked across the kitchen to where his mother stood. "When will we go see the colt, Mama?"

Caitlin kissed the top of his head. There was something miraculous about giving birth to a boy—a child of herself and yet nothing like her. "As soon as you find your sweatshirt. It's cold outside. Bring Annie's as well."

"I won't be cold in the car," said Annie.

"We won't be driving."

Annie looked surprised. "How will we get there?"

Caitlin bit her lip. It wasn't the first time Annie had inadvertently pointed out the disadvantages of her new home. "We'll walk."

"But why?" Annie wailed. "Gran has a car."

"I don't know how long we'll be gone," explained Caitlin patiently. "I can't ask Gran to give up her car."

Annie pouted. All traces of the serious, thoughtful child who, ten minutes before had wanted to please her grandmother, had completely disappeared. "We wouldn't have to worry about any of this if we were at home."

"Oh, Annie. I'm sorry that you're unhappy here. Please give it a chance."

"Why can't we just go home?"

Caitlin felt her right temple throb, an indication of a migraine coming on. Another few minutes of this and she wouldn't be walking anywhere. "We've been over this before," she said, trying to ignore the nagging ache. "Daddy and I are divorcing. You'll go back to Kentucky to visit him but your home will be here with me. I'm your mother."

"I wish you weren't." Annie's voice cracked. "I wish anyone but you was my mother."

Caitlin moved toward her, reaching out. "Annie—"

"Don't come near me," the child sobbed, backing away. "I hate you."

Caitlin watched helplessly as her daughter turned, ran into her room, and slammed the door. Every instinct told her to march into Annie's room and demand an apology. But then what? Annie had blurted out her feelings instead of allowing them to rage inside of her, something Caitlin had always encouraged. Should the rules change because her daughter had expressed emotions that Caitlin found intolerable? Could a ten-year-old girl actually hate her mother?

The pain had crossed her forehead. Now both temples were on fire.

"What's goin' on here?" Brigid stepped into the room and sniffed appreciatively. "It's a lovely smell, whatever it is you've made."

"Pancakes," said Caitlin tonelessly, rubbing her head.

Her mother frowned. "You look pale as milk, lass. Are you ill?"

"It's a migraine. I'll take a pill now and maybe it won't get worse."

Brigid's lips tightened. "Since when have you had migraines?"

She really couldn't stand much more. "Since Sam decided to diddle every woman between sixteen and sixty."

"Caitlin Keneally! There's a child present." Her mother's eyes were narrow with disapproval. "We may not be sinfully rich like the Claibornes, but surely you never learned such language in this house."

Her vision was going. Tiny blasts of light flickered behind her eyelids. "Perhaps not in the house."

"Mama?"

Ben looked frightened. Caitlin forced a smile and pulled him close, burying her nose in his hair. It smelled like strawberries, Brigid's shampoo. "Don't worry, Benjie," she murmured. "It's just a headache. Gran will know what to do."

"Will we still see the colt?"

"Don't worry about that," Brigid replied. "After I attend to your mother, I'll take you."

Somehow her mother did know what to do. Brigid crossed the room, scooped ice from the freezer, sealed it in a plastic bag and pressed it against the back of Caitlin's neck. Blessed coolness met the pain, and a voice, incredible in its softness, whispered, "Don't say anything, love. I'll take you back to bed. You can visit the foal another day."

"My pills," mumbled Caitlin. "They're in my bag."

"Hush," her mother soothed her. "I'll find them. Everything will be all right."

"Annie, she's—"

"Annie will be fine. Don't worry so much, Caitlin. You're not alone here. Rest now."

With that comforting thought swimming through her haze of pain, Caitlin gulped down her Imitrex capsule, turned her face to the wall, and prayed for sleep.

It was three days before she could bring herself to swing her legs over the side of the bed and look into a mirror. What she saw made her groan. Her hair was wild and her skin and eyes had a jaundiced cast that resembled detox patients from the hospital in Louisville where Lucy Claiborne volunteered. The smell of leftover bacon from the kitchen gagged her.

Shakily, she gathered her clothing and headed for the shower. Thank God the bathroom was free. She needed to find a place to live, somewhere private, preferably with a barn, a large kitchen, and at least two bathrooms.

The inadequate trickle of lukewarm water, so different from the steaming, powerful spray in her Kentucky bathroom, barely managed to revive her. She'd forgotten how cold Ireland could be. Shivering from the lack of heat she toweled herself dry, wrapped her wet hair in a turban and quickly pulled on her clothes. She was weak as a cat, and knowing her mother's shopping habits, there probably wasn't enough in the refrigerator to feed a ghost.

The house was unusually quiet. Slipping her feet into fleece-lined moccasins, Caitlin walked down the stairs into the kitchen, turned the heat on under the kettle, and opened the refrigerator. The contents actually looked promising. She pulled out eggs, cheese, mushrooms, and a ham-bone with enough meat left on it for a decent omelet.

The familiar tasks of cracking eggs, slicing meat into neat, even cubes, and grating cheese restored her balance. The mindless routine of cooking always worked its magic on her. Through the colors and textures of food, she assuaged an appetite that had nothing to do with hunger. The sharp blade of a knife slicing through the skin of a tomato, the crisp tartness of an apple, the flaky sweetness of a cobbler laced with cream, the subtle hint of rosemary and sage lifted her above hurt and loss, regret and shattered confidence. Cooking brought Caitlin serenity, the glow of accomplishment. Each time, each new creation, like the act of contrition, restored her badly damaged pride.

By the time she added mushrooms, ham, and grated cheese to the sizzling eggs, and efficiently flipped the omelet on to a plate, her spirits had lifted enough to consider taking Annie and Ben with her to see *Kentucky Gold*. Food in her stomach improved her spirits even further.

Caitlin frowned. Where were Annie and Ben?

Carrying her dishes to the sink, she unwrapped the towel from her hair. Fingercombing her curls, she walked out of the kitchen and down the hall to the pub.

Kirsty, the part-time help, was serving Guinness to two patrons in the wool slouch caps typical of Irish men. She called out to Caitlin. "If your lookin' for your mum, she's in the store."

Caitlin nodded, walked back down the hall and through the door to the convenience store where her mother had spent the better part of her life. There was no sign of Annie and Ben. "Where are the children?" she asked.

Brigid, reading glasses perched on her nose, looked up from the order she was filling. "They wanted t' see the foal. Martin came by t' see you and offered t' take them. How are you feelin'?"

"Better." Caitlin frowned. "Mum, the next time someone

wants to take my children somewhere, please ask me." She sounded ungrateful and petulant. Why did her mother always bring out the worst in her?

"I would have if it was anyone but Martin," said her mother, "but you were asleep and I thought you needed the rest."

"I haven't seen Martin in fourteen years."

Brigid entered another figure in her ledger. "He hasn't changed much."

"He's a priest."

Again Brigid looked up, her blue eyes level and steady. "All the more reason t' trust him."

Caitlin stared mutinously at her mother. There was no reasonable rejoinder to such a statement. She was being absurd and she knew it. Martin O'Shea would never hurt anyone, least of all her children. "I think I'll join them."

"What a good idea. Take the car if you're still feelin' weak."

"I'll walk."

Brigid nodded. "Nothin' like fresh air t' clear up a headache."

Frowning at her reflection in the mirror, Caitlin rubbed out the worry lines between her brows. What would Martin think of her after all these years? She hadn't exactly come home a wild success story.

Dividing her hair into three sections, she wove the unruly curls into a French braid, twisted a colorful elastic band around the end and pulled out a few strands at her forehead and the sides of her face. She turned her head first to one side and then the other. Her spirits brightened. Three days of rest and a ham and cheese omelet had definitely improved her appearance. "Much better," she said to herself.

Walking down the familiar streets of her childhood, it appeared to Caitlin that fourteen years hadn't changed

Kilcullen Town much with the exception of the McDonald's and Gyro fast-food restaurants facing each other on Main Street. It was like any other small Irish town—no bigger than an American football field, only linear, with houses backed up to the main street. A church, a news agent, an off license, a chemist, a restaurant, a branch of Ulster Bank. A relatively new Superquinn market, the inevitable Irish bookmaker, a hardware store, various clothing and gift shops, and, of course, her mother's pub and convenience store.

Even the faces were the same, a bit older, perhaps, more grizzled, with a few more lines, but basically the same. Mr. Murphy, the butcher, waved at Caitlin through his glass window. She waved back. Paddy Byrne's shoe shop was now a bright lemon yellow instead of white, Brown and McCann Solicitors boasted an engraved sign, and inside Kathleen Finch's cafe, round tables with white cloths had replaced the vinyl-covered booths. Caitlin didn't recognize her patrons but she did recognize the plump young redhead in blue denim slacks and a white apron, pouring tea. She stepped inside the restaurant.

"Hello, Lana," she said.

The woman's eyes widened. Then she grinned and nearly lost the teapot she was carrying. "Caitlin Keneally, is it really you?"

"In the flesh."

Lana Sullivan laughed delightedly, set down the teapot and opened her arms. "Come here, love, and let me fold these around you."

Caitlin moved forward into a welcoming hug. "I thought you'd gone to Dublin," she said, stepping out of her friend's embrace.

"I came back. Billy Doyle found someone else," Lana said pragmatically, "and I couldn't afford the rent on my own. Kathleen needed the help, so here I am."

"I'm sorry."

"Don't be," said the redhead cheerfully. "It's good to be home. Besides, there are a few more interesting faces since we left, Brian Hennessey for one. He took Mr. O'Shea's place at the stud farm."

"We've met," said Caitlin. "I brought a mare home with me."

Lana's eyes clouded. "I'm sorry for your troubles, Caitie. I heard you've a wee lad and lass."

Caitlin nodded. "Annie and Ben. I can't stop to talk now. Martin has the children. I've got to claim them, and I'm a bit nervous about seeing him again."

"Nervous?" Lana's eyes widened incredulously. "Of Father O'Shea? Whatever for?"

Motionless, Caitlin stared at Lana. "I don't know really. I suppose it's because I haven't seen him for such a long time. I never knew Martin the priest."

"Martin hasn't changed," said Lana. "He's a dear lad, always thinking of others. His sermons could use a bit of humor but then I'm not complaining."

"What aren't you complainin' about, Lana?" an amused voice broke in on them.

Lana blushed furiously.

Caitlin turned to see Brian Hennessey, a portfolio under his arm, standing near the signpost. "We were having a conversation about an old friend," she said. Why was the man looking at her so intently?

"Anyone I know?"

Lana regained her composure. "Father O'Shea was a friend of ours when we were children."

Brian kept his eyes on Caitlin. "I believe Father O'Shea is at the stud farm with your children as we speak, Mrs. Claiborne."

"I was on my way there when I saw Lana," replied Caitlin.

"I'm going there myself. Shall I walk with you?"

She would rather have gone alone, but Caitlin was Brigid Keneally's daughter, raised on a diet of good manners. There was no possibility of politely refusing.

Lana picked up the teapot. "Bring the children to visit me, Caitlin, and stop by for tea. Mum would love to see you. You're welcome as well, Brian.

"I will," Caitlin promised and fell into step beside the lean, black-haired young man who made her uncomfortable in a way she couldn't quite explain. The silence deepened, became awkward, then embarrassing. Frantically, she searched for something to say. "Where are you from, Mr. Hennessey?" she said at last.

"Inishmore."

She looked puzzled. "Where on the Aran Islands did you learn about thoroughbreds?"

His hands were deep in his pockets. "I thought we were on a first name basis."

"You're the one who called me 'Mrs. Claiborne.' " The wind whipped a strand of hair across her cheek. She pulled it away.

"I'm thirty-four years old, Caitlin, plenty of time to leave Inishmore and learn about thoroughbreds."

"My father was from the islands."

Brian's head was down, against the wind. She saw the quick lifting of the corner of his mouth. "Was he now?"

Caitlin nodded. "So they say. He died before I was born."

"I'm sorry, lass," he said gently.

"It was a long time ago."

His lips twitched. "An eternity."

Startled, she looked up at him. "You're making fun of me."

His eyes twinkled. "You asked for it."

"How?"

They stopped in the street to face each other.

"Your melodrama for one thing."

Her cheeks burned. "You aren't very polite, Brian Hennessey."

His eyes narrowed to thin blue lines. "If it's polite you want, Caitlin Claiborne, you're on your way to see the right man."

She turned away and continued walking. "What have you got against Martin?"

Brian looked genuinely astonished. "Nothin' at all. Did I give you the impression I had?"

He had or she wouldn't have noticed. "Not really."

Brian caught her arm. "Caitlin. Just so there's no misunderstandin'. Martin O'Shea is the best friend I have in the world."

Caitlin stared at him. There was no mistaking his sincerity. Was he warning her? "I'm not surprised," she said softly. "He was mine, too."

7

He was out of his league. Brian knew it as surely as he knew the daily schedule of races on opening day at the Curragh. Caitlin Claiborne not only had the look of a woman used to very dark coffee served in tiny cups on the private terrace of an expensive villa, she obviously had depths he couldn't begin to probe. She was also very skilled at hiding what was on her mind, a lethal combination where women were concerned. He wondered if she saw herself the same way Martin saw her, or if the two of them viewed their mutual past with their own unique set of blinders.

They walked in silence past the ornamental gardens, crossed behind the paddock, and continued down the long road to the Tully Walk where the foaling stable stood apart, protected on all sides by green meadowlands. The door was open. Inside, peering into *Kentucky Gold*'s stall with Martin O'Shea between them, were Caitlin's children.

In unison, the three of them turned toward the entrance as

Caitlin walked in. Brian stepped back into the shadows without speaking, preferring not to participate in the reunion of two old friends.

"Mama." Ben's voice was reverent. "He's so pretty. Annie said we could name him."

"You said so, Mama," Annie piped up. "You said Daddy wouldn't mind."

Caitlin was silent. Brian watched as her gaze met Martin's. He didn't know what he was looking for, a connection perhaps, disappointment that the real person didn't live up to Martin's memory. He held his breath. Seconds passed. Nothing happened. Slowly, he exhaled.

"Welcome home, Caitie," Martin said softly.

"Thank you, Martin. It's good to be home."

Martin laughed nervously and spread his hands. "Well, what do you think?"

She said nothing for a long moment. Finally, "You look wonderful in black."

This time they laughed together and the tension lifted.

"Can we get past the clothes?" Martin pleaded.

Caitlin reached out and hugged him briefly. "I'll manage. Lord, Martin. You really did it."

Annie's words cut through the tension between them. "Mama, look at the colt."

"In a minute, Annie."

Brian stepped into the brightness thrown by the skylight. He extended his hand first to Annie and then to Ben. "I'm Brian Hennessey," he said. "Have you decided on a name?"

"*Irish Gold,*" Annie said, "because he was born in Ireland out of *Kentucky Gold.*"

Brian stroked his chin. "It sounds like a fine name. With your mother's permission, provided Weatherbys agrees, it looks like you'll have a match."

Annie smiled and Brian found himself staring. Normally,

he had little interest in children. But this one was exceptionally attractive. She must be the image of how her mother had looked at the same age. He turned to the boy by her side. Ben had the same dark eyes, hooded instead of round, light hair, a missing front tooth, and features that, except for his freckles, did not look at all Irish.

"Are you the boss, Mr. Hennessey?" the boy asked.

Startled, Brian looked over at Martin who merely shrugged. "The boss?" he asked.

Ben nodded. "My daddy is the boss at our farm. Are you the boss here?"

Brian recalled the Claiborne millions and laughed. "No, lad. I'm not nearly as important as your da. I work here at the farm. That's all."

Ben nodded as if he understood the concept of work. "I worked at Gran's pub," he said. "Maybe I can work here."

Brian was enjoying himself. Caitlin's children were a step past the ordinary, although he doubted that either of them had an accurate concept of the term *work*. "Do you enjoy carin' for horses, lad?"

Annie broke in. "He likes riding better than working, Mr. Hennessey. I'm the one who helps with our horses."

"Most of us prefer the ride, Annie. You're a rare one if you enjoy the labor as well as the sport. Perhaps your mother will allow you to help us around here from time to time."

Annie's pleasure was so strong he could feel it radiate until even the dust motes around her head seemed electrified. "Mama won't mind," she said without once looking at her mother.

Ben thrust his lower lip out. "What about me? I can work, too."

"You've the look of a lad who knows his way around muckin' out the stalls, doesn't he, Martin?" Brian asked, looking back over his shoulder.

"I would say he does," the priest agreed.

Brian considered the matter. "Shall I put you to it right away, Ben, or do you want a day to think about it?"

Ben stepped forward earnestly. "Now, please."

"Ben, love." His mother laughed, exasperated. "Mr. Hennessey hasn't had a chance to think about this. Why don't you wait a bit?"

The boy's chin tightened obstinately and when his mouth opened, Brian stepped in before he could get the words out. "Your mother's right, lad. I'll look over things and see where you might be useful."

"Me, too?" asked Annie.

"You, too," Brian repeated emphatically. "Now, move aside so your mum can see her foal."

He watched as the children reached out to tug Caitlin gently into the space between them. Annie held on to her mother's hand, while Ben leaned against her, slipping his arm around her narrow waist, fingering the belt loops. Her hand rested naturally, easily, on the little boy's head while she massaged her daughter's hand with the tips of her fingers. There was no doubting the affection between this woman and her children. He liked the way she treated their comments as seriously as if they had been adults.

She was a good mother, Brian decided, a bit indulgent but that was to be expected with the Claiborne fortune. With money like theirs it would be difficult to justify refusing children a luxury now and then, unlike his own family where it was understood from the time a lad could crawl out of his crib that there was no point in asking for anything at all.

"I'll be leaving you now," announced Martin as he moved toward the door of the foaling barn. "I'm to say five o'clock Mass at the church."

Caitlin turned. "Come by and see us, won't you?"

"Soon," Martin promised. "Perhaps you'll come to one of my Masses."

She looked embarrassed.

"We'll come, Father O'Shea," Annie said. "Mama said she would take me."

"Good." The relief on Martin's face was complete. "I'll expect you."

"Not today," Caitlin said after Martin's retreating figure.

Brian hid a smile. He approached the stall where the colt suckled, and looked over Caitlin's shoulder. She'd worn perfume today. He knew nothing about the scents women preferred but this one was very subtle, French, he guessed, and expensive. He wondered what she would do when she ran out of it, most likely order another case from Paris.

He had mixed feelings about Caitlin Claiborne. He couldn't decide whether he liked or disliked her. She was a portrait in contrasts, wide-eyed, knowing, quietly fierce, and when she spoke to her children, utterly feminine.

Hiding his thoughts behind a pleasant expression, he broke the silence. "What plans do you have for him?"

He sensed her discomfort, as if the innocent question he posed was one she'd been waiting for, yet dreading.

"I don't know," she said warily. "I suppose I've the same plans that anyone does for a thoroughbred. I hope he'll prove fit to race and eventually to stand at the Stud."

Brian took a long measuring look at the colt, at his promise of deep shoulders, the good strong bones, the barrel chest and extra layer of muscle beside the tail and down to the hocks that meant unusual strength and speed. His heart beat more quickly. "Here in Ireland?" he asked casually.

"Only in Ireland," Caitlin answered in that fierce quiet way he'd noticed earlier. "Are you interested, Mr. Hennessey?"

"Possibly, if everything turns out the way you expect."

She looked sideways at him. "You might ask the good father to offer up a little prayer."

Brian shook his head. "Prayer isn't to be wasted on the likes of this."

"Really?" She was on the verge of a smile. "On what do you consider important enough to waste your prayers, Mr. Hennessey?"

Was she laughing at him or did the lights always dance in the darkest part of her eyes? "Why life and death matters, of course, Caitlin."

Her eyes lost their laughter and her voice, when she spoke, was clear and serious and filled with purpose. "Then I suggest you start praying immediately because that's exactly what you'll be praying for."

Brian turned off his alarm and rolled out of bed. Today Caitlin's colt would be turned out into the pasture with the other mares and their foals. For thirty-five days he would survive on mother's milk and then the weaning process would begin, milk supplemented with sweet feed and crushed oats. Six months later he would be separated from his mother entirely. Shortly before that, samples of his blood and six suggested names would be submitted to Weatherbys.

After a shower and a quick cup of tea, Brian walked into his office and looked at the basket under his fax machine. It was filled with papers where it had been empty the night before. The light on his computer flickered announcing four unread e-mail messages. He decided to put them aside until later. The training of the farm's most promising colt, *Indigo Blue*, was more important. The rare colt that Brian still accepted for training was always chosen carefully. Managing the Curragh Stud required more hours in a day than he had, but occasionally a colt was too promising to pass on. *Indigo Blue* was such a colt.

Brian had already worked with him for days, picking up his feet again and again, playing with his ears, talking and soothing, caressing and patting to accustom him to the idea of a man in his stall. Three days ago the colt had accepted the bit and tolerated Brian's arm lying across his back. It was time for the next step.

Deciding against the fiberglass helmet and indoor ring, Brian led *Indigo Blue* outside and climbed up on his back, straddling him with both legs. The horse sat quietly, ears forward. Crooning softly, Brian walked, stopped, and started him again, over and over, until the colt was comfortable. Then he urged him into a slow trot. The animal felt strong and promising under his legs. Today he would begin to canter and then gallop. For the next week Brian would canter him first in one direction and then the other, teaching him to use both the left and right leads. Irish racecourses ran both counter and clockwise. *Indigo Blue* would learn to lead with his right foreleg going around a turn then switching to the left lead on the straights.

Davy Flynn walked with him, leading another yearling to the training track, past fences, hurdles, and grass so green and rich and dripping with dew that it looked painted on the dark turf with a wet brush. At the track, Brian flattened his tongue against the roof of his mouth to make a clucking sound. Immediately, *Indigo Blue*'s ears pricked and the horse broke into a jog.

Brian coached him through his figure eights, to respond to the reins and the sound of a human voice, to the slightest touch on the lines. Three hours passed. By the time he handed the reins over to the exercise boy, he knew he had a potential winner. *Indigo Blue* was a good, solid colt—large, responsive, well-mannered, winning-purse material.

He stopped at the inside pasture and leaned on the fence to watch the Claiborne colt frolic beside his mother. Caitlin was in the paddock with both children, too intent on her task to notice him. Brian couldn't hear her words but he could tell she was speaking by the way Annie nodded occasionally. Ben wasn't as attentive. Every few minutes, he would spread his arms, flight fashion, look up at the sky, and turn in circles until he fell into the loamy grass.

Caitlin walked to where *Kentucky Gold* grazed and ran her hand down the mare's nose, her mouth close to the twitching ear, while Annie approached the colt. *Kentucky Gold* took a nervous step forward but Caitlin twisted her fingers into her glossy mane and held on. Meanwhile, Annie handled the colt, touching his silky ears, the velvet spots in his nostrils, smoothing her hand over his withers, down his legs, across his back.

Ben stood watching from his spot in the middle of the paddock. Only once did he start forward only to stop immediately when his mother shook her head.

Brian's first impression of the Claiborne children and of their mother completely reversed itself. Caitlin wasn't an indulgent mother, not where it mattered. Annie and Ben understood when it was important to behave themselves.

He continued to watch as Annie returned to her mother. This time Caitlin and Ben played with the colt, rubbing his neck, his ears, the top of his head where the mane hadn't yet begun to grow. All the while, Annie held tightly to *Kentucky Gold*, smoothing her mane, stroking her nose, resting her head against the satiny neck.

It was too soon to tell but every instinct told Brian the colt would be a stayer, good for the long hauls but slow to start at the gate. From the looks of him out there with the other colts, he spooked easily but recovered quickly and completely. Brian's mouth twisted humorlessly. The colt was the last of his line, a *Narraganset* foal out of *Kentucky Gold*. Speculation was foolish. The mare and her colt would most likely be on their way to America by Christmas. Meanwhile, he'd intruded upon this family scene long enough. He had a stud farm to run.

If he had turned away an instant later, he would have missed Caitlin's advance on her unsuspecting son. Tossing him over her shoulder, she turned around and around until the boy shrieked with laughter. Together they tumbled, a tangled mass of arms and legs, into the grass.

Annie left the horses to run toward them. She was nearly there when Caitlin jumped up quickly and tackled her. Ben rolled into his mother and sister, sending shrieks of laughter to all corners of the paddock.

Impulsive, Martin had called her, light-filled, joyous, lacking inhibition. Brian recognized what had escaped him before. With new eyes he saw the girl she once was, the woman she could be, loving, intimate, playful to those she trusted with her heart.

Several hours later, Brian opened the door and stepped into the large dining hall, the social hub of the farm. Here, around large wooden banquet tables, employees played cards, tipped a pint or two, smoked, and swapped stories over tomato and onion sandwiches and steaming tea. It was nearly time for the afternoon rush.

"Brian, over here." Davy Flynn waved to him from a nearby table.

Making his way through the smoke-thick room, Brian stopped several times to talk briefly before sliding into the chair Davy held out for him. Tom McMahon, the veterinarian, sat across from him nursing a cup of tea.

"How's *Indigo Blue* coming along?" he asked.

Brian shrugged out of his jacket. "He'll do. We'll have to interrupt his trainin' for the wormin'. Are you ready for it?"

"Aye," answered the vet. "I planned on this Friday."

Davy scratched his head. "There was a lad up to see you this mornin'. Said you were expectin' him."

Brian frowned. "I wasn't expectin' anyone."

"Did you forget about young Ben Claiborne then?"

Brian groaned and ran his hands through his thick hair. "Sweet Jesus. I did, Davy. What did you tell him?"

Davy grinned. "I told him you'd make it right."

"How shall I go about that?"

"He's a wee lad who misses his father. Go see him, Brian. Tell him you'll have somethin' for him tomorrow."

A woman with wind-burned cheeks dressed in a fisherman's sweater and calf-length denim skirt placed a tea tray on the table. "You look terrible, Brian Hennessey," she said, matter-of-factly, pouring milk and tea and stirring in sugar. "Are you sleepin' at all?"

"Not enough," replied Brian, "and our Davy here has volunteered me for yet another task."

Mary Boyle pursed her lips disapprovingly.

"I only thought he should apologize to Caitlin's wee lad for forgettin' him today," Davy explained. "It seemed like such a small thing."

"Why Brian Hennessey." Mary planted her hands on her hips. "Are you tellin' us that you can't be bothered with the dear wee lad, our Caitlin's boy, who's homesick and lonely for his da?"

Brian gulped down a mouthful of scalding tea. "I haven't said anythin' yet," he gasped.

"Well?" Mary demanded.

Admitting defeat, Brian sighed. "Apparently the decision's already been made."

Caitlin's look of dismay when she opened the door and saw Brian standing on her doorstep almost made up for his inconvenience. For some reason it pleased him to see Caitlin

Claiborne discomfited. He smiled pleasantly. "I've come to see Ben."

"He's dressing for the *cruinniú*." She stared pointedly at the clothes he'd worn since morning. "I thought everyone went to these things."

Brian looked forward to a *cruinniú* as much as the next man. After a pint or two of the Harp, his self-imposed limit, it didn't matter much whether the gathering was the authentic version or the tourist-filled, anglicized replica found here in Kilcullen Town. But tonight he'd completely forgotten. "I'll be there, but first I must speak to Ben."

"Is that you, Brian Hennessey?" Brigid Keneally called out from the kitchen. "Come in and tell me why I haven't seen you in the pub for nearly a week."

"I'm not a drinkin' man, Mrs. Keneally," Brian said, stepping forward so that Caitlin was forced to move back.

Brigid came into the sitting room carrying a mixing bowl and spoon. "It never stopped you before," she retorted.

Brian grinned. "Sometimes it's hard to resist temptation. The best thing to do is stay away."

Caitlin was staring at him. The disapproving line between her eyes annoyed him. Perversely, he wanted to shock her. "Have you never seen a man better off without the drink, Mrs. Claiborne?"

She lifted her chin. "I've seen many, Mr. Hennessey. But I've never heard anyone admit it."

"You just did."

"Congratulations."

"Caitlin!" Brigid's cheeks were pink. "Where are your manners?"

Caitlin's jaw tightened stubbornly.

"No offense taken, Mrs. Keneally," Brian cut in smoothly. "May I see Ben now or shall I wait until tomorrow?"

"I'll tell him you're here," Brigid said, hurrying down the hall.

He wondered if Caitlin would excuse herself and leave the room or if she would engage in conversation with him. He waited.

She surprised him. "Please, sit down, Mr. Hennessey."

He sat down on the sofa.

"Did you have a chance to look in on *Kentucky Gold* and the foal today?"

He nodded. "Both are grand. The colt is exceptional—long legs, deep chest, good bones. He looks like a stayer."

She groaned and sat across from him in a high-backed chair. "Lord, I hope not. I can't bear it when a horse is slow at the gate. My insides feel like they're slipping out."

Brian laughed. "Perhaps I'm mistaken about him. It's too soon to tell."

Caitlin's eyes widened wickedly. "Is it possible that you, Mr. Hennessey, could actually be wrong?"

Brian was beginning to enjoy himself. "There is the remote possibility."

She shook her head. "How disappointing."

Her smile was lovely. He wanted to see it again.

"Were you truly planning on attending the *cruinniú*, Brian?" she asked.

Words he never intended came from somewhere deep inside of him. "Only if you dance with me." Across the room his eyes challenged her.

Slowly she nodded her head. "I can manage that."

Ben Claiborne ran into the room and planted himself in front of Brian. "Where were you today?" he demanded.

"Trainin' a colt," replied Brian. "I didn't expect to see you so soon or else I would have waited."

"Gran said I should phone first," Ben admitted. "But I couldn't wait that long."

Brian rose from his chair and ruffled the boy's hair. "Come around tomorrow mornin' and bring your sister. I'll be expectin' you."

He glanced at Caitlin. "I have a few things to do before I collect my dance."

"Don't wait too long," she warned him. "There are more men in this town than women."

He laughed. Somehow he knew she wouldn't make it easy on him. "Then I'll have to show up and take my chances like the rest of the lads," he said, winking at Ben.

He stopped at the door. "I don't expect you to wait for me, lass."

"I wouldn't dream of it," said Caitlin dryly.

8

❧❧❧

Brigid dipped her finger into the marble font of holy water, felt its cool wetness against the warmth of her skin and crossed herself. Then she walked through the double oak doors, into the small sanctuary reserved for those who had special requests, and knelt before the altar. She looked up briefly at the gentle, doe-eyed face of the Virgin Mother and then at the candles flickering in the scented darkness. Bowing her head she began to pray.

As always, the familiar ritual soothed her. Brigid took comfort in rituals. She lived her life by the ringing of church bells, the rumble of the milk truck, the whistle of the train on its way to Tralee, the howling of Margaret O'Hare's tomcat on his nightly prowl. The Mass had its own rituals: the melodic chanting of the priests, the monotone responses of the faithful, the sweet smell of incense, the stale dryness of the communion wafer, the numbing ache of knees spent too long genuflecting, and the final, hopeful blessing, "Peace be with you always."

Young people who abandoned the church didn't understand the power of ritual. They thought by missing Sunday Mass they could escape what they called "the cloying grip of an outdated clergy." Brigid knew better. Once a Catholic, always a Catholic, she maintained. One could no more escape tradition than one could deny one's father. She frowned. Better to leave that one alone.

Traditions were the heart of a people. If the Catholic church allowed half of what the Protestants introduced into their folds every day, it would no longer be what it was; the strength, the rock of millions of its faithful. If only she could convince Caitlin of the peace and comfort to be found in true faith.

Brigid felt rather than heard the movement behind her. It was no more than a stirring of the air. Whoever it was disturbed her devotions. She needed the peace of the sanctuary this evening, especially after the phone call she'd received earlier in the day. Deliberately, she stiffened her body and bent her head over her folded hands, the picture of a true pilgrim in communion with her God.

This time she heard it. The rustle of stiff material against wooden floors. She sighed, lifted her head and turned to look around. Father Michael Duran sat directly behind her.

"Hello, Brigid," he said.

She nodded. "Father."

"How are Caitlin and the children settling in?"

"As well as can be expected, Father, considerin' the circumstances."

"She always was difficult."

Brigid nodded. "She had more cause than most, growin' up without a father."

The priest sat unmoving behind her. The silence stretched out between them. Why did he make her so uncomfortable after all these years?

"Is there anything I can do for you?" he asked at last.

She stood and moved out into the aisle. "I don't think so, Father," she said primly.

"You're in the sanctuary," he insisted. "There must be a reason. Are you troubled, Brigid?"

Brigid stared at him, amusement clearly stamped on what were once lovely features. "You've known me for a long time, Father. I'm not one t' be advertisin' my troubles." "Good day t' you."

She felt his eyes on her until she reached the doors. When she turned around her breath caught in her throat. What a picture he made, tall and lean in his flowing cassock, white haired, strong featured, his hand holding the flame-lit taper near the candle wick, his lips moving in silent prayer.

Brigid hurried out of the church and down the road toward home.

Caitlin had readied the children for the *cruinniú*. They waited in the kitchen, eyes shining, faces scrubbed, dressed in clothing that no Irish family in Kildare could spare the money to buy.

Even Annie was excited. The rare smile flickering across her features nearly broke Brigid's heart. While Ben was a love, a helpful, mischievous, sparkling, uncomplicated child young enough to make the adjustment from Kentucky to Ireland, Annie was her real challenge.

Sensitive, moody, startlingly intelligent, mature beyond her years, Annie was a child whose spirit needed cultivating. Brigid was very afraid that this move had done irreparable damage to her. The trouble was that Annie didn't fit in. Neither did Caitlin for that matter. She'd married into another class, assumed another style of speech, a way of dressing, an air of refinement. America and money had changed her. The Irish were a proud people. They would forgive her for it but they would make her pay.

Reaching out, Brigid smoothed her granddaughter's shining hair. "You look lovely, lass," she said, emotion making her voice gruff.

Caitlin, who had just come into the kitchen stared at her mother. Brigid flushed as if caught with an embarrassing secret. She had never been one for compliments. Pride was a sin she had actively discouraged in her daughters. But she was a grandmother now. Surely a grandmother could loosen up a bit and leave the molding of a child's character to the parents.

"I look nice, too," piped up Ben.

Brigid smiled. She would tell Caitlin about the phone call later. No sense in upsetting her before the *cruinniú*. "That you do, love, very nice indeed. There's no need t' wait for me. Run along. I'll change and be there shortly."

Caitlin frowned. "I'd rather wait for you, Mum. It might be a bit awkward for us going by ourselves."

There it was, that edge in her voice. Had it always been this way between them or was there a significant moment where she could pinpoint exactly when she had fallen out of grace with her youngest daughter?

Brigid's sharp-eyed gaze moved over Caitlin's slim figure. She wore a long dark skirt and a ribbed sweater, red, with a scooped neck that brought out the ivory color of her skin and snugly molded her waist and breasts. Black hair, the sides pulled up and secured with a clip, curled around her shoulders. Silky wisps framed her forehead and temples. Her face was heart-shaped, her features small and fine. She wore red lipstick, a deep rich russet, the same red as her sweater. Only the exotic slant to her dark eyes proclaimed her Celtic heritage. Had she always looked this way or had America changed that too?

"You were born here, Caitlin," Brigid said. "Nothin's

changed. Take your children and introduce them around. It's the only way. You've nothin' t' be ashamed of."

Caitlin opened her mouth to speak, looked at Annie's anxious face, and thought better of it. She summoned a bracing smile and took both children's hands in her own. "You're absolutely right. We'll go on ahead and wait for you there. Don't forget the bread pudding. It's in the refrigerator."

Brigid helped the children button their jackets and ushered them outside, waiting a moment at the door. The night was icy cold and crisp, and the moon hung low, large, and white over the distant hills. She could hear the sound of their voices, individually at first, Caitlin's low and soft, the children's eager, before they blended with others on their way toward the *cruinniú* at Kathleen Finch's cafe.

With a sense of relief, Brigid filled the tea kettle and sat down at the table. Caitlin would do much better on her own. She always had. These were the same people, a bit older now but otherwise the same, who had followed her lead when she was a child. Annie and Ben were attractive children. They would be an asset to her. The Irish were a friendly race, formal on occasion, slow to forgiveness, but there was a kindness in them, too, and a fierce love for children.

The kettle's shrill whistle interrupted her thoughts. Automatically, she went through the motions of rinsing the teapot, filling it with hot water, spooning in loose tea leaves, pouring milk into the pitcher and then into her cup. The tea steeped, coloring the water a lovely dark amber, the color of wet turf turned up from the ground before the sun shriveled it into the dull brown sticks that sustained Ireland through her long, frozen winters.

Brigid poured her tea and added sugar. She wasn't much for late night reveling. Besides, she'd heard what everyone in Kilcullen had to offer in the way of talent years ago. And no one would miss another dessert. The tables fairly groaned with food at Kathleen Finch's *cruinniú*. She would much rather sit here quietly and figure out how many of Sam Claiborne's threats on the phone this afternoon were serious.

She really should have mentioned his phone call. But Caitlin had seemed so happy lately, almost like the girl she'd been before she left for America. Brigid sighed.

So deep were her thoughts that she didn't hear the first two double rings of the telephone. She picked up the receiver on the sixth ring.

The voice on the other end had a distinctive southern drawl. It was also quite rude. No Irishman would have addressed her in such a way. "Brigid, it's Sam Claiborne. I've been waiting for hours. Where in the hell is Caitlin?"

"She took the children out," Brigid replied bluntly. "They won't return for some time."

Claiborne swore under his breath. "I specifically asked her to call me as soon as she got the message."

Brigid threw herself into the fire. "She doesn't know you called."

"What?"

She didn't answer.

"Listen, Brigid. This isn't a joke. I need to speak to my wife immediately."

Brigid Keneally's temper was slow to rise but when it did those who knew her stayed away. "You listen t' me, Sam Claiborne," she said fiercely. "I don't know who you think you are but I don't take orders from you. Caitlin is my daughter and in case you have any ideas about my loyalty, let me lay them t' rest. It is Caitlin's welfare I am concerned about, not yours. Perhaps if you were a bit more civil I might give my daughter your messages. As it stands I see no reason t' upset her."

"I might just fly over there and upset her a whole lot more if I show up in person."

Brigid's hand tightened on the phone. She willed herself to remain calm. No need to let Sam Claiborne think she was afraid of him. "You must suit yourself, of course," she said quietly. "Be sure you phone for lodgin's first. It's racin' season in County Kildare."

"I know that." Sam was clearly exasperated. He tried another approach. "Please, Brigid. This is important. Caitlin wants to see this finished as much as I do. We need to talk."

Perhaps Caitlin did want to be finished with Sam Claiborne, but Brigid would have wagered the pub that Caitlin's desired result looked nothing like her husband's. "I'll tell her," she said at last, "but not until tomorrow."

She could hear his frustrated sigh across four thousand miles of telephone wire. "Thank you," he said tersely before ringing off.

The *cruinniú* was well under way when Brigid arrived with Caitlin's bread pudding. She recognized the two female fiddlers and the young man playing the harmonica, but the guitarist was a stranger. Children from toddlers to teens chased each other, weaving in and out of the dancers on the wooden floor. Plates of food—boiled ham, sandwiches, salads, scones, breads, cakes rich with icing, biscuits, and puddings—covered a long picnic table. Along the sides, men and women who had given up dancing to observe and drink tea gathered to chat with each other. The room was very bright and very loud.

Kathleen Finch greeted Brigid, took the dish, set it on the table, and led her to a row of chairs near the back of the cafe.

"We nearly gave you up, love," she said. "What kept you?"

Brigid sat down gratefully. "I had a bit of a rest. It's not easy bein' on your feet all day."

Kathleen nodded in sympathy. "You need more help.

Kirsty's a good girl but she can't be workin' all the time and you're not gettin' any younger, Brigid."

"I'm not on my last legs either," remarked Brigid dryly. "I thought with Caitlin home, she could take over a bit."

Kathleen laughed out loud. "You're jokin', aren't you, love? That girl won't be of any help anywhere but in the barns. She lives and breathes horses just as she always has."

Brigid looked around the room. Annie was seated at one end of a long bench playing a board game with two other girls. Ben was pouring brown sauce over a plate of steaming crisps. Good lord, the lad had an appetite. Where did he put all of his food? "Have you seen Caitlin?"

Kathleen pointed to the center of the floor where couples were dancing to the lyrics of the Clarke Brothers. "She's there. Our Caitlin took up right where she left off, the belle of the ball."

Caitlin was circling the floor in Brian Hennessey's arms. "I don't recall that he was even here when she left," observed Brigid.

Kathleen shrugged and laughed. "It makes sense that she would take up with a man who makes his livin' on the horses."

"She's only dancin', Kate," Brigid objected. "She can't be takin' up with anyone at the moment. She's not yet divorced."

Kathleen threw up her hands. "Will you listen to yourself, Brigid Keneally? There are forty thousand people waitin' to be divorced. We've only been allowed the formality for two years. Half of Ireland is livin' in sin and has been for centuries. What difference does it make if she's divorced as long as she's not cheatin' on her husband?"

Brigid winced. Was it really so cut and dry, the severing of vows made between a man and a woman? Why hadn't she seen it that way thirty years ago? Why were things never so simple for her as they were for women like Kathleen Finch?

The answer came to her instantly. Because she wasn't anything like Kathleen Finch. She was complicated, like Caitlin. She eyed her daughter resentfully. Not that anyone had allowed her the freedom to indulge in her own natural tendencies. Married at twenty, widowed at forty, with six daughters in between and a business to run left little time for introspection. No one had ever asked if she was happy with her life or if she would have done things differently.

"Brigid." Kathleen prodded her shoulder. "Are you fallin' asleep on me?"

Brigid kept her eyes on her daughter's graceful figure. Even from across the room she could see that Caitlin was different. She moved with a confidence that comes early and only to women secure in their beauty. Her clothing was exquisitely cut, fitting her body in ways no off-the-rack department store specials ever could. The small makeup bag in the bathroom was evidence that Caitlin used cosmetics, but no one looking at her would ever guess that her skin and eyes were anything but flawlessly natural. Only the finest, most expensive products were that undetectable.

Brian Hennessey was a serious lad with the thin dark features found in the pure Celtic strains of the western isles. Just now there was a look on his face that Brigid had never seen before. "She's changed, hasn't she, Kathleen?" she asked softly.

Kathleen's forehead creased in consideration. "I don't know that she's changed so much, love. She was always one to take the eye. Half the lads in town were in love with her, as much for her pranks as for her looks." She placed her hand over Brigid's to reduce the sting of her next observation. "Perhaps you didn't know her as well as you should have."

"I knew her, Kate," answered Brigid. "I just didn't know what t' do with her. I still don't."

"Give it a bit of time," advised Kathleen. "She's only just come home. Caitlin's a mother now, and she's made her mistakes. There's no point in remindin' her of them."

"What am I supposed t' do when her past intrudes on the present?"

"Are you speakin' of something in particular?" Kathleen asked shrewdly.

"Her husband called. He's fair t' flyin' into a fit over this entire mess."

Kathleen shrugged. "It's her problem, Brigid. Let her sort it out. Our Caitie has always managed to surprise us. Why should she be any different now that she's grown up?"

"Why indeed," answered Brigid.

Later, Brigid hovered in the kitchen waiting for Caitlin to tuck the children into their beds. Ordinarily she would have been asleep hours ago, but she'd deliberately waited for the *cruinniú* to end. It was past time to deliver Samuel Claiborne's message.

Caitlin paused at the entrance to the kitchen. "You're up late, Mum."

"Would you like some tea?"

"No, thanks." She turned away. "I'll see you in the morning."

"Caitlin."

"Yes?"

"Sam called."

"And?"

"He wants you t' call him back, tonight."

Caitlin shook her head. "I don't think so."

Brigid picked up a dish towel and twisted it around her hands. "It isn't the first time he's called."

"Oh?"

"I didn't want t' ruin the party for you," her mother explained.

"I see."

Across the kitchen their eyes met and held.

"I don't blame you for bein' angry." Brigid felt like a child desperately afraid of a reprimand. Better to get it over quickly.

Caitlin was the first to break eye contact. "It's all right, Mum," she said at last. "You meant no harm and I'm not angry. But it's five o'clock in the morning in Kentucky. More than likely Sam, wherever he is, wouldn't want me to disturb him."

Something wasn't right. But Brigid was too tired to examine exactly what it was. She sighed with relief. The important thing was that Caitlin wasn't angry after all, or else she hid it well. Either way meant reprieve. Hesitantly, she broached the subject both of them had, by mutual consent, left alone. "You never talk about why it didn't work out."

"What?"

"The marriage."

For an instant, Brigid thought she saw something flare in the shadowy darkness of her daughter's eyes.

"No, I suppose I don't," Caitlin said.

Brigid ran her tongue over her bottom lip. It felt dry and cracked. "If you should ever want t'—"

She didn't miss the sharp, quick motion of the girl's hand.

"I've found a house, Mum. I've been to look at it already. We won't be crowding you anymore."

Brigid's heart numbed. She'd been dreading this moment. "When will you move?"

"Not for a few months. The tenants have a lease."

She wanted to say, "Please, don't go. Stay forever. I love havin' you with me." Instead she said, "That's all right, then."

"Good night, Mum."

Brigid sank down into the straight-backed kitchen chair. "Goodnight, love."

9

❧❧❧

Caitlin blew on her fingers, grimaced at the fleeting warmth and cursed the unnatural length of time it took for the turf to catch and offer up its flame. It was four in the morning, bone-chilling cold and she desperately needed a cup of tea before venturing out into the predawn fog to check on her mare and colt.

The old wood stove rumbled and coughed. The pilot flickered and the range lit, throwing light and a feeble flow of warmth into the room. She set the kettle on the flame and held her hands, palms down, over the heat source. Her glance settled on the wall phone.

She had no intention of returning Sam's call. Just the thought of hearing his voice again made her stomach queasy. Her lawyer had advised her against all communication with her husband until after they had reached a property settlement and custody agreement.

Zipping up her jacket, she poured boiling water into her

mug and held the cup between her frozen hands, waiting for the tea to steep. Deciding against milk, she sipped tentatively. The hot liquid seared a fiery path down her throat, warming her chest. Immediately she felt better, drank down the entire contents, and, careful not to wake anyone, stepped out into the blue-gray dawn. A light rain dogged her path. Head down, Caitlin trudged through the muddy streets to the stud farm.

Inside the yearling barn, the morning had already begun. Fifteen box stalls were connected by a walking path. Beneath the bright lights, grooms with pitchforks moved in and out of stalls probing and stabbing the beds for mats of urine and manure. Exercise lads talked, sipped at mugs of tea, smoked, and led horses, one at a time on leather lead shanks, around the path to cool them off. Stacked above the stalls, bales of hay, clover, and straw scented the air with herbal perfume. Outside, the metallic clip-clop of hooves signalled the coming and going of horses on their way to and from the track.

Caitlin walked to the stall where *Kentucky Gold* and her colt were stabled. Dust motes rose from the golden layer of new straw spread across the floor. A bucket of fresh water and a bag of grain hung at exactly the right level for the mare. Caitlin opened the door and stepped inside. The mare nickered.

Crooning softly, Caitlin picked up a brush and rub rag. "Don't fuss now, love. I'm going to brush you, that's all. It's been quite a week for you, hasn't it, my darling. Well, it's over now. There's no need to worry any more." As she talked in the gentle murmuring code of the horse lover, she worked carefully, purposefully, brushing and rubbing up and down the mare's coat—the rub rag following the sweep of the brush, the brush following the rag. The brush crisp, clean and practiced, the rag, slower, kinder, more sensual. The brush sending the dust flying, the rag burnishing the coat into a rich gleaming chestnut. Backed into a corner, the colt looked on, eyes too large and legs too long, the promise of speed to come.

Caitlin stepped back to survey her handiwork. "There you are, you lovely thing. Now you look like a champion."

"She's lovely indeed," said a voice from behind her.

Caitlin turned to see Brian Hennessey leaning over the door.

"Is it common in the Claiborne stables for owners to groom their horses?" he asked.

"It depends on the owner."

His eyes moved over her slowly, assessingly. Caitlin colored, wishing that she'd spent a bit more time on her appearance, and then wondering why she cared at all.

"You're up early," he said when his perusal was finished. "I didn't expect to see you until noon at least."

"You're here."

"This is my job. It doesn't stop for a *cruinniú*."

Caitlin waved her hand toward *Kentucky Gold* and the foal. "These are my horses. I wanted to be sure they were well taken care of."

"Are you satisfied?"

She smiled and looked around at the exquisitely maintained barn. "Very. You're doing a fine job here, Brian. John should be pleased. Do you see him often?"

Brian shook his head and a look of genuine regret flickered across his face. "John O'Shea doesn't get out much, not since Assumpta died."

Caitlin rubbed the mare's satiny back. "Martin and I haven't really spoken since I've come home."

"Does it bother you?" Brian asked bluntly.

Caitlin's eyes narrowed. "Are you under the mistaken impression that there was something between Martin and me, Mr. Hennessey?"

Brian grinned. "Are you goin' to freeze up on me every

time somethin' bothers you, Caitlin? That's no way to build a friendship."

"Is that what we're doing?"

"I'd like to." He nodded at her mare and colt. "It would make all this easier."

"Then answer my question."

"I have no reason to think you and Martin shared anythin' but friendship."

Caitlin rubbed her hand against the mare's side, testing for smoothness. "How did the two of you meet?"

"We went to the Jesuit College together. He went on to the seminary. I didn't."

"Why not?" It was out before she could stop the words. "I'm terribly sorry," she said, embarrassed at her breach of etiquette. "It's none of my business."

He stepped inside the stall and reached out to stroke the mare's velvety nose. "Perhaps it isn't. Still, there's no harm in a question," he said easily. "I'm not cut out to be a priest. That's all there is to it. Many who start don't make it through. It's better that way." He smiled. "If you're done here, would you care to share a cup of somethin'?"

Caitlin looked at her watch and shook her head. "I really have to be going. My mother needs help and the children will be up soon."

"Ah." He nodded. "Annie and Ben. They're expected here this mornin'."

Caitlin followed him out of the stall and pulled the door shut. "You can't really want them," she said. "They'll only be in the way."

He stared at her. "You've an odd idea of your children's abilities, Caitlin. They're old enough to be useful. You should know that. You were born here."

"Annie and Ben were born in America," she replied. "They aren't accustomed to being useful."

"Perhaps it's time they learned."

She tossed the brush and rag over the stall into a bucket and rubbed her hands together. Her temper was very near the surface. "Are you criticizing the way I've raised my children, Brian?"

"Not at all. They're splendid children. What I object to is your regard for their capabilities. If you believe they've nothin' to offer, they'll believe it as well."

"It's not that."

"What is it, then?"

She drew a deep breath. "My husband wouldn't be happy if he knew they were mucking out stables."

"I thought they did that at home."

"That's different. Claiborne belongs to them. Not now," she amended, "but it will."

Brian frowned. "I don't see why he would mind if they gathered a bit of experience elsewhere as long as they're willing."

"You don't know Sam."

"I won't go back on my word to your children, Caitlin. As long as you don't object, I'll take full responsibility."

He took her arm and led her out of the barn toward the kitchen. "I've had nothin' to eat all mornin' and I doubt you have either. Sit down with me for fifteen minutes. Then I'll drive you home."

The kitchen Caitlin remembered had been remodeled into a bright room with wooden tables and food served cafeteria-style. The breakfast rush was over and it was nearly empty. Without quite knowing how it happened, she was seated across the table from Brian with an enormous platter of eggs, bacon, toast, and a pot of tea in front of her. Tentatively, she tasted the eggs and her appetite kicked in full force. Oblivious to everything but the hot food, she ate and drank without looking up or saying a word, until her plate was empty.

Wiping her mouth with her napkin, she pushed away the plate and glanced across the table to find herself the subject of Brian Hennesey's amused regard. "I was hungry," she said defensively.

"Obviously."

Instantly she was on guard. There was something unusual about this man, a quick intelligence, pride, and a cultivated sense of humor that didn't quite fit with his loose corduroy trousers and wool shirt—traditional garb of the working class. Brian Hennessey was a loner: tough-minded, warm-hearted, bright—more so than she'd first imagined—a man more perceptive than most because he took the time to listen and read between the lines.

It came to her suddenly. She wanted his approval. The flame-red flag of embarrassment colored her cheeks. She'd eaten like a pig. "I haven't had much of an appetite lately," she said. "More than likely I was catching up today."

He grinned. "Don't apologize. If I hadn't wanted you to eat, I wouldn't have offered to buy you a meal."

"In America, in the south, it's impolite for a woman to have a hearty appetite outside of her own kitchen."

"I suppose Sam Claiborne encouraged that misguided notion."

Caitlin looked surprised. "Do you know my husband, Brian?"

He shrugged. "We've met. I doubt if he'd remember. You might say I know him by reputation."

"What does that mean?"

"It means that I know somethin' of how the Claiborne Farms got started and I'd be a liar if I said that I didn't resent it. I don't believe your husband is particularly talented when it comes to knowin' a good horse, but he doesn't have to be. He's the lucky heir of men like Bull and James Claiborne, men who knew horses down to the bone. I'm not particularly pleased that the Claiborne empire began with an Irish horse. It should never have happened. Old Bull Claiborne stole *Nasrullah* right out from under us, clever bastard."

"I wouldn't call it stealing," said Caitlin. "He *bought* the horse fairly."

"Believe what you will. I happen to know that he cashed in on another's misfortune. Since he acquired *Nasrullah*, every leading American sire since, and a good many European ones, have stood at Claiborne." He ticked them off on his fingers, "*Narraganset, Tiny Dancer, Bold Runner, Princiquillo, Darcy's Pride* and *Cimmaron*, all Claiborne stallions, all champions out of *Nasrullah*."

Caitlin stared at him curiously. "You sound bitter, as if something personal was taken from you."

The line of his jaw was tight and angry. "Somethin' personal *was* taken from Ireland, from all of us who are Irish."

"Do you hate us, Brian?"

He looked across the table, saw the frown between her eyes, and shook his head. "I don't hate anyone, lass. Certainly not you. Besides, you're not really a Claiborne."

She could have mentioned that her divorce hadn't even begun yet. She could have reminded him that Annie and Ben had their fair share of Claiborne genes. She could have explained that she was, most definitely in the eyes of the law, a Claiborne. But she did none of those things. Instead, she asked, "How does a man from the western isles fall so deeply in love with horses?"

"There are horses on the islands."

"Not this kind."

He laughed. "No, not this kind."

"Don't tell me if you'd rather not."

"It's no secret," he replied. "I've family here on the mainland, near Cashel. When I was a wee lad, I spent my summers with them. They followed the races. The first time I went, I was hooked. It's as simple as that. I wanted to be a jockey, but there was never any hope of that. I was never big, but too big to hold on to that dream."

"Why a jockey and not a trainer?"

"Speed," he said simply. "It feels like flying."

She caught her breath. He knew what she did: that none of it mattered, not the money, not the glory, not even the sport—just the power, the exhilarating speed, and the horse finding a window, taking the bit in his mouth, and running to win. Brian's arm was on the table. She wanted to touch him, to stretch the bond that had sprung up between them, to make it physical as well as spiritual.

Slowly, she inched her fingers across the surface to touch the dip in his palm. His hand closed around hers, pulling her closer. The contact was intense, emotional, deeply personal.

Davy Flynn's thick Irish brogue interrupted them. "Caitie Keneally, what are you doin' here this time of the mornin'? We're takin' good care of your horses, aren't we, Brian?" He slapped Brian good-naturedly on the back.

"It's past time for me to be going home," Caitlin stammered. Flushed with embarrassment, she rose from her chair and headed for the door. "Thank you for the food."

Pushing himself away from the table, Brian lengthened his stride and caught up with her at the door. "We agreed that I would take you home."

"I'd rather walk," she said quickly, avoiding his eyes, "really I would."

"All right then," he said quietly. "I'll see you later. I've enjoyed the company and the conversation."

She smiled, a quick reluctant twisting of her lips, and then she was gone, out the door before he could say anymore.

"God help you, Caitlin Keneally," she muttered to herself, covering the ground twice as fast as she normally did. "Are you really so desperate for a man's attention that you'd make a fool of yourself over the first one who pays attention to you?"

The truth, bare and stripped clean of excuses, wasn't flattering. She felt inadequate. It was all Sam's doing, she concluded bitterly. He'd made it clear enough that she didn't have the necessary attributes to keep him interested, whatever those were. Yet he'd been interested enough in the beginning and for a long while after until the glow had passed and it was clear to everyone that she was woefully outclassed by the women in his social circle.

Those snubs in the early days of her marriage had left more than a few scars, bitter reminders of how far she'd come. A business degree, her own abilities, and Bull Claiborne's confidence had resolved most of her issues but the wounds had been slow to heal.

Her pace began to lag as she analyzed her marriage squarely, honestly, something she had avoided until now. To be fair, Sam had been an attentive husband in the beginning and after Annie was born. He'd been truly delighted when she told him she was pregnant with Ben. It was only after she relaxed a bit and allowed the real Caitlin to surface: the woman who had a better than average grasp of finances and invested wisely in the commodities market even though Sam had warned her against it. The woman who understood supply and demand and forced up the price of Claiborne stud fees. The woman who refused to endorse Sam's lifelong friend, gubnatorial candidate Dave Gastineau, because his politics would harm small breeders desperately trying to survive in an industry that was slowly crowding them out. It was only after all of that that Sam had cooled toward her.

When she turned down the trip to Paris, a trip that was supposed to be their second honeymoon, he stopped trying altogether. But sales had been slow that year and she was waiting to hear whether *Suliman,* a Claiborne stallion commanding enormous stud fees, had successfully covered the Brockman mare.

Caitlin had deliberately kept the number of brood mares down to twenty, half as many as a healthy stallion could cover in a season, in the hopes that it would drive up the stud fee. In Britain stud fees were paid whether or not a colt resulted from the mating. Not so in America. Unless a broodmare produced a healthy colt, the fee was forfeit.

Her ploy had been more successful than even she had imagined it could be, but it had required a diplomatic hand to turn away those who assumed they would automatically have access to the Claiborne stallion. She could not have left it to anyone else.

Perhaps the failure of their marriage was as much her fault as Sam's. She slowed down even more, suddenly in no hurry to get home.

Once, this small village and the Curragh had been her world. Memories came back to her, fond, comfortable memories of Martin and his brother, Dylan, of years before either of them knew the meaning of conscience. Memories of chubby cheeks and scraped knees, of grubby fingers and solemn promises, of confidences shared and hurt feelings soothed.

She'd fallen in and out of love with the O'Shea brothers a hundred times. Caitlin remembered the exact moment when innocence became something else, something that made her cheeks flame and her chest ache and her breath shorten. Then it would go away again and the old familiar closeness would return.

She missed her sisters. In the room she had shared with Kitty and Mary sleeping so close she could reach out and touch them, she'd learned more than she ever had at Saint

Patrick's. They would tell secrets and stifle laughter, pressing hands over each other's mouths to muffle the revealing sounds that would bring Brigid marching down the hall. It seemed like a lifetime ago.

Had she ever really cared for Sam? Never with the soul-strangling, uncompromising depth of passion a woman should feel for a man. But there had been a time, however brief, when she thought they could have made a go of it together. He had given her Annie and Ben, and for that, if nothing else, she would be forever grateful. The thought of her children brought a smile to her lips.

"Caitlin." Lana Sullivan dropped the cigarette she had finished, ground it out on the pavement, and ran across the street to catch up. "You're up early," she panted, falling into step beside her friend.

"I went to see the horses."

"Ah, the horses." Lana glanced at her thoughtfully. "Did you happen to see Brian Hennessey?"

Preoccupied with other thoughts, Caitlin nodded absently.

"What do you think of him?"

"Who?"

Lana laughed. "Where's your head, lass? We were speaking of Brian Hennessey, of course."

"What about him?"

"He's a bit of a dish, don't you think?"

It came back to her instantly, that moment in the kitchen when she'd touched his hand. Caitlin could feel the blush rise up from her neck. "He's all right," she said tentatively, "if you like the dark, intense type."

Lana linked her arm through Caitlin's. "He can be rather fierce looking," she agreed, "but I like him well enough. You never were one for the lads here in Kilcullen."

Caitlin opened her mouth to tell Lana that she knew

nothing about it, but the woman wouldn't allow her an opening.

"I know that's all water under the bridge," Lana chatted on companionably. She pulled a strand of flyaway red hair from her mouth. "You aren't still in love with your husband, are you, Caitie?"

"No."

Lana's blue eyes warmed with sympathy. "That's wise. No sense in rehashing what's over, unless there's a chance of going back."

"No," Caitlin said again. "There's no chance of that."

"You never answered my question."

"Which one?" Caitlin asked. Had there been a question?

Lana's expression was open, her eyes honest. "Once, we were close enough to share our thoughts. Would you like to have that again, Caitie?"

In the interminable seconds that followed Lana's question, Caitlin searched her mind for an answer. The truth was, other than Martin and her sisters, she couldn't remember having a friend, not in Kilcullen and certainly not in Kentucky. Had she ever wanted one? Lord, she was hopeless. Did she want one now? Caitlin swallowed. Everything was so different. She was so different. "Sharing thoughts means an exchange," she said slowly. "Is there something you wanted to tell me, Lana?"

The young woman's sturdy body suddenly lost its rigidity and she sighed gratefully. "You always were a clever one, Caitie. The thing is, I'm interested in Brian Hennessey. But I know that I haven't got a chance with him once you decide that you fancy him as well. So, I've come to ask if you do."

"You want to know if I'm interested in Brian Hennessey?" Caitlin asked incredulously.

"Aye."

"For pity's sake." Caitlin stopped dead in the street. This

entire conversation was absurd, much worse than the gossip at Lucy Claiborne's bridge parties. "I'm trying desperately to get out of a dreadful marriage. The last thing I need is another man."

Lana grinned and once again linked arms with her friend. "I'm glad to hear it."

Caitlin lifted her face to the sky and felt rain on her cheeks. This time of year it fell suddenly and relentlessly, in horizontal sheets accompanied by wind that made an umbrella useless. They'd be soaked to the skin if they didn't find shelter in the next few minutes. Lana was clinging to her like a mosquito stuck on fly paper. For her the crisis had passed. She meant well but just now Caitlin would have preferred her own company. Her friend's disclosure had shocked her into offering up a quick, albeit, incomplete answer. She didn't need another man. That part was glaringly evident. The rest of Lana's question, the part about Brian Hennessey, she'd deliberately left unanswered for very good reasons.

She needed time to sort out her thoughts, to analyze exactly what it was about Brian that appealed to her so intensely. By reliving that moment in the kitchen, by refracting it into separate events and exposing it through repetition, by minimizing the magic of that sudden, terrifying attraction that leaped to life between them, she would ensure that it never happened again.

10

❧❧❧

Without waiting for the Newberry racing train to come to a complete stop, Brian jumped lightly off the steps and headed toward the track. It was a clear golden Saturday, rare for October, and the stud farm was relatively quiet. He'd taken the weather and the respite as an auspicious sign and flown *British Midlands* across the channel to bet on four flat and two English jump races.

It was still early. Brian walked into the bar, ordered a Harp, and found a small table near the back. He didn't recognize anyone until a large, callused hand gripped his shoulder.

"Brian Hennessey, lad," the booming Yorkshire-tainted voice reverberated throughout the lounge. "How's the breeding business, and what brings you to Newberry?"

Brian tipped his head back, recognized the balding, red-faced, barrel-chested frame of Robert Tilton, sports writer for the *London Times,* and offered him a seat. "Business is grand," he replied. "I'm havin' a bit of holiday. What about yourself?"

"All in a day's work for me, lad." He pulled up a chair and held up two fingers to the barman before turning his attention back to Brian. "What's this I hear about a court battle over *Narraganset's* last foal?"

Not by the flicker of an eyelash did Brian's expression reveal his thoughts. "I've no idea. What have you heard?"

Tilton waited until the barman delivered his whiskey and walked away. "Come now, lad. It's common knowledge that the Claiborne divorce is stalled over the colt."

"That's all there is," Brian said woodenly. "You've got the entire story in a nutshell."

"Sam Claiborne has millions," said Tilton bluntly. "It could go badly for the Curragh if you go against him."

Brian downed the last of his beer. "I'm aware of that. The colt was born at the farm. As far as I know he belongs to Mrs. Claiborne. When I know for a fact that he doesn't, I'll return him. Until then, he stays."

Tilton studied him shrewdly, bushy eyebrows drawn tightly together. "He must be an exceptional colt."

"He's good-lookin' enough," said Brian noncommittally. "But he hasn't proven himself."

"A colt out of *Narraganset* and *Kentucky Gold* won't have much to prove."

"You've been around long enough to know that bloodline is only one factor. There have been at least a dozen *Narraganset* foals born every year for the last decade, and only a few were Triple Crown winners."

"But this one is out of *Kentucky Gold.* All *Narraganset-Kentucky Gold* foals are champions, Brian. Even if they haven't won every cup, they've brought in enough money in the last ten years to retire their owners. Nominations are priceless and practically impossible to get. You know the figures. Do the arithmetic."

"I've done it," said Brian quietly. "When the colt finishes his trainin' and starts winnin', he'll be worth his keep, somethin' I'm sure Mrs. Claiborne will appreciate."

Tilton laughed, pulled a handkerchief from his pocket and blew his nose loudly. "Difficult, is she? Wealthy Americans usually are. Can't blame Sam Claiborne for wanting his horse back."

Brian couldn't explain the impulse that made him leap to Caitlin's defense. "Mrs. Claiborne is Irish, and I believe *Kentucky Gold* belongs to her."

The sports writer shook his head and held up his hand for another double shot of whiskey. "It won't wash, lad. She'll have to buy him out. There isn't an attorney on either side of the Atlantic who will award the colt to either of them scot-free."

Brian shrugged, uncomfortable with the conversation. "That remains to be seen."

"Sooner than you think." Tilton pulled a mangled periodical from his pocket and handed it to Brian. "Claiborne's featured in the *Racing Gazette*. It says here he plans to be in Antrim to preside over the last flat race of the year at Down Royal. I imagine he'll stop over in Kildare to see the colt."

Brian opened the magazine and stared at the black-and-white print. "I imagine he will," he said slowly, wondering if Caitlin knew. "It would be foolish of him not to."

Tilton downed his drink. "The race is beginning. Shall we go down?"

Brian stood, stuffed the periodical in his pocket, and followed the sports writer through the gate to the center of the course to find a position at the last fence. "You never mentioned why you're here, Rob," said Brian. "This is a small race, certainly not important enough for the *London Times*."

Tilton nodded toward the gate. "*Angel Light* is running. I'd bet my pension on him. He's the horse to watch. After the race tell me I'm wrong."

Brian recognized the name. *Angel Light* had been the favorite for some time now. The two year old could be counted on for speed from the starting gate to the finish line. He'd won every race he'd entered and was on his way to becoming a household word in the equine industry.

The gates shot open and eight horses streaked toward the first turn. *Angel Light* in the number two position immediately struck out in front, running unchallenged to claim the first straight. Brian could see that the horse hadn't yet hit full stride nor had he taken a deep breath.

Seconds passed. Silence gripped the crowd like a chokehold. Then came the thunder of hooves. *Angel Light* raced around the second bend with seven other horses following, their jockeys looking for an opening, chirping, urging their colts forward. Once more he led the others around the seven-eighths pole, around the three-quarters pole, picking up even more speed. With only 660 yards to go, the jockey let out a notch. The horse responded by pulling ahead nearly two lengths. Collectively the crowd leaped to its feet. The jockey rode furiously, using the whip, demanding the last ounce of strength from the dun-colored colt. Twenty yards from the wire, *Angel Light* grew wings and flew across to lead by more than three lengths.

Brian nodded approvingly. "A magnificent animal."

"A champion," Tilton agreed. "There won't be another like him this season." He looked at Brian. "I hope you placed your money on him."

Brian grinned. "My money's safe. I do know a bit about horses."

Tilton laughed. "Sorry, lad. The excitement never stops for me, especially here, at such close quarters."

It was nearly time for the second race. The jockeys, bigger this time and resplendent in their colors, galloped the horses onto the course for the three-mile steeple chase. Again the gates opened and the horses leaped forward over the fence, colors brilliant in the afternoon sun.

The crowd roared its approval while the pounding turf reverberated in eardrums, hearts, and throbbing pulses. The air rang with the shouts of jockeys, the sighs of the disappointed, and the hammering hooves of massive bodies pulling at their bits, straining through the openings, racing around their first loop to the finish line.

Silence swallowed up the endless seconds until once again the ground rumbled and the sweat-stained powerful animals came around into the straight, running at incredible speeds toward the winning post. The final fence was in sight. The inevitable question rose in the throats of every betting man, choking the blood to his brain. Which horse would claim the cup?

Then it happened, the inevitable variable, always a strong possibility in a steeple chase. The bay shied away from the jump, twisting his back and making a complete u-turn on the track. His jockey fought for control, to no avail. The chestnut, two-lengths behind, couldn't turn in time to avoid the bay's flying hooves. Both horses and jockeys went down in a confusion of jewel-bright colors and two thousand pounds of heaving, sweating bodies. The sing-song whine of an ambulance broke through the moans of the crowd. One jockey was on his feet, the other sat up, cradling his head in his hands. Both horses were still down, one with legs thrashing, the other completely still.

Tilton shook his head. "I played that one badly. What about you?"

Brian shook his head. "I make it a habit to never bet on a steeple chase. Too many variables can crab a race."

Eyebrows raised in astonishment, Tilton mocked him. "You're not really a gambling man are you, lad?"

"Only when the odds are in my favor. This time they weren't. I didn't know any of the horses and I didn't get here in time to look them over."

"Is that how you do it?"

"Aye." Brian nodded. "It's the only way to be sure."

Two hours later, after an inadequate ham sandwich, he left Robert Tilton at the track and boarded the train back to Gatwick with a light heart. His pockets were richer by a hundred pounds but that was of little consequence. It was early in the season but already he had a good grasp of the competition. A few more races and he would know the extent of it, except for the upcoming crop of two year olds, of course, and no one would know about them until the first race.

Robert Tilton's news had thrown him. Caitlin hadn't mentioned that her husband intended a stopover in Kildare which probably meant that she didn't know. He didn't relish telling her. Her initial coolness following the *cruinniú* and their breakfast together the next morning had settled into a tentative camaraderie. He looked forward to their conversations when she came to the barn in the morning. He hadn't expected her to be as knowledgeable as she was about the training of yearlings, and wondered if Sam Claiborne was feeling the pinch of her absence from his stables.

He almost stopped in at Kathleen Finch's for a proper dinner but changed his mind when he saw that Lana Sullivan was working the tables. The girl was fishing for a man and Brian had no intention of taking the bait. With a brief wave he hurried past, ignored the disappointed look on the waitress' face, crossed to the other side of the street, and headed home.

The barns were quiet in the evening, clean and uncluttered. Blankets, baskets, linseed oils, and liniments were stored away in tack rooms. Brian walked down the aisle of C-Barn, inhaling the odors of alfalfa, sweet grass, hay, and leather that never failed to excite him. Unlike a racing stable where a groom or exercise boy was responsible for one or two yearlings, a stud farm exerciser cared for a number of horses, simultaneously, at different stages of maturity. Mares could be with their foals out in the paddocks or in their stalls, either in heat or readying to foal. Colts, depending on their need to grow into themselves or put on weight, were still with their dams grazing in the lime rich pasturelands. Some preferred the stalls at night and were brought inside while others stayed out in the open. An exerciser had to be intuitive to the needs of his horse, watching for mood swings and body language. A reluctant gait could mean a desire to stay inside. Ears perked forward could signal a colt's excitement for the rich pasturelands outside the training areas.

Kentucky Gold and her foal were in the paddock just outside the barn. Brian leaned over the top rail of the fence and studied the pair. The colt, Brian noted with satisfaction, was growing into a beauty: muscular, graceful, a shapely head, and more importantly, the strong straight legs, short canon bones, smooth knees, and forty-five degree pastern angle of a champion. He also had something else that made the adrenalin surge through the stud manager's veins. He had a wide jaw which meant good airflow. Only five percent of all thoroughbreds were born with a jaw like that. Now, if inbreeding, the foe of a thoroughbred's healthy respiratory system, hadn't already predetermined his air passages, this colt might very well live up to Caitlin's expectations.

Brian had made a detailed study of speed relative to thoroughbreds. Conformation, gait analysis, heart score, muscle fiber, and bloodline were not nearly as important as airflow, the ability of a horse to take in air as it ran. Airflow was something that could not be accurately measured until a colt was at least a year old. Not all racehorses who were born with that identifying trait were winners, but all who *were,* without exception, had the generous jaw signifying wide air passages. A horse needed air to stay the pace, and this one, he predicted, would have the staying power to last the distance and run to win.

Rounding the back corner that led to the training track, he stopped abruptly, unprepared for the rush of pleasure that washed over him. Caitlin was riding *Indigo Blue*.

He watched as she walked him first and then tightened the reins, chirping gently, trying to give the colt a feel for her weight, her experience, and the bit in his mouth. Heading down the backstretch, she leaned forward, mouth beside his ear, rump above the saddle.

Indigo Blue responded, taking the bit in his mouth, pulling out, increasing his tempo. Caitlin bent double at the waist, her legs completely straight, boots dug into the stirrups. She waved the whip in front of the colt's eyes. He lunged forward, hooves tearing up the turf, sliding by the three-eighths pole, striding hard.

Brian whistled and pulled out his watch. Caitlin was rounding the final length now. He set the second hand. Faster and faster she urged the colt. He was running at top speed now. Her head was close to his ear. Another burst of speed and he was through the wire. Brian looked at his watch and then looked again. A perfect twelve-clip, a record. By God, the woman could ride!

Later, after she'd cooled him down, he joined her in the barn. He could hear her voice, soothing and warm. "Don't worry, love. You'll have your supper soon. You deserve it after the way you ran."

He watched the slender fingers rub and knead and stroke the animal into quivering ecstasy. "He's spoiled enough," Brian said at last. "There'll be no livin' with him."

Caitlin looked up, smiled serenely, and went back to rubbing down the colt as if she knew he'd been watching her all the time. Once again Brian was struck by her poise and wondered how long it had taken a poor Irish girl from Kilcullen to acquire such confidence, and at what price.

"I've nothin' in my refrigerator, but I could offer you a cup of tea," he said, prepared for her usual refusal.

Surprisingly, she agreed. "I'll finish here and then see if your refrigerator truly is bare."

After he fed the colt and she washed her hands, they walked to his cottage. He opened the door, allowing her to precede him into his small cottage. Brian filled the tea kettle, crossed his arms and settled back against the counter to watch her work. "You're good at this," he said approvingly.

Caitlin handed over the vegetable peeler and looked at him skeptically. "I need four carrots peeled and sliced. Can you do that?"

"I'm not an idiot, Caitlin," he said. "How do you suppose I feed myself when you're not here?"

Her eyebrows rose and once again he noticed the darkness of her eyes against pale ivory skin, Irish skin that not even the sun of fourteen Kentucky summers had darkened.

"I assumed you ate in the stud kitchen."

Brian shook his head. "Only for lunch and tea. The rest of the time I'm on my own."

She turned back to the counter, picked up a knife and proceeded to chop celery into small half moons. "Then you won't botch up the carrots."

He finished his task and watched in awe as she scooped the carrots into a pot, sauteed them with celery and onions, dropped in chicken bouillon cubes and boiling water, all the while adding spices he didn't know he had, sprigs of coriander, crushed garlic, ginger. Then she pureed the entire mixture in his blender, ladled out two soup bowls, splashed a dollop of cream on top of each and carried them to the table. "If you have bread we're in good shape," she pronounced.

Brian produced a loaf of wheaten bread and a butter dish, and sat down across from her. He did not have an adventurous palate but after the first suspicious taste, he needed no further encouragement. "You're incredible," he said when the last delicious spoonful had joined the others. "Is there anythin' you can't do?"

Her eyes darkened and her lips parted. For a minute Brian thought she was about to disclose something of herself. But the moment passed with a nod of her head and a brief laugh. "There are many things I can't do. I'm glad you enjoyed the soup."

"Have you always been this creative in the kitchen?"

She appeared confused by the question and it took her a full minute to answer. "I don't know, really," she said slowly. "Not here in Ireland. There was never enough time for it. The only thing I ever thought about was horses."

She looked over his head at the clock. "I've got to run. Sorry to leave you with the dishes."

He lifted an eyebrow. "It's fair, I think. You cooked."

She nodded and stood.

"Caitlin." He tried to keep his voice light. "There's somethin' you should know."

Standing in the doorway, her face shadowed by the halflight from the porch lamp, she looked about twelve years old and very vulnerable. His heart contracted. He swallowed and rushed the words to get them over with. "Your husband is comin' to Antrim to preside over the flat races."

She stood erect, motionless, allowing the words to wash over her. Finally she spoke. "How do you know?"

He pulled the *Racing Gazette* from his pocket and crossed the room to hand it to her. "They've written him up."

She read quickly and gave it back. "Damn Brits," she

muttered. "I suppose they couldn't find an Irishman to run their bloody race."

He bit back a grin. "Apparently not."

Caitlin laughed. "Thanks for the warning."

"Is that what it is?"

"There's no love lost between Sam and me," she confessed. "Our meeting, if there is one, won't be pleasant. If he tries to take *Irish Gold* I won't be able to stop him."

She looked resigned rather than miserable or outraged. Brian's curiosity was aroused. Brigid Keneally didn't wear the appearance of a stern parent. Why had her daughter learned to expect so little? Without thinking he reached out to her, his hands closing around her shoulders. "No one will take your colt without legal authorization and that takes a great deal of time. *Irish Gold* could very well be a four year old by then. Do you understand me, Caitlin?"

He held his breath while her eyes moved over his face, judging him, gauging his sincerity, skepticism etched on every lovely, discriminating feature. Caitlin was not a woman who trusted easily. For reasons he couldn't explain, the very thought of the heartache she must have endured brought him to a dangerous level of compassion. He had been known to do foolish things, things he regretted, when he allowed emotion to take over.

Slowly, Caitlin released her breath, nodded, and stepped back through the doorway. Reluctantly Brian released her. Something wasn't quite settled despite her nod and the look of relief on her face.

"You're not afraid of him, are you?" Brian asked gently.

She looked startled. "Sam? Good Lord, no. He's harmless. The worst he's ever done is bluster absurd insults and he only does that when he's had too much to drink. He never even raises his voice."

Brian wondered if she was in a state of denial or if that

pride she held before her like an ancient battle targe wouldn't allow her to voice just how much her husband's insults had affected her. She'd obviously forgotten that he knew Sam Claiborne. The man had a lethal temper. "I'll walk you home."

"No!"

Her hand was pressed flat against his chest. Brian couldn't deny the panic in her voice.

"I mean, no thank you," she amended quickly. "I need a few minutes alone."

He refrained from reminding her that she was alone and probably had been for quite some time before he returned from Newberry. "Good night, then," he said formally. "Thank you again for dinner."

His cottage, traditionally owned by the stud manager, was set back beyond the roll of a hillock. Assumpta O'Shea had planted a circle of pines that, over twenty years, had grown into a thicket ensuring peace and privacy in an environment that was rarely either. Brian was at the crest of the hill whistling for Neeve when the shrill double ring of his telephone broke the quiet. He jogged down the path and answered on the fourth ring. The voice on the other end made him wish he'd allowed the message machine to take the call. "Hello, Lana," he said, keeping his voice neutral. "What can I do for you?"

"I'm having a party, Saturday next. It's my birthday. Will you come? Everyone will be there," she said babbling over his silence.

"I'll be happy to come if I can get back in time from the Tattersall auction."

"You were first on my list," she confessed. "I don't mind if you're late."

He closed his eyes. Why this, the last complication he needed and the worst he was at managing? "What time?"

"Eight o'clock, at my mother's. Don't worry about bringing anything. It's all arranged."

He hung up the phone and sank wearily into the cushions of the shabby sofa. Now, on top of everything else, he needed a gift. What did a man buy for a young woman whose attentions he wished to discourage? Immediately he thought of Caitlin and just as quickly rejected the idea. A man did not ask a woman to buy a gift for another woman, no matter how desperate he was. It was possible she would select exactly the right kind of nominal present or, if she were unhappy with him and had the barest hint of spitefulness in her nature, she could choose something that would have him walking down the aisle by spring. No, he would find something on his own, something completely neutral, that could in no way be misunderstood.

11

Brigid deposited the last item into Siobhan Callanan's basket, rang up the total and handed over the change. "That's two guineas, three shillin's. Will you be needin' anythin' else?" she asked the woman politely.

"Not today, unless you have somethin' for my wrist. It aches now that the weather's turned."

Brigid took a measuring look at the hand livered with brown age spots and made her pronouncement. "Soak it in hot water, love, or wrap a heatin' pad around it. No sense spendin' money that won't see results."

Siobhan nodded. "I hate feelin' the years." She smiled and the change of expression lit up what had once been attractive features. "It seems like just yesterday that the chaps were lined up for a dance. Do you remember how it was, Brigid?"

Brigid murmured something suitable. Through the store window, she could see Annie walking slowly down the street. Frowning, she looked at the clock. School wasn't out for another two hours. "Let me help you with the door, Siobhan," she said, lifting the basket and coming out from behind the counter.

Ten minutes later, after her friend's usual lengthy good-bye, Brigid hung the CLOSED sign on the door and hurried home. Annie was barricaded in her room. "Annie," Brigid called out, "are you all right?"

For a long time there was no reply. Finally, the muffled reply came through the door. "I'm fine, Gran."

"Why are you home so early?"

Again nothing. Brigid chewed her lip. If Annie had been one of her own daughters she would have marched right in and demanded to know what was wrong. The absurdity of such a thought hit her immediately. More likely if Annie had been one of her own, she wouldn't even have noticed the child was upset. She had been too preoccupied with putting food on the table to keep an eye on anything so trivial as a child's moodiness.

Caitlin was at the stud. Perhaps she should find her and bring her back. On the other hand, Annie hadn't been very receptive toward her mother lately. Brigid resolved to try this one on her own. She turned the knob.

Annie lay on her stomach on the bed, her face buried in a pillow. Brigid sat down beside her and gave in to the urge to stroke the dark curls. "What is it, love?" she said gently. "Did somethin' happen at school?"

The child shook her head but a tell-tale sniff gave her away. Brigid leaned over and kissed her granddaughter's head. Life was difficult for children today, what with people divorcing, moving, pulling them in different directions without so much as a by-your-leave. They had no control over their own lives, forced to make the best of whatever was decided for them.

She'd never considered the matter before, but even with all her money worries, the responsibilities, and not enough time to think things through, she would much rather be an adult than live her childhood over again. It was criminal to tell the young that childhood was the best time of their lives. More likely it would make them end it all prematurely by jumping into the River Liffey. Perhaps Annie needed a bit of grandmotherly wisdom.

"I know none of this has been pleasant for you, Annie," she said, brushing away hair from the girl's flushed cheeks. "In fact, it really is unfair."

Brigid could feel some of the tension leave the girl's rigid body. "You've had to move away from your home, your friends, your father, and grandmother t' come here, a place you've never been before. I certainly wouldn't want t' do it. Your mother did, but that was her decision. No one even asked how you felt about it."

Annie was actively listening now. Brigid continued. "The thing is, your mother couldn't leave you and she couldn't stay where she was. A woman can't leave her children, Annie. There's somethin' in us that can't make such a separation, not when children are young."

Annie turned over and Brigid's eyes widened at the girl's tear-swollen face. Something was terribly wrong. "What happened t' you, lass?"

"I hate that stupid school," the child sobbed, fresh tears brimming over, spilling down her cheeks. "The girls hate me. They make fun of my clothes and the way I talk. No one will play with me. I eat lunch in the bathroom all by myself."

"Oh, Annie. Perhaps it will get better with time," Brigid offered helplessly.

"It's getting worse," Annie wailed. "I left because I couldn't stand it anymore. I'm not going back, Gran, not ever. No one can make me, not my mother and not you," she finished, her voice cracking miserably.

Something told Brigid this was no childish tantrum, solved by a piece or two of shortbread and a cup of hot tea. Annie was moody but she wasn't defiant. Brigid's heart ached. Strange how one could see things more clearly when one skipped a generation. "Hush, lass, hush," she crooned, cradling the child against her chest as if Annie were no more than a toddler. "If it's that bad you shan't go back. I'll speak t' your mother."

"She won't listen to you," said Annie bitterly. "She doesn't listen to anybody. My daddy didn't want us to go away. He told me." She snuffled into Brigid's neck. "I just want to go home, Gran. Nothing's right here."

Brigid thought carefully before she spoke. "Is there no compromisin', love?"

"What do you mean?"

"Can you think of no way t' meet your mother in the middle?"

"Why?"

Brigid bit her lip. "Be reasonable, Annie. Your mother isn't goin' back t' Kentucky. Do you really want t' live so far away from her?"

"You said she wouldn't leave us." Annie said after a minute.

Clever child. "I don't think she will, but it's a risk you'll be takin'. She was very unhappy livin' with your da. I don't think I've ever seen her so unhappy. Do you want to send her back t' that?"

"I'm unhappy, too," mumbled Annie.

"Your birthday's comin' up, isn't it?"

The child nodded, a slight, imperceptible movement of her head.

"You'll be eleven years old. In another seven years you'll be grown. Then you can decide where you want t' live."

Annie drew back in horror. "Are you saying I can't go home for seven more years?"

"Of course not." Brigid didn't know whether to laugh or cry. "You'll go back t' visit your da as often as you want."

"I want to go now."

Brigid tried another approach. "Ben doesn't want t' go back to Kentucky."

Annie's face crumpled. She drew a deep hiccupping breath. "I know."

"What if you went t' a different school, made a fresh start?"

"There isn't another school."

"Aye, there is. But I'll have t' speak t' your mum about it first."

"Where is it?"

"It's the parish school, the school your mum and aunts attended. If I can get Caitlin to agree, will you give it a chance, for me?"

Annie's feeble, "I guess so," wasn't the response Brigid had hoped for, but beggars couldn't be choosers and acquiescence was a long way from where they had started.

She wasn't prepared for Caitlin's flat denial later that afternoon.

"Absolutely not. I'll not have my daughter going to school in that place. I hated it when I was there."

"I can't imagine what you're talkin' about."

Caitlin stared at her mother from across the gleaming oak table. "No," she said softly, "I'm sure you can't."

Brigid's hands clenched on the arms of her chair. Trust Caitlin to make more of something than there was. Forcing herself to remain calm, Brigid crossed her arms. "Your daughter is miserable, Caitlin. She's in her room right this minute, two hours earlier than she's supposed t' be, cryin' her eyes out because she doesn't fit in."

Caitlin's cheeks flamed and her eyes were very bright. "I'll talk to Annie."

"Do you care about your daughter, Caitlin?"

"You're not serious?" Caitlin's voice cracked.

"You'll have t' do more than talk," Brigid pounded relentlessly. "You'll have t' put yourself in her place. Everythin' that's happened t' you, you've brought on yourself. You ran away t' America and married an unsuitable man. When you couldn't stand it anymore you ran back here, but this time with two innocent children who've been snatched away from everythin' familiar, everythin' they love. You aren't the only victim here, Caitlin, but you're the only one with any control. Show the child some compassion."

"Compassion." Caitlin rolled the word around on her tongue. "I don't think either of us are very good at that."

For the space of a single agonizing heartbeat, Brigid froze. Time stopped and she wondered if all she'd endured, all she'd given up had been for nothing. Long seconds passed. The sick feeling in her stomach receded. Wetting her lips, she spoke. "Whatever it is you think I did, surely you can't say that I ran away from anythin'. I worked myself t' the bone t' take you and Kitty out of the National School and send you t' Saint Patrick's. You had the choice t' go on t' university but you refused it. Was that my fault as well?"

Brigid waited but Caitlin remained silent. "All right, then, don't be like me. Learn from my mistakes. I'm tryin' t' make up for them. Annie isn't like you, Caitlin. She needs somethin' other than herself t' believe in. Most of us do. Let her go t' Saint Patrick's. Let her have a choice."

Silence stretched out between them. John Hurley came to deliver more peat but Brigid waved him away.

The quiet had gone on too long. "Say somethin', lass," demanded Brigid.

"I'm going to see Annie now."

"What if she wants t' go back t' Kentucky?"

Caitlin paled. "I'll work something out with Sam. If it's school she doesn't like, maybe I can teach her at home or hire a tutor or she can attend school in Kentucky part of the year." She sat down in the nearest chair and buried her face in her hands. "I don't know what to do, Mum. Maybe I'll just have to give up and go home."

Brigid's heart ached. Caitlin was an adult but why did she seem no different than the little girl who came home all those years ago with scraped elbows and bloody knees? "I'll take over in here," she said gently. "It's nearly time for Kirsty's shift anyway. Go t' Annie and I'll walk down t' school and tell Ben he doesn't need to wait for her."

Caitlin found Annie squatting on the sidewalk in front of the pub with a half-filled jar of worms by her side. "What are you doing, love?" she asked, kneeling beside her. Annie's red-rimmed eyes spoke volumes as did the resistant look on her face. Caitlin recognized that look. She would have to step carefully. This wouldn't be the first time that Annie refused to be patronized.

"It's rained and the worms are out," the child replied. "I'm collecting them to put in the yard."

"But why?"

Annie looked up at her mother scornfully. Her pupils were very large, filling up most of the iris. "So no one will step on them."

Caitlin's heart broke. "Oh, Annie," she whispered. The urge to wrap this frail girl in her arms and never let go was so strong only the look on Annie's face stopped her. She dug her nails into the palms of her hands. "Perhaps people will walk around and not disturb them," she suggested.

Annie shook her head.

"How do you know?"

"At school all the boys were stepping on them. I told them to stop." Annie's voice cracked. "But they wouldn't and the girls just laughed."

Rage blurred Caitlin's vision. She closed her eyes briefly, drew deep breaths, and willed herself back in control.

"I was late to school," Annie confessed, "because I stayed to throw them into the grass. Mrs. Sutcliffe said I was in trouble, that you would be mad, and I wasn't to be late again." She looked up. "Are you mad at me, Mama?"

"Not a bit," replied Caitlin promptly. "I think you did exactly right."

Annie brightened. "Really?"

Caitlin didn't trust herself to speak. She nodded instead. "Here," she said, "picking up a brown earthworm from a puddle. "I'll help you. We'll work together."

They worked in silence for several minutes. There was an art to rescuing worms, Caitlin found. Thumb and forefinger worked best initially. Occasionally the creatures would wind themselves around other fingers or her palm and then she needed two hands. Annie was far better at it than she was.

When the last worm had been deposited in the grassy area by the woodshed, and a small degree of silent communion had been established between them, Caitlin spoke. "Would you like to change schools, Annie?"

Her daughter's eyes filled with tears. "I want to go home," she whispered.

Caitlin brushed away the ones that spilled down her own cheeks and gathered her daughter into her arms, moving back and forth in the gentle rocking motion instinctive to all mothers. "Oh, Annie," she murmured against the soft hair, "I'll take you home if that's what you really want. But I can't leave everything up in the air just now. Can you wait for awhile, at least until the school term is over?"

The child sniffed. "Are you coming home, too?"

"This is my home. I can't live at Claiborne anymore. But if you still want to go back at the end of the term, I'll take you home to Daddy and Grandma Lucy."

"But where will you live?"

"I'm not sure. Let's wait and see. Whatever happens, I'm not leaving you, Annie."

"Until then, can I go to Saint Patrick's?"

Caitlin tightened her arms around her daughter. "Of course you can, love, if it's that important to you. I'll enroll you tomorrow."

To save time, Brigid had left the road and crossed the bog on foot. Overnight it seemed as if autumn had colored the land. Gorse, wild mustard, and heather blanketed the hills. Frost colored the leaves red, gold, orange, and brown. Clouds hung low, heavy, and gray in a slate-colored sky. Darkness rolled in early and lingered late. Smells of peat and burning leaves filled the air, and if one breathed deeply, the sharpness of smoke and frost and pollen stung the inside of noses sensitive and red from unaccustomed rubbing.

Mud oozed up around the sharp marsh grasses, caking the soles of Brigid's boots, sending forth the sucking sounds of swamp muck, larvae, insects, and late-flying birds taking a brief respite from their journey south. Seventy-one seasons had passed her by, seventy-one autumns just like this one, warm air turning to cold, green leaves deepening to rust, all of them uneventful, busy, unnoticed, all except one.

Students were just beginning to come out of the old wood building that served as the National School for children whose parents preferred a secular education over a parochial one. Honesty forced Brigid to admit that just as many National School students went on to pass their O levels, earn their leaving certificates, and attend university as did those from Saint Patrick's.

She felt the exact moment Ben's dark-haired, sturdy figure came through the exit. She saw him look up, recognize her, and grin as if the sheer sight of her standing there waiting for him was his greatest wish. Her heart contracted. Had any of her daughters shrieked with delight when she'd entered a room after a day's absence? What was it about this wee lad that turned her resolve to mush? She held out her arms and watched him run like a homing pigeon straight into them.

She pressed her lips against his forehead. "Hello, love. Was it a good day?"

He nodded. "My spelling words were all right and Mrs. Tott says I shall learn arithmetic tomorrow."

Already, his speech was acquiring Irish nuances. "Wonderful," Brigid said approvingly. "You're a bright lad."

He tucked his hand into hers. "Where's Annie?"

"She wasn't feelin' well and came home early. Your mum's home with her."

"I'm hungry. What's for tea?"

"Cheese sandwiches and tomato soup," Brigid improvised. They were his favorite. "There's trifle if you can manage to wait until I whip the cream."

Ben nodded, satisfied with the menu. After a minute he tugged on her arm and pointed to a spot across the quiet street. "There's Mr. Hennessey, Gran. Can we ask him about the colt?"

Brigid recognized Brian coming out of the bank with Martin O'Shea by his side. Both men crossed the street and came toward her.

"How are you and this fine lad today, Mrs. Keneally?" Brian asked.

"Very well, thank you," Brigid replied. "Ben has a question for you."

Brian ruffled the boy's dark hair with a gentle hand. "What can I do for you, Ben?"

"Mum says you're going to start weaning *Irish Gold* this week."

Brian nodded. "I am."

"May I watch, Mr. Hennessey, if I'm no bother? I'm allowed to watch at home."

Brian glanced at Martin. "What do you think, Father? Can this lad be trusted to sit quietly and watch while a skittish colt is brought out for his first day of weanin' from his dam?"

Martin appeared to consider the matter. "I've no idea, Brian. The decision is yours. Still, if the lad has watched at home—"

Brian knelt down to where he was eye level with the boy. "You've done a good job for me at the farm, Ben. I think you've earned yourself a place in the yard to watch. Tell your mother to bring you around as soon as school's out, startin' tomorrow."

Ben's face lit up from inside. "I will, sir," he breathed reverently. "Can Annie come, too?"

Brian kept a straight face. "You're a hard man to drive a bargain with, wee Ben. If you must have Annie then bring her along." He stroked his chin. "Come to think of it, she's done her share of work around the place as well."

Ben rushed to explain. "Sometimes Mum is busy in the afternoons. If Annie is to come, we won't have to wait."

Martin laughed. "A reasonable argument, although I can't remember a time when Caitlin would rather do something else than be around horses. Have you become a taskmaster, Brigid?"

Brigid drew herself up to her full height and looked Martin squarely in the eye. "I don't remember givin' you leave t' use my Christian name, young man. Your collar doesn't give you the right t' be disrespectful. You've always called me Mrs. Keneally and that's what I prefer."

The color drained from Martin's face. "I meant no harm, Mrs. Keneally," he stammered. "I'm sorry."

Brigid nodded. "I should hope so." She watched the stud farm manager rise and formally shake hands with Ben. Bestowing a dazzling smile on Brian, she turned her attention to her grandson. "Come along, love. We're late for tea."

Looking back over her shoulder she waved to the two men. To her satisfaction, she saw that Martin O'Shea hadn't quite gathered himself after the setdown she'd given him. Cheeky lad. As if she hadn't turned him over her knee more times than she could count, not that it had done him any good.

Brian Hennessey was another matter. The look of amusement on his face made her wonder if she shouldn't have chosen someone else to figure in her scheme for Caitlin's future. A man who understood too much too quickly would never do. A man like that could not be counted on to behave predictably.

12

Caitlin's hands closed around the carved arms of the chair so tightly that the knuckles showed white beneath her skin. She'd spent a great deal of her youth in the office of Saint Patrick's Catholic Girl's Academy and the memories still had the power to reduce her to a childish state of rebellion.

"We'll need your daughter's transcripts, Mrs. Claiborne."

Sister Mary Lucia, a sweet-faced, petite nun in a modified gray habit that revealed auburn hair without a hint of gray was new to the school, a small detail that didn't mitigate Caitlin's attitude in the slightest.

"Mrs. Claiborne?"

Caitlin swallowed and wet her lips. "I arranged for them to be sent to the National School, Sister. I'm not sure if they've arrived. Perhaps I can send them to you later?"

The nun smiled. "There's no need for that, my dear. I'll write a note and someone will bring them around. We'll also need her baptismal certificate."

The remaining color drained from Caitlin's cheeks. Why had she ever agreed to this? "Annie isn't baptized, Sister," she mumbled.

"Oh." The nun looked startled. "I don't understand. Why then—" she stopped.

"My husband wasn't Catholic. We weren't married in the church. I—" Caitlin faltered, searched for a tactful explanation that would explain her lack of devotion, found none, and decided on the truth. Experience told her that when dealing with women like this one, it always came out in the end. "I fell away," she said simply.

The nun stared at her with shrewd, all-seeing eyes. Her voice was gentle but firm with commitment. "Perhaps this isn't the best place for your daughter, Mrs. Claiborne."

"Oh, but it is," Caitlin blurted out, desperate now that the carrot was being held out of reach. "Annie wants it, you see. She's not like me at all. The National School isn't right for her."

Sister Mary Lucia drummed her fingers on the desk. "There is a participation requirement here at Saint Patrick's. We require that our parents be involved in supporting the school. Can you do that, Mrs. Claiborne?"

"Yes."

"Annie will have to begin religious instruction. Is that also acceptable to you?"

Caitlin deliberately sealed off the memory of her years spent memorizing the dreaded catechism. "Of course."

"There is the matter of tuition."

Caitlin waved her hand. "I'll manage."

The nun stood. "Fine," she said briskly. "Then we shall expect you and Annie at Mass next Sunday. Malone's is the usual place to outfit her with a uniform for school. She's welcome to begin classes as soon as she's dressed properly."

Back on the street, Caitlin leaned against the flagstone-covered wall and breathed deeply. Was this really happening? Had she truly enrolled Annie, her beloved daughter, her child who found joy through light and words and music, in this place of damp stone, plaid skirts that scratched cruelly, and rules created a century ago for women who would never set foot beyond the streets where they were born, women who only a generation before birthed fifteen children and acquired tuberculosis and a cemetery plot by the time they were forty? What had she done? If Sam ever had reason to whisk Annie back to Kentucky, this was it.

"Caitlin Keneally? Can it be you?" A lean, black-frocked figure with a full head of silver hair stepped through the doorway of the rectory.

Caitlin sighed and straightened to wait for the priest to reach her side. Misery came in threes and here she was already at number two. Father Duran had never really approved of her. She couldn't blame him. She'd hardly been a model student.

"Hello, Father."

He stood before her, a proud, handsome man in his early seventies, with the chiseled features and clipped speech patterns of an aristocrat. "Were you here for devotions, lass? I didn't see you in church."

She shook her head. "I was enrolling Annie in Saint Patrick's. She's not happy at the National School." A perverse impulse goaded her on. "I hope she's happier here than I was."

Father Duran's lips tightened and the eager, hopeful look he'd worn when he first saw her disappeared. Instantly, Caitlin was ashamed. She had disliked him as a child for reasons she could no longer remember. But childhood was no longer an excuse. She'd behaved badly. "I'm sorry, Father," she said before she lost her courage. "That was poorly done."

He looked surprised and then amused, as if he actually approved of her, a first between them. She would have walked away but he fell into step beside her, hands clasped behind his back, silvery head bent in a thoughtful position.

"What's the difficulty at the National School?"

Caitlin hesitated.

"It's only a question, lass, not confession."

She laughed. "When did you acquire a sense of humor?"

"Perhaps you never gave me a chance."

"I wonder why," she said out loud.

He smiled. "I don't take it personally. As I recall, you didn't want any part of us here at Saint Patrick's."

Caitlin stuffed her hands into the pockets of her jacket. It was true. Her dislike for the parish school was a feeling she'd accepted as normal when she was a child.

The priest was saying something. She lost the beginning of his sentence. "I'm sorry, Father. What were you saying?"

"I was asking about our Annie."

"What about her?"

Father Duran looked at her curiously. "You said she wasn't happy at the National School," he reminded her gently.

"The move has been difficult for her," Caitlin explained. "She misses her father and her friends. Apparently the girls haven't exactly welcomed her."

"Will you be staying in Kilcullen permanently?"

Not for one minute did she believe his question was as casual as it appeared. He disapproved of her. She was divorcing her husband. The entire Catholic church disapproved of her. Father Duran would like her to pack up and move back to Kentucky with Sam.

Caitlin had grown up believing what he did, that marriage was a sacrament that only death could dissolve, but no longer, not when a marriage was so wrong. "I'm divorcing my husband, Father," she said bluntly. "Whatever happens I won't be returning to Kentucky."

He ignored her implication. "In time, I'm sure that Annie will be comfortable here."

"At least her clothing won't be an issue."

They reached the intersection of the street and stopped to watch as two women with the small bums, muscled legs, tightly slicked hair, and sun-leathered faces of the English racing aristocracy rode through. Their horses were high-stepping, nearly unmanageable, their eyes wild, their sleek, satiny coats evidence of generations of inbreeding, their hooves kicking up the unmistakable odors of hay and manure and road dust. Caitlin felt a pang. Once that life had been hers. She pushed the thought aside. That life included Sam. Personal happiness had its price.

Father Duran's elegant high-bridged nose wrinkled slightly. He looked down at the woman by his side. "This is as far as I go, lass. It's been a pleasure talking with you. I hope it won't be the last time."

Caitlin sighed and, without thinking, spoke her mind. "You know it won't be, now that you've Annie in your clutches."

Michael Duran threw back his head and laughed. "Caitlin Keneally," he managed at last, "will you never learn diplomacy?"

She considered his question. "Probably not. I think I'm hopeless."

He sobered instantly. "You should, at least when dealing with issues regarding your children. Your husband is a pow-erful man. I believe you've some difficult times to weather. Keep that in mind."

He had a point. Chastened, she nodded her head. "I'll do that."

His voice softened. "There's something else you should

consider as well. You're a bit weak when it comes to church doctrine. I take no position on your marriage, Caitlin. Because you're a Catholic and your marriage was not sanctified by the church, I'm not supposed to recognize it."

"What are you saying?"

"We have no quarrel with your secular divorce. May it bring you the peace that you seek." He smiled and touched her cheek lightly. "Goodbye lass."

She stared at his retreating figure. What on earth had happened to the Father Duran she remembered?

She caught up with her children on the tree-lined road leading to the stud farm. Annie was holding Ben's hand but he was clearly in the lead. Her daughter's forlorn little figure dragging after Ben brought painful tears to Caitlin's throat. Annie must have had another dreadful day. "Hello, you two," she said, falling into step beside them. Reaching for her daughter's book bag, she took her free hand and laced the small fingers with her own. "Am I late or did you get out early?"

"There was a teachers' meeting," Annie said dully. "We got out at half past two."

"Isn't that a stroke of luck? You'll have more time at the stud. Perhaps if it isn't busy, we can eat in the cafeteria."

"What about Gran?" asked Ben.

"I'll call her," Caitlin replied. "She can join us if she likes." She squeezed Annie's hand. "Would you like to eat out tonight, love?"

Annie shrugged. "I don't care."

Caitlin stepped in front of her daughter. "Annie, please stop for a minute. I want to tell you something."

Annie waited while Ben looked on curiously.

"I went to Saint Patrick's today. They'll take you as soon as we can get you fitted for a uniform."

"When will that be?"

"On Monday morning if you like."

The girl's eyes glistened. "Will I have to go back to the National School?"

Caitlin shook her head. "No, love, not ever again." She hesitated. "There is one condition."

Annie's face closed. "What?"

"They want you to take religious instruction and we're to go to Mass on Sunday."

"Is that all?" the girl asked cautiously, as if not quite sure it could be that easy.

"That's all."

Ben's face crumpled. "I don't want to go to school without Annie," he wailed. "I want to go to Saint Patrick's, too. Can I go, Mum? Please?"

Caitlin looked helplessly at her son. "Ben, love," she began, "you can't go to Annie's school. It's only for girls."

"I want to go," Ben repeated.

Caitlin reached for his hand and kept walking. "I know you do, but even if you could go, think how your friends would miss you."

Ben's forehead wrinkled. He was deep in thought. Caitlin hoped the issue was settled.

Irish Gold was already out in the paddock when they arrived at the stud farm. She noticed Brian Hennessey standing motionless inside the guard rails.

Leaning against the fence, she watched as the colt ran frantically across the limestone turf, lifting his head, snorting, eyes wild, teeth exposed, clearly exhibiting his distress at the separation from his mother. He wanted nothing to do with the old broodmare pastured with the yearlings for the sole purpose of comforting the newly weaned foals.

For thirty-five days the colt had survived on mare's milk alone. After that *Kentucky Gold* had been tied while her foal was given small amounts of crushed oats and sweet feed. He'd grown quickly, Caitlin observed, noting with pleasure his height, the white-stockinged feet, the good shoulders, and straight hind legs. He should be up to six quarts of grain by now, a healthy amount for a colt born only three months ago.

Soon it would be time to name him. In America the Jockey Club administered the naming of all thoroughbreds and rarely accepted a first choice due to its complicated reasons for disqualification. No horse could have the name of an existing horse, a deceased famous horse, a horse who'd raced or served the stud in the last fifteen years, no horse could be named for a famous deceased personality, or a famous living person without his written consent. No horse could advertise a trade name and no name could be over eighteen characters.

The process was nearly as complicated in Ireland. Weatherbys of Ireland managed the General Stud book where horses were registered, bloodtyped, and tested for parentage. It was a formidable process and Caitlin did not relish the experience. She was set on the name *Irish Gold*. Annie and Ben would be disappointed if their chosen name was not accepted. Still, they were Claibornes. They'd grown up around horses and knew, on this matter, that the rules were nonnegotiable.

The colt had settled into a tentative walk and finally stopped to sniff the grass between his long, stiltlike legs. Caitlin watched as Brian approached him holding a bucket filled with grain, a non-threatening, chirruping sound coming from somewhere back in his throat.

The colt lifted his head, swayed slightly on his too-long legs, recognized the man and stepped forward to bury his nose in the grain. Brian ran his free hand over the satiny neck, under the throat and then back and forth across the nostrils and mouth. He waited until the horse lifted his head and moved away toward the broodmare and other yearlings before walking back to the rail and climbing over it.

"He did all right, didn't he, Mr. Hennessey?" Ben called out.

"Aye, lad, he did well enough." Brian set down the bucket, pulled a handkerchief from his pocket and wiped his hands, replacing it immediately. "How are you, Annie?"

"I'm fine, thank you," the girl said, glancing thoughtfully at the tip of the handkerchief sticking out of his pocket. She turned to her brother. "Come on, Ben, let's put the bucket back inside the tack room. Then we'll walk to the other side for a closer look."

Caitlin placed a restraining hand on her daughter's shoulder. "You can see well enough from here, Annie."

"I'd like to speak with you, Caitlin," Brian said tersely. "The children can join us for a bite to eat in the dinin' room after they've looked their fill."

His hands were shaking and there was a taut look around his eyes that she had never seen before. "Run along," she said to the children.

Brian's anger was the furious white-hot kind that rational discussion would never penetrate. Caitlin, walking beside him, recognized the symptoms and wisely remained silent. Brian Hennessey wasn't a man who lost control of his emotions. Whatever was troubling him would come out as soon as he won the battle with his temper.

They walked in silence over the hill and down through the ridge of trees to his cottage. He opened the door and stepped back allowing her to precede him. Still without speaking he opened the antique wooden sideboard, pulled out a bottle of whiskey, poured liberal measures into two glasses, and handed one to Caitlin. Then he sat down on the couch and stared unseeing at his own.

Dismayed, Caitlin turned the glass in her hands. "Please tell me what's wrong."

He raised his head and looked at her, his eyes blazing and blue in a haunted face. Caitlin's throat felt parched as if she'd stood too long under a blast of scorching desert heat without water. Her hand moved to her forehead. She wanted nothing more than to be away from this place. Then she remembered the whiskey and lifted the glass to her lips.

"Your foal is bleedin' badly from the nostrils," he said harshly.

Relief made her weak. "Is that all? Antibiotics will take care of that in no time."

"I don't think so."

She frowned. "What are you saying?"

"I don't believe this is a viral or bacterial problem, Caitlin."

She rejected it immediately. "How can you possibly know that?"

He was very still, his words forced and deliberate as if explaining something basic to someone with impaired mental faculties. "*Irish Gold* has all the symptoms of RLN disease. RLN is recurrent laryngeal neuropathy, palsy of the voice—"

"For God's sake, Brian," she snapped. "I know what RLN is. Get on with it."

"All right. I've seen it in American horses over and over again. The upper airway is obstructed due to a genetic deterioration of the left side of the voice box. If it isn't a severe case, it doesn't show up until the horse is exercised vigorously, usually before a first race."

"That's absurd," she argued. "*Irish Gold* comes from a line of champions. He has no genetic diseases."

The muscle along Brian's jawline tightened angrily. "Ninety percent of American thoroughbreds have RLN. For that very reason some of us have tried to hold out against breedin' programs involvin' North American horses. In case you don't remember, we were overruled." He downed his drink and poured another. "That horse will never win a race, Caitlin. He'll be lucky if he doesn't drop dead in the middle of his trainin'."

Her eyes were wide and dark and horrified in the pale oval of her face. "I don't believe you."

"Believe it," he said bluntly, pulling out his handkerchief and laying it flat on the couch cushion. It was stained an ugly red-brown. "Believe this as well. Until I see the autopsy reports on *Narraganset*, I won't allow *Kentucky Gold* to be covered by an Irish stallion. This lethal inbreedin' has got to stop or we won't have a healthy animal left in the industry."

Gathering her composure, Caitlin set her glass down on the end table. The man was mad. "I have no idea why you're doing this to me," she said carefully. "There have been very few cases of RLN disease at Claiborne and we made sure those animals never competed and never reproduced. If *Irish Gold* is bleeding, then there must be another reason. I'll call the vet right away."

The anger drained out of him immediately. He stood and held out his hand. "You do that," he said gently. "I'm sorry, Caitlin, truly sorry."

She stared at him without moving. Was he unspeakably cruel or a complete fool? *Sorry*. He was *sorry*. What a pathetic little apology for the horror he'd thrust upon her. Did he really have any idea what it would mean to her if his suspicions proved correct?

"If the colt must be put down, I'll help you find another," he said. "We're a bit late for Tatersalls but the Goff's premier foal sale is coming up soon—"

She interrupted him. "Don't be ridiculous. What makes you think I have eleven thousand guineas to throw away? Do you think I'm independently wealthy? I can't last forever without income." Tears burned beneath her eyelids. "This foal means everything to us. He's our future."

He looked bewildered. "I don't understand. Claiborne Farms—"

She waved her hand in a desperate, angry gesture of dismissal, no longer caring that the privacy she preferred and had so carefully cultivated was irrevocably shattered. "Sam Claiborne is Claiborne Farms," she said bitterly. "Even Lucy, my mother-in-law, decent as she is, won't be able to help if he decides to punish me for leaving him."

His face was shuttered, emotions carefully concealed. "What does he want?"

"I don't know." She was close to coming undone. "Annie and Ben, maybe. To have things back the way they were."

"Was it so bad?"

Pressing the backs of her hands against her eyes, she shook with hysterical laughter. "Not for Sam. And maybe not for the children. Not yet, anyway. For me," she dropped her hands and shrugged helplessly, wondering if Sam's reputation extended outside of Kentucky, "I just couldn't do it anymore."

"What will you do if the vet confirms what I told you?"

She reached into her pocket, pulled out a tissue and blew her nose. "He won't. There's nothing wrong with that colt."

His mouth was hard again, all traces of compassion wiped away with his conviction. "If I were you I'd have a strategy to fall back on."

She lifted her chin. "You're not me. You don't know the first thing about me."

Through the open door he watched her walk away, the straight line of her back, the obstinate way she held her head, her hands clenched and tight at her sides. A reluctant smile appeared on his lips. "If that were true, Caitlin Keneally," he muttered under his breath, "I would be an idiot."

13

Brian Hennessey slipped the printed message he had copied from his e-mail into his pocket, pulled on his gloves, and stepped out into a dawn still dark enough that remnants of last night's paper-thin moon hung in the sky. There would be no rain today. The wind had bundled the clouds up and hurled them somewhere out to sea, leaving the promise of light, a soft milky light completely different from the luminous quality he remembered as a boy, in the west.

In the western isles of his youth, a strange kind of light rolled in from the Atlantic, played among the clouds, gathered in the rocky shoals, danced among the Blue Stacks and Twelve Pins, coloring the land a dozen shades of green, celery, mint, jade, pine, turquoise, emerald, until the glow of it changed a man—gave him a mind that was no longer a tidy one with straight and narrow lines, made him believe in ghosts and curses and the myths of his ancestors long buried now beneath the guano-stained Celtic crosses dotting cemetery churchyards.

His people, the Irish of the Isles of the Blessed, those green stepping stones in a turbulent sea, were descended from pastoral Druids, Celtic warriors, and marauding Norsemen. They grudgingly lived in towns, farmed their land, attended Mass, playing out a charade of civilization in its loosest form but they were by no means a *regular* people. They preferred a different kind of life and they'd found it in the isles of the west. There was no softness to break up the horizon, to pacify and soothe it, no waving fields of grain, no turf bogs, no white-aproned haystacks, just the seamless boundaries of sky and sea, wind-hammered rock and lashing waves pounding a disappearing shore.

Caitlin's father had been an island man, another of the banished malefactors forever condemned to make his life away from the light and the land that nourished his soul. What had he done, Brian wondered? What kept an island man expatriated and perpetually numbed with drink in the civilized county of Kildare?

His daughter had escaped the curse. Caitlin was not a woman who turned to alcohol no matter how difficult her problem. But she had her own share of stubbornness as well as a goodly amount of pride, both island traits. He wondered if she would listen to him or if his bluntness had destroyed what had been the beginning of a tenuous friendship.

The truth was she brought out the worst in him. He wanted to impress her but the minute he thought he had, she would look at him with a raised eyebrow, her face still and quiet like an empty canvas, and the words he wanted wouldn't form. Instead, he heard himself saying what she should never have heard, words that were no less honest, but rough and tactless, harsh, outspoken words that a woman courageous enough to survive Samuel Claiborne would not shrink from but should have been spared.

Brian walked down the packed dirt road, past the sign-posted gate to the street that led to the Curragh race track. Caitlin came early to see *Kentucky Gold* and the colt. Often Davy Flynn recruited her to exercise one or more of the two year olds if they were short on help. If Caitlin's night had been anything like Brian's, she would be up even earlier than usual today. He wanted to catch her before she set out for the barns.

She wore a red sweater and gray jodhpers, the expensive kind that a woman from Kilcullen would never own. The color blended with the mist, blurring her outline. Standing a decent distance from the track, he waited for her to finish. There were few things Brian enjoyed more than watching Caitlin take a prize-winning two year old through his paces on the Curragh.

He might have missed her if it hadn't been for her red sweater. The color suited her far more than the muted gray of her jacket. Careful not to alarm her, he stood back away from the track watching her move forward instinctively, head low, rump up, legs straight, urging the colt to greater and greater speeds. She passed the one-eighth pole, easing up on the reins for precious seconds before tightening them again, her hands loose, her body perfectly balanced. He heard her soft chirping sounds, saw the turf fly, and finally, at the three-eighths pole saw the colt stretch out, take the bit in his mouth and lunge. Once again, the animal surged across the wire.

Brian hadn't used his watch this time but he was sure the colt had never performed better. Caitlin was a natural. He waited until she'd cooled down the colt and handed him back to Davy before calling out her name.

Turning, she waited for him, a still figure with black

ringlets curling around her face and a slash of red around her throat where her jacket parted, the same red she'd used on her lips. Reaching into his pocket, Brian pulled out the message he'd received late last night and handed it to her. She read it quickly, her eyes moving down the page twice before she looked up. "What is this about?"

"Robert Farlow has had tremendous success with RLN disease," Brian explained. "He's agreed to look at your colt if you're willin'."

"You've told people that my colt is diseased?"

Deliberately, he curbed his impatience. "Not people, Caitlin. Robert Farlow is the best veterinarian there is. He's a friend of mine and very discreet."

"Why would he do such a thing?"

"Because I asked him, as a favor to me."

"Why would you do that?"

Brian's eyes narrowed. "Are you deliberately being rude or is this a display of American manners?"

Her eyes never left his face but she had traveled somewhere inside herself, away from him, to another place. "I'm sorry," she said at last, her voice low and soft. "Thank you. I accept your offer." She turned and continued down the road. Brian fell into step beside her.

"Where does Doctor Farlow practice?" she asked.

"Outside of Galway City in Spiddal, a small town in the Gaeltacht."

"Near your home?"

She remembered. He experienced a rush of pleasure. "Aye. Just across the water from it."

"When can we go?"

For a minute he was distracted by her mouth, outlined in lush, vivid red. Dark eyes, red lips, cream-colored skin. *Snow White.*

"Brian?"

"I'll make the arrangements today," he said hurriedly. "Tomorrow will be soon enough."

Caitlin shook her head. "Tomorrow is Lana's party. I can't miss it."

Brian groaned. "I'd forgotten."

The flicker of a smile crossed her lips, lips that were driving him crazy. "It's a good thing I reminded you. It wouldn't be much of a party without you."

Again that surging rush of breathless heat. He could barely manage the words. "Do you mean that?"

She glanced sideways at him. "Of course."

He reached for her arm. "Caitlin—"

She hurried on. "Lana has made it clear that you are to be her guest of honor."

He felt like a fool. "You're mistaken," he said shortly, dropping her arm.

"Oh no." Caitlin shook her head. "She was very specific. In fact I was warned away from you."

This time he did stop her. Her gloved hand fit nicely in his. "Why would she feel the need to be warnin' you away, lass?"

Her eyes were huge, laughing, dark as midnight. If he wasn't careful, he could drown in those eyes.

"The way I heard it," she said, "I'm not the only one. Lana's taking no chances and warning all the women away."

He studied her face, definitely out of the common way with a hint of rebellion in the lift of the chin, impossibly dark eyes, a single strand of wavy hair caught in the corner of her red mouth, scooped-out cheeks under high, carved bones, a distinctive nose, lips, parted and waiting for—what?

Like a man going down for the last time, Brian summoned his courage and leaped into dark waters. "I know what love is, Caitlin Keneally," he said softly, "and Lana Sullivan has none of it for me."

Her smile faded. The world around them slipped away. Surrounded by gray mist, dripping trees, and the reverent, muffled silence of breaking dawn, Brian looked down into the startling purity of a woman's face and recognized exactly what it was that he felt for Sam Claiborne's wife. He hadn't asked for it, not now, not with this woman, but here it was. There was no going back.

The relief of knowing why she was the first thing on his mind in the morning and the last before he slept at night, and why her image came to him a thousand times a day when he least expected it, nearly shattered him. A less cautious man would have forced the pace. Brian was wiser than that. Repressing the urge to reach out with his work-callused hand and touch her cheek before his mouth found her lips, he simply looked at her and waited.

The stillness of the moment was broken. The darkness lifted and clouds rolled down from the hills. Slowly, in unison, they turned and walked down the road to the stud farm.

The night of Lana's party was clear and cold. Colorful balloons and a poster signed with the words *Happy Birthday, Lana* lined the walkway and porch of the Sullivan home. Harvest-colored candles around the entrance flickered warm and welcoming in the gathering darkness. Inside the cottage, lamps were lit. Outside, every window appeared to incoming visitors as a cozy rectangle of gold.

Irish Mist, Guinness, and Harp flowed liberally into glasses. A smoke haze from pipes and cigarettes hung in the air and from the kitchen the mouth-watering smells of roasting meat, hot bread, and cinnamon stirred the appetite.

To Brian, who was acquainted with nearly everyone in town, it seemed as if all were there, everyone, that is, except Caitlin. Every corner of the Sullivan's small house overflowed with revelers in various states of holiday spirit. Small groups had already segregated themselves by age and sex— the women holding babies, minding children, serving food; the men drinking, playing instruments, singing, carrying on forehead-wrinkling conversations of politics and philosophy.

Lana claimed him the minute he walked through the door. Brian handed over the gift he had purchased and followed her through the crowd to the makeshift bar. There, he accepted a pint from her brother, Tim, a thickset young man with a meaty fist.

He clapped Brian on the shoulder. Half the Guinness spilled out of the glass on to the floor. "How's the horse business, lad? Any tips for us this season?"

"We've a good crop this year," Brian replied. "Come around and I'll show you a few."

"I'll do that. No sense in all that knowledge of yours goin' to waste, seein' as how you're not a bettin' man."

"I wouldn't say that."

Lana slipped her hand through Brian's arm and gently squeezed it. "Dance with me, Brian," she said coaxingly. "We've live music in the other room."

The dance lasted forever. Caitlin had just come in with her mother and children, and it seemed to him, in all that boisterous, milling, celebratory crowd, that she was the only one in the room.

Ben disappeared immediately with a lad his own age and Brigid was claimed by Lana's mother. Annie slipped her hand into her mother's and showed no inclination to leave her side. Caitlin leaned over to whisper into the child's ear. Lana had asked him something but he couldn't remember what it was.

"Excuse me, lass," he said when the dance was over. "There's someone I need to see and I don't want to keep you from the rest of your guests."

Crossing the room to where Caitlin and Annie stood, Brian set his empty glass on a small table and rested his hands on the little girl's shoulders. "Would you care to dance, Annie? There's a fair group in the other room and the music's quite good."

Annie smiled painfully and shook her head. "I'll stay here with Mama."

"The thing is, Annie, I was about to ask your mum to dance but then I saw you. If you refuse me, I'll have her instead."

"Go along, love," Caitlin said gently. "I'll be right here when you come back."

"Come with us," Brian urged her. "There's no reason the two of you can't share me."

Caitlin laughed. "Are you suggesting that no one else will ask me, Brian Hennessey?"

He grinned. Her lips were red again, the same red as her sweater. "Once you've danced with me, lass, you won't want anyone else."

"I think you should have Annie by herself," Caitlin said, more seriously this time. "Otherwise Lana won't be speaking to me tomorrow."

"I wouldn't have taken you for a woman so easily intimidated, Caitlin Keneally," Brian chided her before taking Annie's hand in his own. "What do you say, lass? Will you dance with me?"

A reluctant smile crossed Annie's lips. "I'll go with you, Mr. Hennessey."

"Call me Brian. It's less of a mouthful."

With his hand at her back, Annie allowed herself to be guided into the sitting room where the furniture had been pushed against the walls and the carpet rolled up to accommodate the dancers. Couples formed without regard for age or sex.

Annie took one swift, surreptitious look around at the other dancers and the tension left her body. Brian stood on the outside of the circle with Annie across from him. When he reached for her hands a pink flush spread across her cheeks.

"I don't know how to dance," she confessed.

He smiled warmly. "Just follow me. It isn't difficult."

The shrill notes of the fiddle signaled the beginning of the set. Annie's hands were wet with perspiration. She stared at Brian's feet. He let go of her hand to slip an arm around her waist, deliberately moving her in the right direction.

She had an ear for music and a natural coordination. Sooner than he expected the steps came to her. Instinctively, she turned, dipped, and twisted in time to the jarring, traditional rhythms of the ancient gypsy tune. Faster and faster the fiddles played. The music took on a fierce, desperate quality evoking images of tinker's caravans, gusts of rain, whistling gales, and lonely hillsides dotted with meager shepherds' fires. When the notes were too lonely to bear, the whistle came into play again. Now the music was quick, light and gay, sun showing gold through morning mist, ponies frolicking in green paddocks, step-dancing in the center of a smoky pub filled to capacity with admiring tourists.

The room tilted and swayed. Through it all, Annie danced round and round as if she'd been born with the steps in her head. It was as if all the disappointments, the slights, the pain of her banishment were washed clean. When the last note died away her cheeks were scarlet, her eyes bright with pleasure. She was breathless with excitement. "I never knew it could be such fun," she gasped. "Thank you for asking me."

Brian grinned at her. "It was a pleasure, lass. You've a talent for dancin'. Shall we find your mother?"

Caitlin came up behind them. She squeezed Annie's

hand. "You were wonderful, love. I had no idea you could dance like that."

The child's face glowed. "I didn't either."

"You must be thirsty," said Brian. "Why don't we find somethin' to drink?"

Caitlin looked over his shoulder. "First we should see what my mother wants."

Brian turned to see Brigid waving at them. Reaching for Annie's hand and motioning for Caitlin to follow, he carved a path through the merrymakers until they reached the spot where the older woman waited. "Hello, Mrs. Keneally," Brian greeted her. "I hope you saw your granddaughter on the floor. She was a sight to behold."

Brigid smiled. "I wouldn't be surprised. You should have seen her mother at the same age. If she'd cared enough t' compete there would have been no one t' measure up t' her."

Brian lifted a quizzical eyebrow and looked at Caitlin. "Is that so?"

"I don't remember it that way at all," said Caitlin, brushing the compliment aside and addressing her mother. "Did you want us, Mum?"

"Aye. There's a young lady from Saint Patrick's who wants t' meet Annie," Brigid explained. "I thought it would be a good idea if the child went in knowin' someone." She rested her hand on her granddaughter's head. "What do you think, love?"

"I'd like to meet her, Gran. Where is she?"

"Come with me." Brigid took her granddaughter's hand. "She's waitin' by the tables."

Brian noticed Caitlin's anxious look. "Is somethin' wrong?" he asked.

She hesitated. When she spoke, the words came haltingly, as if they were difficult to admit. "Annie's having some trouble making friends. My mother means well. I just hope it works out."

"Your mother's an unusual woman, Caitlin. I'd give her some credit."

"What does *unusual* mean?"

He thought of the rumors he'd heard about Brigid Keneally when he first came to Kilcullen Town and how impressed he'd been with the way she'd weathered the gossip. He wondered if Caitlin had heard them as well and decided it wasn't his place to ask. "She's raised a family and run a business on her own. That's unusual enough."

Caitlin watched her mother disappear around the corner. "I suppose it is."

"Will you dance with me, Caitlin Keneally?"

She looked at him, her eyes dark and shadowed. "You know that isn't my name."

"It's more your name than Claiborne. The name you're born with is who you are."

A faint smile appeared on her lips. "You wouldn't expect your wife to change her name?"

"Of course not."

"What about your children?"

"That's different. They carry my blood."

"And hers." She considered the matter. "In fact, they carry more of hers than yours. After all, she carries the child for nine months, nourishes and protects it, and then gives birth. It really is absurd for a child to carry his father's name when a mother does all that."

"You've convinced me. My children will have their mother's name. Now, will you dance with me?"

She took his outstretched hand and smiled with her red, red lips. "After you've conceded so gallantly, how could I refuse?"

This time the music was soft, lilting, alluring, no whistle

this time, only two violins and the flute. The dancers had thinned out, leaving space on the floor for six couples who came together in the soft, smokey, candlelit room.

At first she held herself away from him. But, slowly, as he led her around the floor, she relaxed and settled against his chest, the top of her head coming to just beneath his chin. He was careful to hold her innocently, casually, when what he wanted wasn't the least bit innocent or casual at all.

"You should have danced with Lana," she mumbled against his shirt.

"When you know me better, Caitlin Keneally, you'll know that the word *should* has a strange affect on me."

"What kind of affect?"

"An opposite one."

"Does Lana know that?"

"Of course not. She doesn't know me at all."

"She wouldn't say that."

"It's true. What Lana wants is a man."

"You should be flattered that she's set on you."

"Not at all," Brian countered. "Any one will do. I just happen to be employed and available. Those are her only requirements."

The piercing summons of a whistle interrupted them. The music stopped, couples separated, someone flicked on the overhead light. Reluctantly, Brian let Caitlin's hand slip out of his own.

"I think we're missing something," she said softly.

Without a single regret, he could have shipped the whole bloody lot of them across the Irish Sea. "I imagine that Lana's openin' her gifts."

"Shall we join her?"

Brian considered the matter. "It would be the polite thing to do," he decided.

Caitlin started for the other room. Brian followed her and

took a seat in time for Lana to hold up the gift he'd paid to have wrapped.

"This one doesn't have a card," she said. "Will someone claim it?"

Brian lifted his hand.

Lana beamed and threw him a grateful look before pulling the ribbon and tearing open the wrapping. Nestled inside the small, flat box was a fountain pen. It seemed to Brian that a lifetime passed between the falling of her face, her trembling lower lip, the rallied smile, and the holding up of the pen for everyone to see.

Later, after the remaining gifts had been opened and the party began to fade, Lana walked with him to the door. "Did you choose my gift yourself?" she asked casually.

He pulled up the collar of his jacket and stuffed his hands deep into his pockets. "I did. You can never seem to find a pen when it's time to take an order for a meal," he explained.

Her laugh was forced. "What a lovely idea. Thank you, Brian. You'll have to come in tomorrow to see me use it."

Relief swept through him. It was all right after all, a practical gift but one that wouldn't raise a girl's hopes. "Not tomorrow, lass. I'll be out of town for a few days. Caitlin's colt needs some attention. We'll be leavin' first thing in the mornin'."

Lana's voice was harsh and cracked as if broken glass had wedged itself into the softness of her throat. "Caitlin is going with you?"

Brian was shocked at the look on her face. "Aye," he said uneasily. "It's her colt, you see."

"I do see, Brian," she said softly. "I see very well."

14

Liam Malone's tailor shop was up the narrowest set of stairs in Kilcullen Town. The building was a relic left over from the seventeenth century with the slanting floorboards, thick walls, and high narrow windows typical of the period. Every available space was occupied with tweeds, worsted wool, knit blends, and, in anticipation of the coldest part of the year, satin and velvet for the holidays to come. A long counter with an ancient cash register ran the entire length of the shop and on two racks facing the windows was an array of buttons and ribbons fanciful enough for the most creative seamstress.

Brigid knew every nook and cranny. After six daughters, the oldest who had to be outfitted with a school uniform every year and the others needing various stages of alterations for their hand-me-downs, it would be a miracle if she couldn't walk the floor blindfolded and still find exactly what she needed.

Preceding Annie and Caitlin into the shop, Brigid sniffed and reached for her handkerchief. What the horse dust of Kilcullen had never done to her sinuses, this place with its layers of dust, years in collecting since Maggie Malone's death, would do in good measure. "Mr. Malone," she called out, peering into the dimly lit room with its rolls of fabric. "It's Brigid Keneally. My granddaughter will be needin' a school uniform."

A man with a high domed forehead, slightly hunched shoulders, but still so tall that his head touched the exposed beams of the ceiling, stuck his head out from behind a bolt of wool and stood up.

He was thin enough for a stranger to worry over but Brigid had known him for years. Malones were born looking like scarecrows and they all lived long enough for none of them to complain of their time allotment on earth.

The tailor squinted in the half darkness and then his face broke into a smile. "My, my, isn't it a grand thing to be seein' little Caitie Keneally all grown up. How are you, lass?"

Caitlin ignored his outstretched hand and reached up the entire length of her arms to hug him. "I'm well, Mr. Malone," she mumbled against the white shirt and tie he wore day in and day out whether or not there were customers. Then she stepped back and drew Annie forward. "This is my daughter, Annie. She'll be attending Saint Patrick's as soon as you can have a uniform ready for her."

The tailor bent over, resting his hands on his knees. "Pleased to meet you, Annie. You've the look of your mother when she was a girl. I suppose we'd better measure and have the uniform done quickly. Until then, there's a spare jumper and skirt you can wear for the first few days. How does that sound?"

"Thank you, sir," Annie answered politely.

The old man straightened. "There's a bit of tea left on the

stove if you'd care to pour, Brigid. I made it up for Father Duran but he's late today. You can have his and I'll make more when he turns up."

"You're expecting Father Duran?"

"Aye."

Brigid glanced toward the door. "We can take the spare clothes and come back later if you're busy, Liam."

"Rubbish." The tailor had already reached into his pocket for the measuring tape. "He's only comin' to pick up the cassock I mended for him. It's already paid for."

Brigid watched as he helped Annie up onto the stool in front of the full length mirror. Caitlin had already gone to set up the cups for tea.

Walking over to the window, she crossed her arms against her chest and looked out onto the street. The world was a veil of gray with swirls of smoke from the turf fires of a dozen chimneys, and windows ablaze with lamplight and false cheer. Were they happy, these women who pattered about from table to stove and back again, buttering toast, frying chips, preparing tea for men too dizzy and swaying with drink to want anything more than a bed and a hot water bottle?

The more naive of her friends pitied her when Sean died. A woman without a man to provide for her lived a life of drudgery in their eyes. And yet were their lives any better than hers? When she came in from long days in the store or the pub to lock the door behind her, she had no one to answer to, no loud snoring to keep her awake, no toilet seat up in the bathroom, no mess on the floor, no arguing over money or the children or whether to take a holiday. She was an independent woman with her own business, her own money, answerable to no one. Loneliness was a problem but it wasn't a new one. She'd been lonely long before she was widowed and didn't know many women who weren't. The truth she'd come to know was that men didn't marry for companionship. They married for sex and children and to make their lives easier. When they wanted companionship they took themselves off to the nearest pub to share the *craic* with other men like themselves.

Brigid Keneally knew what it was to be in love. She'd found it on a day that had ended much as this one would, after the exchange of forbidden words, the touch of a hand on hers, the blinding brilliance of a smile that changed a man's face from handsome to approachable.

But love, she could have told anyone who listened, wasn't a constant. It changed daily, ascending and descending, between need and desire and doubt and heartbreak, finally settling into a level of comfort where doubt and heartbreak went by the wayside along with what remained of passion and need.

A draft of cold air pierced the wool of her jumper. Knowing who had entered the shop, she turned to greet him. To Brigid's surprise, Caitlin called out his name first.

"Good afternoon, Father," her daughter said pleasantly. "I've made tea. Would you care to join us while Mr. Malone measures Annie?"

"I would like that very much," he said, seating himself on a low stool. He drew up his legs to accommodate the small chair. His cassock pooled in folds on the floor.

He looked like a vulture dressed all in black with that beak of a nose, thought Brigid uncharitably, turning back to the window.

"Mum." Caitlin held out a cup of tea. "Come over here and join us."

Reluctantly, Brigid crossed the room and sat down opposite the priest.

"How are you, Brigid?" he asked.

"Very well, thank you, Father."

Caitlin stirred milk into her tea and glanced at her mother. Brigid felt her daughter's curiosity.

At last, for lack of anything better to say, Caitlin stated the obvious. "Annie will be attending Saint Patrick's on Monday. Mr. Malone is measuring her for a school uniform."

Father Duran smiled approvingly. "I'm glad to hear it. Does that mean we'll be seeing your entire family for Mass on Sunday?"

Caitlin laughed. "You know perfectly well it does, although this week Mum will be taking the children alone. I've an appointment in Galway with a veterinarian."

"I'll be sure and save my most entertaining homily for your return."

Caitlin lifted her cup. "Do that."

Brigid stared at the two of them. Could she be hearing them correctly? The tone of their conversation was light-hearted, jovial, as if they'd been friends for years. When had Caitlin become so cozy with Father Duran?

She cleared her throat. "Which will be Father O'Shea's Mass?" she asked.

"Nine o'clock as usual."

"I've been meanin' t' attend that one." She felt her own rudeness and hurried to soften the words, to make it seem to Caitlin as if the time was the issue. "It will be better for the children t' go a bit later."

The priest nodded. "Either way I'll look for you. I always assist at Martin's Masses."

Brigid nodded and drained her cup.

Later, after the children were in bed and Brigid was busy with the supper dishes, Caitlin joined her mother in the kitchen. Picking up a towel she began to dry the plates. The silence stretched out between them. Brigid could stand it no longer. "What's on your mind, Caitlin?"

"I thought Deirdre would visit more often," she replied.

Brigid gave a deprecating laugh. "Your sister has six children and another on the way. Besides, livin' in the Six

Counties is like livin' on the moon. She would have to cross the checkpoints and I don't want her riskin' it. She writes occasionally."

"Will she come for Christmas?"

"Anne and Deirdre usually make it home."

Brigid scrubbed a greasy pan vigorously. "Why the sudden interest in seein' your sisters? You've missed fifteen Christmas dinners."

Caitlin ignored the question and continued to wipe the same plate she'd started with. "You never told me how you met my father. Why is that?"

Brigid sighed, pulled the plug and watched the water swirl and drain in the sink. "First Deirdre and now your father. What's this all about?"

The plate forgotten, Caitlin stared at her mother with eyes that were wide and dark and accusing. "I'd like to talk with you, Mum, the way a mother and daughter should talk. Why won't you meet me halfway?"

Brigid dried her hands, pulled out a chair and slid wearily, bonelessly, into it. She was tired, too tired to be defensive, much too tired to hold out against the onslaught of her daughter's probe. "This is about you, isn't it, Caitlin? What is it that you want t' know? This is as good a time as any."

"It doesn't really matter what we talk about. Why don't you tell me about my father."

Staring into the earnest, dark-eyed face of the woman who should have been Sean Keneally's daughter, Brigid knew she had met her Rubicon. This moment had been written in destiny, waiting like a simmering cauldron for that extra bit of heat to boil over its sides. What child, especially one as different from her mother as Caitlin, would not want to know of the man who had sired her. Brigid folded her hands and closed her eyes briefly. Ordinarily she would have prayed, but this was not the time for prayer. Not all the penances doled out within the darkened confines of the confessional would absolve the lie she had lived.

"Sean Keneally was born on Inishmore before there was plumbin' and electric lightin', well before the tourists started comin' over in droves. With only eight hundred people on the island, he was related in some way or other t' nearly everyone there. His father was fond of the drink, as was his father before him, but that wasn't so unusual for a place where winter darkness sets in at three in the afternoon and the rain and the sky and the sea all run together in an endless blanket of gray."

Caitlin was listening intently.

"A woman who married a Keneally man knew what her life would be: up before dawn to walk her man down to the fishin' boats, wave him off prayin' he didn't drown, gatherin' the seaweed and haulin' it back to a field so rocky even the crows refused t' bother pickin' out the seeds." Brigid shook her head. "The worst of it was the waitin'. Sometimes the men wouldn't come home at all until the next day. I was sure Sean was dead, washed over into a ragin' sea after a bout with the drink.

"I tried t' stay, Caitlin. But I couldn't bear it, what with the wind lashin' the cottage and the rain comin' sideways, poundin' against the back wall, water seepin' in under the door until the flagstone looked like a toilet had overflowed. Not that we had plumbin', mind you, just an outhouse in the back. It was so dark. I was always cold, always damp. The wind howled across those stones. Nothin' ever dried. I got sick. My cough wouldn't stop, and that's when he said we could leave."

This part of the story was new to Caitlin. "You never told me you lived on the island."

Brigid shuddered. "I wanted t' forget. It wasn't the place

for me just as this wasn't the place for Sean. Sometimes you can't take a person from where he belongs—he won't survive the leavin'."

"Is that what happened?"

Brigid thought for a minute. "I think so. He was never happy here. There's somethin' about island people. They can never quite manage anywhere else."

"I heard that he died of alcohol poisoning."

Brigid nodded. "That, too."

"Did you love him?"

This was the question for which she could not lie. "In the beginning, I loved him. Later, I didn't."

"Why not?"

"Sometimes it happens. You should know that."

Caitlin looked beyond her to somewhere across the room. Brigid doubted that it was Sam Claiborne who brought that look to her face.

"How did the two of you meet?"

Brigid looked at the clock. It was already half past nine. Caitlin had pulled out a chair and sat down at the table across from her. Resurrecting ancient history was something Brigid did not enjoy. She was not one who believed that dredging up and examining painful secrets was necessary for healing. The least said the better, was her motto. Still, there had been a few good years between Sean Keneally and herself, years when the annual rainfall had been unusually light, when there had only been two daughters to feed, when the thought of her waiting at home for him in a well-scrubbed cottage with a red door and a thatched roof had been enough to keep him out of the pubs.

She felt Caitlin's eyes on her and knew there would be no respite tonight, not unless she wanted to damage the small inroads they'd made toward closing the misunderstandings in their relationship. More than any of the others, Brigid wanted this daughter to be settled within herself. If talking about Sean Keneally would accomplish that, she would do it.

"We met when I was on holiday in Galway," she began, "on a clear spring day. I thought I'd never seen anythin' so beautiful as the blue waters of Galway Bay, the blue sky above it, and the green islands sittin' like sleepin' whales in the sea. I wanted t' see them desperately but I hadn't the money for the ferry so I pawned my watch and bought a one-way ticket. I can't imagine how I could have done such a thing with no regard for gettin' home. All I could think about were those lovely green islands and the stories I'd heard about silkies and mermaids and people who spoke Irish and lived by the old ways." She held out her hands and stared at the thin skin and high ropy veins. Everything had changed. "I know it's hard t' imagine, Caitlin, but I was something of a romantic in those days."

There was no misunderstanding Caitlin's expression. Brigid rather enjoyed bringing that look of wonder to her daughter's face. It occurred to her that Caitlin had never known her as a young woman, not the way Anne and Deirdre had. Perhaps this purging that had been forced upon her would bring the girl closer.

"Sean was standin' on the cliffs below Dun Aengus, spreading out his fishin' nets when I first saw him," Brigid remembered. "The sun blazed down, colorin' him, capturin' the blue of his shirt, his hands and face burned dark from the sun, his hair shiny and dark as a bird's wing." Her voice went reverent and soft as she called up the beauty of him, that deceptive archangel beauty that had knocked her off balance and swept her away as easily and surely as the reversing tide had sucked the sand out from under her feet.

She laughed self-consciously. "He stayed in my mind like a photograph, the spareness of him, the sure capable movements, the liftin' of his hand t' wave in the ferry, his smile as we sailed by. I was sure he'd smiled for me."

"Perhaps he had, Mum. You were beautiful. I've seen the pictures."

Brigid shook her head. "There were quite a few of us on the boat. I doubt he could even see me. We met later that afternoon. I couldn't afford to rent a bicycle so I walked the five miles to the old fort and climbed to the top." It came back to her so clearly that the room tilted the same way the sky had that day when she'd stood on the precarious edge of the Celtic fort and looked down at the crashing waves. One slight misstep, one brief moment of dizziness on that treacherous point and it would all have ended right there. She closed her eyes and breathed deeply until the sick feeling disappeared and she could speak again.

"He called out a warnin' when he was still a distance away, worried that he might startle me. I turned and waited for him t' close the distance between us. He walked with that loose-limbed, toe-turned-in kind of walk that islanders have. I remember thinkin' he was the most beautiful man I'd ever seen and that I wasn't nearly good enough to have him. Not that I was hard on the eyes as far as women went, but nothin' like him." Her mouth twisted. "I suppose that was my undoin'. If he hadn't been so handsome I might have looked more closely at other things. As it was, no two people could have been less alike."

Caitlin challenged her. "Am I like him?"

"No," replied Brigid fiercely. "You're nothin' like him. He couldn't say no t' a pint if he was fallin' down drunk, and there are a good many women who still can't look me in the eye because of his shenanigans. No one on earth had less character than Sean Keneally. Be grateful that you have none of him in you."

A troubled frown appeared above Caitlin's eyebrows. "I don't understand."

"There's nothin' t' it," said her mother, hastily. "You're a hard worker, Caitlin, and honest, never mind the pranks you played in your youth. There isn't anyone living or dead who would call you dishonorable. Sean was another story. He couldn't settle on anythin'. He was always lookin' for an easy way t' make money. The years went by. We bought the pub with money left t' me by my mother. His heart wasn't in it. We grew apart and then he died."

"And then I was born," Caitlin finished for her.

"Aye," said Brigid, avoiding her daughter's gaze. "You were born."

"It must have been difficult for you, a widow with a new baby."

Brigid didn't miss the catch in her voice. "Actually," she lied, "it wasn't as difficult as you might expect. People helped. Assumpta and John O'Shea were wonderful friends. I have no regrets, Caitlin, if that's what you think."

"I'm sorry, Mum."

Brigid lifted astonished eyes to her daughter's face. "Whatever for?"

"For intruding on you like this, for failing at my marriage." She dropped her head into her hands. "Maybe I shouldn't have come home. My degree isn't worth anything here. I'm not trained except to work with horses and the only experience I have was at Claiborne Farms." She laughed bitterly. "Somehow, I don't think Sam will give me a good job reference."

"There's no need t' worry about that now. You can always stay here, you know."

"We need a home of our own, Mum. Annie isn't used to this. Maybe, when we're on our own, when we can keep the horses with us, she'll settle in. Of course, there's the possibility that the horses won't bring in any money at all."

"That's unlikely," replied Brigid.

Caitlin lifted her head. "Brian thinks the colt has a diseased voice box that will prevent him from racing. Because it's inherited he won't let me breed *Kentucky Gold* here at the stud."

"Good Lord." Brigid looked properly horrified. "Is that why you're goin' away together?"

"Of course. What other reason would there be?"

Brigid stared into her daughter's troubled eyes. Could a woman reach the age of thirty-one, marry, bear children, and still retain the naivete of a school girl? She reached across the table and patted Caitlin's hand. "No other reason at all, love. None at all."

15

Twenty years from now what would Annie think of her, Caitlin wondered. Would she consider her mother a failure or would she recognize that it took a fair amount of courage to come back to Ireland? The question hit Caitlin full force in the sitting room of Robert Farlow's white-washed cottage with its narrow stairs and thatched roof, its red door, its tiny windows that framed the sea, and its open hearth fire showering sparks on the icy flagstone floor.

It was in Spiddal, a town in the heart of the Gaeltacht, that she realized how great was the leap between what she'd been taught and what she now believed. Catholic girls from Kilcullen were told that it was up to a woman to shape her husband into a man she could bear to live with for half a century. If a man had no woman to refine him, to polish the edges of his gruff and blundering ways, he would live alone like this man did, this man who was the best equine veterinarian that Ireland had to offer. Or he would find another woman, and another after that, like Sam and her own father had, and the blame would be the woman's. Caitlin was more than a Catholic girl from Kilcullen. She'd fallen into the trap but she was free now. She would make sure that Annie never fell at all.

The veterinarian had left abruptly for an emergency call, a call more life-threatening than the diagnosis of a Claiborne colt—one among many promising, long-legged, high-stepping, well-muscled colts from a rich man's stables. Only, what Caitlin hadn't had time to explain was that this colt was different. This one belonged to her and if Brian Hennessey had his way, it might be the only one that ever did.

She rubbed her arms against the chill and stared out at the Atlantic. Brian had gone out for food nearly an hour ago. The quiet was unsettling. Perched on a hill overlooking the sea, the cottage windows faced west, framing the ocean and the three Aran islands in the distance. The sun was sinking fast and the light, that unusual soft glow that only the finest artists could capture, was fading so that the land and sky, now leached of color, blended together in a swirl of twilight gray.

Here where the boundaries between heaven and earth were not so clearly defined, she could see why villagers saw faeries and wee people along their paths, and why those who needed repairing of the spirit returned time after time to this fey land far enough to the west and remote enough from reality to seem another world. Here, in the absence of city dust, anything was possible and yet nothing mattered, nothing but the comfort of a warm fire and a full stomach and a brown-gray sea that rose to meet the sky.

The lights flickered and came back, dimmer than before. Fear of a black-out spurred her into action. She searched the kitchen and found two thick candles, a book of matches, and a package of fire starter. Banking several pieces of turf so that it formed a pyramid, Caitlin struck a match, lit the starter, and buried it in the middle of the pyramid. Then she added several more pieces to the top, burying the flame completely. There was more than enough turf in the basket by the hearth to keep the fire going through the night, and the doctor's cupboards had a plentiful, if dull, supply of Campbell's tomato soup and saltine crackers. If only Brian would come back.

Bored, she began opening cupboards. Perhaps it was a bit presumptive but Robert Fowler was Brian's friend and he'd insisted they make themselves comfortable in his home. Caitlin pulled out a bag of sugar, a tin of baking powder, salt, and a large bin filled with flour. Inside the refrigerator she found butter, milk, and green apples, everything for apple cobbler. She would make an extra large one and leave the bulk of it for the veterinarian.

She ran her finger down the blades of two knives, chose one, picked up an apple and, working quickly from the top, peeled it until she had a long corkscrew length of apple skin. Six more apples joined the first. Then she cored and sliced them into even segments. Setting a stick of butter in the middle of a square baking pan, she turned on the oven and slipped the pan inside.

Into a glass bowl, she emptied the ingredients, stirring with a wooden spoon until all the lumps had disappeared. Then she pulled the pan of melted butter from the oven, poured in the flour mixture and arranged the apples on top. After placing the pan in the oven, she looked at the clock, set her watch, and washed the bowl and utensils before returning to the sitting room.

The turf had caught fire and the room was comfortably warm. She had settled into the couch with the latest copy of *Irish Field* when the glare of headlights announced the arrival of an automobile. Tossing the magazine aside, she crossed the room to open the door and sighed with relief.

Brian walked toward her carrying two paper bags, one large, one small. Something smelled delicious. He grinned. "Hungry?"

"Starving."

"This should do the trick. I've fish and chips with a bottle of wine to wash it down."

She could have kissed him but settled on removing the larger bag from his grasp. "I'll dish out the food. You can pour the wine."

He followed her inside. "Any word from Fowler?"

Caitlin shook her head. "Not yet. Did you check on the colt?"

Twisting the corkscrew, Brian pulled the cork from the bottle, reached into the cupboard for two glasses, and poured the wine. "He's fine. Robert's compound is the best there is. There's a woman on duty. She'll call us when he gets in."

She had a weakness for chips, salty and rich with oil as only the Irish could make them. Dividing the entire lot evenly between the two plates, she gave Brian an extra serving of fish and decided on the small coffee table in the sitting room.

"It's warmer in here," she explained when he came out of the kitchen carrying two whiskey tumblers.

He nodded, sat down beside her on the couch and held out a glass. "Apparently Robert isn't a wine drinker. This is all I could find. I'm sure it won't affect the taste."

"*Slainte.*" Caitlin touched her tumbler to his and sipped tentatively. The wine was very dry, with a smooth finish and a hint of white chocolate and apples. "This is excellent," she said approvingly.

He leaned back, one arm stretched out along the back of the couch. "You sound surprised."

"When I left Ireland, Irish men knew about whiskey and ale. No one would admit to knowing wine."

"Ireland has changed."

The red rose in her cheeks. "Yes, it has."

"I imagine there are a great many things you wouldn't expect of us."

Chastened, she picked up a chip and bit into it. Flavor exploded against her tastebuds. "Ummm," she moaned, "these are wonderful." Ignoring everything but the delicious, gritty pleasure of the grease-soaked Irish praties, she made her way through the generous serving. Not until she'd wiped the last salty morsel across her plate and popped it into her mouth did she look up.

Brian's eyes danced with laughter. He'd left his food untouched.

"Aren't you hungry?"

"Aye. But I can wait. It's entertainin' to watch you eat."

She flushed. "I don't always eat like this."

"You said that the last time."

"The last time we had carrot soup," she corrected him, "and, if I recall, you were the one who had two servings."

"So I did. You're a grand cook."

Caitlin looked at his plate and then eyed her fish. "I'm not especially hungry any more."

Brian laughed and picked up his knife and fork. "Eat the rest of your meal, Caitlin. I went to considerable trouble to find somethin' that was open. There is nothin' wrong with enjoyin' food. Besides, there's a delicious smell comin' from the oven and I'm sure you grew up with the same rule I did, no dessert until you finish your tea."

She watched him work his way through his own meal before attempting the fish. He was a strange one, sometimes so helpful and friendly, other times probing, serious, and difficult to read. An island man, her mother had called him, one of those who never truly adapted to life on the mainland. And yet, he didn't seem out of place in Kilcullen. He was quieter than most. The silver-tongued muse, an Irishman's birthright, appeared to be missing in this man who thought deeply, angered slowly, and chose his words more carefully than most.

No, Brian Hennessey was hardly a typical specimen, despite the wry wit she'd surprised out of him on occasion. Here, on this windswept shelf of land that looked out over the Atlantic, he seemed more relaxed, more comfortable with the silences that settled between them after a long bout of words. Perhaps she'd misjudged him. Perhaps he wasn't really all that content in Kildare's horse country. She resumed her chewing. Pity. John O'Shea couldn't have found a better replacement if he'd scoured the length of Ireland. Brian had magic in his hands, those thin, capable, brown hands, a combination of sun and genes handed down by a remote ancestor washed ashore from a mythical Spanish galleon centuries earlier.

"Do you miss your home?" she asked suddenly.

He considered her question. She liked the way he thought before speaking as if giving her a careful answer was of prime importance. "I miss the way it was," he said at last. "Everythin's changed. I wouldn't go back now."

"What's changed?"

"People for one thing. My parents are dead. My sisters have moved on."

"But surely you have relatives and friends."

"Inishmore is a small place, Caitlin. Only eight hundred people actually live on the island. Everyone who can moves away to the mainland. There's no work there."

"My father was born there. I'd like to see it."

He nodded. "There are a number of Keneallys on Inishmore. If you're not in a rush to get home, we could take the ferry over for the afternoon."

Regretfully, she turned down his invitation. "I've got to be home for Annie's first day at Saint Patrick's. She's expecting me."

He conceded easily. "Next time."

"I suppose so." Her disappointment was great.

"Do you think whatever you cooked up while I was out is ready?" Brian asked hopefully.

"You're not such a light eater yourself," Caitlin observed as she collected the plates and headed into the kitchen.

The cobbler was perfect, buttery and thick with apples. Folding a towel several times, she pulled the dessert from the oven and spooned two servings, one generous, one small, on to saucers, the only small plates she could find. Then she filled the kettle, settled it over a burner and while the water heated, dusted the cobbler with cinnamon and poured a tablespoon of thick cream over the larger serving.

Brian stood in the doorway. "Can I help you?"

She handed him the plates. "Take these in while I fix our tea."

"Which one's mine?"

"The small one," she said with a perfectly straight face.

"Well then," Brian countered just as seriously, "if you don't mind, I'll have a bit of cream on mine as well."

"There isn't any more."

He nodded to the carton on the counter. "What's that?"

"It's empty."

"I'm sure there's another drop or two. Be a love, Caitlin, and shake it over my cobbler."

She burst out laughing. "All right. I give up. Yours is the large one. I couldn't possibly eat any more after all those chips."

"Do you have somethin' against cream?" he asked.

"Just the calories. I have to watch them," she admitted. "I'm not twenty any more."

His glance was brief but appreciative. "You've done a good job of it," he said softly before turning back to the sitting room.

It was no more than a offhand remark, nothing like the comments she'd endured from Sam's acquaintances after they'd spent an afternoon swigging down bourbon, but it flustered her as if he'd offered the most intimate of propositions and walked away, leaving it hanging between them.

She rinsed the tea pot with boiling water, threw in loose tea leaves and refilled it. Then she assembled the tray and followed Brian into the other room. On his face was a look of wonder. When he spoke, his words disarmed her completely.

"If you weren't still married, Caitlin Keneally, I would propose to you on the spot. I have never in my life tasted anythin' like your apple cobbler."

She laughed, sat down beside him, and set the tray on the table. "Be careful what you offer a woman. You may find yourself at the altar when you had no such intentions at all."

His voice changed, became softer, with a silky, breath-stealing edge. "Are you tempted, lass?"

Her heart skipped a beat. "Not yet." She kept her answer light and poured milk into the cups, grateful that her hands remained steady. "However, desperation often leads us in strange directions."

He took the tea cup from her hand, drank it down in one swallow and set it back on the tray. "Desperation, is it?"

She took a deep breath and looked up to find his eyes on her—narrow, serious, the clear fey blue of the islands. "It would be the only logical explanation if I were to do something so foolish, so soon."

"I can think of another reason or two." His voice, that low purring lilt, was like a caress.

She couldn't think. Dear God, was that his hand against

her cheek? She was at a place between fear and desire, somewhere beyond the first, leaning toward the second, not quite sure where she wanted to end up. Instinctively, she knew the remedy. Turning her lips against his palm, she tasted him.

And so it began, warm hands sifting through her hair, callused fingertips stroking her cheeks, firm lips touching her temples, her brow, her jaw line, and finally, closing over her mouth.

Her first sensation was an absence of awkwardness. There was no bumping of noses, no lips attempting to meet and missing, no embarrassing thrust of a tongue before the other was ready. It was as if she'd always known this man, as if his thin, sure hands and sensitive mouth had practiced a lifetime on her lips, her throat, her cheeks, her breasts.

She wanted to feel him against her. The urgency of her want shook her. Her mouth opened beneath his and she slid her arms around his neck, her fingers finding and kneading the smooth hot skin under his shirt.

He whispered something against her throat, kissed the point where her pulse throbbed erratically, and eased her down on the couch, covering her body with his own.

His hands and mouth were magic. Caitlin was done with thinking. Her body had been invaded by a maelstrom of heat and need and sheer physical passion, the magnitude of which she had never before experienced. She wanted nothing more than to wrap herself around this man and beg him to make this moment last forever, to never stop loving her as sweetly, as tenderly, and unconditionally as he was doing at this moment.

Rain drops sizzled against the smoking peat in the fireplace. Outside a tree branch lashed against the door and a fierce wind rattled the windowpanes. The lights flickered, dimmed, and went out completely.

Brian chuckled. "Convenient, isn't it?" His breath was warm against her throat.

"I found candles," Caitlin offered.

"Do we need them? There's light enough from the fire."

The shrill double ring of the telephone drowned out her reply. Brian sat up and reached for the phone. After a few monosyllabic responses he handed the receiver to Caitlin. "It's Robert. He's examined the colt."

Robert Fowler was brief and to the point. "I need to speak with you, Mrs. Claiborne. Can you come down here right away?"

"Is it bad news, Dr. Fowler?"

"It is."

"I'll be right there." She handed the phone back to Brian. "He wants to see me."

"Do you want me to come with you?"

She shook her head. "I'd rather go alone."

He reached into his pocket and pulled out the keys. "I'll be here when you get back."

By the time she'd negotiated the narrow, dark road and pulled into the parking lot of the animal hospital, Caitlin's nerves had reached the point where her emotions had gone the way of the clear afternoon skies. Rain poured down in buckets and flashes of light zigzagged across a sky black with menacing clouds. She struggled with the umbrella, gave up, and made a run for it.

Dr. Fowler held the door open, watching as she dashed across the lot into the shelter of the compound. Her hair, drenched with rain was already curling around her face.

"I'm sorry to call you out in weather like this, Mrs. Claiborne, but you said you wanted to return home as soon as possible. My offer still stands. You're welcome to my spare room. I'll be here until morning."

"Thank you."

He led her into a small kitchen, poured steaming tea into a mug, and handed it to her.

Caitlin shrugged out of her jacket, hung it on the back of a chair, and reached for the cup. "Is there any hope?" she asked.

Rob Fowler, a massively built man with a round face, a full beard, and eyes that would disappear behind the folds of his cheeks when he laughed, smiled sympathetically. "That depends. The news is both good and bad. If you want a champion flat race horse, I would say, no. There isn't the slightest hope. But if you can be content with waiting an extra two years, I believe something can be done, enough so that he might attempt the steeple races as a four year old."

"Dear God." She slumped against the counter and passed a hand over her eyes. It was worse than she'd imagined. She couldn't wait four years, not with Annie's tuition and the house she'd rented, not when Brian suspected *Kentucky Gold* of carrying RLN disease. Despair settled over her in thick suffocating waves. The veterinarian was speaking again. Forcing herself to focus, she listened.

"Your colt," he explained, "has congenital recurrent laryngeal neuropathy on the left side of the voice box. In other words, a portion of the voice box is partially paralyzed." His voice was kind, professional, completely impartial. "This will eventually result in something commonly called *roaring* and bleeding of the lungs. RLN reduces the ability to open the voice box during exercise and to close it when swallowing. The symptoms are progressive, worsen over time, and are irreversible. Horses with RLN that are forced to race drop dead on the track."

Caitlin set down the cup and lifted her chin. "You said there was good news."

He nodded. "A large percentage of thoroughbreds are

born with RLN. Those that aren't go down in history as our winners. The others die trying or become something less than we would wish. Are you willing to support an animal that will bring you no income?"

She straightened to her full height and looked at him steadily. He was an enormous man. "My children have named that colt."

Robert Fowler grinned. "My name is Rob."

All at once she liked him. "What do you suggest we do for my colt, Rob?"

He pulled out a chair and waited for her to sit down. Then he sat down across from her. "I've developed an experimental technique that locks the glottal cartilage into a neutral position."

"What good will that do?"

"Wait here." He stood and walked out of the kitchen, returning seconds later with a white folder. Opening it, he spread out a diagram on the table before her. "The vocal cords are elastic ligaments that run between the glottal cartilage and the thyroid cartilage," he explained. "By releasing the ligament from the thyroid and threading it through a hole in the voice box, it can be moved from the inside to the outside of the box. By applying traction to the ligament, I believe I can graft it to a new position and resist the collapsing force of suction on the glottal cartilage."

"Does it work?"

"Not always," he replied honestly. "But one thing I'm sure of, it won't hurt him. He'll be able to swallow normally after surgery and the throat muscles will be spared. It's worth a try."

"Is it expensive?"

"Do you have insurance?"

"Insurance doesn't cover experimental procedures."

"This isn't exactly experimental. We'll work something out."

"Everything has to be completely legal."

Robert Fowler's thick eyebrows drew together. "It will be."

Caitlin bit her lip. "Is there an alternative?"

"Not unless you put him down."

She shook her head emphatically. "I wouldn't do that."

Again he smiled, a full separating of the lips that revealed his teeth and a healthy measure of gum. "No, I didn't think so."

"When can you do it?"

"There's time."

Her voice cracked. "But he's already bleeding."

"Only when he's extremely agitated. Keep him in the paddock. Register him as usual. Next year will be soon enough."

She pushed her chair away from the table and stood up. "I'll catch the late train back home. I'd like to use your phone, if I may."

Brian answered on the first ring. "It's me," she began and stopped. Tears crowded her throat.

"Caitlin?"

"I can't—"

Brian's voice, warm and soothing, traveled through the wire. "It's all right, love. Don't cry."

"You were right."

"Oh, lord, Caitlin. I didn't want to be. I'm sorry."

"I'm going back to Kilcullen tonight on the train. I'll leave the truck here for you."

"What about the colt?"

"Rob thinks he can save him but not for flat racing. He wants to operate next year."

She could feel him take in her words. He would think them over carefully, deliberately, as only Brian could, and then he would formulate an answer that was every bit as thoughtful and cautious as the man himself.

After a lengthy interval he spoke. "I'm scheduled to stop in at the Ballinasloe sale tomorrow but I'll be happy to bring the colt home."

"Thank you," she said, relieved that it had gone so easily, that she could return home alone and that he hadn't mentioned what had taken place between them on the couch in Robert Fowler's living room.

She would have long hours to herself on the train, hours when she must come up with a solution to the downward trajectory that her life had taken. All her hopes were now pinned on *Kentucky Gold*. The mare would have to be tested. Sam would also have to be contacted. If RLN disease was prevalent among Claiborne bloodstock, his reputation, the reputation she had helped to create, would be destroyed. He would be out of business before the year was out.

Despite her personal antipathy toward her husband, the magnitude of such a tragedy and what it would mean to the American thoroughbred industry filled her with despair.

16

❧❧

Irish Gold was surprisingly docile when Brian led him into the trailer before dawn the following morning. It was one of the new and improved model trailers recently purchased by the Curragh Stud. Horses walked in from the side instead of backing in and stood at an angle with a window view of their surroundings. The new style better accommodated the yearlings and colts who could stand without the restricting lead rope tying down their heads.

The sky was a dismal leaden gray. Overnight the frost had silvered the grass so that every blade stood stiffly erect in its coat of armor. Brian was scraping the residue from his windows when Robert Fowler hurried out to say goodbye, clapping his arms, his breath smoke-white in the bitter cold air. "You should have an easy drive to Ballinasloe. The weather's good."

"Aye." Brian stripped off his gloves. "Caitlin said you were goin' to operate on her colt."

Fowler nodded. "It's what she wants."

Brian scraped the last of the frost from his window. "There's no hope of racin' him after the hobday operation, not in the flats anyway."

"I won't be trying the hobday, but the results are the same. She knows that."

"What of the expense?"

"I wouldn't think a Claiborne would be concerned with that."

Brian frowned. He was reluctant to betray Caitlin's trust.

"You've heard the Claibornes are divorcin'."

Fowler frowned. "Are they now?"

"The colt is part of the disagreement, or he was," Brian amended, "before this happened. I can't imagine Sam Claiborne fightin' for a defective animal."

"You wouldn't happen to be the reason for their divorce, would you, mate?"

Brian was genuinely shocked. "Whatever put that idea into your head?"

"She's an attractive woman," Fowler observed.

"I've noticed."

"It would be difficult for a man not to."

"Are you interested for yourself, Rob?"

Fowler held up his hands and backed several steps away. "I never said that. She's unusual, that's all I meant. And she took it quite well, about the colt. It had to be quite a blow."

Brian knelt to check a tire. "She had a bit of warnin'. It wasn't hard to figure out after he bled all over my hands."

"His chances are good," Fowler said emphatically. "Only one side is defective."

Brian stood and leaned back against the truck. "She's in a financial bind, Rob. This colt was to be her ticket. There won't be any Claiborne money comin' this way."

"It won't break me." The vet had come close to the trailer

to stroke the colt's velvety nose. "There's something odd about this one, Brian."

"How?"

"I've followed *Narraganset* ever since he was put out to stud. He's never thrown a colt that looks like this one. His genes run truer than any stallion I've seen, small muscles, large head, nothing Arabian about him. This one doesn't look like he has *Narranganset* bloodlines at all."

Later, after Brian had negotiated the maze of round-abouts leading out from Galway, after he'd waited patiently for endless minutes while a road bowling game dispersed, and after he'd waited for a flock of sheep to be herded off the road by a redheaded lad with so many freckles they appeared to stand up on his cheeks, his mind finally cleared, and the ramifications of Rob Fowler's casual comment came to him. It was preposterous, of course. Not even Samuel Claiborne could get away with such a fabrication. Not unless he'd expected the colt to be born in the privacy of the Claiborne stables. Not unless he planned to control every aspect of his bloodtyping and his registering. He couldn't do it alone. Others would have to be involved as well, others who'd worked for Claiborne for years, those whose liveli-hood depended on the reputation of the Claiborne stables.

It occurred to Brian that if his suspicions were true, Claiborne must be feeling rather desperate now that only two months remained before the colt's required blood tests and registering. He looked out of the rearview mirror. The narrow road hugged the edge of the cliff and wound snake-like behind him into the distance. He tightened his grip on the wheel, grateful that Caitlin had decided to go home by train. A desperate man was often a dangerous man.

The Ballinasloe horse sale was located on a flat piece of land resembling the Burren, that ancient limestone shelf that covered a good portion of Connemara and western Ireland. Rows of trailers lined the perimeter of the field and men in wool caps known as middlemen stood arguing the merits of a particular horse to buyers while reminding the owner of his defects. The familiar open palmed, hand-slapping between middleman and seller, and then middleman and buyer, and the rubbing of soil on an animal's hindquarters to indicate an agreement, had been part of the Ballinasloe tradition ever since Celtic warriors raced their steeds at the Curragh a thousand years before.

Brian parked the trailer and checked on the colt before making his way across the long wet grass to where the most promising horses were corralled. Ballinasloe attracted all breeds, from the small, wiry Connemara pony to the Irish draft horse, heavy with muscle. Occasionally a bankruptcy or divorce would force the sale of a thoroughbred of high enough quality for Brian to consider training at the Curragh Stud, but that was a rare day indeed. He came to these events to keep his finger on the pulse of the true Irish horse world.

The Curragh Stud and other farms like it were Ireland's treasures—architectural masterpieces with manicured grounds, state-of-the-art neonatal units, pristine stables, and horses worth millions in worldwide currency, worlds as far away from the backyard horse trainer's reality as the Ballinasloe sale in the middle of a horse pasture was from the Goff's auction in its modern building surfaced with glittering mirrors.

Ballinasloe was the common man's auction and despite his association with the Curragh Stud, Brian considered himself a common man. A horse lover who had learned everything he knew from the kind of grass roots training acquired by trial and error and hanging on the heels of those with experience—just the same as a thousand other lads like himself who had empty pockets, horses in their blood, and hands that weren't afraid of an honest day's work.

"Well, if it isn't our lad, Brian Hennessey." A heavy hand slapped his back nearly knocking him off his feet.

Brian turned, grinned and held out his hand. "How are you, John?"

John Connelly with his bowed legs, mismatched clothes, curly gray hair, and scruffy beard hardly looked the part, but he was a man known the length and breadth of Ireland for his shrewd horse sense and razor-quick wit. He was seventy years old, a middleman, known for bringing buyer and seller together and sticking with a promising transaction until both parties were equally satisfied. His commissions were substantial and Brian had never regretted acting on his advice.

"Well enough, lad," the man replied. "What brings y' t' Ballinasloe?"

"I haven't missed a Ballinasloe sale since I was a boy."

Connelly stroked his beard. "No, I don't suppose y' have. Why is that, I wonder, when you've enough on your plate takin' care of the diamonds of the thoroughbred world?"

Brian narrowed his eyes, and for an instant the years fell back and he was a boy again with imagination enough to feel what it must have been like for a Celtic warrior to race his stallion on the flat plain of the Curragh. The feel of it stayed with him, through summers as an exercise boy at stud farms, as an amateur jockey, as a groom's assistant, and then trainer's assistant and finally, thanks to John O'Shea, a position coveted by every boy in Ireland who ever sat on a horse: manager of the Curragh Stud.

Brian was under no illusions that his talent for training winners would have brought him to the point where he now was. There were many men in Ireland as talented with horses as he was, but only he had managed the good luck of rooming with Martin O'Shea. "This is where it all began for me, John. I wouldn't miss it."

The old man's eyes misted. Unashamed of his emotion, he squeezed Brian's shoulder. "I remember well enough the first day y' came with your da. A scrawny dark little lad y' were with that black hair and those eyes that looked liked all the sea in Galway was locked behind them."

Brian remembered. "He wanted a horse for his wagon."

"Aye. And I found it for him, didn't I?"

"You did, John. We brought home a fine horse that day."

"I remember takin' a good look at your face and thinkin' this lad will never be a fisherman."

Brian laughed. "Right you were, John. I'll not be makin' my livin' from the sea."

"I was sorry to hear about your da, lad. He was a good man who should have had another ten years in front of him."

It seemed to Brian as if the din surrounding them had lessened, and the noise and crowds and color receded to a different plane.

He was at his father's funeral again. His mother had reproached him for missing the Rosary as if that were more important than the years of silence between them. He'd watched the throng of mourners pass by the closed coffin and for the first time saw something in the women of Inishmore that he'd never seen before.

Without exception their foreheads were pinched in the center and the skin around their eyes was stretched with lines that could only have come from long hours spent squinting at the sea, fingering Rosary beads, scrubbing floors that were already bleached to an unnatural purity, beating rugs, washing windows, wringing linens, praying until the fishing boats were sighted again, signaling a fresh catch and a husband who hadn't been washed overboard and swept away.

The sea was both savior and nemesis. It put food on a woman's table and widowed her before her time. The sea had claimed Kevin Hennessey during an unexpected storm, kept him hidden for six long days, and finally washed him up in the nets of another fishing boat, so bloated and disfigured that his sweater, the distinctive Aran with its blackberry stitch representing the Holy Trinity, was his only identifying mark.

No, Brian would not go the way of his father, despite his love for that wild and lonely island off the coast of Galway Bay. Give him the settled beauty of Ireland's horse country: leaves crimson and gold, piled in heaps along winding country roads. Gravel paths leading away from wrought iron gates, hedge rows and oak trees, spruce-lined fences. Sleek horses munching in rich pastures, rare November sunlight picking out diamond-bright raindrops in water-slick grass. Turf fires, pungent, white steam against a pewter sky. Low foamy clouds that hung like stiffly beaten egg whites over the peaks of green hills, an orange sunrise coloring the patchwork quilt that was Ireland. Women in bright anoraks who walked the roads with healthy dogs for no reason other than that the day was a lovely one.

He cleared his throat. "He was a good man."

"Aye, that he was." John pulled his pipe from the inside pocket of his jacket and dug around for his matches. After an exhaustive search he found them in the same place where they always were, beside his pipe. Striking the match against his shoe he lit the tobacco and sucked in deeply. "I hear you've stabled a Claiborne mare and colt," he said casually.

"That's right," answered Brian. John Connelly wasn't one for idle conversation. Sooner or later he would come out with his reasons for throwing a particular subject out on the table for discussion.

"Word has it that Samuel Claiborne has come to Ireland to take them back."

Brian shrugged noncommittally and kept his eyes on a promising bay with black legs and mane. She was giving the boy holding his lead rope a difficult time of it, twisting and pawing the ground. "I haven't heard from him."

"Word has it that Mrs. Claiborne has broken the law bringin' the mare t' Ireland the way she did."

Brian's eyes never left the bay. "Do you know Sam Claiborne, John?"

"Not if I was t' see him face t' face."

"If I were judge and jury," Brian continued, "I'd lay odds that it wasn't Mrs. Claiborne who broke the law, but rather the other way around."

Before the old man could answer, Brian gripped his shoulder and nodded in the direction of the bay. "What can you tell me about that two year old?"

John immediately picked out the horse. "That's Jamie Dempsey's filly. She was passed over last year. Her da was *Satan's Madboy.*" He looked at the leaping, snorting horse. "It appears that she's inherited some of his tendencies."

Brian groaned. *Satan's Madboy* was possibly the fastest horse to come out of Ireland since *Simba Kahn* but he was unpredictable. No jockey would ride him. Even after he was retired to stud, he mauled an exercise boy, crippling him permanently. Eventually he was put down.

"Sometimes it isn't the animal, lad," John offered. "Y' know that. If he's been treated badly y' can't blame him."

"How much is Dempsey askin'?"

John was already counting his commission. His forehead wrinkled. "Two thousand quid, fifteen hundred if we work it right."

"Let's see what he says."

The old man beamed. "Follow me," he ordered, shouldering his way through the masses to where the filly stood shackled and tied to a fence post. "Jamie Dempsey," he roared over the crowd noise. "I've a buyer for your horse. If y' know what's good for y', you'll be here by the time I'm through countin'."

Instantly Dempsey appeared at his side. "I'm here, John."

"Good lad. What are y' askin' for this bag of bones y' call a horse?"

"Three thousand quid," the man replied promptly.

John shook his head sadly. "Brian here will give you one thousand, not a pence more."

"She's worth more."

"Come, lad." John waved his finger at the boy. "Last year y' couldn't give this horse away. I don't see anyone lined up t' buy this year. Mr. Hennessey will give y' a fair price." He lifted Dempsey's hand, slapped it and let it fall. "What do y' say, lad?" Again he picked up the young man's hand and slapped it. "One thousand pounds and you've sold the nag."

"Two thousand pounds," the boy said. "I'll take two thousand for her."

Regretfully, John shook his head and slapped Dempsey's hand harder. "Fifteen hundred. My buyer will give you fifteen hundred dollars and no more." He leaned close to the boy and removed the pipe from his mouth. "This isn't goin' to get any better, lad. Y' didn't really come here today thinkin' y' would sell your horse, now, did y'?"

Dempsey's face fell. "He isn't goin' to pay anymore is he, John?"

"No, Jamie. He isn't. I won't let him."

"All right, then. It's a deal."

John picked up a handful of mud and smeared it on the filly's rump. "Brian, lad. Reach into your pocket and bring out your checks. You've got yourself a horse."

*　　*　　*

Brian had never cared for Sam Claiborne. The man's arrogant disregard for the small horse breeder was enough to raise a fair-minded man's contempt. But now that he knew Caitlin, and after Rob Fowler had raised his suspicions, he could barely look at the man without a slow-boiling rage gathering in the pit of his stomach.

Seated in the stands in the center of a group of fawning Americans, Caitlin's husband with his expensive flannel trousers and tweed jacket looked every inch the wealthy breeder.

The auctioneer, immaculately dressed in the customary suit and tie suitable for the Goff's annual yearling action, took his place in the box. Brian turned his attention to the filly in the center of the ring. Then he looked at his program. She was a *Suliman* filly out of *Aran Light,* a nervous, fine-boned yearling, small for a foal born in January, but with the bloodlines for enormous potential. Brian pulled the pencil from behind his ear and marked her number. The auctioneer started the bidding at ten thousand pounds.

Out of the corner of his eye he saw Sam Claiborne hold up two fingers.

"Ten thousand pounds has been offered," the auctioneer reported, "do I have eleven thousand?"

Brian raised his hand and nodded.

"Eleven thousand pounds," the auctioneer droned, "do I have twelve?"

Claiborne held up another two fingers.

"Twelve thousand pounds," said the auctioneer. "Twelve thousand pounds has been offered."

Brian looked at his program. As much as he wanted to foil Sam Claiborne, the *Suliman* filly wasn't worth more than ten thousand guineas. Reluctantly, he kept silent while the auctioneer finalized the Claiborne offer and the filly was led out of the ring.

Six more horses were brought to the block, all with flaws that an experienced trainer wouldn't miss. Brian didn't bother bidding on them. To his intense satisfaction Claiborne Farms acquired four of the six.

When the next colt was brought before the crowd, Brian wasn't the only one who caught his breath. *Indian Summer* was a March foal but he was large, sleek, and well-muscled with the canon bones of a flat racer. Under the golden light thrown by Goff's reflective panels, his cinnamon coat gleamed like living flame. This time, Brian resolved, he would not allow Claiborne to outbid him.

The auctioneer spoke into the microphone. "*Indian Summer* out of *Donovan's Lady* by *Sorley Boy*. Champions, ladies and gentleman, winners of the One and Two Thousand Guineas races, the Saint Leger's, and the Darby. The bidding will begin at fifteen thousand."

Claiborne raised his hand.

"Fifteen thousand pounds offered by Mr. Sam Claiborne," the auctioneer said. "Am I offered sixteen? Who will give me sixteen for this splendid animal?"

"Eighteen thousand," someone called from the back. Brian recognized Seamus O'Connor, a neighbor from nearby Naas.

"Eighteen thousand is on the table," the auctioneer's voice broke through the murmurs of the crowd. "Mr. O'Connor has offered eighteen thousand punts. Am I offered twenty?"

Deliberately, Brian remained silent as the bidding continued. His reputation was well-established. He intended his offer to be the last and the highest. Sam Claiborne wasn't out of cash but he would be shortly. He'd already spent close to a hundred thousand guineas for untried horses. No stable, not even Claiborne's could sustain that kind of expenditure.

O'Connor's last bid was twenty-six thousand. Brian watched Sam Claiborne and the man beside him engage in a swift and animated conversation. They appeared to come to a decision. Claiborne's hand remained at his side. Unless someone stepped in, O'Connor would walk away with the *Sorley Boy* colt.

Brian pitched his voice for the auctioneer's ears. "Thirty thousand pounds."

The room went silent. Few had the prestige and money of the Curragh Stud. It was an Irish stable owned and run by Irish men and women, its land rented from the Irish government. If Brian Hennessey was willing to spend thirty thousand pounds on a colt, he could just as well spend forty or fifty. There was no point in a man wasting his time or the Curragh's money for a result that was already a foregone conclusion.

The auctioneer's voice came through the microphone. "*Indian Summer* sold to the Curragh Stud for thirty thousand pounds."

Brian stood and walked to the exit. He would finalize the paperwork before he left and in the morning send someone from the Curragh to take possession of the colt.

Ian Cummings, the acquisitions clerk at Goff's, congratulated him on his choice, accepted his check and sent him on his way, keeping the small talk to a minimum. Auction days were his busiest.

Brian folded up his receipt, stuffed it into his coat pocket, and walked through Goff's impressive glass doors to his car. In the adjoining space, Sam Claiborne, arms crossed against his chest, leaned against the door of a late model BMW. He straightened, dropped his arms, and nodded at Brian.

"Brian Hennessey?"

"Aye."

"I'm Sam Claiborne." He didn't offer his hand.

Brian waited.

"I understand that you're stabling a colt that belongs to me."

Brian shook his head. "You're mistaken."

"You're Brian Hennessey, manager and trainer of the Curragh Stud, aren't you?"

"I am."

"*Kentucky Gold* and her colt belong to Claiborne Farms."

Brian opened his car door. "Your wife has a different interpretation. Unless I hear otherwise, from a legal source, I'll go along with her."

Claiborne sneered. "I'm sure you will. Caitlin has no money. Just what kind of arrangement do you have with my wife that keeps you so loyal, Mr. Hennessey?"

The arrogant drawl of the southerner's speech enraged Brian almost as much as his insinuation. His hands clenched around the door handle and the familiar adrenalin rushed to his brain. Ten years ago, Claiborne would have been on the ground with his mouth bloodied and at least two of his perfectly capped teeth beside him. But Brian had since learned something about self-control.

"Mrs. Claiborne pays her boardin' fees like everyone else," he said deliberately, "but if I were you, I wouldn't go spreadin' it around that my wife had no money. Here in Ireland we don't look kindly on a man who refuses to support his wife and children."

Claiborne growled menacingly. "Damn you, Hennessey, that's my horse—"

The Irishman's eyes blazed. His arm snaked out, grabbed the American by his collar and twisted it until the man's mouth opened to suck in needed air. "Don't even think of threatenin' me, lad," Brian said softly. "Here, your money means that you can buy a good horse, nothin' more. Understand?"

Claiborne, his face a dangerous mottled red, nodded desperately.

Brian released him, slid behind the wheel of his car and rolled down the window. "I won't say it's been a pleasure. If our luck holds we won't be seein' each other again. Goodbye, Mr. Claiborne."

From his rearview mirror, Brian could see Sam Claiborne leaning weakly against his rental car. Swearing under his breath, he changed lanes and accelerated. He'd made an enemy, something he resolved never again to do, and for the worst of all reasons, a woman.

17
❧❦❧

For Caitlin, there were moments so powerful, so rich, so filled with quivering breathless joy that everything leading up to them, all the worries and disappointments, the annoyances and failures, the losses and late starts could be looked back upon without regret. This was one of them. She glanced at Annie, standing motionless on the edge of the track, oblivious to the cold, her breath mingling with the morning mist.

The Curragh at dawn, the flattest plain in all of Ireland, the course where the ancient Celts had raced their horses two thousand years before, was a sight that few outsiders were fortunate enough to experience. Caitlin reached for Annie's hand and gently squeezed it.

Out of the mist forms took shape, equine and human: jockeys, cheeks red with cold, standing in stirrups, whips in hand; horses neck-and-neck eating up the green turf, cut grass flying beneath trimmed hooves; the wide open space of it; the control, the speed; the sheer exhilarating power of standing less than ten unobstructed meters away from the finest horses in all the world. Effortlessly they ran, hooves pounding the turf, nostrils quivering, sides heaving, breath steaming in the frigid air.

Caitlin felt the energy run through Annie's slight body. The child's eyes were closed, her face tilted reverently. She looked to be in communion with the sky, the fog, the cold, and the thundering hooves pounding around the track. This, she had given her daughter and she was glad. This she would always have, always remember. Nothing could take this intensity away.

"Will *Irish Gold* train at the Curragh?" Annie asked when she came out of her trance.

Caitlin hesitated. She hadn't told the children about the colt's affliction. "It takes a great deal of money to train at the Curragh," she said, "and *Irish Gold* is still very young."

Annie appeared to accept her mother's statement. "Thank you for bringing me, Mama," she said. "It was a lovely idea."

"You deserve a reward. Does the new school suit you, Annie? You never speak of it."

The child nodded. "I like it better than the National School. Still, I'd rather go home."

Caitlin sighed. "Gran would miss you a great deal."

"Like my other grandma," she said wisely. "Before, no one missed anyone at all. Now Grandma Lucy is sad because we're not there and if we leave, Gran will be sad." She turned her dark eyes on her mother. "None of it would have happened if you hadn't moved us."

Sometimes the child's profoundness shocked Caitlin. Annie thought and spoke as if she were a sage in the body of a ten-year-old girl. "Can't we just try and get through this, Annie? Please?"

"That's what Gran always says."

"Maybe she has a point. Maybe we should think of this whole difficult time as something we can work on getting through instead of just the way it is."

Annie's brow puckered. "I don't understand."

Caitlin bit her lip. How much could a child Annie's age absorb? "Sometimes things look different when you're on the other side. It's possible, in a few years, that you might think I was right to come here."

Annie shook her head. "That won't happen," she said emphatically. "I'll never think it was right for us to leave Daddy."

"Maybe," Caitlin conceded. "But I'm your mother, Annie, and I wouldn't be setting a very good example if I allowed you to grow up believing a woman has to stay in a marriage that isn't good for her. I would never want you to live with someone who makes you unhappy. Do you want that for me?"

Slowly, Annie shook her head.

Caitlin slipped her arm around her daughter's waist. Something still needed clarifying. "You didn't leave Daddy, love. You're still his daughter. He'll always be your father. That won't change. Do you understand?"

"Yes."

It wasn't much, certainly not the whole-hearted acceptance Caitlin wished for. Still, it was a start.

She smiled. "We should be getting back. You'll be late for school and we haven't had breakfast yet. Would you like to eat at Kathleen's before I drop you off."

Annie nodded.

Kathleen Finch's restaurant was nearly empty when Caitlin pulled her car halfway up over the curb on the pedestrian walkway to allow for two-way traffic on the small main street. John Guthrie and Kevin Foley were comparing their heating bills. She nodded to them and took a seat across from Annie at a small table near the window.

"Good mornin', Caitie," Kathleen called out from behind the double doors leading to the kitchen. "How are you, Annie, love?"

"I'm fine, Mrs. Finch," Annie replied.

"We'll have a full breakfast, Kathleen," Caitlin said. "Bacon, sausage, eggs, tomatoes, everything."

Kathleen laughed. "Where have you been to work up such an appetite so early in the mornin'?"

Annie spoke up. "At the Curragh. We saw the horses train."

"My goodness." Kathleen brought out the tea. "You had to be up at dawn to see such a sight. Do y' love horses that much, Annie?"

"I do," the child answered. "I love them more than anything else. Except for my family," she added conscientiously.

"Well then, I suppose risin' with the dawn was well worth it. I'll bring your breakfast right away." She winked at Annie. "If your mum will help me slice the bread you'll have it that much faster."

Annie looked inquiringly at her mother.

Caitlin laughed and stood. "Have a cup of tea and pour me one as well."

The two women worked quickly, Kathleen frying bacon and sausage in one pan and eggs in another, Caitlin slicing the hearty brown bread that was Ireland's second staple.

Kathleen's voice was a shade above a whisper. "You just missed him, Caitie. He was in here no more than ten minutes before you stepped inside the door."

Caitlin plied the knife expertly through the thick crust. "Who?"

"Why, Sam Claiborne, himself," said Kathleen, sliding the eggs on to two plates. "He ate a platter full of eggs and sausage and washed it down with enough coffee to give him the runs for a week. Then he asked where he could find you."

"What did you tell him?"

"Your mum has the only pub in town," Kathleen said reasonably. "He would have found you no matter what I told him."

"I can't really avoid him. He's my children's father." She frowned. "Mum promised to see Ben off to school. I suppose it's better that Annie and Ben won't be with us until we settle things enough to be civil to one another."

Kathleen arranged the bacon and sausage beside the eggs, dished up two stewed tomatoes and released the button on the toaster. "He seemed a pleasant enough chap."

Caitlin nodded. "Sam can be very pleasant."

"Don't you miss bein' married even a wee bit, Caitie?"

"No. Do you?"

Kathleen's forehead wrinkled. "Sometimes, in winter when the nights are long the way they are now and I've forgotten the feel of the sun on my skin. I can't seem to get warm. Do you ever feel the same?"

Caitlin's mouth turned up in a half-smile. "Keeping your feet warm isn't a very good reason to wish for a husband, Kathleen."

Kathleen chuckled. "I suppose so. Aren't we serious for so early in the mornin'? I'll bring out the plates or Annie will be wonderin' where we've put her breakfast."

Caitlin's car was one of the last to pull up in front of the red brick building that had served as Kilcullen's Catholic girl's school for nearly a century.

Annie brushed her mother's cheek in a quick kiss, pulled her book bag over her shoulder, and ran for the entrance.

Watching until her daughter had disappeared behind the

carved wooden door, she negotiated a U-turn on her way back to the pub. Caitlin wasn't feeling her usual self. A strange sort of lethargy had settled over her. She didn't want to see anyone today, not her mother, not the regulars at the stud and most especially, not Sam.

The morning had been fine with a hint of sunlight but now clouds had gathered and the rain was coming down in tiny gusts that clouded the windshield, stopping long enough for the wipers to restore visibility before obscuring it again. Caitlin's hands tightened on the steering wheel. What if she didn't go back just yet? What if she took the day to go into Naas or Lougrea, to look in the shops and stop in for a roll and a pot of tea or a bar meal?

The roundabout toward Naas loomed ahead. Caitlin checked her rearview mirror and merged into the left lane passing the first exit and then the second before turning onto the third. She smiled. A rare sense of adventure lightened her mood, turning her cheeks pink. How long had it been since she had a day to herself? She'd forgotten. She would pick up a jar of chocolate spread and peanut butter at the Superquinn. They were Ben and Annie's favorites. Normally, she wouldn't let them eat the stuff, not the chocolate anyway, pure fudge without the slightest nutritional value. But rules could sometimes be bent and today she felt like bending them.

Her mother bent them all the time, a habit that continued to amaze Caitlin. She couldn't remember when her mother had shown the slightest bit of softness toward her own six daughters. Annie and Ben could do no wrong. Caitlin's mouth turned up in a half smile. Lucy was the same way. Perhaps a grandmother's relationship with her grandchildren was intended to be easier, more indulgent than a mother's with her children.

At ten o'clock in the morning, Naas, like any other Irish

town at the onset of winter, was barely waking. The chemist was still closed and Gogarty's Furniture and Hardware was dark inside, but the Manor Bar and Restaurant had a sign out and a young woman with an earring in her nose was sweeping the pathway in front of Evita's Boutique.

Older women dressed in woolen mittens and caps, divided pleated skirts, and Aran sweaters walked purposely down the rain-wet streets carrying home the day's groceries. It would be another hour before men in business suits and women in fashionable leather jackets and pumps, their faces artfully made up with the latest that Chanel and Lancôme had to offer, would be up and about. Everyone knew that hours were irregular in winter. No one but the occasional American traveler expected otherwise.

Caitlin pulled into a parking spot opposite the Bookends Bookstore and sat for a minute. Her breathing came faster now and the blood beat erratically in her throat. Now that her moment of freedom was upon her she felt strange, almost fearful, as if she were committing an illicit act.

Pushing the feeling aside, she buttoned her coat, reached into the back seat for an umbrella, and stepped out of the car.

Three hours later, armed with packages and flushed with the pleasure of doing exactly as she pleased, she entered the Manor Pub and Restaurant and sat down on a padded bench near the fire. Annie would be pleased with the knit cap and maple syrup. Caitlin found Panda's chocolate spread and a tin of crayons with seventy-two colors for Ben who had lately displayed an artistic streak. She'd indulged in a bottle of hand lotion and bath salts for Brigid, and when the saddlers opened at noon and the gloves she wanted were discounted, she purchased them without a twinge of conscience. It had been a productive morning, every bit as much fun as shopping in Louisville with a balance-free platinum card had been.

Lunch hour was just beginning and the pub, a cozy place with an open-beamed ceiling and picture-covered walls, was beginning to fill up. She looked at the menu and her stomach rumbled. Cottage pie with chips and vegetables would go nicely with a glass of Harp and a pot of tea.

A capable looking young man took her order and returned immediately with her ale. Sighing happily, Caitlin sipped her Harp and closed her eyes, allowing the warm fire and the golden alcohol to relax her.

A low, amused voice broke through her daze. "What a surprise. We missed you at the Stud this mornin'. How are you?"

Her eyes opened and she smiled. Were eyes as blue anywhere else outside the Aran Islands? "Brian. How lovely to see you. I'm well, thank you. Will you join me?"

"I will if I won't disturb you. You look quite content sittin' here all alone."

A lightness had taken hold of her, probably the Harp. She pointed to the chair on the opposite side of the table. "I'd rather have company."

He glanced briefly at the nearly empty glass in front of her before settling himself in the chair. "What brings you to Naas on this fine day?"

Caitlin turned to look out the window. "You must be on the good side of a piece of news. It's been wet since morning."

"Aye, so it has." Brian nodded at the man waiting tables. Before long a pint of Guinness had joined Caitlin's Harp at the table.

She looked thoughtfully at the dark brew. "Do they know you here?"

"I eat here at least once a week." He sipped through the head of his ale. "I don't normally tip one durin' the day but as you're obviously in a festive mood, I thought I'd join you."

She nodded, wondering if she would ever look at a man with a drink in his hand and not be suspicious. "I took Annie to the Curragh track to see the horses train. We had breakfast at Kathleen's and I dropped her at school. After that I just couldn't seem to face the normal routine. Besides—" she hesitated.

He prompted her. "Besides what?"

She felt very warm. The strange lethargy that had plagued her this morning had turned into a warm relaxed glow and the words rolled off her tongue. "Kathleen told me that my husband had arrived in town."

"You'll have to face him eventually."

"I know that. But not now." She smiled brightly. "Maybe not today."

The look in his blue eyes should have warned her away, but she chose to pay no attention to it or maybe it was more than that. Maybe she wanted what came next.

"When did your marriage start to go bad?"

Caitlin thought. It was a question she'd asked herself often enough. "Sam wasn't right for me from the beginning. I saw that soon enough, but I thought if I improved myself, things would change."

Brian's forehead wrinkled. "Improved yourself?"

"We didn't move in the same circles. He was educated, a fraternity man, with educated friends. Everyone he knew, everyone the Claibornes knew, was wealthy and professional, even the women. I didn't fit in."

"Did he see it the same way you did?"

Caitlin finished the last of her Harp. "Oh, yes. I'm sure we would have split long ago but there was Annie, you see, and then Ben."

"So you decided to improve yourself."

She nodded. "I went to college and earned my degree." The alcohol had loosened her tongue. "I watched carefully, especially the women. I learned how to dress, how to speak, and then I did what I wasn't supposed to."

"What was that?"

"I learned to play better than they did." She was quiet for a minute, remembering her moment of triumph when Bull Claiborne had approved her changes in the covering schedules, announcing that she would be the final authority from that day forward. Sam had been furious but it was Bull's corporation, not his. Memories in Kentucky were long. After Bull's death, the major breeders continued to look to her, not to Sam. "Are you surprised?"

"Not at all," he said smoothly. "You're an intelligent woman, Caitlin. It seems you always were. I wonder why you had to go all the way to America to discover it."

She'd often wondered that herself.

Her lunch arrived, an enormous casserole of ground lamb and mashed potatoes with a steaming plate of cauliflower and chips on the side. Brian's order, mushroom soup and a cheese and tomato sandwich looked spare in comparison.

His eyes twinkled. "I see you haven't lost your appetite. Will you be eatin' all of that, Caitlin?"

"Every bite."

He signaled the barman. "You'll need another Harp to wash it down."

The relaxed glow was still upon her and she didn't protest when another drink appeared at her place. "I don't blame Sam for his faults," she observed. "Growing up an only child with a mother who believed he was perfect, and all that money, it would have been a miracle if he'd turned out unspoiled. I shouldn't have married him." The cottage pie burned her tongue. She swallowed a healthy measure of Harp.

Brian's eyes were narrow blue lines in his dark face. "You have Annie and Ben," he said gently.

Caitlin's mouth softened. "I do and I'm grateful. Sam wants them back, you know. He has a great deal of money and I don't."

"An Irish court may see it differently."

"It doesn't matter. The children are American. They've lived their entire lives there."

"What will you do if the children are ordered back to Kentucky?"

Caitlin looked surprised. "I'll go with them."

Brian's soup was cold, his sandwich untouched. "What about the horses?"

"I haven't figured it out yet," she admitted. "I didn't count on *Irish Gold's* condition."

Brian finished half his sandwich. "What if the foal hadn't survived? It's always a possibility. You must have taken that into account."

"I did. But *Kentucky Gold* would have been in foal again by that time, not by *Narraganset* but definitely by another horse with champion bloodlines. What I didn't count on was a defective colt *and* a mare who couldn't be covered."

His eyes were clear as glass. "I'm sorry, Caitlin. Truly I am."

She believed him. "I know you are. I don't blame you. I just hope you're wrong about *Kentucky Gold.*"

"So do I," he said grimly, "more than you think." Leaving his soup and most of his Guinness, he stood and pocketed the bill. "I'll be leaving now. Enjoy the rest of your holiday."

Later, after she'd drunk several cups of strong black tea, gathered her belongings, and braved the wet to climb back into her mother's car, a thought occurred to her. Today was the first she'd seen of Brian since their night in Rob Fowler's cottage and he hadn't mentioned it. She hadn't really expected him to. That would have been too awkward. What nagged at her was that he'd behaved as if nothing had happened between them. Why that bothered her, she couldn't say. She didn't really want anything to happen with Brian Hennessey, or did she?

Pulling down the shade she glanced into the small clip-on mirror and made a face. "You're absurd, Caitie Keneally," she said out loud, "absurd and juvenile. You don't want to fall in love with him, but you would very much like him to fall in love with you."

18

He looked dreadful. What had she ever seen in him? Was it possible that he'd always been like this and her six-month absence had opened her eyes, or had he gone to seed after she'd left Kentucky? Worse still, was she comparing him to someone else, someone whose days were filled with the kind of labor that discouraged excess, someone without a whiskey and rye belly, a loose neck and broken veins spidering up his nose, someone whose voice wasn't the grating rasp of metal on sandpaper and whose breath didn't smell like kerosene. There was no sugar-coating it. Sam Claiborne was an alcoholic and it showed.

"I'm taking the colt back to Kentucky," he said, cutting to the chase.

"Annie and Ben are well. So nice of you to inquire," she said sweetly.

"Damn it, Caitlin. Don't twist this into something it's not. We're going to settle this once and for all."

"Is that what we're doing, settling it?"

"What else?"

Slowly, methodically, she picked up a dust cloth and moved it in even circles on top of the wooden bar. "Settling implies something that both parties agree to," she said carefully, "a bit of a compromise for each of us. It sounds to me as if you're issuing ultimatums and I'm supposed to accept them."

Angrily he stalked to the bar and sat down on a stool. "Have you got any bourbon?"

She lifted her chin and looked him straight in the eye. "It's early and I know you're uncomfortable, but let's not confuse this by adding alcohol to the picture."

"I don't expect anything on the house if that's what's bothering you."

"We both have lawyers," she said patiently, refusing to be drawn into an argument. "What are you doing here?"

"I told you. I came to pick up my colt and take my children home."

A cold fist closed around Caitlin's heart. "The custody hearing isn't for another month."

"If you bother to show up for it."

His remark didn't deserve an answer. She stared at him, a slim straight figure in wool slacks and an Aran sweater, dark hair curling around her shoulders.

He stared at the dust cloth she clutched in her fingers and looked around. "I can't believe you'd actually prefer to stay here, working as a barmaid."

"I'm not a barmaid, but that's splitting hairs so I'll bite and ask, instead of what?"

"Instead of living at Claiborne."

"Believe it," she said evenly.

"Where are the kids?"

"In school."

"I won't have them here, Caitlin," he said vehemently. "You can't possibly believe they're better off than they were at home. Good God! My children, Claibornes, living above a pub."

"I'm better off, Sam, and I'm their mother. Besides, we're moving shortly. I've rented a house with a barn. I can't live with you and your—" she hesitated, "your outside interests."

He snorted. "As if you cared."

"Maybe not," she conceded, "not any more, but it won't be long before Annie and Ben know what you're up to. I don't want my children thinking our relationship is normal."

"Have you got something going on here, Caitlin? Is that the *normal* relationship you're referring to?"

She flushed, mentally cursing the tendency of her fair skin to color at the slightest provocation. "This may be difficult for you to understand, but sex doesn't determine my direction."

"It isn't difficult at all. You never were very interested."

Stung, she snapped back. "You never were very good."

"I haven't heard any complaints."

"You're hearing one now."

He slid off the stool and walked to one end of the bar, stuffed his hands into his pockets, turned, and walked back again. "We're getting nowhere. I want the colt. You aren't going to stop me."

Her fists clenched. "It will be handled legally," she said struggling to remain calm. "If you're the rightful owner, you can take him home."

"When are you registering him?"

She frowned. "What's that got to do with anything?"

"Damn it, Caitlin, just answer the question."

Throwing down the towel, she stood, hands on her hips, eyes blazing. "Don't swear at me, Sam Claiborne. This discussion is over. The children will be home at four. You can come to the house if you want to see them." She pointed at the door. "Now get out."

His mouth twisted strangely and his hands shook as he approached her. "You stupid little fool," he growled. "You have no idea what this is all about, do you?"

Frightened, she stepped back.

The door opened and a wash of sunlight momentarily lit the pub as a tall man with a Roman collar passed through the door. "Caitlin?" he said uncertainly, his eyes adjusting to the dimness.

"Martin." There was no mistaking the relief in her voice. "Come in. This is my husband, Sam Claiborne. He was just leaving."

Martin looked confused but following Caitlin's cue, he stretched out his hand to meet Claiborne's. "It's a pleasure to see you in Kilcullen, Mr. Claiborne. Will you be staying long?"

"My plans aren't definite," Sam replied, withdrawing his hand.

"Well now, perhaps we can convince you to lengthen your stay. I'm sure Annie and Ben will be pleased to see you."

Sam's eyes rested on Martin's collar and narrowed. "What did you say your name was?"

"O'Shea. Father Martin O'Shea of Saint Patrick's Church."

"O'Shea," Sam repeated slowly, "Martin O'Shea. Where have I heard that name before?"

"Caitlin and I grew up together Perhaps she's mentioned me."

Sam shook his head. "Caitlin never talks about her early years in Kilcullen." He smiled pleasantly. "I'm sure it'll come to me. A pleasure to meet you, Father." He nodded at

Caitlin. "We've unfinished business. I'll be back later to see the children."

She didn't answer and he walked out.

Martin waited until the door closed. "He seems a decent enough chap."

"Does he?" Caitlin's smile was brittle. "How can I help you, Martin?"

He laughed self-consciously and again the thought occurred to her that when it came to men, her judgement had been seriously impaired.

"This is a bit embarrassing," he began.

Now she was curious. "Go on."

"The purpose of my visit may no longer apply."

"Let me be the judge of that."

He fidgeted with the change in his pockets. "May I sit down?"

"For pity's sake, Martin. You don't have to ask. This is a pub, not a sitting room. It's a bit early but do you want something to drink?"

"No, thank you." He sat down at a small table and fell silent.

"Say it, Martin," she said, exasperated. "It can't be all that dreadful."

"It isn't a good idea to go away with a man overnight, Caitlin," he burst out. "This is Kilcullen. Ireland isn't America."

Her eyes rounded with surprise and the corners of her mouth twitched. She would make him say it out loud for the sheer pleasure of teasing him. Surely she was allowed that much. After all, they'd grown up together. "I don't know what you're talking about," she said innocently.

Martin spread his hands in a gesture of supplication or perhaps it was a plea for guidance. He could barely get the words out.

"I'm talking about you and Brian Hennessey," he said miserably. "You went away together for the weekend. Don't tell me you didn't, Caitlin. Brian told me himself and he's no braggart."

"Brian Hennessey told you we went away for the weekend together?"

"Aye."

"Did he tell you the reason?"

"He's not a man to volunteer his words and I didn't ask."

"Didn't you?" Caitlin sat down across of him. "What *did* you do, Martin?"

His forehead wrinkled.

"Did you lambast him as well or did you pat him on the back and rush over here to take me to task, a fallen woman with two children and no husband who lured the poor innocent man into evil ways?"

Martin protested. "It was nothing like that, Caitlin."

"What was it like, Martin, or should I say Father O'Shea?"

"Lana told me first," he confessed. "I was having a bite to eat when she saw Brian through the window and called out to him. She asked how the two of you had gotten on. He said the weekend was a satisfactory one."

"That's it?"

"Aye."

"That's all he said and you left it at that?"

Martin's fair skin was stained a dark red. "I couldn't very well question him in front of Lana."

She was beyond angry. A cold rage froze and shortened her words. "So you ran over here to accuse me."

"Not accuse you, Caitlin, warn you."

Caitlin pushed back her chair and stood, two flaming streaks of color beneath the sharp edges of her cheekbones. "Thanks for the warning, Martin. If that's all, I've work to do."

He took a long time to stand, rearrange his chair, button his coat. Finally he looked at her. "When I saw your husband here, I wasn't going to speak at all."

"Why is that?"

"I thought he'd come because there was a chance of your reconciling. But I was wrong, wasn't I?"

"Yes."

"It would be better for the children, you know, and for you."

She was weary of the conversation. If only he would hurry and be done with it. "Why, Martin?"

"You don't really belong here, Caitlin. You aren't happy in Kilcullen. You never were."

You don't belong here, Caitlin. You don't belong here, Caitlin. You don't belong here, Caitlin. The words drummed in her head and the repressed rage she'd carried for years, ever since Lucy came to her after Sam announced their engagement, broke. She was tired of people telling her that she didn't belong. It was time to fight back, to cry out that she did belong, that she must belong somewhere.

"I do belong here, Martin," she said gently, reaching out to smooth the bright hair back from his forehead as if he were no older than Ben. "I didn't before, but I do now. I'm going to have a stable of racehorses. That's always been my dream."

"It's that bad for you in Kentucky with your husband?"

Caitlin nodded. Had he always been so childlike or had the priesthood stunted him, kept him inexperienced, innocent, at the place where they'd been as children?

"Well then, I'm sure Brigid is happy to have you. It can't be easy on her with all her daughters gone."

"I'm sorry about your mother, Martin."

Quick tears sprang to his eyes. "She went quickly but I miss her. Da isn't the same now that she's gone. I'd only been back a short while before she died." He looked hopefully at the bottles lined up behind the bar. "Something smells grand. Would you have a bowl of soup and a bit of the spirits to go with it?"

She felt lighter somehow, as if things were settled between them. "It's mushroom soup today. Would that bit of something be whiskey or ale?"

He sat down again. "Ale, please."

She walked back to the kitchen where the huge caldron simmered appetizingly in preparation for the lunch hour to come. Ladling out two bowls, she carried them out to the table along with several slices of bread and sat down across from Martin.

He bit into the bread and his eyebrows lifted. "This is delicious. I've never tasted anything like it before. It doesn't even need butter."

Caitlin sipped at her soup. "It's rosemary olive bread."

"Where did you find it? I wouldn't mind having a loaf or two around the rectory."

"I made it this morning."

He stared at her in amazement. "I would never have imagined you this way, Caitlin, not after knowing you as a wee girl."

"Why not?"

He finished his bread before speaking. "You were always with the lads. It seemed to me that you resented being a girl."

"Is that the way you saw it?"

"It was." He dipped into his soup. "People change, don't they."

"I suppose." She stirred her soup to cool it. "It might interest you to know that I didn't at all mind being a girl."

"Didn't you?"

"No." She pushed away her soup, crossed her arms and

looked directly at him. "What I wanted, Martin, more than anything in the world, was to train thoroughbreds. Girls can do that."

He scooped up the last of his soup, swallowed it, and nodded. "Would you have that ale for me now, Caitlin?"

She walked back to the bar, poured a pint of Guinness from the tap, let it stand for a minute and then filled the glass to the brim and brought it back to him. "You loved horses as much as I did, Martin. Why did you become a priest? Didn't it bother you to give it all up?"

He picked up his glass and drank half of it down. "I never loved the life as much as you did, Caitie. No one did. You were so taken with the idea that you couldn't see what the rest of us were suited for at all. I was bothered that you might be disappointed in me until my mother made me see things differently."

"How did she do that?"

"She told me you were too smart to let a mere person stand in your way. She said you would get what you wanted no matter what I or anyone else did. She was right, wasn't she, Caitie?"

This was Martin, the boy she'd grown up with, confided in, the boy she once thought she knew better than her own sisters. He was very simple after all, but he'd been blessed with a wise mother. They all had. "Yes, Martin, she was right."

He smiled. "I'll be leaving now, Caitlin. What do I owe you?"

"There'll be no charge this time. Don't tell Mum."

He laughed and headed for the door.

"Martin?"

"Aye?" He turned expectantly.

"Brian and I went to Galway to see a vet. That's all there was."

Martin looked down at the floor, hesitated, and then

walked back to where she sat. Taking her hands he pulled her to her feet searching her face intently.

He was very close. "What is it?" she asked uneasily.

His mouth tightened briefly and then relaxed. He released her hands and stepped back. "Perhaps that's all it was for you, Caitie, but it may have meant more for Brian."

She did not pretend to misunderstand. "How do you know?"

"Brian Hennessey is my friend. There isn't a great deal I don't know about him."

"Are you warning me again, Martin?"

He shook his head. "I'm appealing to you. If you're not in this for the long term, don't toy with him."

"I've never toyed with anyone."

He smiled sadly. "Perhaps not intentionally, but there were a few broken hearts when you left Kilcullen."

She flushed angrily. "Don't be absurd. I was a child."

"And now you're a woman, a beautiful woman."

Caitlin was torn between exasperation and amusement. One minute he disapproved of her and the next he flattered her. "Go away, Martin," she said, waving him off, "or I'll be ranting at you again."

He grinned. "You were a hellion, Caitie, do you remember that?"

"Surely that's a bit harsh."

"Not the way I remember it. Give my love to your mum. Perhaps I'll see you at Mass come Sunday."

She groaned. "You know you will. I'm actually quite reverent now that Annie's attending Saint Patrick's."

His smile faded and the serious look came back to his face. "You're a good mother, Caitlin Keneally. No one can deny you that."

He'd noticed. She was deeply touched. "Thank you, Martin."

It wasn't until after Kirsty arrived for her afternoon shift that Caitlin passed the locked post office and thought of her mother. The store was never closed on a weekday. Where was Brigid?

She crossed the street and stepped into the cafe. Lana was sweeping up after her last customer. "Have you seen my mum, Lana?" Caitlin asked.

"Not today." Lana's voice was unmistakably frosty.

Kathleen Finch came out from the kitchen. "I saw her this mornin'. She had breakfast here after you drove Annie to school."

"Has anyone seen her since?"

Kathleen's eyes widened. "Has she been gone all this time?"

"I'm not sure. I've been working the pub since morning."

Lana spoke up. "Don't be worrying over nothing. She took the day to do a bit of shopping. The holidays are coming up, you know."

Caitlin relaxed. Lana was right. Her mother had lived alone for a long time. She wasn't accustomed to announcing her plans to anyone. "If you see her tell her that I'm on my way to the Curragh."

Lana stiffened.

"The children are meeting me there after school," Caitlin said hastily, backing out of the restaurant.

Back on the street, Caitlin sighed, pulled on her knitted hat, and rolled up the brim. Her weekend in Galway had resulted in more than a dressing down from Martin. There was no mistaking Lana's hostility. She saw Caitlin as a rival for Brian Hennessey's affections. Their time away could be easily explained, of course, but Caitlin wasn't convinced that a few chosen words in Lana's ear would solve the problem.

The truth of it was that she *was* attracted to Brian Hennessey. That night on the vet's couch in Galway was proof enough if she'd ever doubted it. She tingled, her body flushed with the memory of his tongue parting her lips, his mouth and hands moving across her skin, awakening a desire she hadn't known existed, not for her anyway.

She wanted him. That part was undeniable, but was it enough, her wanting without offering more? Martin insinuated that it wasn't, that Brian Hennessey was a man who should not be trifled with. Was it fair to make him love her unless she loved him in return, and if not, was it honest to offer a man the promise of love some time in the future just because he knew the secret of lighting a flame inside of her?

19

He wasn't concentrating. Deliberately pushing aside all thoughts except the horse beneath him, Brian rose instinctively in the saddle, allowing the full weight of his body to balance on the balls of his feet. *Graybeard's Lady*, the horse he'd taken a chance on and purchased at Ballinasloe, responded like a champion and sailed over the hurdle as if she were born for the Grand National, the most important steeple chase in the world. Recovering, she moved into a slow gallop, running easily.

On Brian's cue, Davy Flynn leaned over, yelled and prodded her in the rump. The filly would need to become accustomed to shouting, bumping, and quick movements, the world of horse racing. Brian liked the way she moved— confidently, deliberately, more like a veteran three year old than the two year old she was. It was time to teach her how to run like a racehorse, to level out and reach for ground.

Brian clucked to the horse, urging her to pick up speed

slowly. At the quarter pole he chirped. She leveled and reached out, stretching, her body lower to the ground, accelerating rapidly, gathering speed. "Steady, girl," the trainer crooned, "give yourself time. No need to rush into anything."

Responding to the soothing voice, the filly stabilized, synchronized her legs and gathered momentum. It was raining steadily by the time she reached the three-eighths pole, the midpoint, and the track was muddy. Brian felt her fall against the bit. He eased down in the saddle, reached forward with his whip and waved it in front of her right eye. Immediately she increased her speed, striding hard against the bit, breathing easily, all the way to the wire. The time was 0.36, a perfect twelve clip. Brian's heart pounded. At Ballinasloe, for an absurd price, he'd found his champion.

Walking back to the stalls, Davy kept up a flow of conversation. Brian heard none of it. Cursing his lack of discipline, he dismounted, ran a hand down the colt's trembling flank and held out the reins. "Let's call it a day, Davy, lad. I'm not thinking clearly."

Davy threw him a curious look, nodded, reached for the leather, and maneuvered the filly in the direction of the hotwalker.

Brian watched as they disappeared around the whitewashed walls of the foaling pens, his attention once again claimed by his meeting with Caitlin the day before. Their tentative relationship had turned into something he hadn't expected, something stronger, deeper. Brian wasn't a believer in miracles. He knew it would take just that for a woman like Caitlin, hurt as she'd been to risk her heart again.

Brian took a long time checking the stallion's boxes. There were eight of them left. The mares had been sent back to their owners for a brief respite before they came into season again. The stallions were unusually silent, libidos calm, muscles relaxed. Brian spoke to them all, soothingly, caressingly, as a man does who understands the potential of arousing eighty stone of deadly power.

After slipping in the bolt on the last stall, Brian turned off the light and walked up the paved walk, through the copse of trees to the small whitewashed cottage where Neeve waited patiently for her evening meal. He refilled her water dish, set down a bowl of kibble and opened his refrigerator with disinterest. Tonight his own cooking didn't appeal to him. He could go into town and have a meal at Bernie's or he could make do with what he had in his own cupboards. Venturing into Kilcullen meant risking a meeting with Lana. She was everywhere these days.

He frowned, looked at his watch, and once again surveyed the contents of his refrigerator. Brian didn't pretend to be a creative cook. Food was a necessity, a means of satisfying the hunger pangs in his stomach, nothing more. The less time he spent in the kitchen the better. He couldn't run from Lana for the rest of his life. It was Tuesday and still early for dinner. With luck he could be in and out of Bernie's before anyone knew he was there.

Bernie Lewis, the proprietor of Kilcullen's only fine restaurant, opened the door for him. "Have you tired of your own cookin' so soon, lad? You were in just last week."

Brian grinned. He was the only customer. "Are you turnin' away business, Bernie?"

"Not a bit. I wasn't plannin' on openin' up the restaurant but if you don't mind the bar, I'll put you in a chair by the fire."

Pulling his cap off, Brian impatiently fingercombed his hair. "As long as the food's hot, I'm not particular."

"I've salmon tonight and leg of lamb, if you can wait. It's not quite done."

Brian sat down on a stool near the fire. "Salmon will do,

along with some of those potatoes and a green salad if you have it."

"I have it." Bernie set a glass of Guinness in front of Brian. "Word has it we've important visitors in town."

The ale was mellow and creamy against the back of his throat. He savored the flavor before speaking. "This is Kilcullen, Bernie. We're less than five miles from the most important race track in Europe. We always have important visitors."

"This one's different. He's Caitie Keneally's husband come to take back his colt."

Brian could feel the tendons swell and stiffen in his neck. "Is that so?"

"Aye." Bernie leaned over the bar, eager to impart his information. "So they say."

"They?"

An icy breeze swept through the restaurant. Brian turned toward the door, words of welcome dying on his lips.

Sam Claiborne, his voice dripping with sarcasm, spoke to the man beside him. "Is this the best you can come up with, Fahey? The clientele really isn't up to standard. Eating with the hired help won't do at all."

Fahey looked uncomfortable. He moved closer to Claiborne. "Be reasonable, Sam. This is the only place in town," he muttered under his breath.

Brian swallowed more of his Guinness. Keeping his expression neutral, he waited for Claiborne to make a decision. Long minutes passed. From across the room the man's eyes challenged him. Unperturbed, Brian met his stare. No one was chasing him away. Sam Claiborne would have to lower his standards or go hungry.

Claiborne was the first to look away. Without a word, he walked to the opposite end of the bar and sat down. Fahey glanced apologetically at Brian before taking the seat beside him.

Brian was in the middle of an exceptionally good cut of salmon when once again he heard the door open and felt the cold on his neck. This time the voice that greeted Bernie froze his fork in the air, halfway to his lips. He turned to see Caitlin framed in the doorway, her slender figure wrapped in something long and red and definitely more elegant than the town of Kilcullen was accustomed to seeing on one of their own.

It was the first time he'd seen her since her revelations when they'd met in Naas, and he was more than a little curious as to how she would behave when she saw him again. He needn't have worried. She didn't so much as glance in his direction, but went directly to where Sam Claiborne and the man he'd called Fahey waited. Brian glanced over his shoulder. Obviously she was expected. The men shifted to make room for her.

The salmon tasted like ashes in his mouth. He would have given an enormous percentage of his next winning purse to know what the topic of conversation was on the other side of the room.

Before long, the sound of chair legs scraping the floor alerted him. Casually, he glanced in their direction. Fahey was standing, clearly calling it a night. Caitlin had turned so that Brian could see her profile. What caught his attention was the expression on her face. Clearly she was disturbed, not an unexpected emotion considering her circumstances, but she was looking at Fahey, not at her husband. Could she be upset that the man was leaving? And where in bloody hell was Bernie? The man was never around when you wanted him.

Brian debated with himself. Should he stride across the room, interrupt their conversation when Caitlin hadn't even acknowledged him? He was fairly certain she hadn't seen him. She wasn't the kind of woman to snub a man who moved in a different social circle. Perhaps it was time to notify her of his presence.

Leaving his salmon and potatoes, Brian stood and crossed the room to stand behind her chair. "Hello, Caitlin," he said.

She looked both startled and pathetically relieved. "How long have you been here?" she asked.

It was a coat. She was wearing a coat, a long red coat with sleek lines and a stand up collar, the kind he'd seen on magazine covers. His glance met hers and held. "Long enough to finish most of my meal."

Blushing under his intense regard, she gestured toward Fahey's empty chair. "Please, join us."

Brian hesitated. Before he could refuse, Claiborne spoke up. "This is a family matter, Caitlin. I think Mr. Hennessey would only be uncomfortable, not to mention being in the way."

There was nothing Brian wanted more than to leave Sam Claiborne's presence but he couldn't resist the appeal in Caitlin's eyes. "I've my dinner to finish," he said, ignoring Claiborne completely, "but I've a few matters to discuss with you. I'll wait until you're done and then drive you home."

"I'll take my wife home, Hennessey." Claiborne's voice dripped with insult.

Caitlin turned on her husband. "Actually, I don't believe we can settle anything here tonight. You've made your position quite clear. We obviously need a mediator. I'll be in touch through my lawyer."

Sam's lips paled with anger. Throwing down his napkin he pushed back his chair and rose. "I suggest you find yourself a good Kentucky lawyer who knows the risks involved."

"I'll stick to the one I have," replied Caitlin. "He's less likely to be influenced by Claiborne money than a *good* Kentucky lawyer."

"Suit yourself." Without a word to Brian he strode across the floor and out the door.

Caitlin stared after him, her eyes wide and dark and mutinous.

Brian waited.

"I apologize," she said at last.

"For what?"

"My husband's rude behavior."

Brian sat down beside her. "No need. You aren't responsible for him."

She looked down at her hands. Her lids were tinted a delicate mauve. "No. I suppose not."

"Are you hungry?"

She looked up. "Not really. Sam has a way of ruining my appetite."

He grinned. "Mine, too."

"You said you had something to discuss with me?"

Brian shook his head. Red wool, dark hair, ivory skin, French perfume. His senses were reeling. He wet his lips. "Nothin' in particular, just a feelin' that you needed rescuin'."

Her face stilled, all expression erased. "Is that why you came over?"

"What other reason would there be? Your husband wouldn't be my choice for a dinner companion."

Tilting her head, she studied him. Candlelight bathed her face, sculpting her cheekbones, shadowing the hollows beneath them. "You've rescued me, Brian Hennessey," she said quietly. "I can find my own way home."

Disregarding the voice in his head warning him that no good could come of this, he reached for her hand. It was cool, her fingers slender with space between the bones. "I've a better idea. Come with me to Naas for a drink and some real Irish music."

"Why?"

He looked surprised. There was no time to think of a clever response. The truth would have to do. "Because I want to dance with you."

The brilliance of her smile shattered him. "I hoped that was it."

"Will you?"

"Yes."

Still holding her hand, he stood, pulling her to her feet, and fished in his pocket for money to pay his bill. He nodded at the drinks on the bar in front of them. "Is this taken care of?"

"No."

He threw down a ten punt note. "Shall we go?"

Caitlin nodded. "First, I need to call home. Otherwise, my mother will worry."

She was thoughtful. He liked that. "I'll wait in the car."

By the time she climbed into the passenger seat, Brian's nerves had taken on the seesaw swinging of a pendulum. No good could come of taking his relationship with Caitlin to another level. Heartache was the inevitable outcome. He knew she wasn't indifferent to him. Their night in Galway had proven it beyond all doubt. But Caitlin wasn't a green girl. She was a woman with experience behind her, a woman who wouldn't be swept away by mere words, not the second time around.

She saw him waver and, because she was Caitlin, nailed him to the dashboard. "You're very quiet. Regretting me already, Brian?"

He had nothing to lose. "Not for the reasons you think."

"How do you know what I think?"

He dimmed his headlights as another car approached on the divided road. "It isn't difficult to guess. You're wonderin' if I expect a replay of the other night and how you're goin' to refuse without insultin' me."

"No. That isn't it."

Brian glanced briefly at her profile. It told him nothing. He turned his attention back to the road. "No?"

She shook her head. "If I were going to refuse I wouldn't have agreed to come."

It took a full minute for her words to register. When they did, the imperceptible shaking of his hands on the wheel nearly forced the car into the opposite lane. Swerving quickly to the left, he righted the car and drove for several minutes in silence.

He was at a loss for words. Normally such a condition signalled him to slow down, evaluate, plan a course of action. Instinct told him that this time, with this woman, his normal pattern wouldn't work. For some inexplicable reason, Caitlin was behaving unlike herself and if he took the time to settle his mind, organize his thoughts, it would be too late. He would never again be on the other end of such an offer.

Again his thoughts had distracted him. The blare of a horn and the bright beam of headlights sliced through his concentration. Abruptly, he pulled off to the shoulder of the road and turned off the motor. "I'm likely to kill us before this night is over," he muttered.

"Why is that, Brian?"

Shifting so that his back rested against the door, he studied her. Across the space that separated them it was too dark to see more than her eyes, black pools in the pale oval of her face. Christ, she was cool. Once again the terrifying sensation that he was dealing with something bigger than he could handle washed over him. "You're drivin' me insane," he said softly.

She moved slightly. The beam of an oncoming headlight lit the interior of the car and for a few timeless seconds her face was caught in golden light.

Brian's throat closed and his hands clenched. His chest felt tight and hot. God help him. He knew what that look meant. A man would give up years of his life to inspire such a look on a woman's face. Could a woman like Caitlin, a woman who had the power to change her life at the snap of her fingers, really call up that kind of wanting for a man like him?

"Me too," she whispered. "I'm insane, too."

He said something. He was sure of it. The words came from a place deep down in his throat. But somewhere, after he reached for her and their lips met, after the frantic search for buttons and the delicious shock of cold fingers against wool-heated skin, after the warm, weighty melting of her breasts against his chest, and the slide of his palms down all the curves he'd fantasized about for months, he forgot what it was he meant to say.

Later, when their exertions had fogged the windows beyond visibility, when his breathing had gone raspy and labored, when his hands and mouth had touched and tasted every inch of bare skin he could uncover within the space of his narrow compact, he remembered it again. Lifting his head he stared down at her kiss-bruised mouth, at the swell of ivory flesh above her lace-trimmed bra, at the dreamlike expression in her eyes.

His arms tightened around her. Lowering his head, he set his mouth on the spot where she was most sensitive, a fraction above her right nipple, and sucked gently, then not so gently. As the intensity of his onslaught increased, she gasped, arched against him, and buried her face against his neck.

"Take me home with you, Brian," she whispered.

He lifted his head. A faint strawberry marked the spot where his mouth had been. "Tell me you won't change your mind."

Her brow wrinkled.

He forced her chin up so that her eyes met his. "I'm no good at this kind of thing. No matter what happens, I have to know that you mean this, that you want me, that you'll want it with me tomorrow and the day after that. I don't need a fling."

Her voice was sultry, soul searing. "What do you need, Brian?"

"You," he muttered against her mouth fiercely. "I need you, the girl who ran away to Kentucky, Annie and Ben's mother, the woman who lives and breathes horses, the woman who is Brigid Keneally's daughter and Sam Claiborne's wife. God help me, Caitlin, but I need all of you and it terrifies me to think that this might be a game to you, a midpoint between leavin' your husband and winnin' your freedom."

She sat up, moved out of his arms and spent more than enough time adjusting her clothing. Finally she spoke. "I'm flattered," she said quietly, "more than you'll probably believe."

"Go on."

"I want us to be honest with each other."

He nodded.

She looked directly at him. "My marriage wasn't honest. I don't know if what I feel for you is permanent. It's possible that it could be, but I don't know yet. It's too soon."

Surely he had seen women far lovelier than this slender girl with her stern beauty and night-dark eyes, but he couldn't recall them. Brian was very much afraid that he never would again.

"Please say it's enough, Brian." Her voice cracked on his name and his heart broke. "I need it to be enough for you."

20

❧❧❧

Caitlin leaned against the fence and watched the jockeys file out, small men, perfectly proportioned, narrow as strips of leather, their silks hot flashes of color in the winter grayness. The horses came next, stud chains taut against their tongues, warming blankets covering the sleek coats, legs wrapped, hooves shining, eyes wild. The black filly caught her attention. She was calm, expectant, every nerve under control, a winner. Caitlin marked her race card.

"Mum?" Ben tugged at her sleeve. "I like the red one. Will you bet on him?"

"Her," Caitlin corrected him. "These are fillies, Ben, and this is their maiden race."

"Will you bet on the red one?" he repeated, undeterred.

Brigid ruffled her grandson's hair. "Give your mother a chance t' think, lad. She's the one whose money will be lost or won."

The chestnut was magnificent: large, showy, nerves on edge. Caitlin bent down and kissed the top of her son's head. "Look at her, Ben. I don't think she's got what it takes to win. Look at the way she's resisting the bit. Do you see it?"

Ben nodded.

Caitlin looked around. "Where's Annie?"

"She went to the barns."

Caitlin sighed. The Punchestown race was too large for a child to be wandering about alone. Sam would find out and he would have yet another complaint against her.

Deciding quickly, she marked her second and third choices: the bay to place and the gray to show. Long ago, John O'Shea had warned her away from caution on a maiden race. Still, John had been reaping the benefits of a comfortable monthly draft from the Curragh Stud. She wasn't so fortunate. Handing her race card to her mother along with a fifty pound note and the admonition, "Be sure to get there before the window closes." She held out her hand to her son and smiled. "Come along, Ben. We need to find your sister."

Plowing through the wet turf, more sodden than usual because of a thick mist that had settled over the track the night before, Caitlin surveyed her boots and grimaced. They were black with mud. She led Ben into the barn. Under the casual swipe of her hand she felt her hair, unruly as usual, the strands escaping from her clip to curl riotously around her face, and sighed. She'd tried for a more dignified look but the weather wouldn't cooperate.

The barns were warm with horse breath and smelled sweetly of hay, alfalfa, and oats. Ben extricated his hand from hers and pointed to several shadowy shapes standing near an open door. "Annie's there, Mum," he said, "and she's found Brian."

Caitlin's heart sank. After her embarrassing seduction attempt, the last person in the world she wanted to see was

Brian Hennessey. The Punchestown race was an important one which he would surely attend but as far as she knew, he didn't have a horse running.

Reluctantly, she followed Ben to stand beside her daughter. "You didn't tell me where you were going, Annie," she said reprovingly. "I was worried."

"*Graybeard's Lady* is running in the third race," the child announced excitedly. "I wanted to wish her luck."

Caitlin gave the horse a quick, appraising glance. "I haven't seen her before. Is she new?"

Brian nodded. "She was an impulse buy. I bought her at Ballinasloe. Her sire is *Satan's Madboy.*" He glanced sideways at Caitlin. "I took a chance on her."

"You certainly did." She'd heard of *Satan's Madboy.* He was legendary for his temper and his inability to conform.

"This one runs like a dream, with speed and nerves of steel. I think she'll make it."

Reaching out, Caitlin stroked the shining neck. The horse suffered her touch without so much as a twitch. "She's lovely. I hope you won't be out much if she doesn't come through."

Grinning, Brian shook his head. "I bought her for a song."

Envy rose in Caitlin's chest. It wasn't fair. She so desperately needed a winning horse. *Irish Gold* had the finest pedigree a colt could hope for yet he wasn't fit to race while Brian, on a hunch and at a price he could well afford, had found a winner at the Ballinasloe sale.

Battling her uncharitable thoughts, she forced a smile. "Congratulations," she said lightly, "and good luck."

"Caitlin?" He hesitated.

"Yes."

Placing one hand on Annie's head, he reached into his pocket with the other and pulled out two coins. "Will you do me a favor, Annie love, and buy your brother and yourself a plate of chips while I finish up with your mother?"

Annie lifted her chin. "I suppose you have something to tell her that you don't want us to hear."

"Annie." Caitlin's cheeks were pink with embarrassment. "What will Brian think of your manners?"

"It's nothin' like that, lass," Brian reassured her. "Your welcome to stay if you like. I didn't want to bore you, that's all."

Annie sniffed. "Come on, Ben. The race is about to start. Let's see if we can find Daddy."

"I'm terribly sorry," Caitlin said, after the children were out of hearing. "Annie isn't usually rude."

Brian nodded. "I've been around her enough to know that's so."

"I can't seem to get through to her," Caitlin admitted.

"Sometimes it happens with mothers and daughters."

"You sound experienced."

"I've two sisters," he said simply. "Sometimes the tension in our house was so thick, the only safe place to be was the barn."

Caitlin relaxed. He wasn't going to bring up their last disastrous meeting after all. "It was that way in our house as well," she said, stroking the filly once again.

Two men walked into the barn, opened up the door of the stall on the far right, and stepped inside. Brian looked up, dismissed them, and turned back to the horse, his profile toward Caitlin.

"I should be getting back to the children," she said when they'd stood there several minutes and he hadn't resumed his thread of conversation. "Good luck with the filly."

"Caitlin." He reached out, his hand circling her arm.

At his touch, she froze. He dropped his hand quickly.

"I've a business proposition for you."

"Oh?"

"It may be a long time before *Irish Gold* is fit to race. How would you feel about buyin' *Graybeard's Lady?*"

Her mind raced with the possibility and quickly rejected it. "I couldn't possibly afford her."

"I'd sell her to you for what I paid."

"How much?"

"Fifteen hundred quid."

She was stunned. "You're joking."

His eyes were impossibly blue and steady on her face. "No."

"Why would you do such a thing?" she burst out, and then her face flamed. She had as much as asked for another declaration. "Never mind," she stammered. "I'm sorry. It's out of the question."

Caitlin couldn't read the expression in his eyes. His words were formal, impeccably correct. "While I can't blame myself for the condition of your colt, I am responsible for not allowin' *Kentucky Gold* to breed this season. I'd like to offer *Graybeard's Lady* as a replacement."

"You're handing her over at a pittance of what she's worth."

"Her worth hasn't been established. If you buy her now, before she wins, the sale will be perfectly legitimate."

"What if she wins?"

"Her price will be ten times what I paid for her. I'd give her to you, Caitlin. God knows I don't need the money. But if I do, there will be questions asked and I don't think you need that right now."

Caitlin chewed her lip and considered the dwindling balance of her bank account. Under normal circumstances, or if she were alone, she would be a fool to refuse such an offer. But the custody hearing was coming up and she had to consider appearances. The purchase of a race horse would be looked upon as an act of irresponsible negligence.

Regretfully, she shook her head. "I appreciate the offer, Brian. I mean that sincerely, but I can't."

"If it's a matter of money, I could loan it to you."

"That would only give Sam more ammunition against me. I can't risk it, not with the children involved."

"Are you sure that's the reason?" he asked casually.

She wouldn't insult him by pretending ignorance. "Yes."

He searched her face until she was sure he'd committed every feature to memory, and then he smiled. "I understand. Will you let me give you a tip?"

Relieved, she laughed. "Of course."

"Bet on number five in the first race."

The black was number five. "I already did."

He nodded. "Good girl. Tell Annie and Ben I'll expect them with me when the jockeys mount."

It was a tremendous honor, one they hadn't experienced since Kentucky. "Thank you, Brian," she said warmly. "They'll like that."

"They're grand children, Caitlin. You're doin' a fine job with them."

His consideration shamed her. She didn't deserve it, not after so firmly dismissing his feelings. Drawing a deep breath, she plunged into dangerous waters. "About the other night—"

He waited, neither helping nor impeding.

She continued. "If I seemed abrupt, I'm sorry."

Still he waited, eyes impersonal, lips turned up in a polite smile. If only he would say something. Her temper flared. "Perhaps I'm being presumptuous and you never gave it another thought."

Amusement, or something close to it, glinted in his eyes and then disappeared. "You're being absurd," he said simply.

Chastened, Caitlin found herself halfway to the stands

before she realized that she hadn't so much as noticed if her children were anywhere to be found. Squinting against the glare, she shaded her eyes and surveyed the stands, her gaze moving across the crowd, stopping briefly to linger on each small dark head before moving on.

Someone called her name. She turned toward the sound and saw Brigid waving at her. Changing direction, Caitlin met her mother at the fence.

"Where are the children?" Brigid asked.

"I was hoping you'd seen them. Brian sent them to buy chips."

Brigid looked around, randomly at first and then her eyes focused. She nudged Caitlin. "Isn't that Sam with Annie and Ben?"

Caitlin stiffened. "Where?"

"Near the startin' gate, with the man in the gray coat and the other one wearin' the odd hat."

Caitlin recognized the man called Fahey. He appeared to be deep in conversation with her husband. She watched Ben struggle against the stranglehold Annie had on his arm. Brushing aside Brigid's restraining hand she started across the green, anger lending her speed.

Her mother ran along beside her. "Don't make a scene, Caitlin. He's their father."

She fought back tears of rage. "A father who's so oblivious he doesn't even know they're alive. Look at him, Mum. He hasn't seen them in months."

"Whose fault is that?"

"Are you on my side or not?" Caitlin demanded angrily without losing her stride.

"Yours." Brigid increased her speed and stepped in front of Caitlin, forcing her to stop. "They won't thank you for it, love. It's best t' let this one go."

Pressing her fingers tightly against her eyelids, Caitlin

took a restoring breath. "He won't get them, Mum, not unless it's over my dead body, and not even then." She gripped her mother's arm. "Promise that if something happens to me, you won't let him have them."

"Nothin's goin' t' happen t' you."

"Promise me."

Brigid rubbed her arm. "You've given me a bruise."

"Promise me, Mum."

"There isn't anythin' I wouldn't do for you and the children. You should know that."

Some of the tension left Caitlin's body. She stepped around her mother. "You don't have to come with me."

Brigid fell into step beside her. "I've come this far."

"I'm not going to make a scene, Mum," Caitlin said, exasperated. "I'll simply remind them that unless we hurry we'll miss the first race."

"You promised me lunch," Brigid reminded her.

Ben noticed them first. "Mum," he shouted, breaking free of Annie's hand and hurling himself into Caitlin's arms. "I'm hungry but Annie says we need to stay."

"Does she?" said his mother, keeping her voice light. "Annie, I've a place on the grass and a lunch basket. Daddy can come for you when he's finished."

Sam broke off his conversation and lashed out at her. "For God's sake, Caitlin. It's about time. I'm in the middle of something here. Can't you control them?"

Annie's face whitened with hurt.

Caitlin felt her nails break through the skin of her palms. "It looks like everything is already under control, thanks to Annie." She turned her back on her husband and smiled at her daughter. "Come along, love. It's time for the race to begin."

Reluctantly, Annie fell into step beside her mother. "But Daddy said we could watch it with him."

Caitlin's pace picked up so that the others had to jog to keep up with her. "Obviously Daddy had other priorities."

"Caitlin," Brigid warned under her breath.

Sighing, Caitlin stopped, rested her hands on her daughter's shoulders and concentrated on keeping her words impartial. "Annie, today is a work day for your father."

"What kind of work?"

"He's in the thoroughbred business. You know that. This is a big race. People he needs to see are here. I'm sorry that he doesn't have as much time for you as you'd like, but he has promised to take you out next Saturday." She smiled bracingly. "You'll have to be patient, love. Do you understand?"

Annie sniffed. "I'm not a baby."

"I know you're not—" Caitlin was interrupted by the announcer's voice. The horses were at the gate. Grabbing her children's hands, she ran toward the fence for a better view just in time for the break.

The track was flat, treeless. Every stumble, every gain, every flick of a jockey's whip could be seen by the bystanders. Moving at incredible speeds, the jockeys stood in the saddles, hunched over, their silks streaks of color bleeding against the gray sky.

From the beginning the black was in the lead. Caitlin watched as she moved gracefully, efficiently over the soggy turf, her head stretched, legs reaching out in a glorious, ground-eating stride. Effortlessly she made the turns, increasing her lead by two leagues and then by three as if the sheer joy of being in front was what she lived for. Caitlin held her breath as the riders disappeared behind the stands and came out again. The black was still ahead, crossing the finish line a full four leagues in front of the bay and five in front of the gray.

Caitlin stared at her racing card. "I've won," she said

unsteadily. "The black to win, the bay to place, and the gray to show. I've won." She stared at Brigid. "You did place the bets."

Brigid held out the ticket. "I did and I added a bit for myself as well. Will you bet on the next one?"

Caitlin shook her head. "John always told me if I was lucky enough to double my winnings on the first race, I shouldn't throw it all away by hoping for the same luck on the others."

"John O'Shea always was a wise man," Brigid observed.

"Besides," said Caitlin practically, "I haven't the money to lose." She smiled at her children. "I spread a blanket on the green. Who's hungry?"

"I am," Ben shouted, his voice drowning out Annie's more subdued one.

Brigid's thick woolen blanket kept out the chill of grass still wet with morning dew. Caitlin passed out napkins, poured stew from the thermos into paper cups and handed out slices of what looked like a cold cheese pie.

"What's this?" Brigid asked, biting into it tentatively.

"Tomato-cheese frittata," her daughter answered absently. She was busy wiping Ben's mouth after he'd found his first ambitious mouthful of stew to be too hot.

"It's delicious," Brigid pronounced. "Who would have thought cold cheese and tomatoes would do the trick on a day like this?"

Caitlin laughed. "It's easier to manage than sandwiches, and just as healthy. How's the stew, Annie?"

Annie tilted her head, considering her answer. "Too many green things," she said, "but still good enough to eat."

"Thank you." Caitlin's eyes twinkled. "The green things are fresh parsley, a rare find this time of year."

"Lord, Caitlin," Brigid marveled after tasting several bites of stew. "You're amazin'. This is wonderful."

Ben smiled engagingly and once again Caitlin wiped his mouth clean.

"How would you like a cookie?" she asked. "They're Annie's favorite."

"Mine, too," said Ben.

"You like everything," Annie scoffed. "It wouldn't matter what Mama cooked."

"How accommodatin' of you, love." Brigid nodded approvingly at her grandson. "I wish your mother had been so easy t' please."

Annie perked up. "Was Mama a picky eater?"

"Aye." Brigid nodded. "The worst kind."

"Tell us, tell us," pleaded Ben.

Caitlin stood and brushed off her calf-length skirt. "I've heard this story before. I think I'll collect my winnings while you destroy my character." She smiled. "The next race should start soon. Pay attention. Brian's filly is running in the third."

With her mother's promise that they would be at their places near the fence, Caitlin set out for the betting windows. Men and women were already queued up in anticipation of the next race. She took her place, keeping an eye out for other windows that might open.

A hat caught her eye. She turned to see Sam's friend, the many called Fahey, talking to a thin, narrow-faced boy she recognized as one of the exercisers at the Curragh Stud Farm. They were deep in conversation. The older man's thick hand gripped the exerciser's shoulder. Casually, oblivious to the milling crowd around them, he slipped an envelope into the boy's jacket pocket.

For some reason the encounter struck her as odd. Caitlin knew that transactions were commonly handled at races the size of Punchestown. But something bothered her about this one. Brian and her husband had an adversarial relationship.

Money was not an issue for the Curragh Stud nor was it one for its manager. What could Sam and his henchman, Fahey, want with Brian's exercise boy?

Smiling at the man in the window, Caitlin watched as he counted out her cash. It wasn't unusual to win fifteen hundred pounds at the races, but for a small fifty pound bet, it was a windfall. Pocketing the money, she walked toward the fence where her mother and children waited. Her thoughts were elsewhere. Fifteen hundred pounds, once a meager fifty, burned a hole in her pocket.

Minutes ticked by. Horses in the second race leaped from the starting gate. She paid no attention. Her pace slowed. A certain bay-colored filly weighed heavily on her mind. Fifteen hundred pounds. The offer of a lifetime. Too tempting to refuse.

Caitlin turned and began to run toward the mounting yard. Her boots, heavy and stiff with mud, were awkward and slow. The barns loomed before her, stall doors opened. Horses were led around the block before being saddled and walked out to the yard where jockeys would be wished luck before mounting. She had to find Brian. Her eyes scanned the crowd once and then once more. Where was he? Where was *Graybeard's Lady*? Once the horses were out of the starting gate, it would be too late.

The door to the jockey room opened and he stepped out. Caitlin breathed a sigh of relief. She walked toward him, saw him frown and look around as if something wasn't quite right. Then his gaze settled on her. He straightened, smiled, and waited.

She ran the last few steps and clutched his arm. "I've changed my mind," she said, breathlessly.

His eyes warmed and the grooves that lined his cheeks deepened with his smile. His hand found hers and covered it.

"I've fifteen hundred quid and I want to buy your horse."

His smile faded. "I see."

"She's still for sale, isn't she? You haven't changed your mind?"

He shook his head. "I haven't changed my mind. She's yours if you want her."

Caitlin reached into her pocket and handed him the money. "I want her. Is it a deal?"

Brian held out his hand. "It is," he said formally. "Congratulations and good luck with her."

21

Caitlin Claiborne was the kind of woman a man came back to, a woman with a streak of wildness running through her, a woman of hidden depths and great reserves. She'd come into his life when he least expected it, bringing to him a sharp-edged, clear, finely-honed awareness—the kind that forced a man with any character at all to stand up, take a good look at himself, and ask the painful, pointed questions he'd always managed to avoid.

Checking the last of the feed buckets, he locked down the stall of his newest acquisition, a stallion from a wealthy breeder, a Kuwaiti prince who took a personal interest in his horses. Then he checked on *Graybeard's Lady*. She was resting easily, her demeanor as calm as if she hadn't been sired by the infamous *Satan's Madboy*. He wasn't at all surprised that she'd won her maiden race nor did he regret practically gifting her to Caitlin. Stabling three horses at the stud was quite an expense for a woman on a limited budget, even when she assumed all responsibility for their care.

Brian held no hope of *Irish Gold*'s winning a race or of ever being allowed to run in one. Surgery was a bandaid at best. Horses with RLN disease didn't have the stamina for racing. The colt had been blood-typed yesterday, his paper work and samples sent to Weatherbys a good three weeks earlier than was customary. Brian wanted the results back and documented before Sam Claiborne knew the applications had been sent out.

Davy popped his head around the corner of an empty stall. "Will you be needin' anything else, Brian?"

"Not tonight. Go home, Davy. I'll finish up."

Without bothering to turn on the lights, Brian closed up the tack room and checked each stall to be sure it was securely locked. He'd grown up with the soft glow of gaslight and the deep purple shadows thrown by its gentle illumination. The glaring, offensive white of electricity was fine for a veterinary clinic or a foaling unit but it had no place in a stable at dusk.

Behind him, he heard the barn door creak. Instinctively he stiffened, waiting for the caller to declare himself. Nothing happened. Tension roiled in the pit of his stomach. His hand closed around the handle of a pitchfork.

"Brian," a soft voice called out. "Brian, are you in here?"

Relief swept through him. His suspicions about Caitlin's colt were making his imagination run wild. Replacing the pitchfork, he straightened and looked over the top of the stall. "I'm here, Annie."

"Is something wrong with the lights?" Her voice quavered.

Brian flicked the switch and light flooded the barn. He blinked against the brightness and waited for his eyes to adjust. "I'm sorry, lass. I didn't know you planned to visit. Darkness doesn't affect me as much as most."

Annie came all the way into the barn, pulling the door shut behind her. "Why not?" she asked when she reached his side.

Brian lifted her to the top of several stacked bales of hay and took the stool across from her. "Where I was born there was no electricity until I was older than you. I grew up accustomed to a different kind of light."

"What was it like?"

He thought a minute. "Golden, instead of white, warmer and dim, like candlelight."

Annie nodded. "It's like that at Gran's when she lights the fire just before dark."

"There you have it, exactly the same." He waited for her to explain her reason for seeking him out when it was late enough that she should have been at home.

"I came to see *Irish Gold.*"

"You'll have to do better than that, Annie. You're in the wrong barn."

"I wanted to ask you a question first," she said hurriedly.

"What's on your mind?"

"You know my mother better than anyone here."

He swallowed and cleared his throat. "Do I?"

Annie chewed on her bottom lip, a gesture so similar to her mother's that Brian winced. "You don't know her as well as Gran does, but she doesn't count."

"Why not?"

Annie shook her head impatiently. "None of us count, not Gran or Ben or me. We knew her before."

"Ah, I see." And suddenly he did.

"Do you think she's happy?"

Christ, what next? He knew nothing of children. Why was he chosen to be this particular child's confidante? "Sometimes, Annie," he improvised. "She's happy sometimes, like most of us."

"Do you think she's as happy as anyone is happy?" the child persisted.

Brian frowned. "What's this about, lass?"

"Gran says Mama wasn't happy living in Kentucky and that she's happier here."

"What do you think?"

Annie shrugged. "I don't know. I can't remember the way she was. I never really thought about it." She looked at him. "That's why I'm asking you."

Recognizing that the child needed comforting and that words alone wouldn't do it, he stood and lifted Annie from her perch. Then he pulled down the bales until they were level with each other and sat, pulling her down beside him, keeping hold of her hand. "I didn't know your mother when she lived in Kentucky, lass. But I know this. She's got a lot on her mind. I'm goin' to tell you somethin' and it's up to you whether you share it with your mother or not. *Irish Gold* is sick. He's goin' to have an operation but he may never race. Your mother is very worried about that. She's also in the middle of a divorce. That isn't easy on anyone but it's especially hard on her. She's got quite a bit on her plate but it won't last forever. Do you know what it is I'm tellin' you, Annie?"

"I think so."

He reached for her other hand and faced her. "Don't look so serious, love, and tell me what you think I just said."

Annie concentrated. "Mama is worried over a lot of things but it's not as bad as it seems."

"Good girl," Brian said approvingly. "She won't be worried when things are settled."

"How long will that be?"

He considered the matter. Three months was forever for a child. He decided on the truth. "I can't say exactly, but you can help."

"How?"

"By talkin' to her when you're troubled. Talkin' is the only way out of worries."

"Is Mama worried about me?"

"It appears so."

Annie gnawed on her thumbnail. "Why?"

"She told me you were homesick, so homesick that you weren't sleepin' well or makin' friends at school."

Annie looked skeptical. "Why is Mama worried about that?"

Brian laughed. "All mothers worry when their children aren't happy. That's their greatest worry of all. Nothin' else is right for a mother if a child is unhappy."

"What about fathers?"

"What about them?" Brian hedged.

Annie kicked her feet against the bale of hay. "Do they feel the same as mothers when their children are unhappy?"

He was in over his head. What did he, a childless bachelor, know of mothers and fathers? His own, inhibited isolationists who'd lived out their lives on an island with eight hundred inhabitants, were hardly standards by which to gauge the rest of the world.

Annie's hand rested easily in his own. She looked up through her lashes and his heart contracted. This Claiborne had nothing at all of her father. She was Caitlin's clone, skin as pure and fair as carved ivory, wide dark eyes, the centers bright with emotion, thick lashes, curly hair, fine delicate features, and that bow of an upper lip that in her mother made his knees weak. Seeing it on Annie had an altogether different effect on him. He wanted to protect her, to take the hurt away. She needed the right words from him and she needed them now.

Brian drew a deep breath. "Fathers are different, Annie. They have a different kind of love for their children than a mother does."

"How is it different?"

If he ever needed the gift of a silver tongue, he needed it now. "A mother's life is her home, her children," he began, "while a father thinks more of his job and makin' a livin' for his family. He doesn't worry about the same things your mother does."

Her head was against his shoulder. She appeared deep in thought. Encouraged, he continued. "When you lived in Kentucky, who spent more time with you, your mum or your da?"

"Mama did."

Brian nodded, satisfied. "That's the natural way of things, Annie. Your mum takes care of you when you need her. She feels sad when you do."

Annie was deep in thought.

"You know what I think, Annie?"

She leaned against his shoulder and looked up at him with her mother's eyes. "What?"

"I don't think you dislike it here as much as you say you do. If that's so, it would do your mum a great deal of good to hear it."

Annie stared at him with wide, unblinking eyes. He held his breath wondering if he'd done any of it right at all.

When she smiled and he could breathe again he thought his lungs would burst.

"I'll be going home now, Brian. But first I want to see *Irish Gold*."

"Run along then. You know where he is. If you can wait for a bit until I finish closing up, I'll get my coat and a blanket for you and then I'll drive you home. Your mum is probably wondering where you could be now that it's already dark."

Annie stood up and stretched. "I'll wait for you in the colt's stall."

"I won't be long. Holler if you can't find the light

switch." Brian watched until she disappeared inside the yearling barn and light flooded the open door. Picking up his clipboard, he took a quick inventory of the supplies Davy had ordered. Linseed oil and penicillin were low. He checked both boxes and moved down to the feed section. Alfalfa and oats were higher than he'd ever seen before and it wasn't even the dead of winter. Frowning, he put a question mark in the margin, hung the board on its nail, picked up his coat, and made his way to the yearling barn where he found Annie asleep in the hay outside the colt's stall. He looked down for a minute at her dark head. Her arm was curled, pillow-like, under her cheek. Brian wondered, not for the first time, how Sam Claiborne could be such a fool to let all that was important get away from him.

The child looked dead to the world. Deciding against waking her until he brought the car around, he left the door open and jogged back to his own driveway. Even at a steady clip, it was a good five minutes before he reached his front door and another five to call Caitlin, reassure her that Annie was safe and that he would bring her around shortly. By the time he found his keys, turned on the ignition and drove back to the barn, fifteen minutes had passed.

He didn't notice the smell until he drove to the top of the rise. At first the orange glow surrounding the barn didn't register but when he saw flames leaping over the roof, his heart stopped and for a single agonizing moment he was sure that nothing on earth would jumpstart it again, that he was permanently paralyzed and doomed to watch as fire spread up the walls and across the roof, beam by beam, until there was nothing left of the barn where ten-year-old Annie Claiborne lay asleep in the hay.

With a painful, lurching thump that threatened his chest cavity, Brian felt his heart resume its beating. With the rush of fresh blood came a surge of adrenalin that activated his instincts, propelling him into action. In seconds the truck was down the knoll to within twenty feet of the burning barn. Willing himself to remain calm, he flung open the door and, exercising every ounce of his discipline, turned away from the flames and raced toward the stallion barn and the telephone.

Sirens broke the peaceful stillness of the night even before he hung up. Offering a silent thank you, he threw two blankets into the sink and turned on the water. Endless seconds passed. When the blankets were saturated, Brian ran to the yearling barn, dragging them behind him. Dropping one of the blankets, he wrapped the other around him and pushed against the door. It was locked. Why in bloody hell was the door locked? "Annie," he called out, "are you hurt?"

There was no answer. Flames danced and crackled, consuming the old wood, plank by plank. Smoke curled up from the floorboards. Brian hurled himself against the door. "Annie," he shouted, his voice raw with desperation, "answer me. Damn you, Annie, say somethin'."

Heat blistered his hands and forehead. Clearing his mind, he thought. The barn doors were solid, built for purposes of security. He couldn't possibly knock them down himself. There was only one other way. Picking up the remaining blanket, Brian ran for the truck. The keys were in the ignition. The engine turned over immediately. Aiming straight for the side of the barn that had already been weakened by fire, Brian buckled himself in, pressed down on the gas, and drove straight through.

The impact shattered the windshield and nearly tore the steering wheel from his hands. But he was through. Flames surrounded him on all sides. Behind him he heard noises, men shouting, the shriek of a siren, a strange roaring. Reversing the truck he backed out leaving a six foot hole in the barn, plenty of room to go in after Annie and bring her out. Wrapping himself in a wet blanket, he gingerly tried the door handle. The metal was branding-iron hot. Keeping his hand beneath the wet wool, he forced it down and kicked the door open.

"Brian," a voice shouted from a distance. "Come away from there. We're bringing on the hoses."

Without responding, Brian pulled the blanket up over his head and ran into the barn. Smoke filled his nostrils and burned his eyes. Visibility was zero. Dropping to the ground, he crawled forward using his forearms. Horses screamed and the pungent smell of singed hair turned his stomach. Where was Annie? How far had he come? Desperately he moved faster. Surely he was almost there. If there truly was a God, he should be there. His arm landed on a soft mass. Afraid to hope, he reached out and felt human skin, hair and clothes. Annie. Water poured from his eyes, salt and soot mixing, running down his cheeks. He moved on pure instinct. Gathering the child against his chest, he tightened the sodden blanket around them both and stood. Turning back from where he had come, he took a chance and ran for the opening.

Immediately the air cleared. Every breath seared his throat but he could actually breathe again. A firetruck stood in the courtyard and men in yellow slickers operated high pressure hoses that even now had the terrifying flames under control.

Brian pressed his ear against Annie's chest. Her heartbeat was strong. She was unconscious but she didn't appear burned.

Yellow-clad arms took the child from him and placed her in the ambulance that had suddenly materialized beside the fire truck. "Smoke inhalation knocked her out," pronounced Keith Murphy, the fire department captain. He watched the ambulance circle the courtyard and drive away. "She'll need to be looked at in Naas. You could use a going over yourself."

"The horses," Brian managed out of stiff lips.

"We got them out, all except one. I'm sorry, lad."

"Which one?" asked Brian, although he was sure of the answer.

"The Claiborne yearling. It looks like he was gone before we even got here."

"Do you have any idea how it started?"

"We'll do a complete investigation. The smoke was thick and oily. I'd say gasoline but that remains to be seen."

"Arson?"

"Aye."

Brian ran a filthy hand through **his** hair. "Can you keep that quiet for a bit?"

"Have you got a lead?"

"I do."

"I'll do the snooping myself," said Murphy, "although we've got more than a few experienced men on board. They'll know it was gasoline."

"Do the best you can. I'll need a week."

Murphy clapped him on the back. "You've got it. Let's get you to a doctor just as soon as I break the news to Caitlin that her daughter is in the hospital. I'll let you tell her about her colt."

22

(faint text visible through page from reverse side)

"Answer the phone, will you, Caitlin?" Brigid called from the kitchen as she ladled healthy servings of soup into bowls. Minestrone, Caitlin had called it. It looked and smelled like vegetable although it did have some strange looking beans and noodles floating among the greens. By now Brigid was willing to take Caitlin's word for it. The girl had a gift. The soup would be delicious.

"Sit down, Ben." Brigid tucked a napkin into the front of her grandson's shirt. "Eat while it's hot. I'll save some for your sister. No, love, use this one." She picked up the smaller of the spoons and exchanged it for the one Ben had chosen. "The other is too hard for you to manage."

"Grandma Lucy says the big spoons are for soup."

Brigid looked down into her grandson's twinkling brown eyes. Sometimes it was difficult to remember that he was six years old. "I'll be sure t' tell her you know that. However, I'd like some of it t' find its way into your mouth and not down the front of your shirt."

Ben's cherubic smile split his face in two. "Are you having some?"

"In a minute, love. Let me just check on your mother."

Brigid pulled her jumper over her chest against the draft and stepped into the long hallway. Caitlin stood at the door. She had wrapped a muffler around her neck and was pulling on her coat. The white cast of her face signalled alarm bells in Brigid's brain. "Where on earth are you goin'?" she asked. "Dinner is on the table."

"There was a fire at the Curragh," Caitlin said woodenly. "Annie's in the hospital."

"Dear God." Brigid's hand flew to her lips. "Is she badly hurt?"

"She's alive, thanks to Brian. Keith Murphy is waiting for me in Naas."

"I'll find someone to stay with Ben and follow you."

Caitlin's face crumpled. "Oh, God, Mum. What have I done? She never wanted to come here. I should never have brought her here."

Brigid crossed the floor and folded her daughter in her arms. "Hush, love," she crooned, holding the dark head against her shoulder, marveling at the unfamiliar feel of it, wishing she'd felt comfortable enough to do it long before. "You mustn't blame yourself. It isn't your fault. It must have been an accident."

Caitlin pulled away, scrubbing at her eyes. "I've got to go. Annie needs me. I want to be there when she wakes up."

Brigid walked her to the door. "I'll follow you as soon as I find someone to care for Ben." She watched Caitlin back the car into the road and winced as she rounded the corner too quickly and nearly clipped the right fender in her haste to be on her way. Praying that her daughter would arrive in one piece, Brigid returned to the kitchen. Ben was nearly done with his soup.

"Where's Mum?"

She sat down across from him. "There was a fire at the Curragh. Annie's been hurt. Your mum is goin' t' see her at the hospital. I've got t' get Mrs. Finch t' look after you so I can help your mother and Annie for a bit."

"What happened to Annie?"

"Come here, love." Brigid held out her arms to him. Ben slipped out of his chair and climbed into her lap. "We don't know yet. That's why I have t' go and find out."

"Will you come back and tell me?"

"Of course. Go t' bed for Mrs. Finch tonight and I'll be back here in the mornin'." She hugged him. "Not t' worry. We'll sort it all out."

Annie lay curled up on her side in the hospital bed with one hand under her cheek. Caitlin pulled the blanket up over her shoulders and smoothed out the wrinkles. She bit her lip. Annie looked so peaceful, ethereal almost, like an angel.

Her eyelids fluttered and opened. Her eyes met Caitlin's. She smiled. "Mama?" she whispered.

Caitlin leaned forward. She breathed in the sweet, warm breath that was her daughter's. A lump formed in her throat. "Yes, love. I'm here."

"Sleep with me, Mama."

Careful not to disturb the IV, Caitlin climbed over the guardrail, nestled in beside Annie's slight body, and wrapped her arms around her daughter.

"My throat hurts."

"I know." Relief swept over Caitlin. "Oh, Annie. I'm so glad you're all right. You scared me to death."

"I'm sorry, Mama." The child's voice grated like sandpaper.

Caitlin soothed her. "None of this is your fault. Go to sleep now. I'll stay here with you."

"I need to tell you something, Mama. Brian told me to tell you."

"What is it, love?"

"It's not so bad here anymore. It's different and I like my school in Kentucky better, but I don't hate it like I did in the beginning."

"Do you mean that, Annie?"

"Yes. Brian told me to tell you."

"Did he?" Caitlin felt a surge of warmth flood her chest. "Daddy's expecting you and Ben back in Kentucky for Christmas. You haven't changed your mind about that have you?"

Annie shook her head. "No. But, I'll miss you."

Tears choked Caitlin's throat. "I'll miss you, too, but I can stand it if I know you'll be back."

The child turned to her, fit her body against her mother's, and buried her face in Caitlin's shoulder. The steady beating of the small heart, the charred smell of her hair, the trusting fingers curled around her mother's hand—all that she had nearly lost terrified Caitlin. Pressing her lips against her daughter's forehead, she whispered tenderly. "I can't live without you, Annie. Nothing is worth that."

Annie smiled and closed her eyes. Caitlin looked at the small face with its promise of beauty, at the thin eyelids delicately etched with a faint smudging of blue veins, at the small vulnerable mouth and obstinate chin. Annie, lovely, difficult, misunderstood Annie. Her heart broke. She began to weep, silently, shoulders shaking, tears coursing down her cheeks.

John O'Shea was not much for conversation but he could be counted on in any emergency. Brigid didn't hesitate to call when she needed him for a ride. He came immediately, without asking a single question. She told him what she knew of Annie's condition.

He clucked sympathetically. "Poor little lass," he said when she'd finished. "Call me when you're ready to come home."

"Thanks so much for everythin'."

"Don't mention it. I hope everything goes well for the child."

She waved him off and hurried into the hospital lobby. Caitlin was at the desk talking to a man with a white coat and a face that looked much too young to be trusted with the care of her granddaughter. At least Caitlin didn't look as if her world had fallen apart. Brigid breathed a sigh of relief. Annie's injuries couldn't be too serious.

Caitlin introduced her. "Dr. Moore, this is my mother, Mrs. Keneally."

Brigid nodded. Close up he looked even more like a teenager. "How is Annie?" she asked.

"I've just gone over her condition with your daughter," said Dr. Moore. "She'll explain it to you. If either of you have questions, please ask. I'll be here for the night."

Brigid sniffed. "He's a bit young, isn't he?" she asked after he'd left them.

"He seems all right." Caitlin's mouth quivered. "Annie is going to be fine, Mum. She's asleep now. They've given her enough to sedate her for the night. She has a sore throat from the smoke but that's all. We're very lucky. You can look in on her if you want but they told me to go home for the night. I'm going to stop by the Curragh and see Brian. He's been hurt and he's not picking up the phone. I won't be long."

"Don't worry about me. John will pick me up. Be careful," her mother said automatically, her mind already in the hospital room with her granddaughter. "The roads are wet."

Caitlin's soft kiss startled her. Brigid touched her cheek in disbelief and watched the daughter who was least like her walk down the hall to the exit. How long had it been since Caitlin had kissed her? Twenty years? Twenty-five?

Brigid smoothed the covers over the sleeping child. Deep in her own thoughts, she never heard the door open or the harsh intake of breath behind her. The first indication that someone else was in the room was a firm hand on her shoulder. When she heard the voice that went with it, she stiffened.

"I heard what happened and came right over," said Father Michael Duran.

Quickly, she pulled two tissues from the pack beside Annie's bed and held them to her nose. "Annie's not dyin', Father. There was no need for you t' trouble yourself."

"Martin told me what happened. He met Brian Hennessey on the way to the doctor." He looked down on the sleeping child. "Is there anything I can do?"

"No, thank you."

His hand fell from her shoulder. "For God's sake, Brigid. You're a hard woman. Let me do somethin'."

Brigid turned on him, her eyes throwing blue sparks. The old Michael Duran, the one who refused her when she needed him most was back. Like a vulture with black wings he stood there, eyes remote, cheeks carven, waiting for the worst that could happen. "We don't need your help, Father, not this time."

"Martin told me about the fire. I've grown close to Annie since she's come to Saint Patrick's."

"Annie's a lovely child."

Shaking his head, he smiled painfully. "You always did have your share of pride, Brigid. You were wasted in Kilcullen."

She stood silently, her posture stiff and straight, her arms folded, the look on her face that told him he wasn't welcome.

He moved to the other side of Annie's bed and looked down on the sleeping child. Reaching out he touched the dark curls spread across the pillow, twisting a single strand around his finger. Then, ever-so-gently, he rubbed the back of his hand across the small cheek. "She's like you," he said, under his breath. "Not the coloring but the bone structure."

Brigid was having none of it. "Have you eyes in your head, Father? Annie is the image of Caitlin."

He nodded. "Caitlin is also like you."

It was true. Not many saw it because of the differences in eyes and hair but from the moment Caitlin's features began to take shape, her lineage had been impossible to deny. Brigid had forgotten that or perhaps she'd chosen to ignore it over the years. Caitlin with her love for language, her tenacity, the quick intelligence that had lifted her above her classmates, her rejection of the boring, the mundane, the unnecessary, and backward portions of her lessons at Saint Patrick's, shared many of the same qualities as both her mother and daughter. How ironic that Michael Duran, of all people, had noticed.

"I haven't been a good priest for you have I, Brigid?"

She stared at him in amazement. Regret, she could have told him, was part imagination, a net woven during long dark lonely evenings, as much a part of her life as his. "Don't be so hard on yourself," she said instead. "It wasn't a priest I needed, but you've helped a few."

"Name one."

"Martin," she said promptly. "You've been a help to Martin O'Shea. You gave him peace when he sorely needed it. It's because of you that he's a priest."

He laughed. "You always did manage to have the last word, Brigid. It's one of the qualities I admire in you."

"Why are you really here, Michael? I need to know."

Bending his head he told her, forming words she'd wanted to hear thirty years before, words that no longer mattered.

23

Caitlin stood on the porch, her face pale, her hands trembling. "May I come in?"

Wordlessly, Brian stepped aside and closed the door behind her. Neeve lifted her head briefly before settling into her original position.

Caitlin kept her back to him and clenched her fists to stop the shaking of her hands.

"How is Annie?" he asked.

"She'll be all right." Her voice cracked on the last word.

"I'm makin' tea," he said to the back of her head. "Would you care for a cup?"

She still wouldn't look at him. "Do you have anything stronger?"

"Will whiskey do?"

She turned and something in her face must have shocked him.

"Are *you* all right?"

She nodded. "Are you?"

He held up a bandaged hand. "Nothin' serious, accordin' to the doctor. Sit down. I'll be right back."

He returned with two glasses filled with a liberal amount of amber liquid. She was seated on the couch, her face warmed by the heat of the hearth fire. Friendly light it was, copper colored, slightly aromatic, safely contained. He sat down beside her.

She took the glass from his hand and swallowed more than she should have.

"Easy now," he warned her. "There's no hurry."

"I can't—" She stopped.

He waited.

She stared into the fire, not looking at him. "I wanted to tell you—" Again she was unable to continue.

He set down his drink and took her hand in his. It was ice-cold against his warmth and she was still trembling. Carefully, he drew her into his arms.

She buried her face against his shoulder and sobbed. From deep within her the sound came up—the guttural, wrenching, primitive cry of a woman uncomfortable with tears. She felt his hands move up her arms, tenderly, soothingly. Cradling the back of her head in his hand, he pulled her tightly against him and pressed his lips against her temple. He muttered words in Gaelic, words she'd forgotten and would have no memory of beyond this moment. Over and over he stroked and soothed and kissed and spoke, and all the while she sobbed and shook in his arms.

When there was nothing left, when the tears had battered her face so that her eyes disappeared and no one outside of her own mother would recognize her, she relaxed.

Somehow he knew what she needed, a reaffirmation of life—Annie's, his, her own. He must have felt the change in her at the exact moment it happened. She felt his hands, no longer soothing, slide beneath her jumper to caress the bare skin of her back. His lips moved from her temple to the hollow of her cheek, the line of her throat, the curve of her mouth. Circling his neck with her arms, Caitlin pulled him down on top of her and parted her lips.

She was a woman who'd gone too long without and it all came together quickly. For Caitlin it was as if she'd never known the intimacy of a man's tongue in her mouth, never felt her bare breasts filling his hands, his leg urging hers apart, his fingers sliding down her belly, moving against her, inside her. His words, urgent, whispered, encouraging. For the first time she understood the building intensity, the ache of rising heat.

Meeting his mouth eagerly, she arched her back and held his head to her breasts, to the dip of her waist, the inside of her thigh and when it was time, she took the hard length of his swollen flesh in her hand, guiding him in until her body closed around him, every nerve heightened, exposed, waiting for his thrust and that first delicious rush of pleasure that would begin it all.

She loved the way he slept—effortlessly, thoroughly, without motion or sound. She loved the texture of his hair, the black shine of it, the way it fell across his forehead and grew down unevenly to the base of his skull where his spinal cord began. She loved the feel of his ribs and the play of hard muscle beneath his skin when he moved his arms. She loved the way he smelled of linseed oil and hay, leather and horse. She loved his voice, kind with rough edges, amusement lifting the ends of his sentences in a lovely Irish lilt. She loved the rise and fall of his smooth chest, the lean spareness of his shoulder blades, the clean line of his nose, the firm, no-nonsense cut of his lip. In fact, decided Caitlin, she could not have designed a man to be any more appealing than Brian Hennessey was to her at this moment.

He'd fallen asleep on top of her. Shifting carefully so as not to disturb him, she maneuvered his weight so that she could breathe comfortably. He muttered something inaudible and moved his hand to cup the underside of her breast, but didn't wake.

She saw the back of his hand and winced. It was badly blistered, burned because of Annie. If it hadn't been for Brian, Annie would be— She couldn't face it, not yet. That was why she'd come. After Annie had been sedated and fallen asleep in her hospital bed, Caitlin had come to see Brian, to reassure herself that he was alive and well, to tell him just how much what he'd done meant to her.

Those had been her intentions, nothing more, despite what had passed between them that night on the Naas Road. But when he opened the door and she saw the bandages on his hands, the raw scrape across the plane of his cheek and the weariness in his eyes, she lost what was left of her control. She hadn't planned to seduce him. She would never have done such a thing. He was particularly vulnerable just now. Perhaps she should have been the strong one, the one to step away. It would have been the fair thing, the right thing to do. But she desperately needed comfort and she'd waited such a long time for a man, this man, to want her.

"Admit it, Caitlin," she said under her breath, "he's not like anyone else." Not that admitting it changed anything. She was in the middle of a bitterly contested divorce that could drag on indefinitely. She could be forced to change her domicile from Ireland to Kentucky at the whim of a judge and she was nearly out of money—not an appealing package for a man who had choices. What they'd done was rash, foolish even, because neither of them was a casual kind of person. Sex meant more, a great deal more, than a relieving of tension. But she wouldn't take it back, not now, not for anything.

Brian lifted his head, bracing himself on his hands and looked down at her. "Regrettin' me already?" he chided, softly mimicking her own words.

"Not for the reasons you think."

"For what then?"

She hesitated.

"Tell me, Caitlin."

"I'm afraid to start something that may not play out."

He traced her jaw with his finger. "Doesn't everyone begin that way?"

She frowned. "Not in the same sense."

"Meaning?"

Suddenly self-conscious, she turned her head to the side. "I'm still married and it looks like it may be some time before I'm divorced."

"I can wait."

"If the judge finds in Sam's favor at the custody hearing, I could be forced to return to Kentucky."

"No one can force you to do anythin'."

"I can't lose my children."

"Of course not." The amusement was back in his voice again. "Is there anythin' else?"

Her voice lowered to a whisper. "I'm not in the best position financially."

Brian chuckled low in his throat, winced and swallowed painfully, lingering effects of the fire. After a minute he spoke. "I rather like havin' you dependent on me."

"You know what I mean."

"I do."

"Doesn't it matter to you?"

He kissed her nose, then both eyelids, and finally her lips. "Things have a way of workin' out."

She sighed and closed her eyes, only too willing to give up her objections and revel in the feel of his mouth moving across her skin. Much later, when he'd found an afghan and wrapped it around the two of them, she whispered into his ear, "Thank you, Brian, for Annie. I can't tell you how grateful I am. There are no words for what you've given me."

His eyes were bright. "You're very welcome," he replied gently. "I'm happy that it all worked out."

"Gratitude isn't the reason I'm here with you, like this."

"No?"

"No."

Laughter deepened the lines around his eyes. "It's settled then."

Relieved, she rested her cheek against his chest. Somehow he understood and it was enough.

Succumbing to the combined effect of alcohol, darkness, and warmth, Caitlin's eyelids drooped. She was nearly asleep when Brian's words jarred her awake.

"There was a casualty of the fire, Caitlin."

Her eyes flew open. "What do you mean?"

His arms tightened around her. "*Irish Gold* died in the flames. I'm sorry."

Her lip trembled. Tears welled up in her eyes and spilled over. She wiped them away. "Poor little thing. He never had a chance. You never told me how the fire started."

Brian shook his head. "We don't know yet. There will be an investigation."

"Were any other horses injured?"

"No."

Something was wrong but she couldn't put her finger on it. Her brain was too muddled with drowsiness and drink and the afterglow of sex to think clearly. "I should be getting home. I said I wouldn't be long."

"I'll know more after the fire chief looks into things."

"What things?"

He kissed her shoulder. "The cause of the fire."

Caitlin sat up and pulled the blanket around her shoulders. He was too close and she was too vulnerable. This conversation required space between them. "You would tell me if there was anything else, wouldn't you, Brian?"

She could see the indecision in his face and pressed her advantage. "Because if you didn't and we weren't careful and something happened—"

His hands slid up and down her arms. "You're a clever lass," he said, his mouth against her neck. "Rest assured, if I thought you were in any danger I would tell you and the garda."

"Why was Annie in the yearling barn?"

"She wanted to see the colt."

"Was she with him when you found her?"

She felt the sudden tensing of his jaw.

"I can't be sure," he hedged. "The barn was filled with smoke."

He was lying. She was sure of it. But why? "It's odd that *Irish Gold* was the only horse killed."

"We were lucky."

"I wasn't so lucky, Brian."

He sighed, sat up, reached for his clothes and began to dress. "*Irish Gold* was crippled, Caitlin. He was facin' a serious operation and an uncertain future. The expenses would have been enormous. Even then—" He stopped suddenly, as if he knew he'd already said too much.

Caitlin frowned. "Please, finish that thought."

Brian tucked in his shirt. "I don't believe he would ever have made a race horse."

A cold miserable lump settled in her stomach. "What makes you more of an expert than Robert Fowler?"

"Fowler's a vet, not a trainer," Brian replied. "He cures sick animals, he doesn't judge them for racin' potential."

"Please don't repeat those sentiments to anyone else."

He stared at her. "What is that supposed to mean?"

She swallowed and forced the words through her lips. "*Irish Gold*'s condition was no secret. I wouldn't want to be suspected of burning down your barn for the insurance money. My children would be taken from me for good." A thought chilled her blood. She could no longer feel the warmth of the blanket between her fingers. "I hope you don't think I started the fire for that very reason."

A thin white line appeared around Brian's lips. His face went completely still. Averting her eyes, Caitlin found her clothes. Her fingers shook as she pulled on her underwear, sweater, and slacks. If only he wasn't staring at her. "It's late," she said shakily. "I've stayed too long already."

He interrupted her. "You didn't start the fire, Caitlin, but someone did. It's too soon to speculate but when I know more I'll tell you. I promise you that."

"Did someone deliberately set out to kill my colt?" she demanded.

"I wouldn't rule out the possibility."

"What about *Graybeard's Lady*? Is she in any danger?"

"I don't believe so. The important thing is that you and the children aren't in any danger. Annie's presence in the barn was coincidental. She wasn't supposed to be there."

Caitlin shook her head. "I don't understand." Suddenly she remembered. "Sam's man, Mr. Fahey, gave your exercise boy an envelope at the Punchestown races."

"Davy?" Brian sounded incredulous. "Are you sure?"

"Not Davy Flynn. The new one. Tim, I think. I'm not sure of his name. I remember thinking how strange it was that you and Sam would do business together. Didn't the boy mention it to you?"

"No."

He was too abrupt, shuttered against her. "I know you're keeping something from me. Please tell me what's going on," she pleaded. "I'll only think the worst if you don't."

He hesitated.

"Why won't you trust me?" she cried out in frustration.

Neeve lifted her head and whimpered.

"My daughter was nearly killed and my horse is dead. Don't I have a right to know who hates me enough to do such a thing?"

He swore under his breath, turned to face the wall, and turned back again. "If it turns out not to be so, I'm goin' to look like the worst kind of fool, the worst kind of jealous fool."

It was her turn to look puzzled. "What are you saying?"

"I think your husband wanted *Irish Gold* dead."

She laughed and stopped herself in the middle, shocked at the hollowness of the sound. "Don't be absurd. Sam wants the colt back, or at least he did before we found out about the RLN problem. I'm still waiting for the right time to tell him his stable might be infected."

"Have you ever wondered why your husband would go to such trouble to retrieve one colt when he has so many others?"

"Probably to spite me."

He brushed aside her response. "I don't think so. I don't believe *Irish Gold* had any *Narraganset* blood at all."

Caitlin stared at him in shock. "Are you insane? How could such a thing happen? It's completely illegal. Sam would know it was illegal. Something like that couldn't happen at Claiborne."

"It could indeed. Sam would also know when the results of the blood-typin' came back, he would be facin' some serious charges, serious enough to put him out of business."

It was too outrageous. "But, Brian," she said helplessly, "why would he do such a thing in the first place?"

The line in his forehead deepened. "I can't answer that. Perhaps *Kentucky Gold*'s coverings by *Narraganset* weren't successful. Maybe *Narraganset* was ailing even then and couldn't perform for mares whose stud fees were already paid. It would explain a great deal, Caitlin. Robert Fowler suspected it first. *Narraganset* foals have no history of RLN. *Irish Gold* had a different kind of conformation altogether. Then there is your husband's irrational behavior over one colt. Now that colt is dead. Everything is too coincidental."

"He would never have gotten away with it," Caitlin protested. "People would have known."

Brian shrugged. "In his own barn, with his own people, maybe not. I don't pretend to have all the answers. Why Sam would go to such lengths I have no idea. For some reason it was important to him that the world believed *Kentucky Gold* was carrying *Narraganset*'s foal. Do you have any idea why?"

She remembered how frightened she'd been in the pub alone with Sam before Martin interrupted them. "Not the world," she said slowly, "just me. He wanted me to believe it."

Brian waited, giving her time to think.

"He was furious when he found out I'd taken *Kentucky Gold*. He wanted her to foal in a Claiborne barn." She looked up at him with horror in her eyes. "He wasn't going to let the foal live. He couldn't because I would know the truth when the colt was blood-typed."

"That still doesn't explain why he would consider such a charade in the first place. Why wouldn't he simply tell you the coverin's didn't take?"

"*Narraganset* commanded a larger stud fee than any stallion in North America." She was thinking out loud, trying to see the logic in it. "When Sam gave me *Kentucky Gold* he promised, in writing, that every year I would be guaranteed the proceeds of one foal out of her by *Narraganset*."

"Why wouldn't he honor your agreement?"

Caitlin shook her head. "I don't know. Maybe you were right when you said that *Narraganset* could no longer perform the way he had in the past. Sam never was very good at managing money. Most of the stud fees were spent before we even received them. It's possible he didn't want to waste the stallion on my mare when there were paying customers. He hasn't been thinking too clearly the last few years." She shrugged. "It's a stretch. We'll never know anyway now that *Irish Gold* can't be blood-typed."

Brian stared into the fire, both hands thrust deeply into his pockets. Caitlin noticed his balled fists. "I'll be leaving now."

"First, tell me what you saw at the Punchestown races between Fahey and our Tim."

Caitlin repeated her story and answered his questions until he was satisfied. Finally, he nodded. "That should be enough for now."

She stepped in front of him, arms folded against her chest, her back to the fire. "What will you do?"

"Nothin' yet. I'll wait until Keith finishes his investigation. He'll determine whether the fire was an arsonist's doin'. If so, I'll tell him what you told me."

"It isn't much, is it?"

He smiled and her heart turned over. Reaching for her, he held her against his shoulder. "We'll sort it out, love," he murmured against her hair. "Don't worry. I won't let anythin' happen to you."

It was an absurd vow. He couldn't possibly keep it, and yet, she was comforted just knowing that he wanted to.

It was after midnight but she decided to stop in at the hospital to check on Annie. The carpark was nearly empty when Caitlin drove in as close to the emergency entrance as possible and turned off the ignition. The nurse on duty at the desk looked up, smiled encouragingly, and waved her past.

She hurried down the long corridor to the room where

Annie slept, opened the door, and stopped abruptly. Her husband was seated in a chair by the bed, his head buried in his hands.

Rage, hot and violent, rose in her chest. His greed had nearly killed Annie. He was the reason her daughter lay there, small and white and sedated, in a bed with bars. A sob rose in Caitlin's throat. She swallowed it, struggled against her temper, and felt the soothing fingers of sanity calm her nerves. There was no real evidence. Not yet. Brian had told her to wait until the fire chief finished his investigation. No good would come of accusing Sam before there was proof.

She walked into the room and took her place on the other side of Annie. Sam looked up. Despite her anger, Caitlin was moved to pity. She had never seen him look so haggard. The knowledge that his actions nearly cost him his daughter must be taking its toll. He looked years older than when she saw him last.

"How long have you been here?" Caitlin whispered.

"Not long."

"Has Annie opened her eyes?"

Sam shook his head and ran his hands over his face. "God, Caitlin. I wonder if I should call Mama. If anything happens to Annie—"

"Nothing's wrong with Annie," Caitlin replied sharply. "She's been sedated to help her sleep and she'll probably have a sore throat, but that's all."

"Thank God."

Guilt. That's what he was feeling. Pure guilt. She didn't want to be around him. "I'll take over now, Sam. You look like you could use some rest."

His face worked. "I'm sorry, Caitlin, so sorry."

She froze, waiting for him to continue, wanting him to confess. And when he did, she would kill him. He deserved nothing less. No one would blame her, not after hearing the story.

His voice changed, became waspish, self-pitying. "None of this would have happened if you hadn't left me. We could have worked it out. Why in the hell did you have to go and file for a divorce?"

She felt the white heat rise in her cheeks. "You know why and it's pointless to go over it again." Lowering her voice, she spoke in hushed tones. "I'd like to talk to you about something, but not in here."

He stood, picked up his coat, and followed her out of the room. Caitlin closed the door firmly behind them.

She came right to the point. "My horse was lost in the fire today." Was there the tiniest change in his expression? She couldn't tell.

"I'm sorry."

"Only sorry? Not upset, outraged, even disappointed?"

He ran a shaking hand through his hair. "What do you want from me, Caitlin? Of course I'm disappointed, but if I fell apart over the loss of one yearling I wouldn't stay in business for long."

"This is the colt we've been squaring off over since before he was born."

"I told you I was disappointed but there isn't anything I can do about it. Annie's alive, that's the most important thing."

"I agree. But it changes the terms of our divorce."

"How?"

"The colt is no longer an issue. I assume that even you can't dispute the ownership of *Kentucky Gold.*"

"You can have the damn mare," he said angrily. "I want my children in Kentucky with me. If they were home where they belong none of this would have happened."

Her voice was cold, deadly. "How dare you say such a

thing when you know perfectly well there would have been no fire if it hadn't been for—" She stopped.

"Go on."

She turned away from him. "Go away, Sam. Go home. You bring out the worst in me."

"You won't win this one, Caitlin," he said before walking away.

Shaking off the frightening thought, she sat down in the chair Sam had vacated and rested her head on her arms. Something nagged at her, something that hadn't sounded quite right when Sam first said it, but she was too angry to examine why. It came to her just as she was dozing off. She had *three* horses stabled at the Curragh Stud. Sam never asked which one hadn't survived the fire. He hadn't asked because he already knew.

24

Mary Boyle pursed her lips and surveyed the damage before her. She avoided eye contact with Brian. "It could have been worse. At least it was only one barn and one horse."

"Where's Tim?" Brian asked abruptly.

"Tim Sheehan? Our exercise boy?"

Brian nodded.

"I don't believe we'll be seein' him today. He's feelin' a bit under the weather, poor lad."

"Is he now?"

"Aye. His mother called in for him."

Brian looked at his watch. "I think I'll look in on our Tim. If Mrs. Benedict calls, tell her to leave a number. I'll get back to her before the day's over."

The stricken look on the cook's face smote him. He draped an arm over her shoulder. "Now, Mary, love," he said soothingly, "you're not to think of her as an ogre. She's bound to be a bit upset. After all it's her stud farm. But she won't be blamin' you for the mess we're in."

"Easy for you to say," Mary retorted. "She's always had a soft spot for you, Brian Hennessey. It's the rest of us who get the sharp edge of her tongue."

With a final comforting squeeze, Brian dropped his arm and headed for the compact parked in his gravel driveway. Hillary Benedict could be difficult. To her credit she had taken over her late husband's business empire two years ago and done a respectable job of maintaining its profit margin, not too bad for a woman who had grown up in a Limerick row house with nine families to a single latrine. He had to admit that she was much warmer with him than she was with her other employees. For the most part he declined her invitations, aware that their similar upbringing gave her cause to believe they still shared commonalities, a misconception he had gently, with limited success, tried to correct.

Tim Sheehan lived outside of Kilcullen in a three room house kept by his mother. Mrs. Sheehan opened the door and welcomed Brian warmly. "Please come in, Mr. Hennessey. It's kind of you to be lookin' in on our Tim. Will you have a cuppa while it's hot?"

"No, thank you, Mrs. Sheehan. I'd like a word with your son, if you don't mind."

"Not a bit, not a bit." Hands fluttering, she shuffled ahead of him, down the hall to the back of the house where Tim lay in his narrow bed.

At first glance Brian thought his suspicions were unfounded. The lad sported the flushed cheeks and glittering eyes of a serious fever.

"Tim, love," his mother said, "Mr. Hennessey is here to cheer you up."

The flame in the boy's cheeks burned deeper. "H-hello, Mr. Hennessey."

Brian nodded and smiled at his hostess. "I believe I will have that tea after all, Mrs. Sheehan."

She beamed. "I'll fix a fresh pot and bring it in."

He waited until she disappeared into the kitchen before closing the door. Pulling a chair close to the bed, he sat down. "Have you heard about the fire we had at the Stud, Tim?"

The boy shook his head.

"Your mother said you'd heard," he improvised. "The word is all over town."

"Oh, that." Tim hedged. "Maybe I did hear something."

"It would be a difficult thing to forget. After all, you're an employee of the Stud." Brian met the boy's shifting gaze with his own direct one. "I imagine it's the fever talkin'."

Tim grabbed on to the excuse. "Aye. It's the fever."

"There's talk of arson," Brian said casually. "The fire inspector plans an investigation. We'll know soon."

"Know what?" Tim's hand was at his throat, his voice a painful sounding croak.

Brian nodded. "There's always evidence left behind that points to the guilty one."

Mrs. Sheehan knocked on the door. "Let me in. My hands are full."

Brian opened the door and took the tea tray from her. "I'd like to speak with Tim for a bit longer, if you don't mind, Mrs. Sheehan."

"I don't mind at all, Mr. Hennessey." She backed away. "If you need anythin', I'll be in the sittin' room."

He set the tray on the nightstand and once again took his seat. "Where was I?"

"You were saying there was evidence left behind." Tim appeared to have snapped out of his fever haze.

"I'm told there always is." Brian held out a cup. "Shall I pour the tea, lad?"

"N-n-no, thank you."

Brian poured himself a cup. He took his time adding the milk and sugar. "I was wonderin' if you could help me out with somethin'?"

"What's that, Mr. Hennessey?"

"Mr. Fahey gave you an envelope at the Punchestown races. Would you tell me what was in it?"

The exercise boy's face was leached of all color except for two red circles on his gaunt cheeks. "The envelope, sir?"

"Aye."

"I-I don't remember."

Brian drained his tea and stood. "I think you'd better, lad, and soon."

The boy shrank back in the bed and swallowed. His breathing became labored. He barely managed the words. "I don't want to go to jail."

"Have you a criminal record?"

"No."

"If you're honest with me you may get off with less."

"What shall I do?"

"Tell me what you know."

"Nothing much," the boy said miserably. "Mr. Fahey asked to buy me a drink. He said how Mrs. Claiborne had stolen her husband's colt and how the Stud would be shut down after he sued. He said I'd be out of a job at the least." He was hurrying now, his words tumbling over each other in an oddly disjointed confession. "He told me I could earn some cash. He said it was the least I could do. It would go easier on me if I did what he said."

"Did he tell you to set fire to the barn?"

"No."

Brian's hand tightened on the china teacup. "Did he tell you to bolt the door?"

The boy hung his head.

"Answer me, lad." There was something in Brian's voice that demanded an honest answer.

Tim's reply was a mere whisper. "No."

"Did you know there was a wee lass asleep in the barn?"

Now the lad truly looked wasted. "I swear not, Mr. Hennessey."

"Annie Claiborne was in that barn when you bolted the door and set fire to it. What do you think Mr. Claiborne would have done to you had you killed his daughter?"

Tears streamed down the boy's face.

Brian continued relentlessly. "You're a lucky man, Tim Sheehan. We were in time. Annie Claiborne didn't burn to death but she spent last night in hospital. Did you even bother to ask why you were set to such a task?"

The boy fidgeted with his covers, unable to meet Brian's eyes.

"Out with it, lad. You're hidin' somethin' and I'm in no mood to be generous."

"I didn't bolt the door and I didn't set the fire."

Brian frowned. "Someone did."

"I don't know his name but Mr. Fahey sent him. He was in the barn when I got there, inside the colt's stall. He'd done something to him. One minute *Irish Gold* was standing and the next time I looked he was on his side in the straw. The chap told me to do what I'd been paid to do. I swear it, Mr. Hennessey. All I did was keep watch to be sure no one came around and then get rid of the cans. I didn't see him leave or bolt the door. I didn't know the girl was inside." He was desperate. "If I'd known I would never have done it."

"Why did you, Tim?"

He looked surprised. "I needed the money."

A wave of fury swept through Brian. The boy was contemptible. "You knew what he intended. You've cared for those horses for weeks. Have you no feelin's at all for them? Wasn't there one you felt partial to?"

No answer.

"Doesn't the idea of charred horse meat make you want to vomit?" Seconds ticked by.

Tim's voice was barely a whisper. "I thought they'd get out."

"You didn't think it through, lad. Otherwise you would have asked yourself why someone would do such a thing." Brian stood. "I think you're in the wrong profession, Tim Sheehan. When you're up and about, come in for what's owed to you. Don't come back to the Stud again and don't use me for a reference."

Despite his stricken expression, the boy hadn't lost all of his wits. "What about Mr. Murphy and the investigation? Will something be done?"

"You can be sure of it," Brian replied grimly. "I'll tell Murphy what you told me. It might go easier on you if you agree to stand witness. That's for you to decide." Turning his back on the boy he left the room.

There were two messages on his cell phone display. One was from Keith Murphy, the other was Hillary Benedict's secretary. Ignoring both, he dialed Brigid Keneally's number. Caitlin answered.

The sound of her voice flooded him with images, images he had no business having on a winding country road slick with rain. He pushed them aside and identified himself. "How's Annie?"

Caitlin's voice was giddy with relief. "She's fine, Brian. I think she may be well enough to go back to school tomorrow."

"May I talk to her?"

"Of course."

There was a brief silence and then he heard Annie's voice, slightly hoarse but unmistakable. "Brian?"

"In the flesh."

"Were you hurt in the fire, Brian?" she asked anxiously. "Mum says you were, not too badly, but more than I was."

"No more than a bad sunburn and a sore throat. Tell your mother not to give it another thought. A good night's rest fixed me up."

Annie's sigh was audible. "I didn't feel anything so I was never afraid. I guess it's a good thing."

"A very good thing," Brian agreed.

"Will you come to see me?"

"As soon as I'm allowed."

Another silence with muffled conversation in the background. Annie's voice came on again. "Mum says to come for dinner at six if you can. We're in the new house now, you know, the Sullivan's old house. We weren't supposed to be in until after Christmas but Mama surprised us. All of our things are here and my room is perfect, all pink, just like it was in Kentucky. Ben likes it, too. Would you like to see it, Brian?"

"I would. Thanks for the invitation. I'll be there at six."

Keith Murphy wasn't surprised to hear Brian's news. "It was definitely arson," the fire inspector said, "and the job of an amateur. The petrol cans were thrown in a nearby dumpster, fingerprints all over them. The horse is still at the clinic, scheduled for an autopsy. We're waiting to hear the official cause of death. I'll wager my mother's rosary that it won't be smoke inhalation although I wouldn't go spreading it around just yet."

"I'm not sure Sheehan can be counted on not to talk to Fahey."

"I'll make it easier for him," Murphy promised. "As soon as I hear word on the horse, I'll call you."

Hillary Benedict wasn't so easily appeased. "What do you mean you don't know how it happened?" she fumed. "It was negligence, pure negligence. How else does a fire start in the middle of the rainy season?"

"We're still confirmin' the cause, Hillary," replied Brian.

"I can't believe this is happening." He heard a deep sucking silence and the breathless pop that indicated she'd lit a cigarette. "All of my horses will be pulled. What idiot would take a chance on boarding his thoroughbred at my stud after this catastrophe?"

Brian lost his patience. "We lost one horse, Hillary, one horse. I'd say we were lucky. Now if you've got anything else to contribute, say it now."

"I need to see you as soon as possible, Brian. It's urgent."

"I'm free now."

Her voice grew sharp. "Now isn't possible. Tonight is better."

"Tonight isn't good for me. I've made dinner plans."

"That shouldn't take long. I'll wait and see you after."

Damn the woman. What could possibly be so urgent that wasn't urgent yesterday? "You'll have to come here."

"I will. Where and when?"

"Come to the cottage at half past nine. I'll leave the door open in case I'm late."

"Don't be too late," she ordered before hanging up the phone.

Perhaps she would fire him. It wasn't the first time the thought had crossed Brian's mind but never before had the prospect of being on his own again appealed to him so. He would open up his own training yard. It might be slow at first, but not for long, not when the word got out. His reputation for creating winners had exceeded even his expectations. Breeders beyond the borders of Ireland were contacting him. Even so, he had enough put aside to make it through more than a few lean years.

Brian fingercombed his hair and ran a hand up the side of his jaw, testing for smoothness. Deciding against a shave and the fancy cologne his sister had sent him for Christmas, he dug through his bottom dresser drawer for his favorite sweater, an oatmeal wool Aran, and pulled it over his head.

He'd wasted too much time at the off license debating between red or white wine and ended up buying both. If he didn't leave now, he would surely be late.

Caitlin's house was two miles north of Kilcullen, a pleasant gray two-story with gables, white trim, and wide lawns. At his knock, Ben opened the door. "It's Brian, Mum," the boy shouted over his shoulder.

"May I come in?" Brian asked.

Ben stepped aside. "There are starters in the sitting room. Annie made them. Mum helped," the boy confided, "so it's okay to eat them."

Brian's lips twitched. "Such an uncharitable thought never crossed my mind."

Annie knelt beside a small table and set down the tray she had carried in from the kitchen. To Brian's relief he was able to recognize nearly everything on it.

"These are fried cheese sticks," Annie announced, pointing to several steaming brown wedges, "and this is marinara sauce to go with it."

Ben immediately reached for one, dragged it through the sauce and popped half of it into his mouth. He was nearly at the sauce again when Annie stopped him. "Don't you dare double dip or I'll tell Mum."

"My sauce is all gone," he said, ever practical.

"That's what the plates are for." She left the room returning with a stack of five small plates, tiny spoons, and forks with three tines. "You can use a spoon to put the sauce on your plate. Then you can dip all you want."

"What an idea," said Brian, shrugging out of his coat and laying it over the back of his chair. "The sauce is delicious, Annie. Did you make it yourself?"

"I made everything here," the child said proudly.

Ben reached for the carrots. "Where's the dip?"

Annie ignored him. "Would you like something to drink, Brian? Mum told me to ask you. She'll be out in a minute."

Brian handed over the wine bottles. "Take these in to her. I wasn't sure what she was servin'. I'll wait until she can join me." He looked around for Brigid. "Is your grandmother here tonight?"

"I am." Brigid walked down the stairs choosing her steps carefully. She stopped Annie to inspect the wine labels. "Very nice. Very nice, indeed. Show these t' your mother, Annie. She'll know what t' do with them."

"I've left Caitlin on her own," she explained when Annie had left them. "She does a much better job in the kitchen than I've ever done. I believe she's servin' lamb tonight."

Brian's stomach juices came to life. "I look forward to it."

Caitlin stepped out of the kitchen, an apron around her waist and smiled. "Hello, Brian."

He nodded. "Thanks for the dinner invitation."

She addressed her son. "Ben, this is the second time I've asked you to come and set the table for dinner."

Something green held her hair up and back, away from her face. A few loose tendrils curled around her temples. Her neck looked impossibly long and creamy white. Brian wanted nothing more than to press his lips on the exact spot where her shoulder met her throat and kiss her. Damn Hillary Benedict.

Another mozzarella stick found its way into Ben's mouth. A stern glance from Brigid sent him scurrying into the kitchen. Brian grinned. There was nothing like an Irish grandmother to turn a lad in the right direction.

"Are you all right in here?" Caitlin asked. "I've the salad to make and then I can join you."

"Can I help you, love?" Brigid asked.

"No, thanks. Everything's nearly done." She smiled and returned to the kitchen.

Brigid sat down in a chair beside the fire. "It seems we are in debt t' you, Brian Hennessey."

"You may feel that way, Mrs. Keneally, but there's no need. I'm pleased no harm was taken."

"No harm at all, thank God. Have you any idea how it started?"

"I do, but I'm not at liberty to say just yet."

Brigid leaned forward. "So, it wasn't an accident."

"I never said that."

"You didn't say it wasn't either."

She was quick. Brian would give her that. Older people were supposed to be less keen but there was nothing at all feeble about Brigid Keneally's faculties.

"I know how t' keep my mouth shut if that's what's worryin' you."

"I would never dream of askin' you to do so, Mrs. Keneally. The fire marshalls will be done with their investigation soon and then I imagine the cause of the fire will be public knowledge."

Brigid fixed a cold blue stare on his face. "Is my family safe, Brian?"

"They are, more now than ever."

She hesitated "I believe you."

Something wasn't right. "But—?"

"I need a favor."

He'd been down this road before. "What can I do for you, Mrs. Keneally?" he asked warily.

"I'd like you t' make an inquiry about Father Duran's health?"

It was a request he hadn't expected and his surprise showed.

"Martin will tell you," she said.

"Martin would tell you, too, if you asked him."

"No." Brigid shook her head. "I don't want t' be the one askin'."

He was about to cross the line and ask if there was a particular reason for such a question when Caitlin called them into the dining room. One glance at the feast she had prepared wiped all other thoughts from his mind. "Caitlin," he said in awe, "you're an artist."

She brushed aside the compliment but her flushed cheeks told him that his words had pleased her.

"Sit down, Brian," Brigid said dryly, waving him into a chair. "We eat like this all the time. If you came around more often every available woman in town wouldn't feel the need to feed you."

Caitlin sighed. "Don't listen to her, Brian. Kathleen Finch tells me she gets more outrageous every year."

His chest ached with emotion. Give him another minute and he would embarrass himself. There was something about a table groaning with food, shining silver, well-scrubbed children and a woman, lovely and smart, talented and giving. He wanted it, all of it, even the omniscient old harridan who pretended ignorance when all the while she knew exactly what she wanted and exactly what it took to get it.

This was the answer, the master plan, the reason he'd ended up here in Kilcullen. It all came down to this moment, this woman and all the years that would follow. Brian was thirty-four years old. Finally, he'd found his destiny.

Hillary's BMW wasn't anywhere in sight when he pulled into his driveway. It was past nine-thirty. He waited until ten before dialing her number. She answered on the first ring.

"I'm here, Hillary. I cut my dinner plans short. Where are you?"

"I have a guest," she said, keeping her voice low. "I won't be able to make it tonight. Tuesday will be better. I'll drive over Tuesday night."

"You said it was urgent."

"I don't care for your tone, Brian. Please remember that you work for me."

He could feel his jugular throb. "That can be remedied."

She laughed, the false, tinkling laugh of a woman who knew she was being watched. "Don't be absurd. I'll see you Tuesday."

He hung up the phone. Neeve padded in from the kitchen and rested her head on his knees. He stroked her where she was most sensitive, under her chin. She whimpered and he gave in. "You win. We'll go for a run. I don't know who needs it more, you or I."

25

❧❧❧

Michael Duran was dead. Black clad mourners passed by his open coffin paying their respects in death as they had not in life.

Brigid sat in the back of the mortuary, her fingers frozen in the twisted strands of her rosary beads, her voice whispering familiar words of the litany that no amount of grief, or time, or resentment could wipe from her Catholic memory. *"Hail Mary, full of grace, the Lord is with thee, blessed art thou among women and blessed is the fruit of they womb, Jesus. Holy Mary, mother of God, pray for us sinners now and at the hour of our death."*

Michael Duran was dead. Was it possible? How long ago had he come to Kilcullen? Thirty-seven years ago or was it longer?

Why must black be the color of death? Didn't they know Michael hated it? Wasn't it enough that he would rest in it for all eternity? Brigid wasn't enough of an optimist to believe that there was another option for Michael Duran. He was a priest who'd lived a lie and was sorry for it, but in the end knew he would have done nothing differently. No white clouds and pearly gates for him, no rubbing shoulders with the likes of Saint Patrick and Thomas More. Michael was a flawed man, a man who stood on the fence to make his life comfortable. No amount of rationalizing would whitewash what he had done.

Martin looked visibly shaken, his handsome youthful face was gray with shock or grief, or both. But he performed his duties well. Assumpta would have been proud of him tonight, officiating at Father Duran's rosary. Assumpta had always been reverent, too reverent, Brigid thought, but then one could never walk in another's shoes.

There would be no wake. Michael Duran hadn't the soul of an Irishman. They wouldn't put him to rest as one. Brigid's fingers tightened around her beads. *"Hail Mary, full of grace, the Lord is with thee, blessed art thou among women and blessed is the fruit of thy womb, Jesus. Holy Mary, mother of God, pray for us sinners now and at the hour of our death."*

Where was Michael's family? He'd mentioned a sister, Mary Rose. Perhaps she was dead as well. People didn't live forever. Her knees ached from kneeling. Martin had begun the Lord's Prayer. Automatically, Brigid followed his lead. *"Our Father, who art in Heaven hallowed be Thy name, Thy kingdom come, Thy will be done on earth as it is in heaven. Give us this day our daily bread and forgive us our trespasses as we forgive those who have trespassed against us. Lead us not into temptation but deliver us from evil. Our Father . . ."*

Brigid closed her eyes and clutched at the words, familiar and comforting in the face of her tragedy. For it was a tragedy. It signalled the end of an era, an irrevocable closing of a chapter that had finally been set in ink, never to be revised or improved. She brushed away a tear. It was time for

Michael Duran to have his day of revelation. She never doubted that it would come. She'd hoped for more time, just a few more years until her own life wound to a close. But it was not to be. Michael would have the last laugh, only this time no one would be laughing. Perhaps she deserved it to end like this, after the way she'd treated him. She only hoped for Annie's sake, and for Ben's, that Caitlin would forgive her.

Even with her eyes closed she knew the exact moment her daughter had slipped into the seat beside her.

Brigid opened her eyes and forced a smile. "I didn't expect you t' make it."

"I'm sorry to be so late," Caitlin whispered, "but I couldn't get Ben to bed, and then Davy was late. He said he wouldn't mind staying with the children." She looked around. "Everyone is here."

Brigid didn't miss the venomous look Lana Sullivan had directed at Caitlin. Now, what ailed the girl? "Aye," she said dryly. "The passing of a priest doesn't happen every day, thank God."

"You didn't like him, did you, Mum?"

Frowning, Brigid shook her head. "This isn't the place."

Martin turned in their direction, smiled, and blessed the congregation. The rosary was over.

As always, the inhabitants of Kilcullen drew together when one of their own expired. It had taken his demise to do it, but Father Duran had finally been admitted into the inner circle. Gathering together on the steps of the mortuary, the priest's mourners discussed his passing.

Caitlin pressed her mother's gloved hand. "You look tired, Mum."

John O'Shea interrupted them. "Will you be openin' the pub for a few hours, Brigid? Kathleen said if you weren't feelin' up to it, she would unlock the cafe."

Brigid hesitated. A few hours meant half the night. She wanted to mourn Michael in the peace of her own house. If she had been a relative or even a close friend they would understand. But she was neither of those. They knew nothing of what had really happened that autumn thirty-odd years ago and she had no plans to tell them.

Caitlin's arm closed around her shoulder. "Mum's been up the last few nights with Annie. She hasn't caught up on her sleep yet."

"Don't think twice about it," said Kathleen. "Lana and I will manage." She nodded at the girl hovering on the edge of a group of four. "You don't mind puttin' in a few extra hours, do you, Lana? Caitlin wants to take her mum home."

Lana's cheeks were a bright pink. "Of course I don't mind. It's up to the poor peasants of Kilcullen to give the princess whatever she wants. Isn't that right, Caitlin?"

Brigid felt her daughter stiffen. Her hackles rose. She reached up and pried away the fingers clutching her shoulder. "Leave off, Caitlin, you're killin' me," she grumbled. Then she turned to Lana and without raising her voice, pitched it for all those around them to hear. "Will you watch your mouth, child, or will you be needing a good bar of soap to wash it clean?"

Lana sucked in her breath and looked to her family for support. The Sullivans were there in full force but no one stepped up to defend her. Without a word, she turned and walked away.

Kathleen sighed. "I'm not sayin' she didn't deserve it, Brigid, but how will I manage without any help?"

Caitlin spoke up. "I'll help you, Kathleen. Let me walk home with Mum and then I'll be back."

Barbara O'Shea, John's youngest daughter, stepped forward. "There's no need for that, Caitlin. We know what it's been like for you and Mrs. Keneally with the fire at the stud farm nearly taking our Annie. I'll help Kathleen tonight."

Brigid relaxed. Despite her Claiborne marriage, Caitlin wasn't without friends in Kilcullen.

"Does anyone know how it happened?" Caitlin asked after she'd checked on the children and come back downstairs to find her mother and Davy Flynn sharing a pot of tea.

Brigid was unusually silent, her eyes on the flickering flames and the curling squares of new peat she'd added to the fire.

"I hear they couldn't get his heart to start up again after the bypass surgery," Davy volunteered. "Imagine, a man like Father Duran, strong as a horse, dyin' on the table like that."

"I wonder why he did it?" Caitlin said.

Her mother looked up. "Did what?"

"I wonder why he took such a risk at his age."

"He was just past seventy, Caitlin, the same age I am," Brigid admonished her. "I'm not ready t' step one foot into the grave. Most likely they promised him a few extra years. Anyone starin' death in the face would take such an offer."

"I suppose so." Caitlin looked unconvinced.

Brigid patted the space on the sofa beside her.

Caitlin sat down beside her mother. "I knew him all my life," she mused, "yet I don't feel like I really knew him."

"He wasn't an easy man to know," observed Davy. "I don't think he had a real friend in all of Kilcullen for all his bein' the pastor of Saint Patrick's for forty years."

"Thirty-seven," Brigid corrected him.

"What's that, lass?" Davy turned his good ear in her direction.

"He's been at Saint Patrick's for thirty-seven years," she repeated.

"I didn't think you liked him, Mum."

"What makes you say that?"

Caitlin shrugged. "Nothing concrete, really. It's just that when we ran into him you made excuses to leave."

Brigid laughed through stiff lips. "I suppose it looked that way."

Davy drained the last of his tea and stood. "I'll be on my way, Caitlin. Thank you for the tea, Mrs. Keneally. Don't get up. I'll find my way out."

Brigid turned down the lamp so the room was dim and shadowed with firelight. She liked to watch the flames leap and dance. Wood snapped. Rain slanted down through the chimney, sizzled, smoked, and rose again something else entirely. She loved the smell of turf, the popping wood, the hiss and crackle and smoke, the anonymity of her face in the shadows, her hands empty and idle in her lap. "He had blocked arteries," she said into the darkness. "He was a smoker when he was young. We all were. But he waited too long to stop."

"Maybe something was wrong with his heart as well," said Caitlin. "He should have come out of it."

"Michael Duran couldn't be counted on to behave predictably."

"I can't imagine why you would say that." There was an odd note in Caitlin's voice. "He's never been anything other than the consummate parish priest, only more intolerant and superior."

Brigid couldn't help defending him. "You liked him well enough."

"Only lately. He lightened up a bit during the years I was gone."

"He's gone now. It's bad luck to speak ill of the dead."

They sat in silence for a while longer. Caitlin spoke first. "Are you all right, Mum? You're unusually quiet tonight."

Brigid intended to assert that she was well enough for seventy-one and lay her daughter's suspicions to rest but the words wouldn't come. Instead she surprised herself. "I feel like a drink, somethin' bubbly and dry."

"Champagne? We'll have to drink the whole bottle."

"If we don't finish it, I'm sure you can find another use for what's left. Didn't you say somethin' about salmon with champagne sauce?"

"The cheapest champagne I've seen in your cellar is forty pounds a bottle. I can't pour that over fish."

"Why not?"

"Mum." Now Caitlin sounded exasperated. "You can't have changed that much."

"I'm seventy-one years old, Caitlin. If I can't drink good champagne with my daughter before I pass on, what have I worked for all my life?"

"So, that's what this is about. Father Duran is dead and you think you haven't much time left."

Brigid stood. "Somethin' like that. Don't go anywhere. I'll be right back."

The champagne she preferred was a *Blanc de Blanc* from California, a dry, small-bubbled, crisper version than the more traditional French variety. Her gnarled hands struggled with the cork but at last she managed it and the satisfying pop exploded in her ears. A misty residue escaped from the bottle, hovered around the top and disappeared. Brigid balanced on a foot stool and chose two Waterford flutes from the top cupboard. Carrying the bottle and a towel in one hand and the flutes in the other, she returned to the sitting room and poured two glasses. Small bubbles, she noted with satisfaction. A good champagne guaranteed to make the following morning a pleasant one.

Caitlin sipped from her glass. Her eyebrows lifted in surprise. "This is delicious," she said, reaching for the bottle to check the label.

"It's been around for some time, only not so much in

Europe. I don't believe it had a market outside of the United States until a few years ago."

"You like this, don't you, Mum?"

Brigid could barely see her daughter's face in the firelight. "Like what?"

Caitlin waved her hand to encompass the room. "This life. Running the pub and the store, sampling new champagne, living here in Kilcullen."

Brigid thought a minute. It was true, with provisions. "I like it much more now that you're here. I was goin' through the motions until you came with the children. Now I have the three of you t' look forward t'." She bit her lip. Vulnerability made her uncomfortable. She plunged forward anyway. "You will stay the night, won't you? The children are already asleep."

Caitlin nodded and rested her head on her mother's shoulder. "I wish I could tell you for sure whether or not we can stay here in Kilcullen. The hearing's coming up. I should know after that."

"When do you leave for Kentucky?"

"The day after tomorrow."

"I thought it wasn't until next week."

"Mr. Marston wants me to meet his associates in Lexington before we go to court. I think it's a good idea since they'll be handling most of the case. He thinks a lawyer from Kentucky will have an advantage over one with an Irish accent."

Brigid watched Caitlin's fingers tighten around her glass.

"I can't lose this one, Mum."

Closing her eyes, Brigid sent up a silent prayer of thanks. She'd been granted a reprieve. "You didn't say whether you'll take the children."

"Not this time. They have school and I don't want to disturb them unless I absolutely have to. Besides, *Graybeard's*

Lady will be racing in Newry and Annie is determined to be in the owner's box. Brian said he would take her if you can't."

"I didn't see him tonight," Brigid said casually. "Why do you think that is?"

"He had a meeting with Hillary Benedict. She's concerned about the reputation of the Curragh after the fire. I'm sure he'll be at the funeral tomorrow."

The champagne gave Brigid courage. She poured herself another glass and topped off Caitlin's. "May I ask you a personal question?"

"I suppose there's no harm in asking."

"Exactly what is your relationship with Brian Hennessey?"

Caitlin leaned back into the couch and closed her eyes. Once again Brigid was struck by the delicate beauty of her daughter's face, something that even weariness and worry couldn't diminish.

"I'm not sure," Caitlin said at last. "I can't be sure until I know where this is all going to end. Brian is Irish. He belongs here."

Brigid could have told her that love waits for no one, that there is no perfect time for it, that happiness is measured in moments, not days or years, and that wisdom lies in knowing when to reach for it and when to step back. But as usual, with this particular daughter, she did not. Instead, she said, "What about you, Caitlin? Do you belong here?"

She shook her head. "I can't let myself think that way, Mum. If I have to keep Annie and Ben near Sam, then I'll belong in Kentucky."

"What will you do there?"

"Breed and race horses," she said without hesitation. "That's all I know how to do."

"Then why not do it here. If Hillary Benedict can do it, you can. She doesn't have any schoolin' at all."

"She inherited her business, Mum. Starting from the ground up isn't so easy."

"You'll manage."

Caitlin smiled and lifted her champagne glass. Firelight gilded the bones of her cheeks. She'd had too much to drink. Tonight, anything seemed possible. "To the future of my training yard."

Brigid saluted her daughter. "T' your future," she said. Caitlin approved of her. It was a heady feeling and an unusual one. She would hold on to the memory of this night, save it in her mind, bring it out and relive it when she needed it most.

26

Lexington, Kentucky

Lucy Claiborne happened to look up at the exact moment Caitlin walked into the courtroom and her face lit from within. She smiled and beckoned, then remembered what had brought them together again, and hesitated.

Caitlin saw the conflicting emotions pass over her mother-in-law's face. She understood the older woman's dilemma. There was no precedent in Lucy's life on which to pattern her behavior.

Recognizing that it was up to her to set the standard, Caitlin moved swiftly across the space that separated them and, before she could change her mind, drew her mother-in-law up out of her chair and into her arms. Lucy's embrace was long and painful, genuine and healing.

"I've missed you so much." The older woman's voice broke. Clearly embarrassed, she stepped back, pulled a tissue from her purse and pressed it against her nose. "How are my grandchildren?"

"Looking forward to seeing you again."

Lucy looked startled. "Will that be soon?"

"They'll be coming back in the spring when they have a break from school, unless we're forced to come back sooner."

"I understand." Lucy was obviously uncomfortable with their present circumstances.

Sam broke away from his lawyers and joined them. "Hello, Caitlin."

She nodded cooly.

He slid his hand under his mother's elbow. "It's almost time. I think we should sit down."

Charles Malone, Caitlin's American attorney, a fourth generation Kentuckian, opened his briefcase and removed a manila file. He was busy examining the contents when Caitlin sat down beside him. She knew better than to interrupt. Mr. Malone was a stickler for perfection. After leaving his office the first time she'd felt more hopeful than she had in months.

He finished his perusal, put away his pen and smiled at her. "Remember, no matter what happens here today regarding the children we can always appeal."

She blanched. "Has something happened?"

"Custody cases are never predictable, Caitlin. They bring out the worst in people."

"Is there something you're not telling me, Mr. Malone?"

"Your husband's attorney has taken a deposition from a woman named Lana Sullivan. Do you know her?"

Her heart sank. "Yes."

"Mr. Claiborne's attorneys will assert that you are an unfit mother."

She gasped. "Why?"

"According to Miss Sullivan you have entered into a relationship with a man in Kilcullen, a Mr. Brian Hennessey. She claims that you left your children to go away with him overnight."

Rage consumed her. A vein throbbed in her neck. She felt the hot dry heat of injustice sear a path from her chest down to her stomach. Closing her eyes, she drew a deep breath. "Mr. Hennessey is the manager of the stud farm where my horses are stabled. My foal had a debilitating birth defect. Together we took him to a veterinarian in Galway. We did not spend the night together. I came home on a late train. He drove the colt back."

Malone's face softened. "Don't look so terrified, Caitlin. We encounter this type of thing many times."

Her voice was bitter. "I'm amazed that Sam has the nerve to accuse me after his years of philandering."

"I must ask you this question and I need you to answer honestly. Have you ever at any time during your marriage had an affair that you kept from your husband?"

"No."

"Will Mrs. Claiborne support your claim?"

"Yes."

Charles Malone smiled. "Good."

"But—"

He held up his hand. "Don't say anything more. That's the question I'll ask you after your husband's attorney has finished. Respond exactly the way you did for me."

The bailiff ordered all to rise. Judge Phillip Rutherford entered the room. Court was in session.

Sam had been well coached. "Did you ever beat your wife, Mr. Claiborne?"

"No, sir."

"Did you verbally abuse her?"

"No, sir."

"Did you mistreat her in any way?"

"No, sir."

"Isn't it a fact, Mr. Claiborne, that you denied your wife

absolutely nothing that her heart desired, even down to a prize-winning broodmare of considerable reputation."

"Yes, sir."

Elery Hayes, the Claiborne attorney for more than two decades, was in rare form. "Can you think of one, single, solitary reason that your wife deserted you, taking your two children, and stealing two horses from your stable?"

Charles Malone rose halfway out of his chair. "Objection on two counts. Speculation and Mr. Hayes has already conceded that the broodmare was a gift to Mrs. Claiborne."

"Sustained." Judge Rutherford peered through his glasses. "You aren't practicing before a grand jury, Mr. Hayes. I'm the only one you need to impress."

Mr. Hayes regrouped. "I'll rephrase. Mr. Claiborne, do you consider yourself to be a good husband?"

"I do."

"Did your wife explain to your satisfaction why she left you?"

"No, sir, she did not."

"No further questions."

Charles Malone stared down at his file. Then he turned, winked at Caitlin, stood and buttoned his coat.

"Isn't it a fact, Mr. Claiborne, that you were not faithful to your marriage vows?"

Sam appeared outraged. "It is not."

Caitlin watched the blood pound in her wrist and willed herself to remain calm.

Mr. Malone picked up his file and flipped through several sheets of paper. "Isn't it true that on the night of October 17, 1994, you checked into a Charleston hotel with a woman who was not your wife? You are under oath, Mr. Claiborne."

Sam's fists were clenched and his face was an alarming shade of red. "I don't remember."

"Let me refresh your memory. Her name was Rachel Willoughby. Does that ring a bell?"

"No."

"What about June 23rd of the same year? You appeared with the same Rachel Willoughby at a hotel in Paris and signed the guest register as Mr. and Mrs. Claiborne." Malone waited. "Still no recollection, Mr. Claiborne? What about May 16th, 1995, and a Mrs. Catherine Downing?"

Hayes leaped to his feet. "Objection. Mr. Malone is badgering the witness."

"Overruled." The judge sounded amused. "Mr. Claiborne, answer the question and remember that you are under oath."

"I don't recall."

Charles Malone sighed. "Very well, Mr. Claiborne. I have no further questions."

Several witnesses were called to vouch for Sam's character. At last Elery Hayes addressed the bench. "This concludes my client's case, your honor."

"So noted." Rutherford lifted his head and looked through the bottom half of his bifocals. "Mr. Malone. You may proceed."

"I call Caitlin Claiborne to the stand."

Later, when asked to recall what kind of a witness she'd been in her own defense, Caitlin couldn't say. She remembered explaining why she'd returned to Ireland and why, in her opinion, divorce was her only option. The one about Annie and Ben's state of mind had been harder. Somehow she'd managed it. The rest of the attorney's questions and her own responses passed in a blur, leaving her feeling weary, defeated, and powerless, emotions she hadn't experienced since she'd walked out on Sam Claiborne eight months before.

And then it was Lucy's turn. For the rest of her life Caitlin would never forget how her mother-in-law stood up in front of them all and defied her son. No one knew better than Caitlin what loyalty meant to the Claibornes. For Lucy to take a stand against Sam was a testimony to the woman's courage and character. Charles Malone was a genius. Caitlin had no idea how he'd known that Lucy would do what she did. Somehow he had seen something in the woman that no one else had.

"Mrs. Claiborne," he began in his most courteous voice, "would you say that your daughter-in-law is a good mother?"

"Caitlin is an excellent mother."

"Have you ever known her to do anything that was not in the best interests of the children?"

"Never."

"To the best of your knowledge, was your daughter-in-law ever unfaithful to your son during their marriage?"

Lucy's contemptuous gaze flickered over her son and moved on. "No, she was not."

Malone looked down at his shoes. One hand was in his pocket. "This may be difficult for you, Mrs. Claiborne. Your answer is very important. Take as much time as you need before answering." He smiled. "Are you ready?"

She drew a deep breath. "Yes."

"Did you ever caution your son about his extra-marital affairs?"

"Yes."

"To what end?" the attorney gently prodded her.

Lucy lifted her head and once again leveled her son. "He disregarded my advice completely."

"Do you want your grandchildren back in Kentucky, Mrs. Claiborne?"

"I do. More than anything in the world."

Charles Malone smiled. He'd struck pay dirt. "That will be all, Mrs. Claiborne."

"Do you wish to question the witness, Mr. Hayes?"

Elery Hayes shook his head. "No, your honor."

Judge Rutherford nodded at Lucy. "You may step down, Mrs. Claiborne."

During the recess, Caitlin stayed as far away from Sam as possible. Over cobb salad and coffee in the court house cafeteria, Charles Malone summed up the situation as he saw it.

"Some good points were made in our favor, but I wouldn't be too optimistic. Some things are determined by precedent and domicile is one of them. Child and spousal support are another."

"What can I expect?"

"Honestly?"

"Please."

"The court will instruct you to move the children back to where their father can see them on a regular basis."

She swallowed. "I see."

"That can change if you remarry or if an employment opportunity presents itself in Ireland."

"How long do I have?"

His smile was sympathetic. "We'll appeal this, Caitlin. Nothing is set in stone. Meanwhile you'll have to come up with a very good reason for staying in Kilcullen. The court is predisposed to keeping young children with the mother. However, she is expected to act in good faith and allow her ex-husband regular visitation privileges." He hesitated. "I'll do all I can but much of what will happen is up to you and Sam. Is there a chance that the two of you can mend your fences long enough to come to some kind of agreement over this?"

Caitlin thought of the last time she had seen Sam before today, in the hospital in Naas, his head in his hands, distraught over Annie's brush with death. "I'm not sure," she said slowly.

"It's clear that he cares deeply about his children."

She nodded, picked up her fork and meticulously separated the crumbled blue cheese from the rest of her salad. "I think he does, Mr. Malone, more than I thought. But there's more involved here."

"Does it have anything to do with the terms of your divorce?"

"Not really. I don't think so, anyway." If Brian's suspicions proved correct, Sam had committed a criminal act, but she couldn't prove it even if she wanted to. Caitlin had a terrifying feeling that it wasn't the first one he'd committed and it probably wouldn't be the last. In the eyes of the law, Sam Claiborne appeared the successful horse breeder, capable of providing for his ex-wife and children. What would happen to them if he were caught?

The world of Kentucky's upper crust was a small one. What would happen to Annie and Ben if their father was exposed for fraudulent breeding practices?

She couldn't depend on Sam. Better to stay in Ireland and build a life for herself and her children even if it would never be the kind of life Sam could give them. Her mother's words came back to her. She cleared her throat. "I do have a job opportunity, Mr. Malone. I'm going to open a training yard. The expenses are much less in Ireland than they would be here in Kentucky. I might even be able to get a loan."

Charles Malone's mild blue eyes assessed her from across the table. "You've never mentioned this before. Is this legitimate?"

"It is." She leaned forward eagerly. "I went back to Ireland to train and breed horses. My colt out of *Kentucky Gold* died in a fire at the stud where I boarded him. I could breed my mare again but not until I can afford a stud fee. That could take some time. But I've got to try. I need to get on with my life, Mr. Malone. I wasn't going to consider the yard until I was more settled but now I don't have a choice if

I want to stay in Ireland. Kentucky is Sam's world. I won't succeed here. Ireland is a country of backyard trainers.

Charles Malone pushed aside his salad, liberally sugared his coffee, all the while appearing deep in thought. "You might have something here, Caitlin. It won't affect today's ruling but we can try it in the appeal. Meanwhile it wouldn't hurt for you to go home and see if you can make your idea work."

Suddenly her salad looked appetizing. She was even in the mood for dessert, real dessert, not the generic cubes of jello and cornstarch-thickened fruit pies she'd seen behind the glass while moving through the cafeteria line. Caitlin wanted maple-crusted crème brûlée or cheesecake in its purest form, sinfully rich with cream cheese, eggs, and a light topping of sweetened sour cream.

Phillip Rutherford was not unsympathetic but, as he explained somewhat regretfully, his hands were tied. "In the case of Claiborne versus Claiborne, Kentucky law is clear. Mr. Claiborne has requested joint custody of his children and unless a justifiable reason to deny him is brought before the court, his request must be honored. Because all other terms in the divorce settlement have been agreed upon by the Claibornes, including the stipulated amounts of child and spousal support, the court hereby grants Mr. Claiborne the rights of custodial parent every other week and alternating holidays to be agreed upon by both parties. If either party's circumstances change, the court will again look at the matter and reach a determination based on the new facts."

He flipped open the calendar beside him. "In consideration of Mrs. Claiborne's present living arrangements and because the children are currently settled in school, I hereby allow her until June 30th to comply with the court's ruling. The children will spend Christmas with Mrs. Claiborne and

Easter with Mr. Claiborne." He stood, Godlike, all powerful. "Court is dismissed."

Nothing could destroy Caitlin's optimism, not Sam's excess-ravaged face, not Lucy's embarrassment, not Charles Malone's cautious words. The marriage was over, her future was unsure, but she was free, free to go back to her life and what she could make of it.

27

❧❧❧❧

For reasons Brian had never cared enough to explore, Hillary Benedict left him cold. She was good-looking enough, a redhead with pale green eyes, long legs, and enough money to correct any noticeable imperfections—a circumstance she'd not hesitated to take advantage of the instant her husband's estate was settled.

Brian preferred a woman to look the way nature had intended. Hillary's conical breasts, non-existent nose, and laser-smooth skin stretched over synthetically-constructed cheekbones had no effect on him beyond a cynical kind of pity. For an already pretty woman to attempt to halt the aging process by going under the knife again and again, was a lesson in futility. He wasn't one to notice a woman's isolated body parts. It was the entire package that mattered. Either a woman was attractive or she wasn't. Her appeal had little to do with coloring, breast size, or the length of her legs.

He'd never taken the time to analyze exactly what it was that would make him turn around for a second look. It was something that defied explanation: a spark in the middle of shared conversation, a generous smile, a candid response, the curve of a cheek, the movement of a hand. It just happened in the same way he knew that Hillary Benedict didn't tempt him at all.

Her late model coupe was parked in his driveway. Brian stopped beside her car, turned off his ignition, and set the brake. On his way to the door he placed his hand on the boot of the BMW. It was cold. She'd been here for quite some time. Bracing himself for what he assumed would be another haranguing over the fire, he turned the knob and stepped inside.

She stood near the empty firestove, wrapped in an ankle length mink. Her hands were blue.

Without greeting her, he pulled three logs and a sheet of newspaper from the basket near the hearth. Striking a match, he held it to the paper until it caught. "Why didn't you light the fire?" he asked when the blaze was strong and some of the blueness had left her fingers.

"I don't know how."

"Come now, Hillary," he chided her, "give over. We both know you were fixin' oats for a family of eleven before you were eight years old."

"You're wrong. I've never done such a thing."

He let it go. "Can I get you anythin'?"

"A drink if you have one."

He'd hoped she would decline. Hillary wasn't a woman who stopped at one drink. He poured a tumbler of whiskey into a glass and handed it to her.

She raised one eyebrow. "You're not having any?"

Brian shook his head. "What did you want to see me about?"

"May I sit down?"

Ignoring her sarcasm, he waved her into a chair and took the one across from her.

She came right to the point. "Why didn't you tell me it was the Claiborne colt that died in the fire?"

Brian was startled. "You never asked. I suppose I assumed you knew. What difference does it make?"

"It puts us under tremendous liability."

"No more than if he belonged to someone else."

Hillary shrugged off her mink and crossed her legs. Her skirt slid halfway up her thighs, enough so that the tops of her nylons peeked out from below the hem. Brian kept his eyes on her face.

"The colt's ownership was under dispute. The fire inspector says the cause of the fire was arson. My guess is that someone set out to kill the colt. What do you think?"

She was shrewd. He'd give that one to her. "It's possible," he said noncommittally.

Hillary leaned back in the chair and sipped at her whiskey. For some reason his answer had pleased her. But why?

"I understand that Mrs. Claiborne has two more horses stabled at the Stud."

"That's right. However, their ownership is not under dispute."

She leaned forward. Here it was, his ultimatum, the reason he'd been summoned in her usual peremptory, noblesse oblige manner.

"I want you to evict Caitlin Claiborne."

"No," he said evenly.

Her eyes widened. "I beg your pardon?"

"You heard me."

"Aren't you even going to ask me why?"

"No." His mouth was hard, uncompromising. "Your reasons don't interest me, Hillary. I made it very clear when you asked me to stay on at the Stud after your husband died. You gave me full authority."

"I've changed my mind."

"Well, I haven't."

She leaned back again and sipped her drink. "Are you threatening me, Brian?" she asked softly.

"That depends on your perspective."

"Spell it out for me. Exactly what do you mean?"

"I won't evict Mrs. Claiborne's horses."

"And if I insist?"

"I won't stay on."

She frowned. "Do you have a cigarette?"

"No." He watched the nervous play of her fingers against the whiskey glass.

"Sam Claiborne is pressuring me."

"How?"

"He's influential. A word here and there about the unsuitability of my stud could put me out of business."

Brian's eyes narrowed. "You'll have to do better than that. Claiborne is an amateur compared to the Aga Kahn and his friends. They have no intention of goin' elsewhere."

"We have serious damage because of the fire," she insisted. "It won't be as difficult as you think to plant seeds of doubt. I can't risk it."

"For Christ sake, Hillary, have some compassion. Caitlin has nowhere else to go."

"So, it's *Caitlin,* is it?" Her voice—knowing, snide, unattractive—grated on Brian's nerves. "Sam implied there might be more to your relationship than I realized."

Suddenly he understood. This conversation was pointless. It was finished and so was he. Without a word of explanation he rose from his chair, walked to the door and opened it. "Good night, Hillary. I'll clear out by the end of the week."

"You're a fool, Brian. Where will you go? She isn't worth it."

"The drink is on me. Don't forget your coat."

Tight-lipped, she stood, draped the mink around her shoulders, and stalked past him out the door.

Brian held on to the doorknob. His knuckles were white and very prominent beneath the stretched skin of his hand. Deliberately he relaxed, splayed his fingers, wiggled them until he could feel the blood flow again and stepped back, away from the door. Rage wouldn't help him. Caitlin would be home soon. He would have to present her with a plan, a plan that would save her pride and prevent him from looking like the sacrificial lamb.

Martin O'Shea looked around the rectory sitting room. "You can stay here, I suppose. I don't think anyone would mind."

Brian laughed, shook his head, leaned across the table and helped himself to another ham sandwich. "Thanks, but I don't think so. The church isn't a hotel and not everyone would take kindly to your invitation."

Martin relaxed and spread mustard liberally over his ham. "Where will you go?"

"There's a yard up for sale a few miles north of the track."

"Does it have a house?"

"It does."

"Tell me about it."

Between gulps of milky tea and ham sandwich, Brian filled Martin in on the details of the training yard, house, and acreage for which he'd made a substantial offer. "It's vacant," he said. "If everythin' goes accordin' to plan, I can move in now and pay rent until it's officially mine."

"It's a large house for one man."

Brian shrugged. "Beggars can't be choosers."

Martin's blue eyes were fixed on his friend's face. "Are you planning on living there alone?"

"For now," Brian hedged.

Martin turned the subject. "Sam Claiborne's lawyers phoned me earlier in the week."

Brian's face stilled. "What did they want?"

"A statement affirming Lana's deposition that you and Caitlin are having an affair."

Brian swore softly.

Martin winced. "Not here, please. Besides, it's all your fault, you know."

"Would you be good enough to explain that?"

"Lana's been in love with you since she first came back to Kilcullen."

"Why is that my fault?"

Martin grinned. "I've heard 'tis your handsome face that's driving all the women wild—single and married."

Brian felt the heat rise in his cheeks. "I knew Lana was taken with me but this is the first I've heard of *all* the women."

"I can't see it myself," Martin agreed.

"Be serious for once."

The smile left the priest's face. "I am, Brian. Lana's so green with jealousy that she'll do anything to hurt Caitlin. You might want to think twice about staying here in Kilcullen now that you're out of work. Why not start up somewhere else?"

"I'm out of a job, Martin, not out of work," Brian corrected him. "My work is trainin' horses. This is the Curragh race track. Where else would I train them?"

"I was thinking of Caitlin." Martin kept his eyes on Brian's face. "She might find it difficult to live with Lana's dislike. Caitlin isn't accustomed to disapproval from her mates, not here in Kilcullen anyway. When we were small she lorded it over us and we were pleased to let her. We worshipped her, you see."

"Caitlin isn't a child. She's weathered a few trials of her own since she left Kilcullen. I'd worry more about Lana's state of mind. She's not thinkin' clearly. I hope for her sake that she doesn't do any harm. Caitlin would die for her children. I'd hate to see what she would do to someone who helped take them away from her."

Martin frowned. "You don't sound terribly worried about that possibility."

"It won't happen," replied Brian with certainty.

"How can you be sure?"

"Claiborne is a crook. His man set fire to my barn."

"You're not serious."

"I am." Brian's face was grim. "I hope to have proof of that very soon."

"Are you thinking of blackmailing Claiborne?" Martin sounded incredulous.

"If I have to."

"Good Lord, Brian. Do you love her as much as that?"

"I do." It was a relief to finally say it.

Martin hesitated, lifted his teacup and set it down again. "There's another reason Caitlin might be more comfortable somewhere else."

Brian's eyes narrowed to a chilling blue. "What is it?"

Martin shrugged. "Never mind. It was just a thought."

"Where did it come from?"

Martin hesitated.

"Out with it, lad."

"I'm not at liberty to say just yet. But trust me, Caitlin won't be happy about it."

Brian released his breath. "If you're not goin' to tell me why in bloody hell did you bring it up?"

"Because I think you have a chance with Caitlin, if she cares enough for you, but not here, not in Kilcullen. Mark my words, Brian. You don't want to go investing any money in a house and a yard in Kilcullen, not if you want Caitlin Keneally to move in with you."

"Move in with me?" Brian lifted astonished eyes to his friend's face. "Have you not been hearin' anythin' I've said, lad? I want you to marry us. I want to raise her children. I want to give her more children, my children."

Martin smiled sadly. "Then you'll take my advice."

Later that afternoon on his way home, Brian kept his hands on the wheel and his eyes on the road. What in the hell was Martin talking about? Kilcullen was Brian's home. Caitlin was born here, and Annie and Ben were settled in school. This was where she would want to stay.

He would go ahead with the purchase of his training yard and the house with its massive ceilings, tumbling staircase, and a kitchen spacious and well appointed enough for a woman who knew her way around it. Together they would move beyond whatever was troubling Martin.

Brian would make her realize that it was enough just for her to be here, that he loved her, the woman she had become—a dark-eyed girl with a laugh like music, fiercely loyal, tender and vulnerable. A woman who wore old shirts and painters' pants with the same effortless style as lavender lace and diamond studs. The woman who had left Kilcullen, married Sam Claiborne, borne him two children and come home again to find the life she'd been destined to live all along. He would make her understand that the journey was necessary to reach the destination, that none of it was wasted, or wrong or shameful.

He turned down the lane leading to his cottage, stopped by the mailbox, emptied it, and parked in his usual spot near the back entrance. Neeve barked her welcome and Brian opened the door to let her in. Already the cottage had ceased to be home for him. Odd, really, how few were the personal items he'd acquired over the last ten years. E-mail messages waited in his inbox and a stack of papers in his fax tray needed to be sorted through.

Settling back in his chair he looked at his mail first. An envelope with Weatherbys return address caught his attention. He tore it open, read it, and whistled softly. "Son of a bitch," he said under his breath.

Irish Gold's registration had been denied. Would Brian call at his earliest convenience? Turning to his computer screen, he moved the mouse to his mail icon and clicked. Six messages, one from John Chase at Weatherbys. Again Brian read the telling words. *Something of a serious nature has been discovered that makes the timely registering of* Irish Gold *an impossibility. His blood does not match the blood type of* Narraganset, *the sire listed on his application. This oversight must be corrected immediately.* Chase would wait before contacting the owner on the outside chance that the error was the stud farm's mistake.

Brian leaned back in his chair. It was all there, just as he'd expected. The shrill double ring of the phone jarred him. He reached for it. "Hennessey," he said automatically.

"Hello, Brian. It's Caitlin."

Caitlin. As if she need bother to identify herself. "Hello," he said softly, "when did you get back?"

"An hour ago."

Only an hour and she'd already called him. "How did it go?"

"As I expected. I have until June to change my circumstances. We're appealing the decision." She didn't sound disappointed.

"Are you all right with it?"

"Not exactly, but I have an idea, or rather it was Mum's idea. I'd like to tell you about it. When are you free?"

"Now."

She laughed and his heart lifted.

"I'll be there in ten minutes."

Was it just his own biased opinion or did everyone see her as he did? She was beautiful, dressed in something dark blue and above the knee with white around the collar and cuffs. Later, when he thought about it, he could never describe what she wore but somehow it always suited her as if designed especially with her proportions and coloring in mind.

She stood in his doorway, dark hair pulled up in a twist at the back of her head, those tiny curls she could never control wisping around her face, a single pearl in both ears and at her throat. Her legs—Brian allowed himself a good long look at her legs beautifully displayed in neutral-colored nylons beneath her dark skirt. He swallowed, lost his head, pulled her inside, closed the door, and kissed her. Without protest, she followed his lead as naturally and completely as if she'd practiced the move a thousand times before.

"A week can be a long time," she said shakily when he lifted his head.

He tightened his arms around her. "I hoped you'd think of it that way."

"Do you want to hear my news?"

She looked happier than he'd ever seen her. She'd called him an hour after her return and she'd kissed him without reservation. He had nothing to worry about. Brushing her lips once more, he kept hold of her hand and led her to the couch. "Aye. Then I'll tell you mine."

Her eyes sparkled. "I'm going to start a training yard." She clutched his hand. "I need to be able to support myself. One of the conditions for staying in Ireland is that I'm employed here."

Brian was puzzled. He wasn't sure if his lack of understanding was due to her knee intimately pressed against his thigh or if his wits were truly scattered. "I'm not sure—"

"Don't you see, Brian? I can make it here if you help me. I've been helping Davy train at the Curragh for months now."

He did see. This wasn't the time to tell her he was leaving the Curragh. "I may have a few horses for you, an overflow from the Stud."

"I was hoping you would say that." She sat back on his couch and laughed out loud, as pleased as if *Graybeard's Lady* had won the Grand National.

He wanted to prolong this moment, her giddy delight, the flush in her cheeks, the warmth in her eyes and this feeling between them as if the very air itself crackled with a current that needed only the slightest charge to connect them.

Brian thought he'd been the one to move first but maybe she had. He couldn't be sure because it was her words he'd been listening to, the unbelievable words he'd been prepared to wait months, even years for. She said them first, before he declared himself, before he told her about the house and the kitchen and how long he'd waited, and how much he loved and wanted her forever.

Caitlin lifted her lips to the hard edge of his cheek and said them again in her lovely American voice with its flavoring of Irish. "I don't know exactly how or when it happened, but I know that I love you. I hope that's all right."

Somehow, without his quite knowing how, she was in his arms again, the boneless weight of her melting against him, filling up his empty spaces, curve against hollow, cheek against jaw, hip against thigh, her breath warming the pulse point in his throat.

Her absence had made him weak. That could be the only explanation for what was happening to him. Pulling out the clasp that held her hair back, he threaded his fingers in the tangle of her curls and looked down at her face, a face without the classic beauty of Hillary Benedict's but far more lovely because it was uniquely, purely Caitlin's. His gaze settled on her upper lip, bow-shaped, well-defined, slightly chapped, the lip she had given Annie.

She said something. He heard the words but they meant nothing. His hands cupped the back of her head, his thumbs tracing the bones of her cheeks. Her eyes closed, eyelashes dark half-moons against ivory skin. Gently, tentatively, he bent his head and again kissed her mouth.

The flare of her response encouraged him. The pressure of his lips changed, became harder, demanding. She was warm, warm from her laughter, warm from her love, warm from the touch of his lips. A wisp of hair had fallen across her forehead. He brushed it away and kissed her again. Her mouth opened and she kissed him back, thoroughly.

"I can't get you out of my mind," he said, when he came up for air. "I think about you every wakin' hour. You haunt my dreams."

He felt her smile against his throat. Her fingers tickled his ribs, and her words, soft and low, were music to his ears. "Tell me that you want me, Brian. You have no idea how much I need to hear you say the words."

"I've never wanted anythin' more than I want you."

She laughed and his heart nearly burst with the pleasure of it. Pressing her back so that she lay on the couch cushions, he bent over her and kissed her mouth, her neck, the swell of her breasts below the vee of her collar.

He felt her fingers on the buttons of his shirt. Bracing himself with his hands on either side of her, he waited while she slipped the buttons out of their holes and pulled the fabric up out of his pants. Her hands were warm on his chest. The smell of her hair, the texture of her skin, the beat of her heart, the way her blood leaped under his palms and her breath caught in a long, shuddering sigh when his mouth found and settled on a sensitive spot brought him to the edge of a joy he'd looked for his entire life.

This time he would see it through. He would tell her all of it. But first there was this. It took no time at all to remove her dress and hose. The sight of her, all ivory-colored skin and white lace, would have been enough to send him over the edge if she hadn't promised him with velvet fingertips and whispered words that there was more, so much more than he'd hoped for.

Glowing embers from the fire threw off a golden light that lit her skin, washing it in gilt and bronze. Later, he would take off that bit of lace that bound her breasts and kiss every uncovered inch of her but now it was enough to feel her beneath him, to slide deeply inside of her, burying himself in heat and softness, Irish soap and French perfume. She tasted of mint and sweet cream and something herbal he didn't recognize.

Moving against her, he caught her rhythm and matched it. With words found only in the courage darkness brings, with urgent lips and seeking hands he carried her with him, harder and higher, until he felt the slight, nearly imperceptible shifting of her hip. Her breathing changed, quickened, shattering his control. Pressing his mouth against hers, he kissed her until his breath was gone and there was nothing left in him. He kept kissing her until her nails left marks in his flesh, stopping only when she moaned his name into the back of his throat.

His mouth touched the corners of her eyes and tasted wetness and salt. "I love you, Caitlin," he muttered against her hair. "Don't cry, my heart. Everythin' will work out. I'll always love you. I'll wait forever if I have to. Please, don't cry."

"I know," she whispered. "I've always known. But I was worried that you wouldn't tell me."

28

Brigid looked at the clock and tapped her foot. Where was Kirsty? It was past time for her shift. The least the girl could do was have the courtesy to call when she was late. Grumbling to herself, Brigid dried the last of the glasses and set them on the shelf. At this rate Annie and Ben would be home before she had a chance to speak with Caitlin.

The door opened and Kirsty breezed into the room bringing with her the scents of pine and smoke and cinnamon, Christmas smells.

Brigid folded her arms. "You took your time gettin' here."

Kirsty looked guiltily at the clock. "It's only ten minutes past the hour, Mrs. Keneally. I was helpin' with the children at home. Sorry to keep you waitin'."

"Well, never mind then. It's Christmas after all. I just wanted to be home before Caitlin came back."

"You're a wee bit late for that," said Kirsty, tying her apron. "She's already home. We walked down the road together. She's waitin' at your house for the children to come from school."

All at once Brigid found it difficult to breathe. Her hand moved to her throat and she swallowed.

Kirsty glanced up and frowned. "Are you all right, Mrs. Keneally?"

"Aye." The taste of fear was strong in her mouth. "I'll be goin' home a bit early today. Call me if you can't manage alone."

"Make yourself a cuppa and lie down for a bit," advised the girl. "You'll be right as rain tomorrow."

Brigid nodded and walked down the hall and up the small stairs to the living quarters of her house. This was a moment to be dreaded, perhaps not the most difficult moment she would face in the days to come, but certainly one of them.

The house was quiet. Had Caitlin gone out again? The kitchen and living room were empty. She drew a deep breath. "Caitlin, are you here?"

"In here, Mum," her daughter's voice called out from the small sitting room in the back of the house.

Bracing herself, Brigid passed what had once been Annie's room and then Ben's. She hesitated briefly, mustering her courage and walked through the door to the room that served as her study.

Caitlin sat in a deep chair with several opened envelopes on the floor beside her and a week's worth of mail in her lap. She was frowning. "Mum, Father Duran's solicitor wants to see me." She looked up, a question in her eyes. "Isn't that odd?"

Brigid cleared her throat. "It is a bit odd."

Caitlin looked at her watch. "It's nearly three. I won't be able to see him today."

A weight lifted from Brigid's heart. "The children will be home soon. They've missed you."

"I'd rather you didn't say anything about the possibility of our moving back to Kentucky."

"Not a word," Brigid promised.

*   *   *

Brigid drove to her daughter's house the next morning. She was unusually gentle with Annie and Ben, lingering over breakfast and offering to drive them to school. Caitlin looked at her mother curiously. "They can walk, Mum. It's a lovely morning for December." She pulled the curtains aside. "The sun's out. Come and see."

"We want to ride with Gran," Ben informed his mother. "I don't care if the sun's out. It's still cold."

"It's cold in Kentucky, too."

"We rode the bus in Kentucky," Annie reminded her.

Caitlin threw up her hands. "Oh, all right. Do as you please. I thought you might like a few minutes to yourself for a change."

Brigid pulled on her coat. "Hurry up, you two. Remember, Annie. It's Ben's turn to ride in front."

The children raced to the door, stumbled over each other, laughed breathlessly, and raced back to kiss Caitlin before running out to the car.

Caitlin sat down at the table, poured herself a second cup of tea and began to read the *Irish Times*.

Brigid walked to the door and hesitated.

Caitlin looked up from her paper and smiled. "What is it?"

"I was just thinkin'—" She stopped unable to find the right words. Why was it so difficult to say what she meant to this particular child? Determined to finish, she rushed her sentence, jumbling the words together. "You could come with us if you like. We could take a drive to the Curragh and watch them bring the horses in."

Caitlin stared at her strangely. "I'd like to, Mum, but I have an appointment with Father Duran's solicitor."

Brigid looked down at her hands. Slowly she unclenched them. "Of course. I'd forgotten. Will you be needin' a ride?"

"I'll take the bus. What time is Kirsty coming in?"

"Not until two. Why?"

"We might be able to meet for lunch."

By lunch time, this new understanding between them would be completely destroyed. "Why don't we try for tomorrow?" Brigid said gently. "I'll ask Kirsty t' work the mornin' shift."

"All right."

Brigid nodded and walked quickly out the door to the car.

Two hours later she had driven the M1 all the way to the Dublin city center exit and back again. Now she was parked in Caitlin's driveway trying to muster the courage to leave the car, walk into the house, and face her daughter. It was inevitable, really, this final penance, the weightiest of all by far.

Never once, in those dark years when she and Michael had swallowed each other whole and choked on the unpalatable mass of their guilt had she considered what God might ask of her in return for what she'd taken from Him. Discovery she could have handled. Divorce, even scandal would have been manageable, but not losing her daughter. She closed her eyes against the burning tears beneath her eyelids.

Stepping out of the car, Brigid walked through the back door of the house. Curled up on the couch with her legs beneath her, Caitlin waited in the semi-darkness of the living room.

"Hello," Brigid said warily.

Caitlin turned her head. Her face was expressionless, her eyes dark, unreadable, her mouth a slash of red against the clear, poreless skin. A sheaf of official looking papers lay in disarray on the floor. On the table, framed in dark walnut, was an oil painting of a young girl on a horse. "Do you have something to tell me, Mother?" Caitlin asked softly.

Mother. She'd called her "mother," not the familiar affectionate "mum" she'd reverted to months ago. Suddenly Brigid's legs felt wobbly. She sat down in the chair across from Caitlin. "Perhaps it's you who should ask the questions," she began cautiously.

"That would suit you wouldn't it?" Caitlin said bitterly. "Because I don't know where to begin or even what to ask, again you would be spared from telling me the whole truth."

Brigid closed her eyes and leaned back in the chair. Age made its presence known at the strangest times. "All right," she said wearily, "I'll ask the questions. What happened at the solicitor's office?"

"Surely, you know."

The contempt in her daughter's voice nearly undid her. "No," she said, her mouth working, "how would I?"

Caitlin could barely get the words out. "Because of what you were, what the two of you were." Her voice cracked.

For the first time Brigid noticed tear tracks on her daughter's cheeks. "I'm sorry, Caitlin," she said. "It's a poor sort of apology I'm offerin' you, but there isn't anythin' I can do t' take back what I've done."

Caitlin shook her head over and over as if she couldn't bear the pictures in her mind. "How could you? How could you?"

Brigid stared somewhere beyond her daughter's shoulder. "I don't know," she said at last. "I can't imagine what came over me. It was a dreadful thing t' do. Even now it would be dreadful, but then—" She lifted her hands and let them drop in her lap. "I have no excuse except that I was married to a stranger. My life was movin' into its second half and I was afraid I would never again know joy. We were just people, Caitlin. None of us can look back on all we've done and explain why."

"You had five children."

"Aye." Brigid smiled. "And lovely girls they were, too, but

I wouldn't have had the loveliest of them all were it not for Michael Duran." There. She'd said it out loud, finally, and despite her superstitions the roof had held, windows remained intact, and Caitlin stayed in her chair, her fist pressed against her mouth. Brigid relaxed a bit.

"Did you love him?"

Did she love him? A simple question, really. But love had many sides and the answer wasn't at all simple. What if that crisp autumn day all those years ago had begun differently? What if the leaves hadn't piled in drifts along country roads, and the sun hadn't thrown off a light that was sharp and pure? What if the air hadn't smelled of burning wood and the promise of a soft Irish rain. Sunlight was rare in Ireland. It did things to the mind. Sunlight, that day, had given Brigid a raw courage that showed its face at unexpected moments.

Brigid Keneally knew what it was to be in love. It had smothered, wrapped around, and nearly drowned her with the suffocating strength of its addiction. Passion had been new to her despite the children Sean had given her. She had been no match for the sheer power of physical sensation, the tenderness, the magic of a man's hands on her bare skin, his mouth seeking out places no man had ever touched before. She'd felt like a girl again, beautiful, firm, appealing, no matter that she was nearly forty years old, another man's wife, and the mother of more daughters than any woman should have. Without remorse, she'd left them all to go to him, to be with him, to lay in his arms in the long golden grass, to kiss his mouth and feel his lips in her hair, on her breasts, and down the blade of her hip bone where the skin was still stretched and tight, new and young.

God alone knew what had given her the courage to lie to all who asked about her new sense of freedom, to hike up the public road to the glen, to run boldly into his arms, to take off her clothes without the slightest hint of self-consciousness while he looked on, to shamelessly touch him until he gasped with the strength of his own release.

It had rained that day drenching them completely, washing away layers of artifice, leaving what was hidden in their hearts shockingly exposed for the other to see. She would never again feel rain on her face without remembering the heat of those first stolen moments, a hard body, tight with passion, an insistent mouth urging her lips apart, exploring hands lifting her to levels of pleasure she'd never known it was possible for a woman to reach. Even now, just remembering, brought an unaccustomed warmth to her chilled limbs.

Michael Duran had been new to the parish, a man destined for better things than a small country church in an Irish village that survived on the tourist trade, leavings of the more popular Kildare and Naas, one to the east the other to the west. *New,* in Ireland, meant he was still considered a stranger to the villagers despite the five years he'd lived among them. He was invited to supper, spoken of with respect, his Masses were well attended, and his suggestions acted upon, but that was all.

The citizens of Kilcullen were slow to change, and a mere five-year apprenticeship was not enough for them to invite the new priest into their hearts. There were no friendly meetings at the Keneally pub, no street-bowling tournaments where he was invited to take part, no stopping by the rectory for a bit of cheer and an evening of friendly *craic*.

Somehow they knew, without anyone actually spelling it out, that Michael Duran was as different from a working class Irish peasant as a registered thoroughbred is different from a Connemara pony. Father Duran was an aristocrat: one of the anglo-Irish who hailed from the Six Counties; a descendant of those who had kept their land, evicted their tenants, made fortunes during the famine years, and sworn allegiance to the English crown.

Not that their resentment showed, mind you. They were too courteous for that. But it was there all the same. It grew as the years crept up on them and the priest stayed on. They were reminded of their own shortcomings when they listened to him speak in the Oxford educated tones of a well-bred Englishman. When he held out the communion wafer they glanced at his long patrician fingers with their manicured nails and nodded knowingly at each other. His sermons appeared humorless and stern, his subtle gentleman's wit escaping all but a few of the congregation. They looked upon his flat belly and his white, flawless teeth with suspicion, and when he took to walking country roads to visit his parishioners, they shook their heads, pursed their lips, and only guessed as to why a man with a perfectly good automobile would choose to use up the only legs God had given him in such a way.

Brigid was fascinated by him. She'd left school early but everyone knew she would have earned a leaving certificate if her family hadn't needed her in the pub. Reading was her passion. Yeats and Synge, Milton, Shakespeare, new Irish writers like Brendan Behan, Nuala O'Halloran, and Liam O'Flaherty. Writers who used words in ways she'd never heard before—stirring words, words that lifted her soul, opened up worlds, exposed her to ideas no one else had ever heard of, much less suggested.

Over the years the purity of her love for Sean had gone the way of harsh reality, taking on the appearance of a room beautiful and elegant by candlelight, only to be seen the following day in the merciless morning sun, the carpet thin and frayed, the drapes shabby, the furniture marred, in need of repair.

They'd struck up a friendship, the dissatisfied wife who

spent her days dividing her time among the post office, the store, the pub, five daughters, and a man who drank too much, and the lonely priest who ministered to no one's soul but his own.

Brigid knew that he walked alone in the long hours of summer when the sun lit the sky until well after nine. Occasionally she met him, inadvertently at first, but later too often to be other than intentional. Then they walked together—a woman, slim, lovely, her face and hair the color of the first gold leaves that fell from the trees; the man, tall, refined, lean, with distinguished flecks of silver dimming the darkness of his hair, softening the chiseled bones of his face. A handsome couple: graceful, well-matched, arresting, and, no matter how one twisted the view, utterly forbidden.

When Brigid saw him that day, she paused and caught her breath. He'd reached the top of the rise ahead of her. Instead of his Roman collar he wore regular street clothes and even though she was some distance away she could see the fineness of them. What did it mean this breaking of tradition? She stopped by a giant oak, her sepia-toned skirt and sweater blending with the tree bark. He hadn't yet seen her. Brigid watched as he stood, hands in the pockets of his trousers, head lifted toward the sky. He wasn't handsome the way Sean had been in his youth, but no one who saw the two men together would find him wanting in comparison. *Striking* was the word that came to Brigid's mind, *striking* and *discriminating,* a man not easily forgotten, a man wasted on the priesthood.

Moving away from the camouflaging tree, Brigid climbed the hill to stand beside him. He reached out his hand, helping with her last few steps.

He smiled. "Hello, Brigid. You look grand."

She blushed. "Thank you, Father."

"I'd rather not be Father Duran today, if you don't

mind." He stepped back and placed his hands on the lapels of his coat. "I'm not dressed for the part."

"I noticed. Why is that?"

He opened his mouth to speak, looked into her eyes, and closed it again. Shrugging, he started down the path. "No reason. One gets tired of all that black."

Brigid laughed and fell into step beside him. "An odd sentiment for a priest."

Laughing with her, he reached for her hand and held it a bit longer than necessary before tucking it into the crook of his arm. "I'm more than a priest, Brigid."

"I didn't think there was anythin' more than being a priest," she teased him.

"There's a great deal more than that."

This was the best part of her time with him, the bantering, the exploring of ideas, the stretching of her mind. "Such as?"

He tilted his head, dark eyes narrowing, silvered hair falling across his forehead, brow furrowed in concentration. "Being a man is more important than being a priest."

"Are the two mutually exclusive?"

"Yes," he said emphatically.

The road was shaded by a canopy of trees. Shaded, silent, remote—the leafy bower felt like a secluded sanctuary, separate from the world outside. Brigid stopped, her hand still securely tucked inside Michael's arm. "Do you really mean that?"

"I do."

She knew where she was going but she wasn't about to back away from it. Nothing on earth would make her stop now. "Why?"

He turned and the look on his face told her everything she needed to know and more.

"Have you ever wanted something that you know is

wrong?" he asked urgently. "Something so outrageous that it will change your life forever and everything you've done, everything you've worked for may turn out to be meaningless?"

"No," she said honestly, "not yet."

"Brigid." His voice was ragged, raw with wanting. "Do you know what it is that I'm asking?"

She lifted her chin. Never had she felt so confident, so brave, so beautiful. "Tell me," she whispered, "I need the words, now, from you."

He turned to look at her, smoothed the hair from her forehead, and reached for her other hand. "You're an unusual woman, Brigid Keneally," he said unsteadily.

She waited for what she knew would come.

His hand cupped her cheek, his fingers moving over the bones of her face. "Have you any idea how lovely you are?"

Closing her eyes, she leaned against his hand. "Tell me."

"It takes a lifetime to find a woman like you—proud, graceful, curious."

A curious lightness took hold of her. She could do anything, say anything, and it would be all right. "Hold me," she said, "I want to feel you against me."

His arms moved around her, sliding past her ribcage, settling on her back, her waist, her cheek pressed against his chest. Her heart pounded in her ears or was it his? She couldn't tell. Something soft and warm brushed against her temple. Could a man's lips really feel this way? Brigid leaned into the warmth and the feeling intensified, moved to her cheek, her neck, her shoulder, and finally her mouth. Unresisting, she parted her lips and felt his tongue slip in, filling the space in her mouth.

Heat flowed through her. Standing on her toes, she met the thrust of his tongue with her own desire, giving in to a need she'd only allowed herself to think about in the privacy of her dreams. She was surrounded by warmth, hard muscle, fine wool, and a tension she hadn't felt before. Her blood sang and the ache that began in a spot below her stomach moved up and outward, filling her with urgency, capturing her hands, controlling her movements until the barrier of clothing disappeared and her palms moved against the smoothness of hot male skin and rough chest chair. Moaning softly, she lifted his sweater and pressed her mouth against his breast bone.

His soft intake of breath increased her daring. This was something Brigid knew better than he. She was the aggressor, he the novice. Moving down the length of his chest, she pressed furtive kisses on his skin, relishing the trembling of his muscles beneath her fingertips, knowing, because she knew him, that he was drowning, helpless in the throes of longing, fear, and a reckless desire to experience what had always been denied him. She stopped briefly at his navel, her tongue circling, then invading until he gasped, cradled her head, and pressed her firmly against him.

Quickly, her fingers moved to his belt. With the precision of a craftsmen, she worked it apart, releasing the button, pulling at the zipper, until the hard swollen length of him fell into her hands. That first time he came in her mouth, one more sacrilege against Holy Mother Church, the spilling of seed for no purpose other than sheer pleasure. Her lips on his sensitive flesh were his undoing and, like a schoolboy, he came instantly, explosively, unable to control the surging heat, the rush of blood, the curse of Adam.

Because it was only a beginning, because having tasted a pleasure he'd only imagined he wanted more and so did she. His fine cashmere coat spread on the long grass away from the road was warm against Brigid's skin.

She loved him, not that first time, or the time after that, but sooner than she would have thought. A woman of forty was more cautious than one in her first bloom of youth. Love was more than fire in the loins. It was shared thoughts, laughter, knowing the other's failings and loving despite them.

Brigid came to the realization of her love on a cold February night. Mrs. Clarke, the parish housekeeper, was having her holiday, and they had taken advantage of her absence. Two weeks had passed since they'd managed to meet and their first bout of lovemaking in his narrow bed was intense and urgent. Their passion sated, they lay together quietly, neither one in a rush to rise, to dress, to take up the normalcy of their lives.

He combed her hair with his fingers, winding the long golden strands several times around his hand, pulling back her head so that he could look into her eyes. "I love you, Brigid," he said fiercely, for the first time. "You're the best thing that has ever happened to me. No matter what happens, never doubt that I love you."

Caressing his arrogant, strong-featured face, she smiled and pressed a kiss against his jaw. "Has somethin' happened?"

He hesitated. "I'm thinking of leaving the priesthood."

Alarmed, she pulled back. "Because of me?"

"Because of what I've done." He rolled over and stared at the ceiling. "I feel like a hypocrite, saying Mass on Sunday, hearing confessions."

Her voice was hollow, but calm. "Are you tellin' me we're finished?"

"No!" There was no doubting the horror behind the word. "I won't give you up. I can't give you up."

"What do you want, Michael?"

He reached for her, bruising the delicate skin on the inside of her arms above her elbows. "You. I want you with me, always."

"I love you, too, Michael," she said, voicing the truth to herself and to him. "But I'm a married woman with children. We can't be together, not here, not in Ireland."

"I'll think of something, my darling. I promise I will."

They came together once more and this time their loving was slow and so sweetly tender that whenever Brigid looked back, it was this night she remembered and the promises he made, muffled, but unmistakable, against her throat.

Dark days loomed ahead, heavy with gloom amid moments of green hills and bright mornings. There was hope, weighted down by the inexorable pull of reality, the rhythms of long hours spent in the pulse of everyday life. In the end it was that night she would recall above all others, when their love met and was matched and for a single, crystalline moment, everything was possible.

How often had she wished that she could have had a look ahead and seen the way it would all turn out. And yet, what good would it have done her? If she were completely honest with herself, Brigid knew she would do the same thing over again, despite the gossips' knowing looks, the averted eyes from well-meaning friends, those frantic, desperate couplings behind the old arbor when the end was near, and finally, the birth of a child, dark-haired and dark-eyed, so different from the others that even Assumpta, her dearest friend, shook her head, took Brigid's two hands in her own, and pleaded with her, "Be done with it, lass. Nothing in this world can ever come of it."

And nothing had. When Brigid, newly widowed, pressed for more than stolen moments, he refused her, choosing his life and his past over their future together. That was the end of it. Thirty years had passed. They met infrequently, in the streets, at Mass, in her pub, and yet she had spoken no more than a few sentences to him in all that time. But she hadn't forgotten. She would never forget, not the pleasure nor the pain. Only her headstrong, obstinate, late-in-life daughter remained her one regret.

Caitlin sat across from her, cheeks scarlet, eyes accusing, waiting for her mother's answer.

Brigid nodded. "Aye. I loved him, more than anythin'. More than my children, more than my honor, more than the life I'd made. I would have gone anywhere with him." The relief of admitting it was overwhelming.

"Did he love you?"

"Not enough."

Caitlin pointed to the painting. "He left me two hundred thousand pounds and this picture. He had it painted from a photograph. It's like the one in the pub, only a different pose."

Brigid knew about the picture. She hadn't known about the money. Two hundred thousand pounds was a windfall. "That's a great deal of money."

Caitlin glared at her accusingly. "You knew, didn't you?"

"I knew what the two of us were to him, if that's what you mean."

"Did you know about the money?"

Brigid shook her head. "No."

Caitlin rubbed her eyes, fluffed the couch pillow and positioned it behind her head. "Why did he leave you?"

"He didn't. I left him."

"But you said—"

"This is difficult for me, Caitlin. Try t' understand. I wanted him t' leave the church, t' go away with me and the children. He asked t' be released from his vows and was refused. Then he changed his mind." The old hurt, diamond sharp, closed around her heart. "I wanted more than we had. I wanted t' walk down the street with him, smile at my friends, hold my head up in a public place."

"In Kilcullen?" Caitlin was aghast.

Brigid couldn't help laughing. It was good to laugh. It was a start back to where they'd been before today. "Perhaps not in Kilcullen," she agreed.

"I'm not Caitlin Keneally at all," Caitlin said in wonder. "Who am I, Mum?"

"I was Brigid Keneally when you were born. You're as much a Keneally as I am."

Caitlin's brow furrowed. "How long were you together?"

"A year."

"Did anyone know?"

"Assumpta knew."

"And John?"

"I don't know," Brigid said honestly. "Some women can keep what needs to be kept from a husband. Others can't. I wouldn't have minded if she'd told John. He isn't a man for gossip."

"I mind," Caitlin said coldly. "This isn't only about you anymore. It's about me and my children, and I mind very much. I wanted to stay here in Kilcullen with Annie and Ben. The last thing I need is for everyone to know that Father Michael Duran, the pastor of Saint Patrick's, was their grandfather."

"I would hardly call John *everyone*," her mother said.

"Who would you call *everyone*?"

Brigid swallowed. "I don't know. Maybe Michael told someone."

"Who would he tell?"

"Martin, maybe, in confession."

Caitlin shook her head and the ghost of a smile appeared on her lips. "Poor Martin." She sighed, unfolded her legs, and stood. "I'm going out. Tell Annie and Ben I'll be back before dinner."

Brigid didn't really want to know but it was harder not to. "Where are you goin'?"

"I'm not sure. I need to think."

Clasping her hands together, Brigid prayed for patience. "Don't do anything foolish, Caitlin. Perhaps you should take a walk first."

Surprisingly, Caitlin was agreeable. "What a good idea." Buttoning up her coat, she pulled the gloves from her pocket, and disappeared down the hallway.

Brigid heard the door open and close again. She waited until the large hand made a complete circle of the clock before moving to the phone.

He answered on the first half of the double ring. "Hennessey."

"Hello, Brian, it's Brigid Keneally."

"How are you, Mrs. Keneally?"

"At the moment I could be better. There isn't much time, but I wanted t' let you know that Caitlin saw Father Duran's solicitor this morning. She's very upset."

"I see." His voice had changed. It was cautious, probing. "Is there anythin' I can do?"

"We had words," she began.

He interrupted. "How is Caitlin?"

Brigid clutched the phone with both hands. "She went for a walk. I believe she may be on her way to see you."

Brian's voice, low and reassuring, soothed her. "I'll talk to Caitlin and ring you back. Put your feet up, Mrs. Keneally. Caitlin's a sensible girl. She'll come around."

Brigid hung up the phone. There was something about Brian Hennessey that made a woman feel as if she could rest her burdens for awhile. It was absurd, of course. *Sensible*. He'd called Caitlin sensible. Obviously he saw a side of her that no one else had. Intelligent, she'd been called, spirited, profound, complicated, and difficult. Those were the trailers that had at one time or another been affixed to Caitlin during her lifetime, but no one, as far as Brigid knew, had ever called her sensible.

Brigid was the sensible one: an obedient daughter, an accommodating wife, practical, efficient, matter-of-fact, a no-nonsense kind of girl her father had called her. Who would have imagined that she would have done what she did? Who would have known she was capable of such desperate emotion and the ache that followed, an unsettled ache that would last for more years than she could count—cold painful years where it was all she could do to work and sleep and work again, refusing to think at all until a protective scar sealed itself around her heart and she could hear the name *Michael* without flinching?

A wave of nostalgia shook her and with it came the memories: memories of her heavy with the child she would bear, memories of Michael coming up the rise, the lean beautiful length of him framed on both sides by the colors of autumn.

If she tried very hard she could stop it now, concentrate and push aside the memory, just as she had a thousand times before. But the softness of Michael's kiss intruded. Once, the world and the promise of love had been hers. She wanted the way it was back again. Closing her eyes, Brigid welcomed the images that washed over her.

He'd been distant that day, running his hand across her bulging belly over and over as they walked the lonely country roads outside Kilcullen. Finally she'd asked him.

"Is somethin' wrong, Michael?"

He came out with it as if her permission was what he'd waited for. "I've been denied a hearing. They won't let me leave."

"Why not?"

"It isn't easy to defrock a priest, Brigid." He laughed bitterly. "Fornication isn't reason enough. Apparently neither is adultery. That doesn't shock them. There's absolution for that. It's my vow that's irrevocable."

"What about losin' your faith? Is that reason enough?"

Again his long, aristocratic hand moved across her stomach. "Perhaps, but that wouldn't be true. I haven't lost my faith."

"But you no longer want t' be a priest. Your child is about to be born."

"I still believe in God, Brigid."

"For pity's sake, Michael. One lie isn't goin' to condemn you forever. Who made such arbitrary rules anyway? Do you think that Jesus Christ is up there in heaven tellin' everyone that a priest won't go t' hell for fornication and adultery but he will go if he lies about his faith to marry the woman he loves?"

"It's more complicated than that. I can't deny my faith. Please understand, I must be left with something."

"Left with somethin'?" She'd pulled away from him. "What am I, Michael? I'm nearly eight months gone with child. Sean is dead. I love you more than life itself. I'm willin' to leave everythin' I know and go with you to start again with nothin' but the clothes on our backs. You said you loved me, Michael. What does that mean?"

"You have five children."

She felt as if a heavy stone was pressing against her chest. Stopping by a giant oak, she leaned against the trunk to catch her breath. "I've had five children all along."

"We can't be selfish. You have the store and the pub. It's a decent living even without Sean."

"You said we couldn't live here," she reminded him.

He rested his arm against a tree branch just above his head. He wore his Roman collar, something he hadn't done for months. Black suited him, complementing the silver touches in his hair and the dark, nearly black eyes set under soaring eyebrows. She knew he was laboring under something that needed to be said. Words didn't come easily to him, not like it had with Sean, despite his seminary training and his Oxford education.

"We could live here if nothing changed," he began.

No, oh, no. He couldn't mean what she'd heard.

Encouraged by her silence, he continued. "No one would know that the child wasn't Sean's. We could continue as we are, meeting like this." He turned to her eagerly. "It would be better for both of us, love. No nasty scandal, no scrubbing for a living. We have more than most married couples. We talk and touch and laugh. How many have that after the years of living from hand to mouth takes its toll?"

"What happens if I have another child and this time with no husband? Will you marry me then, Michael, after I've given you two children, or three, or four?"

"I'll be careful, darling, very careful. I promise I will."

"No one can promise such a thing."

"There are ways to prevent pregnancy."

He was pulling away from her. He wanted out. She could feel it. "In England, maybe, and in the north. But not in Ireland."

"You could go north."

"With six children and a pub t' run? I don't think so." Her arms were cold but it was nothing compared to the cold inside of her, freezing the life from her limbs. She rubbed her arms. It was late and she should be getting back but she wasn't leaving until it was clear between them. He would have to say it. She would not make it easy for him by walking away, out of his life.

"I don't think this is right for your children."

Her eyes burned with tears. "You didn't think of my children when you stuck your tongue down my throat or when we were rollin' about between your sheets in the rectory," she said furiously.

"Don't be crude."

She read the distaste on his face and something inside of her snapped. It was over. "Goodbye, Michael," she said softly, turning on her heel and walking quickly away.

He did not come after her. Flowers were sent when Caitlin was born, anonymously, of course. Brigid knew who had sent them. When Caitlin was old enough to attend school, her mother considered sending her to the National School instead of to Saint Patrick's with Kitty, but that would have been too obvious. Caitlin's coloring had been the source of enough speculation. Brigid saw no need to point out further differences between her and her sisters. Only Assumpta O'Shea knew her secret, and she was the soul of discretion.

Michael Duran had missed his opportunity. At the end, in the hospital when Annie was hurt, he told her of his regret, but Brigid wasn't so sure. She knew what it was to love. Once, Michael Duran had been on the other end of that love. But that was a lifetime ago. Now her love was caught up, complete in the circle of her children and grand-children.

29

❧❧❧

Caitlin's first inclination was to tell no one, to simply pack up her children and take the first train out of Kilcullen. But then what? Kentucky was the obvious answer. Lucy would take them in, but Claiborne Farms was Sam's home, and Caitlin couldn't live with her ex-husband and his mother for the rest of her life. Besides, she rather liked the idea of being independent, of building a business that was exclusively hers from the ground up. Michael Duran's legacy would make the dream a reality. But not here, not in Kilcullen.

At first Caitlin had considered not accepting his money on principle. But once the horror of the solicitor's revelation had worn off, her own practical business sense prevailed. If she didn't take it, the money would revert to the church and if ever an institution could afford to give up two hundred thousand pounds, it was the Roman Catholic Church. She would use the money for herself and her children and be better off for it.

Caitlin walked through the late afternoon dusk and forced herself to slow her steps and think about the events her mother had described, events leading up to her own conception and birth.

Two hours ago she'd been furious with Brigid, but now she wasn't so sure she had a right to be. Thirty-one years ago her mother had fallen in love and been loved in return.

She did not doubt Michael Duran's feelings for her mother. Caitlin remembered the snapshots. Long ago, before worry and work and children had taken their toll, Brigid had been a beautiful woman. Just because a man was a priest made him no less human. Ideally, a man entering the priesthood set aside the trappings of ordinary men, but perhaps, for some, it wasn't so easily accomplished. Perhaps it was a struggle to be battled and overcome every new sunrise.

Caitlin was thirty-one years old, old enough to understand the magnetic pull of desire. No, it wasn't her mother she blamed, nor was it Father Duran. Blame had no place in what she'd learned at the solicitor's office today.

It was later, in Brian's cottage, that another kind of ax had fallen, one that affected her more profoundly because it was so unexpected.

The massive gate of the Curragh loomed before her. She stood before it, reached out and clung to the wrought iron, her fingers folding over the center pike. For as long as she could remember, this gate had been the entrance to the mainstay of her life.

Lifting the latch, Caitlin pushed it open and walked through the cobbled entrance of the stud farm, past the dormitory, the offices, and the swan pond. Jagged plates of thin ice floated on the surface of the gray water. For once she did not stop at the barns to check on either of her horses, but continued up the path and over the knoll to Brian's cottage.

As if he felt the pull of her presence, he opened the door at the exact moment she started up the long driveway.

"Hello," he said in that low, gravelly voice she would prefer in a man for the rest of her life. "I've been expectin' you."

She reached the steps of his porch and climbed them to stand before him. Her coat was unbuttoned. His eyes lingered on the collar of her blouse edged in white lace and then moved to her mouth. Caitlin felt the warmth of his approval. "Are you omniscient or did my mother call you?"

He grinned. "She called me. Does that bother you?"

The bittersweet honesty of his answer pierced her heart. "It doesn't matter."

"Will you come inside?"

She nodded and he stepped back, allowing her to precede him into the living room.

"I love you, Caitlin," he said, heading her off. "Please believe that."

She did, but it didn't change anything. "I can't be with you, Brian."

His eyes met hers and held. "Don't destroy what we've begun."

She shook her head. "You don't understand."

He frowned, reached for her, changed his mind, and dropped his hands to his sides. "No. I don't understand. Tell me."

Tears closed her throat. "I can't."

"Why not?"

"I don't want to."

"Then don't," he said reasonably. "Tell me later, when you're ready."

Again she shook her head.

He swore softly. "Sweet Jesus, Caitlin. Why won't you trust me?"

"It's not that."

"What is it, then?"

She swallowed. "I'm not ready for this. I don't know what will happen."

"Yesterday you didn't feel this way."

She didn't want to tell him. The horror on his face would kill her. "I'm leaving now. I just wanted to tell you that I can't—, that we're not—"

His eyes blazed. She'd made him angry, no small feat for a man with Brian's patience. "Listen to me, Caitlin Keneally," he said in a controlled voice. "You've done a great deal of talkin' but now it's my turn. I don't know what you think you've done, but it doesn't matter. I love you. I want to marry you. I've never said that to another woman. I know it's soon to be thinkin' of that, but my feelin's won't go away. Don't tell me that between a night and a day you've mixed up yours enough to change your mind about me."

He wasn't all that tall but just now he seemed to tower over her. Backing away from him, she felt the edge of a chair against the back of her legs and sat. He leaned over her, bracing himself with his hands on the upholstered arms. "I love you. Doesn't that mean anythin' to you?"

"Yes, it does, a great deal, but it doesn't change anything. I'm sorry, Brian."

"Are you?" He straightened and moved away. She felt oddly bereft now that he was no longer close to her.

She sighed, suddenly too weary to get up out of her chair. She had spent too many years with Sam Claiborne to trust easily. It would take time to heal herself. "I'm sorry, Brian," she said again, her voice low, her words unsteady. Tears welled up, spilling over onto her cheeks. She lifted her hand to shield her eyes. "I didn't mean to lead you on. I told you from the beginning this might happen."

His face was pale. "I love you, Caitlin. I love your children as if they were my own."

She could feel the sob rise in her throat, blocking the airways. She gasped, breathed, and tried to hold back the waves of pain.

Brian cupped her elbows and lifted her out of the chair, bringing her close to his chest. Dear Lord, had she ever wanted anything this much? Turning her face into the curve of his neck, she breathed in the smell of him, soap, leather, horse, and hay. For an instant she was tempted to put everything behind her, everything but this. Was it possible to want so and turn away from it?

Summoning resources from deep within her, Caitlin stepped back, pushing him away. She couldn't afford another error in judgement, not with two children at stake.

"Don't do this." His voice was raw with hurt.

"I can't help it," she said, and watched the light leave his eyes. "I want to but I can't."

"Tell me why."

"It's too soon after Sam. There are things I don't want to share with you right now." She waited for him to tell her she was absurd, that her concerns weren't legitimate. All of her life people had told her that her feelings weren't important enough, serious enough, worthy enough to think twice about. Bracing herself, she waited, hoping he wouldn't disappoint her. It would be so much easier to walk away if his words proved her right.

He looked at her, exasperated, blue eyes dark with confusion, black hair falling across his forehead, the vein in his neck throbbing against his shirt collar. "Your standards are very high," he said gently. "I wish I was up to them."

"It's not you. It's me. I'm sorry," she said again.

"So am I."

"It wouldn't be right for either of us."

"I suppose not."

So, this was what giving up felt like. "I've Annie and Ben to consider."

He nodded. "You have."

"It wouldn't be right for them."

"Don't say that." The anger was back in his voice again. "Of all the reasons you've thrown at me today, don't say I wouldn't be good for your children."

Too much had been said already. Mutely, Caitlin turned and walked toward the door.

"Caitlin."

She turned, waiting.

He met her gaze steadily. "I had *Irish Gold*'s blood samples sent to Weatherbys. He wasn't a *Narraganset* foal."

"How is that possible? *Irish Gold* died in the fire."

"I sent the samples before the fire."

"You told me you hadn't."

"No. You assumed I hadn't and I didn't correct you."

"Why not?"

"I had no proof. You were goin' to Kentucky. I knew if your husband was capable of settin' fire to a barn full of horses, he was dangerous. Until I had the facts, I couldn't tell you."

She frowned. "Why would Sam do such a thing?"

"That remains to be seen. Will you use the information?"

"I'll tell him I know," she said slowly. "I have no other choice, but I won't blackmail him if that's what you mean."

"Would you like the documentation from Weatherbys?"

"Yes."

Brian left the room, returning with the evidence. Handing it to Caitlin, he hesitated. "Be careful."

"You've been very busy," she said. "Is there anything else?"

"Sam is puttin' pressure on Hillary Benedict. She's afraid for the reputation of the Stud."

"What kind of pressure?"

"You have a month to find another stable."

She counted the days in her head. Apparently Claiborne

money still had influence in Ireland. "Thank goodness I have a barn."

"The stud fees will be higher everywhere else," he warned her.

"How much of a discount have you been giving me?"

"Half."

Caitlin hoped her shock didn't show. Fees had risen enormously since John O'Shea's time. She couldn't afford to spend Father Duran's money on her horses. "I'll manage," she said stiffly. "Thank you for telling me."

"You could take a chance on me until you're up and started."

Her hand was on the door. "I don't understand."

"I've made an offer on a yard near the track. It's time I went out on my own."

From across the room she could see the blue of his eyes. "Please tell me you didn't leave the Curragh because of me."

"Hillary and I haven't been seein' things the same way for a long time."

"All right, then. I'll think about your offer."

"Think about both of them, Caitlin. I'm not going anywhere."

It was after four when she left the cottage. Fog clung to the trees and streetlights, shrouding the branches, blurring the lamps so the light took on the fuzzy quality of candles in the December darkness. Turning up the collar of her coat, Caitlin hurried down the deserted streets of Kilcullen, more miserable than she could ever remember feeling.

She was a fool to think of staying here. There was too much to put behind her. Brian would wear her down before she was ready or, worse still, he would find someone else, an irrational thought considering she'd refused him, but one she couldn't bear to face. Lana Sullivan hated her, Annie still wanted to go home, and every time Caitlin looked into her mother's eyes, she could see the shame in them. Only Ben was unaffected—sweet, chubby, affable Ben who would be just as content in Kentucky with Grandma Lucy as he was here in Kilcullen.

Annie and Ben were eating cheese and tomato sandwiches when she walked into the kitchen of her mother's house. They jumped up and threw themselves into her arms, jabbering a thousand questions all at once.

"Hold on," she laughed, hugging her children fiercely. "I can't answer both of you at the same time." Over their dark heads, her eyes met her mother's. Their glances connected and held as if an invisible force united them, its message clear and unmistakable. *This is what's important,* her mother's eyes said, *this blood bond that ties us together. Nothing matters as much as this.*

Later, after listening to conflicting renditions of the time Annie and Ben had spent without her, Caitlin tickled and kissed them until they were breathless and then left them to do their schoolwork on the round oak table in her mother's kitchen. She returned to the sitting room where Brigid was banking the fire with squares of peat. Caitlin rubbed her arms against the cold, saw the tea tray set for two, and sat down in a wingback chair.

Brigid pulled off her rubber gloves and threw them into the peat basket. "That should do it," she said, before dragging her chair closer to the fire. "I've made tea. Would you like a cup?"

Caitlin nodded. "Please."

Brigid sat down and carefully poured milk and steaming tea into china cups. She stirred a spoonful of sugar into each and passed one to Caitlin. "You're the only one who takes it just as I do," she observed. "Did you know that?"

Caitlin thought a minute. "I don't think I ever really paid attention," she said. "I know that Ben doesn't like it at all and Annie likes hers black with honey."

Brigid smiled. "You know their preferences because they're your children. A mother always knows."

Caitlin cleared her throat. It was awkward, this thing between them, awkward to leave it, awkward to clear the air. "Mum," she began, "I don't blame you for what you did. I was surprised at first, that's all. It's just that I never thought of you that way."

"What way?"

Caitlin felt the color rise in her cheeks. She searched her vocabulary for the right words. *Sexual* came to mind but that would never do. *Sensual* wasn't right either. "Youthful," she blurted out. "I never thought of you as youthful. You were always just my mother."

"I suppose it's only natural." Brigid looked pensive. "I wasn't particularly young when you were born."

"I always knew there was something odd about me," Caitlin confessed. "I didn't look like a Keneally but it was more than that." How did one explain the feeling of sitting at the table, watching common rituals like one's mother dishing up plates, smearing brown sauce on praties, reprimanding a daughter for her table manners or her conversation or her marks in school, and all the while feeling she was different from her sisters?

"You were different, but not because you weren't Sean Keneally's daughter. You would have been different no matter who your father was."

It was time for the question, the one that had haunted Caitlin since the day Ciara Burke whispered in her ear, in lurid detail, how babies were put inside their mother's stomachs. "Why did you have me at all, Mum?"

Brigid looked perplexed. "Quite frankly, Caitlin, I had no choice."

It was not the answer she'd expected. "Yes, you did. You

could have gone north or to England. People did it all the time, even then."

"What are you saying, lass?"

Caitlin's hands shook. Carefully, she set her cup and saucer down on the tray. "You could have had an abortion." There it was, put into ugly, honest words.

Finally, Brigid understood. Her face, pretty still, even at seventy-one, settled into lines of shock. "Why would you ask such a thing?" she gasped.

Caitlin waited until she could trust herself to speak. "You were forty years old, a widow with five children. Isn't that reason enough?"

"It might be for some women," her mother agreed, "but I never once considered it."

"Not even when my father wouldn't marry you?"

Brigid's eyes widened in sudden understanding. "A woman doesn't love a child because of a man, Caitie. Would you love your children anymore if someone other than Sam Claiborne had fathered them?"

Her mind flashed mental images, Annie's face, scrubbed and clean, Ben's cheeks, round, moist and warm when she'd kissed him after his bath. "Of course not." The suggestion angered her.

"Isn't that what you thought, that I loved you less because of Michael?"

Caitlin stared into the fire. Put into words, the idea was absurd.

Brigid left her chair and knelt beside Caitlin, taking her daughter's hands between her own. "By the time Lelia was born, I had no feelin's for Sean Keneally beyond pity. If your logic was sound, it should have been Kitty and Mary askin' the questions, not you. I loved Michael Duran even if he didn't care enough t' marry me. I may not have welcomed the idea of having another child, Caitie, but don't doubt that you were loved, deeply loved, from the moment I knew you were goin' t' be born. Can you understand the difference?"

Strangely enough, she could. Tears were embarrassing but the primal, human need for emotional catharsis was strong within her, and for the first time in her life, Caitlin was grateful for her mother's shoulder. Burying her face against the soft skin of Brigid's neck, she wept. "I don't know what to do," she said at last, sniffing back the last of the tears. "Please, Mum, tell me what to do."

"Oh, love." Brigid's voice was a mix of laughter and regret. "Only you can decide that. But I'll be here while you decide. I promise you that."

30

She was the last person he expected to see. Keeping his face impassive, Brian turned back to check the stirrups on the two-year-old roan he'd acquired yesterday. "Hello, Lana."

"I was in the neighborhood," she began.

He finished with the horse, ran his hand down the withers and turned to look at Lana, his expression unreadable.

"No one has seen you for some time now," she faltered, unsure of herself.

Brian was surprised at the level of animosity that rose inside of him at the sight of her. "Most of my business is in Naas and Kildare Town."

Fidgeting with a buckle on the strap of her purse, she reached out to stroke the horse's neck. "What's his name?"

"*Northern Lights,*" he said shortly. "What can I do for you, Lana?"

She shrank back, pulling her hand away. "I was wondering if you had time for a bite to eat?"

Remorse replaced his annoyance. Lana believed herself to be in love with him. If he had been more direct in the first place, the whole mess would never have happened. "I'm afraid not," he said gently.

"You've friends in Kilcullen, Brian," she said, growing bolder. "It would mean a great deal to us to have some news of how you're getting on."

He couldn't allow her to humiliate herself anymore. Plain speaking was the only way. "My friends know how I'm gettin' on." He emphasized the word friends.

In the dim light of the barn, he could see a wave of red stain her face and neck. "I thought—" she stopped.

He waited, refusing to help her.

"Caitlin won't have you," she burst out. "She's made it plain enough."

"Has she now?"

"You can't deny it."

Ignoring the searing hurt that followed her words, he kept his eyes on Lana's face. "I'm wonderin' how you came by that bit of information. It's not as if Caitlin would take you into her confidence now, would she?"

"You don't know that."

Controlling his temper, Brian soothed the fidgety colt, clucking gently under his breath. Keeping his eyes on the now quiet animal, he spoke deliberately. "I know this. When a woman betrays one of her own, it makes a man wonder how loyal she would be to him."

She gasped. "You've no call to talk to me this way, Brian Hennessey."

"We've no call to say anythin' to each other at all, lass. You know where my heart is, whether or not she'll have me."

He watched her eyes flicker across his face. Something in his expression must have convinced her in a way that words had not. She blinked back tears. Automatically, his hand moved in search of a handkerchief. His nature, the same one that brought him to a love of dogs and horses, and later to children, was moved to pity by her tears. Midway to his pocket, he changed his mind. Better to let her cry it out, to despise him if she was so inclined.

They stayed that way, without speaking, for interminable seconds. Finally, she threw him a last angry, watery glance and left the barn.

Davy Flynn arrived on her heels. He hurried to explain. "I wasn't listenin' at the door, if that's what you're thinkin'."

Brian laughed. He felt lighter, somehow, as if settling with Lana had lifted several stone from his shoulders. Anything was possible. "What are you doin' here?"

"Lookin' for work. I've left the Curragh hopin' you'd take me on."

"In that case take the colt out, will you, Davy, lad? I've some paperwork that needs attendin'."

He'd painted the office himself and refinished the floors, all in the six weeks since the house and grounds had officially become his own. The normally exhausting effort turned out to be a catharsis for long, lonely winter nights, replacing memories of another house rich with children, firelight, conversation, and delicious food smells.

Refusing to pedal backward, he stayed away from the local pub, forcing himself to concentrate instead on improving the first home he'd ever owned. Butter yellow walls blended with gleaming oak floors and molded bay windows, creating the illusion of light and warmth and space. Prints and photos in oak frames filled the walls and a desk with the same golden wood as the floor faced the largest window. Through it he could see miles and miles across the rolling horse country of Kildare.

This was his room, his place of business, part of the house yet separate from it with an outside entrance—a place of solitude, a retreat, a sanctuary, the only finished space in the entire house besides the kitchen. Every time Brian stepped in and closed the door against the outside world, satisfaction and peace welled up within him. He had no desire to complete the other rooms, not yet. This was where he wanted to spend his life, to bring his wife, to raise his children. A woman would have something to say about the color and design of the rooms she would make her own. Not for an instant did he consider that his dream of a life with the woman he wanted might not be realized.

For Brian Hennessey, pure Celt, descendent of a fey, blue-eyed island people who believed in fate and wee folk and answers in the mist, when two people were meant for each other, time and distance and the petty difficulties created in their own minds to keep them apart meant nothing in destiny's overall scheme. He would wait, forever if necessary, until the woman intended for him was ready to accept what he already knew.

Pulling his chair close to the desk, Brian busied himself with his accounts, not noticing the passage of time until a knock at the outside door interrupted him. Lacing his fingers behind his head, he called out, "Come in," and waited.

Sam Claiborne stepped into the room. Brian's face, schooled to keep thoughts to himself, slipped momentarily into lines of disbelief. For a minute he thought he'd made a mistake but when the light fell full strength on the man's tobacco gold hair and whiskey-blurred features, he knew he had not.

He watched Claiborne glance around the room taking in the furnishings, the pictures, the desk, before coming back to him.

"I'd offer you a chair, Mr. Claiborne, but now that you've

had a look I'm not sure you'll be stayin' long enough to need one."

Sam winced. "I didn't come to cause any trouble."

"I thought you'd gone home."

"I'm only here for a few days to finalize some purchases."

"Why did you come?"

"May I sit down?"

Brian waved him to one of the empty chairs. "If you like."

Sam came right to the point. "Caitlin told me."

Not by the flicker of an eyelash did Brian reveal his thoughts.

"I'm here because of Annie and Ben." Sam laughed bitterly. "Despite what it looks like, I love my children. It hasn't been easy living apart, not seeing them for months at a time."

The spring that coiled Brian's stomach into a large restrictive knot eased slightly. "I imagine it hasn't."

Sam looked up. "Does that mean you won't object?"

"To what?"

"To my having them for the summer."

Brian stared at him. Was the man insane? Had he missed something? "I don't understand. Why would I object to any decisions you and Caitlin make regardin' your children?"

"As her husband you should have some sort of influence on her, for Christ's sake, although why I would think so escapes me at the moment. No one I know has ever influenced Caitlin." He sank lower into the chair, as if weighted down by his own words. "She doesn't want me to have the children for the summer months. She says Ireland is beautiful in the summer."

"It is," Brian said automatically. What in bloody hell was going on?

"So is Kentucky," he heard the man reply over the roaring in his ears.

Stalling for time to figure out the root of Claiborne's insanity, Brian opened the bottom drawer of his desk, pulling out a bottle of whiskey and two glasses. Without asking, he poured the drinks and passed one across the desk. Sam emptied his glass immediately and passed it back. Brian refilled it and downed half of his own. Judging the time was right, he probed carefully. "Do you need Caitlin's permission to take the children for the summer?"

Sam, working on his third glass, grimaced and shrugged. "I do now. She found out that I switched the stallions."

Adrenalin surged through Brian, erasing all effects of the alcohol. Whiskey had loosened Sam Claiborne's tongue. He would take advantage of it. "A dangerous business, mate. What made you think you could get away with it?"

"I had no choice."

"Why not?"

"Before he died, my father trusted Caitlin with certain parts of the business. She cut *Narraganset*'s coverings to half. The agreements were contracted. I couldn't do anything about them."

Brian had been in the breeding business for a long time. Limiting stud services was a common practice. It drove up the amount of the fee, the value of the resulting colt, and it prolonged the stallion's stamina. "His fees doubled," he reminded Sam. "Obviously she knew what she was doing."

"We could have kept the number up and charged the same fee," Sam argued.

"What has that got to do with substituting another stallion for *Narraganset?*"

"Caitlin expected one colt a year by *Narraganset* out of *Kentucky Gold*. We had a written agreement. The covering was scheduled months in advance." A tick throbbed in his cheek. "I made some poor investments. Profits were low and someone made me an offer I couldn't refuse."

Brian frowned. The bad investments he could understand but what kind of an offer would make a man risk
everything his family had worked for?

Sam Claiborne was a poor judge of horses and he
couldn't hold his liquor. His hands shook uncontrollably
and his glass was empty. He pushed it back across the table.
"How about a refill?"

Brian hesitated. "I think you've had enough, mate. The
roads are tricky at night."

"I don't need a babysitter, Hennessey," Sam snarled.
"One more drink isn't going to make a difference."

Judging the level of Claiborne's inebriation, Brian filled the
glass halfway. "Tell me about the offer you couldn't refuse."

Sam emptied his glass. Brian didn't press him but he put
the whiskey bottle away. Finally Sam spoke. "Two days
before *Narraganset* was scheduled to cover Caitlin's mare, I
was contacted by the agent of a wealthy breeder."

"American?"

"No," he said shortly. "He offered me a million dollars if I
guaranteed him a *Narraganset* covering."

Brian was incredulous. "Surely Caitlin would have understood that."

Sam shrugged. "We weren't getting along. We barely
spoke to each other. I didn't ask her."

"I see. You substituted another stallion and hoped it would
have a convenient birth defect before anyone found out."

"*Hope* had nothing to do with it. I was prepared to make
sure no one found out. If Caitlin hadn't left when she did, I
wouldn't be in this mess."

Brian was disgusted. Claiborne's morals were those of a
spoiled teenager. He blamed everyone except himself for the
dilemma he had created. "Why come to me?" he asked.

"You're going to marry my wife. I want my children and I
won't get them without your help."

"Caitlin is no longer your wife," Brian reminded him. "The best way through this is to convince her that Annie and Ben will be better off visiting you. After the stunt you pulled, I'm not sure that's possible."

"I would never do anything to hurt my children."

"You nearly killed your daughter."

Sam gasped and paled. "What are you talking about?"

Apparently Caitlin hadn't told him everything. Mentally, Brian cursed himself. It was too late to take it back now. "Annie was in the barn when your man set fire to it."

"Who?"

"Don't deny it, Claiborne. Tim Sheehan confessed to the police. Caitlin knows about your plan to do away with the colt. She won't forgive that one easily."

Sam swallowed and wiped away the sweat above his upper lip. "So help me God, Hennessey, I didn't know what he was going to do. I had no idea what happened until Brigid called me. I admit I wanted the colt gone. He wasn't good for running, not with the defective larynx in his bloodline. I thought that damn vet in Galway would have advised Caitlin to put him down. But I didn't want anyone else hurt. I'd die for Annie and Ben. Caitlin knows that."

Brian's head reeled. He needed a moment to sort it out all out. "How did you know the colt had RLN?"

"His sire had it."

Brian swore softly. "You bastard. How could you do such a thing to your own wife?"

"I told you," he said as if it justified everything, "I needed the money."

Shaking his head, Brian stood. "I wouldn't help you even if I could. My guess is that you're sincere when it comes to wantin' your children, but you can't be much of a human bein'. Grow up a bit first. Clean up your drinkin' and maybe Caitlin will change her mind."

Sam Claiborne was defeated. Brian watched as he dragged himself through the door out to the gravel road where his car waited, dismissing the ugly thought that it might be best for everyone concerned if he perished somewhere along the Kilcullen Road.

Six weeks had passed since he'd seen her. Something was different. He couldn't put his finger on it but the change, subtle though it was, was definitely there. Brian stood outside the paddock and watched her work a black yearling from his jitters. Expertly, she played with the colt's ears until he no longer shied away. Then she picked up his feet, over and over again. At first the colt kicked at her but after ten minutes or so he stopped fidgeting. Sliding her arms around his neck, she patted him, allowing him to carry her full weight. When he was comfortable with it, she pulled herself up over the saddle and laid down on his back. He took a few steps and she slid off. On, off, on, off, over and over, until the colt accepted her with no more distress than he would a fly.

Brian drew a deep breath. Caitlin Claiborne was pretty. He'd forgotten how pretty. Her dark curls were pulled back in a clip. She wore a red highnecked jumper, tight-fitting beige trousers and expensive, broken-in riding boots. Anyone looking at her would guess her age to be ten years younger than it was.

She glanced up, saw him, and for the briefest instant the smile on her face tore his heart out.

"Hello," he said softly.

She hesitated. The joy was gone now. Her eyes had turned wary. "Hello," she said cautiously.

"Do you have a minute?"

"Give me ten. I'll finish with the colt and meet you in the house. Make a pot of tea or a drink for yourself, if you like."

The tea was steeping by the time she came in from the

barn. Brian poured two cups while she washed her hands and sat down across from him at the table. He came right to it. "So, when is it?"

"It?"

His lips twitched. "The date."

"What date?"

"Our weddin' date."

"Oh, that." Her cheeks burned.

"Your ex-husband offered me his congratulations."

"I don't believe you."

"All right," Brian conceded. "*Congratulations* might be stretchin' it a bit."

"I didn't think he'd bother to check up on me," she confessed.

"It wasn't the reason he came. He thought I might be an ally. He wants to see Annie and Ben more than you want him to."

Brian watched the anger rise in her eyes. "He isn't fit to see them, not after what he did."

"I won't argue with you on that one, but—"

"What?"

"If you feel that way, why haven't you turned him in?"

Caitlin sighed, picked up a spoon, and stirred her tea. "I don't know, really. Because he's the father of my children, because of Lucy. Just because I haven't pressed charges doesn't mean I want him around Annie and Ben."

"Ben might be all right without him, but I think that Annie needs her father."

"I'm not a monster, Brian. Annie will see her father. But Sam nearly killed her and even though he had no intention of doing so, I'm not sure his remorse will extend to future behavior. What happens if he needs money again?"

"I imagine you won't be there to stop him from doin' what he thinks is best for Claiborne Farms."

"Are you saying what he did was my fault?" Her voice broke.

Mentally, Brian cursed himself. The last thing he wanted was to hurt her. He wanted to touch her, hold her, reassure her. "I'm sayin' that without you he can run his business into the ground if he wants and he won't be able to blame anyone else."

He held her glance until she looked away. "I miss you, Caitlin."

She swallowed and stared down at her cup. "I miss you, too."

Relief swept over him. "How is the trainin' comin' along?"

She brightened. "It's going well, thanks to your referrals. I've four horses already. I think I'll be all right on my own from now on."

"Congratulations." He meant it, from the heart, but he couldn't help the sinking feeling that came from knowing she no longer needed him.

Something still didn't make sense. "Why does Sam think we're gettin' married?"

She flushed and shrugged. "I told him."

"Might I ask why? After all, I'm the prospective groom."

"Don't make fun of this, Brian. It's serious for me."

"I'm all for takin' it seriously. Just tell me why you said it."

Again she shrugged. "Insurance, I suppose. June isn't that far away. By then I'm supposed to be back in Kentucky or have a very good reason for not returning. Marriage to an Irishman seemed like the best reason."

"Sam will know the truth soon enough."

"By that time I should be self-supporting."

"And here I was, hopin' it was wishful thinkin' on your part," he said, striving for lightness.

She laughed self-consciously. "I would have thought you'd come to your senses by now."

"Meaning . . . ?"

"My life is filled with complications."

It was killing him not to touch her. "Nothin' that can't be sorted out."

"Probably," she admitted, "but I think I need to sort it out myself. I'm afraid of the kind of wife I'd be otherwise."

Now was the time. He could feel it. "I've a few skeletons in my own closet, Caitlin. Who doesn't? What do you say we work them out as we go along?"

She stared at him, her eyes level and serious. "Michael Duran was my father, Brian. By rights, I should never have been born. I don't know if I can work that one out. I've talked to my mother and she's explained, but even so—" She shook her head. "There are moments when I'm not very good company. I can't ask you to live like that."

This time he did touch her. He walked around the table and lifted her out of the chair, his hands curling around her upper arms. "Is that the reason you're givin' up on us?"

She refused to look at him.

"For Christ's **sake**, Caitlin. Don't tell me you think you are in any way responsible for your parents' behavior before you were even born."

He knew her well. She would have chuckled if the subject matter had been different. But it wasn't. "He left me money," she said, her voice low. "I can afford the expenses and advertising for the training yard. Sometimes I feel as if I shouldn't have taken it, as if the money is tainted somehow, because of what he was, because of what he and my mother did."

She looked up. What she saw on his face gave her courage. "I didn't want anyone to know, especially you," she confessed. "I thought you would think less of me."

"You deserve that money, Caitlin." The words rolled off his tongue, clearly, earnestly, without hesitation. There was no doubting his sincerity. "So, a priest was your father. There's no shame in that, only tragedy. Money is the least the man could have left you. The real shame would have been if he denied you, felt no responsibility for you and refused to support you."

She felt better, much better. It was freeing to come clean, to tell a man the worst about you and come out knowing it didn't matter to him after all. It was an epiphany of sorts, one she needed to arrive at on her own, one that needed the weeks of separation between them.

"Don't you see, Caitlin?" he continued earnestly. "Your mother and Michael Duran were meant to be because you were meant to be, for me. I've waited a lifetime for you. Without the two people you came from, you wouldn't be who you are. There isn't anyone else for me. Surely you can see that."

All at once she did, clearly, completely. Keeping her eyes on his, she slid her arms around his neck and brought his head down to hers. "When did you first know you loved me?" she whispered against his mouth.

"That first night in the barn."

"That was a long time ago."

"Aye," he agreed. "Now, please tell me you won't make me wait any more."

Brushing her lips against his, she asked, "How do you feel about taking on a partner?"

Were they both speaking English? "Have you heard nothin' I've said to you, Caitlin Keneally? I want to marry you."

"I mean a business partner."

Straight-faced, he went along with it. After all she deserved a bit of teasing after what she'd put him through.

**Visit the Simon & Schuster
romance web site:**

---

www.SimonSaysLove.com

**and sign up for our
romance e-mail updates!**

Keep up on the latest
new romance releases,
author appearances, news, chats,
special offers, and more!
We'll deliver the information
right to your inbox—if it's new,
you'll know about it.

POCKET BOOKS